A
Lavender
Wedding

D.P. Benjamin

A
Lavender
Wedding

Book Two in
The Mountain Mysteries Series

D.P. Benjamin

A Lavender Wedding
By D.P. Benjamin

For more information, please see *About the Author* at the close of this book and visit benjaminauthor.com

Cover photo by D.P. Benjamin. Cover design by Donna Marie Benjamin.

Elevation Press
P.O. Box 603
Cedaredge, CO 81413

Ordering information: Quantity sales. Special discounts are available on quantity purchases by book clubs, corporations, associations, and others. For details, contact the publisher at the address above.

ISBN 978-0-932624-03-1

1. Main category— [Mystery-Cozy] 2. Other categories— [Colorado]—[Female Detective]

© 2021
Elevation Press
Cedaredge, Colorado

Acknowledgments

Once upon a time...

The stories we hear as children, often read to us at bedtime by an earnest parent, are golden.

The cadence of the classic fairy story—with its familiar opening, its colorful characters, action and dialogue, conflicts and resolutions—form the foundation for our understanding and appreciation of narrative fiction.

Although we age, such stories never grow old. It is the goal of every novelist to write at least one story which is as memorable as these well-loved treasures. And so, I pursue my craft as a spinner of tales and my imagination, ignited by my dear parents, continues to churn.

I've learned that fiction, however fanciful, must be anchored in reality. So it is that my waking life has paralleled my imaginary world. On October 3, 2020, in the midst of a global pandemic, my dear collaborator, Donna Marie Woods, and I exchanged our marriage vows in our own *Lavender Wedding*.

Since that happy day, my life—already rich with creative endeavors—took on new and deeper meaning. The woman sings—I can hear her singing now in the other room. The woman laughs and smiles—cajoles and instructs—critiques and guides. She brightens each day.

My characters have also embarked on a new and richly shared journey. My hero, Anne Scriptor, is an imagined combination of three spirits: my dearly departed mother, my dead sister, and my late friend Tina Elisabeth Kjolhede. A complex young woman, Anne remains feisty and resolute as she continues to battle the demons of her past with her new love, Trinidad Sands, by her side.

As with my debut novel, *The Road to Lavender*, this new book has relied on the help of a host of others. Anonymous critics from Rocky Mountain Fiction Writers provided early guidance, leading me to strengthen my characters and story. Laurie Conner of Hotchkiss, Colorado, hosted a generous tour of Conner Orchards, allowing me to photograph her vigorous plants for our *Lavender Wedding* cover. My dear friend, Jack Casey, helped shape the psychological profiles of my suspects. An essential resource, Mark Petterson, was on-call to help with foreign phrases. Skip Bethurum kept me supplied with fresh ideas. Sharon Grotrian reviewed the accuracy of my law enforcement radio chatter. Katherine Key was the inspiration for Cozy, my intrepid police dog. Art Phillips lent his botanical expertise to my descriptions of Colorado plants and topography and, when I found myself lost in the wilderness, he straightened out my directions. Art and his wife, Janice, also read an early draft of the *Wedding* book.

Other "beta readers" who navigated through early versions were Stacy Malmgren, Cecilia (Cissy) Norton, Kim Taylor, Karen Grant, and Michael Mendocha. As usual, Wayne McKinzie and Rene' Janiece (the musical duo known as *Bittersweet Highway*) nailed down the final read.

A Lavender Wedding is the second book of my *Mountain Mystery Series*. The first book, *The Road to Lavender*, earned a third-place finish in the 2019 Rocky Mountain Fiction Writers' Colorado Gold Contest and also received a 2020 award for cover design from the New Mexico Book Association.

For a full list of upcoming titles, see the final page of this novel.

Donald Paul Benjamin/July 12, 2021

THE KOLLER FAMILY TREE

Esau Noah Koller

First Wife **Chloe Catharine (Quick)**	Second Wife **Hortense Helen (Hapsen)**
Natural Children **Ruth Rachel Koller** **Isaac Elijah Koller** **Naomi Esther Koller**	Step-Daughters **Juliet Ann Koller** **Mildred Alice Koller**

Twin Brother
Jacob Jeremiah Koller

Dedicated to Phil Ellsworth and Wayne Hamrick,
faithful warriors and dearly departed brothers in arms.

Prologue

(Easter Sunday, 2019)

"Can you fix it?" Esau Koller asked, unable to mask the impatience in his voice, but past caring. There were advantages to being eighty-eight years old and one of them was the privileged luxury of no longer caring what other people thought.

His visitor was an intimidating figure, half Esau's age, twice his height, and three times as heavy—rough-hewn and bulky. But the older man felt secure at the top of Denver's exclusive Stevenson Building, snug within the five walls of his immaculate penthouse, surrounded by his things. It hadn't been easy, having those things installed in this lofty abode, not to mention cajoling the reticent builder into remodeling the interior to create a singular five-sided penthouse in a pentagonal shape. But, money talks. And money was the one thing in which the old man was up to his skinny butt. What he didn't have to spare was time and this bumpkin was shaping up to be a temporal drain of the first water.

The man was a menace, yet, clearly, Esau should have the upper hand. After all, it was Esau who'd summoned the reluctant repairman and forced the hesitant rascal to make the unwelcome journey across town, in the heat, on a holiday. Esau was in charge of this interview and yet he'd been unable to extract an answer from the taciturn stranger.

Visitors seldom crossed the threshold of Esau Koller's isolated apartment which was fine with him. He'd never welcomed society.

Despite his increasing fortune and growing fame as a best-selling novelist, his abhorrence to the general public was legendary. Unlike a typical starving writer, he'd had the distinct advantage of starting out rich—a circumstance which relieved him of the burden of making a living. This, in turn, endowed him not only with the freedom to write but also the ability to easily afford all the appendages which came with the writing life. Talent hadn't been enough. He'd needed to hire editors and agents and finance the printing of books one and two before a traditional publisher would give him a second glance. Now the scavengers were courting him, so it goes. Woe unto the naïve wordsmith who believes authorship requires nothing more than talent and a writing stick. It requires money which buys influence which, in turn, fuels leverage.

Leverage, he thought to himself.

Esau seemed to recall that Archimedes of Syracuse had once praised the attributes of the lever. "Give me but a place to stand and a stout rod and I shall move the World." The Greek mathematician might have said something like that. But, then again, the deep thinker also ran naked through the streets shouting "Eureka!"

So it goes. So it goes.

For a moment, the old man forgot his immediate dilemma as thoughts strayed to the words of his favorite author and the incident which had cemented his desire to keep the public at bay. On that traumatic day, two years ago, he'd been standing in his back hallway, clad in his old thread-bare slippers while tossing a much younger man out on his ear. Seeking to reorder his thoughts, Esau looked away from his current visitor and involuntarily glanced at his feet.

He was wearing them now, those same old slippers, even as he attempted to deal with the hulking repairman. He also wore a frayed housecoat and antique nightcap. He looked foolish, he suspected. Like a creature from another century—a throwback—the very image of his alter-ego, the irascible Ebenezer Scrooge, dressed for bed and on the cusp of receiving Dickens' three spirits.

But Esau didn't care how he looked. He had no interest in being properly attired to receive company—in fact he had no interest in company. In his twelve-year journey to becoming a widely-published author, he'd honed his written and verbal skills while simultaneously allowing his social graces to atrophy. Faced with this morning's emergency, Esau had reluctantly opened a phone book and telephoned for assistance. And that call—the first time he'd used the telephone in months—had produced a disheveled man in overalls with dusty boots and a cockeyed ball cap. Now, despite Esau's attempts to drive the man in the direction of a sensible response, the unkempt stranger continued to stand on his plush wool carpet, face to face with the award-winning novelist, and apparently unable to answer a simple question.

For his part, the visitor, Ray Zumberto, proprietor and sole employee of Ray's Jiffy One-Stop Fix-It Shop, was uncertain how to respond to his grumpy customer. Fixing things was his specialty and he was reluctant to turn down a job, but he had a strong notion that working for this old guy would be a pain in the ass. Ray wasn't good at guessing ages, but he was pretty sure this Koller character, with his unshaven cheeks, his unruly white hair, wrinkled skin, stooped posture, and Halloween outfit, was at least eighty.

Moments ago, with a mumbled greeting and languid gesture, the old guy had opened the door, beckoned the repairman in, and stated his problem. The requested repair was outside Ray's wheelhouse and his initial inclination had been to decline the work, but instead of following his instinct and saying no, he'd clammed up like the seized motor on a malfunctioning dishwasher.

For two dozen minutes, the two men had been standing in silence until a huge grandfather clock in the entryway struck the half-hour. Whereupon Ray removed his slanting cap, scratched his bald head, and then replaced the cap again at an even more severe angle.

"I asked can you fix it?" Esau repeated with a tone that reflected his growing irritation with the reticent man.

It was clearly Ray's turn to speak and, after hesitating a moment more, he opened his mouth and gave it a shot.

"Can I fix it?" he repeated. "I gotta say I doubt it," said Ray as he gazed at the ancient typewriter which occupied the table between the two men.

"It's an odd animal and it'll be a chore no doubt gettin' parts for this-here old machine. So, I suppose I might could try heatin'-up that-there type-bar thing-a-ma-bob and bendin' it back in place. Is this a letter you use much?"

"A letter I use much?" The old man was incredulous. Apparently, this backwoods repairman had no idea who Esau Koller was. "All my books are based on the letter 'H' or haven't you noticed?" The offended author waved a hand in the direction of his bookshelf. "A letter I use much? It's only the most important letter in my pantheon."

Ray glanced at the books, but if he was impressed by the nine dozen hardbacks that lined the tasteful hazelnut-tinted wall of Esau's impeccable apartment, he didn't show it. All the prolific author's triumphs were displayed on that shelf: *Hell of a Night, Heavy Water, Horror Wagon, Husk of Satan,* the list went on.

"Well anyhow," Ray said, "this-here machine ain't no Pantheon. It's a Remington and one that's about seen its last days, I reckon. Fixin' this old rattletrap ain't gonna be so easy. Maybe you should switch over to an electric machine or, better yet, one of them laptops or, better yet, one of them…"

As the man droned on, Esau felt his ire rising until he was on the verge of uttering a profanity, but instead he merely repeated his request. "Look—will you agree to fix this machine or not? That's all I want to know."

"Sure. Sure. Sure. I can fix it, but it'll take time, see? It ain't so heavy that I can't lug it back to my shop, but I'll have to lug it back again which won't be no picnic."

Esau hesitated. He'd written all his novels on his vintage Remington and he had every intention of using it to complete the manuscript for his latest masterpiece (working title *Hallway of Doom*). The draft was nearly finished and his long-suffering publisher had already agreed to begin editing the first twenty-seven chapters while trusting his best-selling author to produce the concluding pages. Esau habitually wrapped his stories up in thirty-one concise chapters—no more, no less. This habit, along with his reputation as a hermit, were his trademarks. The number was a nod to his 1931 birth year, so he was nearly finished with Doom and should have been transcribing those final pages today, but he'd been ducking work on his new novel in order to finish a more personal project.

And now, both ventures were on hold, because his usually dependable typewriter had malfunctioned and refused to produce an "H."

"How long for the repair?" Esau asked, suspecting he would not like the answer.

"A week?" Ray ventured. "Maybe longer—I got other customers."

"Six-thousand," said Esau.

"Pardon?"

"Okay—sixty-five-hundred, but that's as high as I go," said Esau and he crossed his arms to signal that the negotiations were closed.

"Are we talkin' dollars here?" asked Ray.

"Yes."

"You're gonna pay me $6,500 to fix a machine that ain't worth twenty bucks?"

"Yes."

"Okay, it's your dough. You pay me that much and I can have this-here machine back in the morning and it'll be fixed so good that you could play music on it."

"That, my friend, is precisely what I do," said Esau. "I'll expect you back on Monday."

Chapter 1

So It Goes
(Dusk)

When Ray was gone, lugging the unwieldy Remington in both hands, Esau took a seat in his den and used the last of the whiskey to pour himself a stiff drink.

So, it goes, he thought as he pivoted on his stool and surveyed the well-furnished room until his gaze lit upon his most treasured possession, a single sheet of correspondence received from Kurt Vonnegut in 2007, just months before the famous author's death.

"And, so it goes," he told himself aloud, repeating his legendary hero's words—a well-remembered catch-phrase from Vonnegut's landmark novel, *Slaughterhouse-Five.* Esau had discovered the 181-page masterpiece late in life, a dozen years ago, when he was rearranging furniture. Having expended considerable energy trying to shove a little-used chest of drawers aside, he found the novel wedged into a corner. The book had been placed there to serve as an improvised shim by someone attempting to level the unbalanced rear leg of the wobbly antique.

Intrigued by the title, Esau rescued the book and began reading. Soon he was captivated by Vonnegut's freewheeling style, which suggested that the man merely sat down at a typewriter and boldly hammered out whatever came into his head—paragraphs be damned. It was an appealing notion to an old man who considered himself an aspiring novelist. Seeking advice, he'd written the author on a whim, asking whether Vonnegut thought 76 might be too old to launch a writing career. In return, he'd received a warm and encouraging letter.

Preserved inside a gilded frame and pressed securely beneath a slice of museum-quality glass, the treasure was visible from across the room. It was a single typewritten sheet—five succinct lines, anchored by Vonnegut's bold and singularly unique signature. The handwritten signature was a dramatic scrawl—a bold cats' cradle of swirling pen lines which was indecipherable even at close range.

Gazing at Vonnegut's poignant letter and recalling the words which provided the inspiration to launch his own prolific writing career, Esau smiled briefly. Then the old man immediately frowned as he recalled what had transpired two Easters ago in 2017—the year which, not counting today, marked the last time he'd allowed a visitor on his property.

The occasion had been Esau's eighty-sixth birthday, which coincided nicely with the debut of his eighty-sixth novel. His publisher had decided to exploit the anniversary by harvesting free publicity. And so, despite Esau's objections, a lanky, pimple-scarred twenty-something reporter had been dispatched to interview the old man. The reporter was clearly out of his depth. The youth's questions had been sophomoric and the old man's boring answers had matched the interviewer chapter and verse. The afternoon had been going nowhere when the reporter made his fatal error.

Half-way through the unproductive interview, the fool had tried to break the ice by eyeing the Vonnegut letter and making a lame joke suggesting that the unusual signature, and by implication the sentiment expressed in the letter, might not be genuine. That accusation had sent Esau over the brink. Surprising himself with his agility, the old man had responded to the smart-ass remark by leaping to his feet with such urgency that his slippers were left behind. Snatching the pen out of the astonished youth's hand, he seized his notebook, ripping out the offending pages. Then he'd hustled the interloper out the side door, tossing the reporter's tools after him.

"Tell your useless bitch of an editor," he'd growled at the neophyte, "if she prints even a comma about me, I'll sue the hound out of her." In the wake of this tirade, it was with tremendous satisfaction that Esau stood in the doorway and watched as the young man gathered his things and, rather than scuttling away, paused to make a note of his subject's unusual threat.

"...the hound out of her," the reporter repeated dubiously as he documented the phrase.

"Get out," Esau intoned, keeping his words level as his copious eyebrows knitted together to form unambiguous messengers of his suppressed rage.

"Okay. Alright. Gee whiz. I'm done." The youth glared, seemed on the verge of saying more, but turned instead, traversed the marble hall, and disappeared around the corniced corner—in search of the elevator, Esau supposed.

He presumed the lad would use the lift because his spindly legs would be incapable of successfully navigating the 264 stairsteps which separated the old man's lofty penthouse from the Denver sidewalk far below.

Esau himself had counted them, walking down one day. Thirteen steps per flight, two flights per story, and twelve floors. It was easy going down and he'd taken all day to make the descent. He'd never have risked the labor of climbing up. Only once in the three years Esau had occupied the penthouse had the building's elevator failed, stranding everyone on the ground floor. When that happened, the other tenants had walked up.

Not Esau.

He'd marched out the front door and hailed a taxi. Riding to the lavish Brown Palace Hotel, he'd flashed a wad of cash, demanded and been given a suite, and instructed the concierge to telephone his publisher to immediately send someone to his penthouse. The underling was directed to hustle upstairs, use the Koller pass key to collect typewriter and notebooks, and deliver those tools posthaste to the waiting author. He had to work, but to climb, he did not. He'd ordered room service and, because he was on deadline, he ordered liquor as well. In his experience, drinking and typing went hand-in-hand. He saw no need to alter his routine just because he was forced to change locations. Whiskey, in moderation, served as a lubricant to get his creative juices flowing. It was a habit which might have compromised a less confident writer with a weak constitution, but it served him well.

On the day of the young reporter's aborted visit, Esau heard the elevator bell and the sliding doors open, then glide shut, and he'd relished the quiet. Even the sound of the young man scribbling in his narrow, spiral-bound notebook had irritated him.

Standing there that day in his marbled hallway, as the vanquished reporter descended to the ground floor, Esau had glanced at the wadded pages grasped in the stiff fingers of his arthritic hand. Now that the young fool was gone, he'd been tempted to examine the boy's scrawled notes. But he'd resisted the urge, speculating that the lad had no future as a journalist. With this final thought regarding his unwelcome visitor, the old man had dismissed the boy from his mind. As for the purloined notebook pages, the waste bin was the best place for those scribbles.

That day two years ago, Esau had intended to cross to the trash chute and toss the paper in. With this goal in mind, he left the warm carpet of his bedroom floor behind, took a single step into the marbled hallway, and winced. The Italian marble was translucent, a dusky white, the color and temperature of December ice. Set into the cold smooth marble were seven circles of inlaid brown and blue, forming a kind of steppingstone pathway which led across the hallway from his bedroom door to the recessed trash chute in the far wall.

For a fleeting moment, he considered hopping from one multi-colored medallion to another, indulging in a kind of rich man's hopscotch. The medallions were indeed warmer to the touch and jumping across would be more expedient than going back inside to put something on his bare feet, but it would have been a risky proposition. He was pushing ninety. It would be a poor time for a fall. He'd turned back that day to fetch his slippers.

He was wearing them now as he sipped his whiskey—those same slippers. *So it goes.* Balancing on the centermost of his nine expensive hand-built bar stools, he drank a cursory toast to Easter. Then, contemplating the empty bottle, he glanced at the back bar and found it barren. Usually, his home bar was fully stocked, but he'd neglected to leave the cook a note.

The bar deserves better, he told himself, *and the cook should have attended to it without being told. I ought to fire the woman, if it weren't for the nuisance of hiring a replacement.*

Hiring someone new would mean interviews and all the attendant rigmarole which the old man despised. Enough was enough. Years ago, while living in Aspen, he'd hired, eternally tolerated, then summarily fired, an entire household crew—landscapers, kitchen staff, maids, gamekeeper—everyone except his man Phillip. Then Esau had boarded-up the manor house and moved to the city and into his custom-designed penthouse. He'd kept the unctuous retainer in harness, not out of allegiance to the man, but simply because he wished to avoid the replacement process.

But, in the end, the arrangement grew intolerable.

Phillip had been a competent manager of Esau's Aspen manor house—a sprawling edifice on a sizable acreage—but he was underfoot in the Denver penthouse. To make matters worse, the live-in manservant was an unwelcome reminder of his master's former life—a past existence which Esau took pains to erase. Besides, Phillip had been caught in a lie, so Esau fired the fellow and endured the inconvenience of hiring two women to replace him.

Esau's new Denver staff consisted of a cook and a housekeeper, but having them on the payroll did nothing to diminish the reclusive author's social isolation. Even when his wives were part of his manor household, Esau had relied on domestics to keep his home in order, but he never interacted with or felt the slightest loyalty to his employees. He'd fired the Aspen staff without a single regret. Ultimately, Phillip too was gone and two new Denver domestics had learned to do as they were told and stay out of the master's way.

The new help came and went and he paid their salaries, but—after interviewing them by telephone two years ago—he'd communicated with both women using written notes and never spoken directly to either. He, in fact, had absolutely no idea what either one of them looked like.

The cleaning woman came in the dead of night—like a vacuuming vampire. She did her work while the old man slept. Luckily for her, Esau, who was deaf as a post, always removed his hearing aids before retiring. Which was just as well, for woe unto her if her nocturnal ministrations had disturbed her employer's slumber. Meanwhile, the cook did the shopping and prepared Esau's meals, leaving them in refrigerated Tupperware containers for the old man to microwave.

His vintage manual typewriter, his prehistoric microwave, his standard telephone, his centuries' old grandfather clock, and his antique coffeemaker —these few devices were the only instruments he knew how to operate. He didn't own a television or radio or computer or cell phone. He never once used his stove and had no idea how to even turn the thing on.

Esau attended no concerts or plays or parties. Nor did he acquiesce to his publisher's demands to promote his books. He delegated public appearances to surrogates, an oddball practice which only increased his mystique among his legions of loyal readers. He never signed his works in public. If someone wanted an autographed book and was willing to pay an outlandish fee, his publisher had strict instructions not to bother his famous author. Instead, a publishing house minion was dispatched to the cellar of Esau's apartment house to crack open a storage crate and pull out a pre-signed volume. In periodic marathon sessions, the quirky author had signed fifty copies of each old title, and whenever a new novel came off the presses, he signed another fifty. When a given batch of signed copies was gone, that was it, because he refused to sign any more. Which made a signed book all the more valuable.

The signature business was a sore point with Esau and his suspicion that Phillip was selling signed copies on the side had been the final straw. With Phillip gone and the other two servants reduced to virtual phantoms, Esau continued to solidify his retreat from the world.

Doing the bare minimum to keep his career alive, he dealt with his publisher by phone and—since parcels were left on his doorstep—he never interacted with couriers who shuffled manuscripts between himself and the publishing house. He had no outside friends and no outside interests and seldom, if ever, left his apartment.

His cook and housekeeper kept their opinions to themselves, although Esau suspected that both pondered the same question which was, *why does an antisocial hermit possess such a sizeable bar?*

The ponderous thing was fifteen-feet across with a mirrored back bar which was eight-feet tall. Esau had purchased the entire set-up from a vintage Denver pub which was being demolished to make way for the latest wave of downtown gentrification. The bar was a solid mahogany masterpiece with beautifully carved wood and lavish mirrors and there was room to seat nine people, but over the years he'd been its only customer.

At first, he'd spent hours sitting there alone, balancing on one of the matching stools, sipping spirits, and making notes for his next novel, until sitting there by himself struck him as ridiculous. Lately, the bar had been gathering dust as he worked sitting up in bed, compiling his notes while propped against a reading pillow. Whenever his preliminary handwritten notes were cobbled into a manageable rough draft, he sat at a broad butcher's table and typed his manuscript on the old Remington, often revising and improving the writing once his arthritic but still obedient fingers came into contact with the familiar keys.

Early this morning, he'd been forced to deviate from his writing ritual. He'd intended to put the concluding touches on a clandestine manuscript—a personal project about which his publisher knew nothing. But, deprived of his typewriter, he'd been unable to finish the final chapter of his hidden work. It was a secret autobiography—the memoirs he'd been struggling with for months and which he'd finally been able to revise after reconciling with his prodigal child. It was a heartfelt story of his personal odyssey from damnation to deliverance—it was his confession, his revelation, and his redemption. Unlike his trade novels which had become formulaic and predictable, it was a highly personal narrative without deliberate plot structure. And he'd treasured the process of conceiving, drafting, and finally rewriting it.

Sitting there at the dusty bar, contemplating a half-full glass and an empty bottle, Esau thought about the two creations which would be his final works. Once *Hallway of Doom* and his memoirs were complete, he'd stop.

Doom would be his last novel, but the memoirs would be his final word and he was content to be ending on a high note. He couldn't recall when he'd fallen so in love with his writing. He'd begun the memoirs methodically, chronicling his parent's early struggles—a true American rags-to-riches story. Then he'd bogged down as he wrote about the years when he was governed by his lesser angels and he'd been on the point of shelving the project until his child's sudden reappearance. The desire to reconcile was strong and meant he could revise his memoirs to conclude with a happy ending.

Feeling wistful, he looked up and considered his reflection in the bar's lavish cut-glass mirror. How many times, as a paid critic for the local writing guild, had he severely disparaged the work of a novice author? How often had he criticized a fledging writer for employing the trite gimmick of having one's character study his or her reflection?

"Humbug," he said aloud, but he continued staring as he got eye-contact with his image and distorted his rather ordinary visage into a sardonic grin. He held the mocking pose for a full minute before allowing that leering face from his past to meld back to its present blandness.

"I am..." he said aloud and with heartfelt conviction, "I am no longer the man I was." Fully aware that he was quoting old Ebenezer Scrooge, Dickens' caricature of a cynical malcontent turned reformed protagonist, he internalized the notion.

I am no longer that man, he told himself. He patted his heart and said aloud, "The proof is here." He studied his hands and added, "Behold, here are the instruments of my salvation."

Resolved to return to work, he drained his glass and searched for his writing tablet and fountain pen. He ought to be putting the finishing touches on his new novel, but time was short and it was more important that he complete the closing chapter of his memoirs—the final stanzas which chronicled his improbable redemption. Deprived of his Remington, he'd be forced to proceed in long-hand. He had much to say and, given his arthritic fingers, writing it out would be a challenge. But he was burning to continue, so he took up pen and paper and, as the chimes of his hall clock sounded the final notes of the waning afternoon, tottered to his bedroom.

Chapter 2

Easter Monday
(7:30 a.m.)

As promised, on Monday morning, Ray Zumberto, known to his friends as 'Mister Fix-it,' rang the bell and spoke into the intercom.

"Typewriter," was all he said.

The buzzer sounded just as a fire truck trundled past, siren and horn blaring. Ray watched the emergency vehicle maneuver awkwardly around a corner to reach the narrow confines of Welton Street. Then he laboriously balanced the heavy typewriter on his hip with one hand while using the other to open the outside door. Squeezing inside, he lugged the 43-pound Remington to the elevator.

He cursed as he read the out-of-order sign and continued cursing as he started up the deserted stairway.

If I was running this here place, he told himself, *for certain no way would the elevator not never work.*

Yesterday, he hadn't encountered anybody when he'd taken the elevator to the top to inquire about the repair job and he hadn't seen anyone when he rode back down and he didn't anticipate seeing anyone today. For all he knew, Koller was the only living soul in the entire towering building.

It was twenty-two flights to crazy Koller's penthouse—twelve damn floors above the sunny Denver sidewalk and it was a hot day for April. Koller was supposedly famous—an important writer of some kind or so he said—but Ray wouldn't climb so high in this heat for some damn writer. He wouldn't make that precipitous climb for somebody who was nobody to him. But for six-thousand-five-hundred dollars plus sales tax—for that he would climb.

Ray was half-way up, wheezing and puffing, when he stopped, put the Remington on the marble step beside him, and sat wearily down. That's when he heard the elevator whirl to life. It seemed to make the whole stair-well shudder. He was between floors with no chance of catching it. There was also no chance that whoever was inside could hear him, but anyway he bellowed a string of profanity as it rumbled past him, heading down.

He looked up the stairwell and decided he would climb no higher. He wasn't one to shun physical labor, but it was too damn far to the penthouse and too damn hot. So, he picked up the Remington and trudged down to the floor below, grumbling and counting the steps as he descended.

"Thirteen," he said aloud. "That sure as hell figures."

Ray was swearing and sweating as he pounded the call button. He shifted the typewriter to one arm, pulled out his handkerchief to wipe his brow, and stared at the lighted numbers above the door. The elevator car was sitting on 'G,' stuck on the ground floor. Stuck on 'G' like a bent type-bar in an ancient typewriter. Ray pounded the button again and, as if in response, the elevator slowly began to rise—its indicator light advancing one number at a time from left to right until it flashed on '5' and the doors slid slowly open.

"Take your got'damn time," Ray hissed. He pushed the 'P' for penthouse and leaned heavily in the corner as the elevator trundled upward. When at last the car reached the top, Ray carried the typewriter across the marbled hall and pressed the Koller doorbell. When there was no response, Ray looked up and down the hallway. The old man owned the entire top floor so there was only one doorbell. Ray rang again. There was no answer. The repairman frowned. He could literally feel the money slipping from his fingers. He shifted the typewriter's weight to rest it against his ample belly. Then he balanced the Remington in both hands and started down the hallway. There had to be another door somewhere. He reached a junction, turned left, and slipped in the blood.

Chapter 3

Marble

"Lucky," was all Ray could think to say as he lay on the solid marble floor. Somewhere he could hear a clock chiming the quarter hour. He checked his watch. It was 8:15 in the morning on Easter Monday and he was flat on his back—a bad way to start the day.

"A guy could really get hurt this way," he observed as he remained supine in a shallow pool of blood, shaken by his undignified tumble, but seemingly uninjured.

Turning his head to one side, he could see the wretched Remington lying nearby. The vintage typewriter had fallen from his grasp as he dropped to the marble floor. One glance told him the thing was a total loss. No amount of time or money would ever restore the wrecked machine and what it would cost to fix the fractured floor, Ray didn't like to think.

Ray was a practical man and so he stayed on the floor alternately flexing arms and legs and torso, making absolutely certain he hadn't broken any bones. He remained there until his curiosity began to get the better of him. He'd slipped and all that blood had to come from somewhere. So, he carefully raised his head, strained to look beyond his shoes, and saw his customer's prostrate form lying a few feet away.

The old man was not breathing.

Ray relaxed his neck and let his head fall back until he was able to look up and study the hallway ceiling while he collected his thoughts. He was a veteran of Desert Storm and he'd seen his share of corpses in combat. Lying there while blood seeped into his overalls, he didn't wonder how Koller had died. The thought never crossed his mind. At the moment Ray had room for only one thought in his head and that thought told him that, given the circumstances, he was highly unlikely to get paid.

Time advanced as Ray lay there, its passage marked by the relentless striking of the distant clock. At last, he sat up. Unlike the rest of the world, he didn't own a cell phone. He'd better uses for his pockets. There was a phone in the lobby. He ought to call someone. Leaving the typewriter and Koller where they had fallen, the disillusioned repairman struggled to his feet and walked back to the elevator where he pressed the call button and waited. After fifteen minutes, the doors opened and Leonard, the building maintenance man appeared.

"What took so long?" Ray asked as he eyed the man's fashionable cap and the handsomely lettered monogram 'Repairs.' *Gotta get me one of those,* he told himself.

"And you are?" Leonard countered, then he frowned at the stranger standing before him. Ray shrugged his shoulders and pointed down the hallway.

Leaving Ray at the elevator, Leonard followed a track of bloody footprints, rounded the hallway corner, and discovered Mr. Koller lying dead. At least he presumed it was Koller. In his two years with the Stevenson Building, Leonard had yet to lay eyes on the occupant of the building's luxury penthouse. In fact, he'd never been inside the Koller apartment, only conversing twice with the mysterious dweller through his closed front door and talking to him once on the phone.

Leonard stood absolutely still for a moment and sighed. He wasn't cavalier about death, but he'd seen enough lifeless bodies in the war to be unmoved by the sight of a cadaver. It wasn't the dead man that bothered him. The flummoxed custodian was calculating the damage to the hallway's floor. The old man's mortal remains lay a few steps from the penthouse's side door and next to a mangled typewriter which had cracked the otherwise pristine marble.

"Damn," said Leonard as he took out his cell phone and called the police.

Forty-five minutes later, Ray and Leonard sat side-by-side on a protective layer of plastic which covered one of the half-dozen luxurious sofas in Koller's spacious apartment. Leonard was giving a statement to an officer, a tall woman who stood ramrod straight and towered over the two men on the low-slung couch.

"I was called-up by residents," Leonard reported. He spoke slowly, pausing at regular intervals as the woman recorded his words.

"Go on," she prompted.

"They all complained that the elevator was busted," he continued. "It's my day off," he added unnecessarily, "which is why I was in a bad mood. I got in the car at the ground floor right off and rode it down to the basement. I stopped there to look over a broken window in the street-level casement, then started back up, testing the buttons one at a time, stopping on every floor until I got to the penthouse level which is where we are now. Did you get all that?"

"Got it," she assured him. "Anything else?"

"Saw the bloody footprints. Saw the body. Saw the typer-writer. Saw the busted floor—that will take some doing to fix," he exchanged a knowing glance with Ray who nodded in agreement.

"Sit tight, gentlemen," she instructed as she closed her notebook and turned away.

The two men exchanged a smile.

"Gentlemen?" Leonard chortled.

"Must mean you," Ray grinned. "So, your elevator ain't broke?"

"Seems like," said Leonard.

"Hmm. You done a good job of recollectin' what you did," said Ray.

"Your story was a better one," said Leonard. "I think the lady police liked your story better."

Leonard had waited patiently as Ray was questioned first.

"Pretty young thing," Ray pointed out.

"And smart too," Leonard observed.

"Yeah," Ray agreed.

Their conversation exhausted, the two sat in silence. From their vantage point in the center of the lavishly furnished living room, the pair watched forensic technicians walk back and forth wearing masks and gloves and little booties over their street shoes. Each time a technician passed from room to room, he or she ducked under skeins of yellow crime scene tape which criss-crossed the apartment like the random web of an overachieving spider.

Ray was bored and wished he had his tools. In particular, he wanted to put his spirit level flush against the marble hallway floor in order to check the balance bubble. He'd bet anything that the floor was at least half a bubble off the horizontal. Otherwise, why had old man Koller's blood flowed one way and not the other? Certain that his sofa-mate would appreciate this observation, the curious repairman was about to pose this question to Leonard when one of the technicians, all of whom had been working silently, shouted across the room.

"Hey, Bobby," said the technician as he motioned to his colleague, "check this out." The technician held up a piece of paper. "This old guy was writing a book and you'll never guess what the title is—go ahead—guess."

"I have no idea, bonehead," said Bobby.

"It's called *Hallway of Doom* and from the look of these pages he was typing the thing on that old busted machine out there. Ironic, huh?" The technician laughed.

"You are one stupid jackass, you know that?" growled his colleague.

"Stupid is right," Ray whispered to Leonard. "It ain't no Ironic, it's a Remington."

Chapter 4

The Hungry Hart
(Tuesday, April 23)

It was early Tuesday morning. Trinidad Sands sipped his cappuccino and watched his beloved Anne as she looked through rows of mystery novels. He was sitting forty feet away, the sole patron of the open and elevated coffee shop situated in the exact center of the Hungry Hart Bookstore. It was precisely where a detective would sit. His strategic position made an ideal observation post because the bookshelves radiated around the circular coffee shop like spokes of a wheel, affording him an unobstructed view of adjacent sections.

Like most bookstores, the Hungry Hart was divided into subject matter sectors with non-fiction arranged by topic and fiction shelved by genre. From his perspective, Trinidad could see all the way down three separate fiction aisles, one to the left labeled 'Romance' and one on the right labeled 'Horror' with 'Mystery' in the middle. The juxtaposition of those three genres didn't escape his notice.

Nine months had passed since the vivacious and lovely Anne Scriptor first entered his life. Two torrid months of dating, a fifteen-week trial separation, and most recently four months of living together. To Trinidad it had been a time of Mystery followed by Romance followed by Horror and now back to Romance again.

So far so good, he thought.

Those fifteen weeks apart had been hard for Trinidad. The separation had been Anne's idea. Afraid of losing her forever, he'd agreed to what he prayed would be a temporary parting. With the object of his affection miles away in Tucson completing her university semester, he'd missed her cooking, missed hearing her laughter and loving her. Busy with her studies, she'd hardly written and when they spoke on the phone, she sounded distracted and distant. The village of Lavender and his big farmhouse had seemed empty and his time alone had been horrible. Was *horrible* the same as *horror?* If not, it was close enough. Now that Anne had returned the romance to his life, he couldn't bear to let her out of his sight.

He didn't like to think of himself as possessive. He simply wanted to be near her—was that wrong? How could it be wrong when Anne seemed to relish his company and when their relationship was much more than a sexual one. Since her return, each night, after the loving, when they were spent and entwined in each other's arms, they'd talk for hours. As the morning birds began to sing, they'd hop up, pull on running togs, and go for a brisk run around the farm. Then they'd spend the day together talking and laughing, sharing chores and meals—fashioning a life together.

There'd been bumps, of course, more like potholes, he admitted.

He and Anne would be cruising along, moving ever-forward on the highway of life, when the past would pull her away. He could see it take her, see it in her eyes—a frightened look, something feral, like a cornered animal poised to flee. During those horrible episodes, when unhappy girlhood memories overwhelmed Anne, sex was out of the question. She'd just want to be held. Now and then, when a dream jolted her awake, she'd leave their bed and seek solitude. If she needed space, she'd arise and pad downstairs to sleep on the sofa.

Anne had shared much about her past and he'd guessed the rest. Most days, she welcomed and delighted in their intimacy. Sometimes, the prospect frightened her. *Romance, Mystery, and Horror*—the themes continued to churn in their lives. And yet he was certain the latter was fading and confident that, in the end, romance and mystery would prevail.

The abuse Anne had suffered as a girl continued to haunt her, but she no longer had to face the spirits alone. He shared her burden—they'd get through it together. Trinidad loved her—vertical or horizontal—he absolutely loved her.

Sipping his coffee and thinking of Anne, he grinned in her direction and she smiled back. She'd left him alone with his morning cup while she browsed through the bookstore. She hadn't gone far, but he wanted her nearer. He raised his cup and waggled it, inviting her to join him.

Anne looked down the aisle at her handsome lover. The shelved books of the mystery aisle formed two parallel rows which neatly framed Trinidad and his table for two. It was, she thought, a bit like looking down a gun barrel at a distant target. To reinforce that vision, she made one hand into a pretend pistol and aimed at Trinidad.

"Pow," she mouthed the word and was pleased to see her playmate clutch dramatically at his heart as he feigned the impact of her imaginary bullet. Then he instantly recovered and inclined his head. It was an unambiguous invitation and he and the coffee looked tempting, but she wasn't quite ready to join him. So, she shrugged her shoulders, sheathed her finger pistol, pulled another book from the shelf, and held it up as a signal that she hadn't yet found what she was looking for. She examined the novel, then put it back and took another, opened that one and put it back. Then she repeated the same motions and repeated them again.

From where Trinidad sat, it looked like she was choosing books at random, skimming the first few pages, then moving on to the next. Curious, he called her cell phone which he was certain she had set on vibrate.

"You quivered me?" she answered.

"Yes," said Trinidad. "What gives down there?"

"You know me—just browsing."

"Browsing is right," Trinidad laughed. "You look like a persnickety little lambkin searching an enormous meadow for one perfect leaf of clover."

"I like to start with murder," she said.

"Pardon?"

"I like my mysteries to begin with a murder, preferably in the first five pages, otherwise I lose interest."

"A blood-thirsty little lamb."

"Now you're getting the idea," she laughed. "Ah! Found one!"

Chapter 5

In Bed
(Wednesday, April 24)

One day later, at four o'clock on Wednesday afternoon, the amorous occupants of Lavender Hill Farm were naked under their gigantic comforter. The day had been unusually warm but, as the sun slanted steadily westward, it had grown chilly and the plush blanket, mingled with their body heat, made a pleasant lovers' cocoon. Trinidad was napping after hours spent checking the season's seedlings in the farm's sprawling lavender field, plus an additional seventy minutes spent pleasuring his willing partner. Anne was awake and reading.

"Have you ever been to one?" she asked.

"Huh?" Trinidad responded without opening his eyes.

"Ever been to an infirmary—a hospital morgue—ever examine a body laid out on a slab?"

"When I wake up in twenty minutes, I promise to thoroughly examine every naked body in the neighborhood."

"Creepy," she said. Trinidad grunted and she quickly added, "Not you...I mean this book. Wish I'd left it alone. The plot is way too creepy, but I can't seem to put it down."

"I thought you preferred to read at night," said Trinidad as he kept his eyes closed and tried in vain to salvage his nap.

"Read this spooky thriller in the dark? Not likely. It's all I can do to get through it in broad daylight."

"Hmm."

"How can you sleep at a time like this?"

"Like what?"

"When I'm sitting here in mortal terror, almost afraid to turn to the next page?"

Anne was silent for a moment, then Trinidad heard a page rustle and opened his eyes. "You turned," he observed.

"I said *almost* afraid..." she began. "Oh—jeepers!" With an impetuous gesture, she hurled the paperback across the room where it collided with the bedroom wall and crashed to the floor. "That's a sure-fire nightmare!"

"What...?" Trinidad began as he sat up in bed.

"I have a good mind to call Harts and lodge a complaint," she interrupted.

"Call the bookstore...?"

"The very idea of allowing a horror novel to be shelved among the mysteries!" she protested. "I call it false advertising and they're going to hear from me."

Trinidad was awake and struggling into his jeans as he walked to the corner to retrieve the book.

"*Hacksaw Fury*," he read the cover title aloud. "That title should tell you something."

"I thought it was a metaphor." She frowned.

"For...?" he prompted.

"Oh, I don't know," she admitted. "Anyway, the cover photo caught my eye."

"It's a photograph of a nickel-plated hacksaw, splattered with blood and hovering diagonally against a pitch-black background," he laughed as he examined the cover. Then he turned to the first page. "Well, I'll say one thing in its favor—there's a murder on page one."

"And on page five and page eighteen and page thirty-two and so on," she sighed. "Fifteen dismembered corpses by chapter six plus a body on a slab which disappears."

"The body or the slab?"

"The body of course!" she said. "Whoever heard of a slab disappearing? Those things are heavy."

"You want this back or not?" he asked holding the book out to her.

"Keep that thing away from me," she said. "I only wish I could disremember the first six chapters. No...don't bring it over here! Throw it out the window!"

"Out the window? Are you sure?"

"Damn it! Can't you do this one little thing for me?" she shouted in mock indignation and tried to suppress a smile while wondering whether her intrepid lover would actually do as she asked.

And she was inwardly delighted when Trinidad shrugged, crossed to the window, cranked the transom open, and tossed the book down into the farmyard. It fluttered through the springtime air and landed among a flock of foraging doves, causing the birds to scatter briefly before returning to the same patch of ground. Trinidad stayed at the window staring down at the discarded book and the persistent doves.

Anne remained in bed. The novel's gory details had frightened her and she was glad to be rid of it, but not at any price. She'd meant to tease her lover, but...

Did I protest too much? she wondered.

"Is this our first argument?" he asked, uncertain of Anne's feelings.

"Come here, my dear," Anne said and he turned to see his lover lounging in the bed with both arms reaching out to him. "And take those silly trousers off."

Chapter 6

Pancakes
(Thursday, April 25)

"How many more, sweetheart?" Trinidad asked as he monitored the bubbles forming on yet another pancake. It was Thursday, the sun was streaming into the kitchen, and the grandfather clock in the farmhouse hallway was just striking noon. More than fifteen hours had passed since Anne asked her lover to toss the Hacksaw novel. Glancing past Trinidad as he labored at the stove and looking out through the kitchen window, she was pleased to see that he must have removed the discarded book from the farmyard. With any luck, her hero had buried it somewhere on the property.

She did not want to know where.

As for yesterday's little spat, she was still smiling as she remembered their passionate reconciliation. After she'd pleaded with him to toss the book out the upstairs window, the two had enjoyed a passionate afternoon. Then came last night's late supper, after which they'd lounged in the living room to watch an old John Wayne movie on DVD.

Just before midnight, Trinidad had carried his slumbering partner upstairs and the couple slept like the dead. At ten this morning, both had jumped out of bed, dressed like firemen answering an alarm bell, and burst into the sunshine for a vigorous run. Now Anne was sitting at the kitchen table feeling tired but satisfied and her lover was at the stove acting chipper and being domestic.

It was beginning to look like a lazy day.

"Just one more cake will be plenty for me," she said as she downed her third cup of coffee.

"You sure?" he sounded disappointed. "I made them special with peaches and walnuts in honor of our anniversary." When Anne didn't react, he added, "Don't tell me you've forgotten."

"Nope," she said. "Nine months since I drove into your life, but I thought we weren't celebrating until July."

"Starting early," he said. "Anticipating more presents that way." He put the spatula aside, reached into his apron pocket, and carried a small wrapped package to the breakfast table. "Here you go."

"Honey," she blushed as she opened the gift to reveal a miniature box of chocolates. "But I didn't get you anything."

"I wouldn't say that." He passed behind Anne's chair, put his hands on her shoulders, and leaned forward to kiss the top of her head. "What about that nice surprise you gave me early this morning?"

His reminder of their pre-dawn passion made Anne blush even deeper. "Shucks, that couldn't have come as much of a surprise," she suggested. "Especially since I was holding onto it at the time. And, by the way, when exactly do you plan to make an honest woman of me?"

"Would today suit you?"

"Now you're just..." She stopped and stared. "Is that what I think it is?"

"Darling..." he began.

"Yes, dear," she answered as she beheld the compact velvet box in Trinidad's outstretched hand. She could feel her heart pounding in anticipation of what he was about to ask. The scene felt like a dream as Trinidad knelt beside her chair, but something seemed wrong. It should have been a perfect experience and all her senses should have been focused on his anticipated proposal—and yet her nose was tingling.

"Honey..." she said.

"Yes, my love," he cooed as he continued to kneel ceremoniously at her side.

"I just want you to know one thing..." she gushed.

"Yes?" he asked.

"My pancake is burning," she declared.

Chapter 7

Old Goat Trail

Anne was grinning broadly as the two of them left the farm and drove toward the county seat. It was just after three on that memorable Thursday afternoon. If they hurried, they'd have time to reach Delta City before the courthouse offices closed. Fortunately, Trinidad was at the wheel, because his newly-minted fiancée seemed incapable of taking her eyes off her luminous engagement ring.

"Well," said Trinidad as he steered along Old Goat Trail to reach the highway. "That was some smoky breakfast, but at least now we know for certain-sure that every single smoke alarm battery in the farmhouse is good to go."

"Uh-huh," Anne cooed. She'd already forgotten the frantic episode in their kitchen as the two of them scrambled to put out the stove fire, then checked every room in the farmhouse, wrestling with a cacophony of blaring alarms in order to re-set the upstairs and downstairs smoke detectors. A narrowly avoided household disaster was the furthest thing from her enraptured mind. The recent past was a dim memory as she surrendered completely to the present, sticking her fingers out the open moon roof, rotating her hand in a slow arc, and surfing it in the passing air to watch her new diamond ring catch the afternoon sunlight.

They'd left her little Nissan pickup behind at Lavender Hill Farm in favor of traveling in his hefty Honda Ridgeline. She'd wanted to tie tin cans to the bumper of her old battered truck and drive it to Delta City, but Trinidad convinced her such a public display was premature. And, besides, he could see that his distracted lover was in no condition to operate a motor vehicle.

Insisting they take his Honda, he also pointed out it might rain. "And we both know how slippery your favorite hill can get," he reminded her.

"If you say so," Anne murmured as she hummed to herself. The tune she was attempting might have been *Hail to the Chief* or it might have been the wedding march—Trinidad tended to get the two mixed up.

The Delta County clerk's office was on the first floor of the courthouse, so Trinidad and his bride-to-be didn't have to go far to apply for their marriage license. Waiting in line, the beaming detective squeezed Anne's hand.

"Nervous?" he asked.

"Not a bit," she declared. "This first step is easy. Now the marriage marathon begins."

"Don't remind me," he said. "What was I thinking?"

"Next," the clerk informed the dawdling couple.

The official form and related process were simple enough. They might have completed their task in record time if Anne hadn't constantly wandered away from the clerk's counter to show everyone—including courthouse workers and arbitrary passersby—her new ring.

At last, the happy couple turned in their paperwork and decided to walk downtown for a celebratory coffee. They were just leaving the building when they encountered Joel Signet ascending the courthouse steps.

"Detective Sands," said Joel as he grasped Trinidad's hand. "Fancy meeting my favorite gumshoe here. And this must be the lovely young visitor I've been hearing so much about." He shook Anne's hand too and introduced himself. "Joel Signet, Esquire, attorney extraordinaire and all-around champion of the oppressed." Joel stood on the steps for a moment regarding the couple and grinning broadly until he asked, "So, you two, business or pleasure?"

"Pardon?" asked Trinidad.

"Your visit to the courthouse, I mean."

"Oh—business *and* pleasure I guess," said Trinidad.

"See my ring," Anne interjected.

"Wow," said Joel and he put on his sunglasses for effect. "What a sparkler! So, I guess congratulations are in order. When's the wedding?"

Trinidad and Anne exchanged a glance as the couple suddenly realized they hadn't planned that far.

"Uh—the wedding is..." Trinidad began.

"Soon," said Anne. "We'll let you know."

"Can't ask for more than that," said Joel. "Say, you didn't ask me if I'm here for business or pleasure?"

"Oh," said Trinidad, "Which is it?"

"All business," said Joel. "You heard about the murder, I guess."

"Murder?" asked the prospective groom.

"Who's dead?" asked the future bride.

"Only one of our most famous Colorado celebrities," said Joel. "Surprised you two haven't heard. The deceased is Esau Koller...the author? Surely, you've heard of the "H" horror novel series? *Husk of Satan*? No? *Heavy Water*? How about *Hacksaw Fury*?"

"That one we know," Trinidad said.

"Do we ever," Anne agreed.

"Well, anyway. The old boy was bumped off two days ago in his Denver penthouse and the cops are looking hard at my client for the murder. My guy was the last person to see Koller alive, or so the police allege. He was questioned, told to stay put in Denver-metro, and then he made the mistake of crossing the mountains to come back here to Delta City, which is his hometown. Denver issued a warrant so the locals picked him up and I'm on the job to make sure justice is served. There's a hearing today and you know how it is—news travels fast and bad news gallops faster—so I rushed here to get ahead of the media and looks like I made it just in time. Ciao, kids."

Joel glanced over his shoulder as he hurried into the courthouse. Following his gaze, Trinidad and Anne saw a convoy of media trucks beginning to jockey for parking spaces along the street beyond.

"This is no place for us," Trinidad decided.

"Speak for yourself, Mr. DeMille," Anne laughed. "Personally, I'm ready for my close-up." She struck a pose, but Trinidad seemed unable to make a logical connection between their present situation and the memorable Gloria Swanson scene from the classic noir film "Sunset Boulevard." *It'll take time,* she thought, *but I'll make a movie buff of my guy yet.*

Trinidad interrupted her thoughts. "I'm serious," he said. "Let's go before the media circus begins."

"Okay, but it's been a long time since I went to the circus," she frowned.

"Believe me," said Trinidad, "in this particular circus, the animals have sharp pencils and long lenses and pointy teeth and they ain't in cages."

"Okay," said Anne. She stared with sudden apprehension at the first wave of determined reporters heading their way and added, "you've convinced me. Let's blow!"

They started down and were soon swimming against the current as they bucked an onslaught of journalists scrambling up the courthouse steps.

"Hey," shouted one reporter as they passed, "are you somebody important?"

"Nobody," said Anne as she held fast to her fiancé's sleeve.

"I'm with her," said Trinidad as the fleeing couple ducked through the surging crowd.

Chapter 8

Duffy's Tavern
(Divine Mercy Sunday)

The phone call was no surprise.

Three days had passed since Trinidad and Anne encountered Joel Signet on the courthouse steps, but the detective had a notion the lawyer would be asking for his help. It wasn't every day that the alleged murderer of a world-famous author turned up in Delta City—not to mention a famous author whose tale of hacksaw mayhem had frightened the crap out of the detective's recently acquired fiancée.

The call came in on the farm's landline—a number which only a handful of people knew. Aware of telemarketer tactics, Trinidad would ordinarily have let the phone ring, but he was pretty sure the call was from Joel. A glance at the caller ID display confirmed his notion, so he picked up the receiver.

"Duffy's Tavern—where the elite meet to eat—Duffy ain't here," said Trinidad.

"Old-time television trivia—I love it. So, your intended is already working her cinema spell on you. What's next I wonder? Foreign films? Well, anyway, they're holding my client without bail," said Joel and he sounded worried. "I'm convinced he's innocent of course—it's what I do—but I'm going to need some crack detective work to prove it. Are you and the missus up for this?"

Trinidad smiled. He'd been waiting for the right moment to suggest to Anne that they might make a pretty good investigative team. Though she herself may not have realized it yet, Trinidad was certain that his fiancée's training as an archaeologist more than qualified her to serve as his detective companion. The ever-perceptive Joel had sensed that such a partnership already existed.

"I'll ask Annie, but I'm pretty sure I can speak for her when I say we're on board," Trinidad assured the anxious lawyer.

Anne had heard the unfamiliar ring and was standing at Trinidad's elbow, listening to only one side of the conversation, and pantomiming the question '*what?*' over and over again as her new fiancé concluded his talk with Joel.

"Okay. We'll be there. See you then."

"What?" Anne asked aloud after Trinidad hung up. "I told you not to get a landline," she continued. "It was a telemarketer, right? Trying to sell you a condo in Cuba?"

"Not exactly," said Trinidad.

"A get-rich-quick scheme in Pakistan involving a disenfranchised prince and dogs and ponies?" Anne asked.

"Sort of," he answered. "It was Joel about a job."

"A job for you or for us?"

"For Sands et al," he said.

"I appreciate the sentiment," she said. "Except, your Latin's wonky since et al typically means 'and others.' Unless you're planning to form a posse and, if you're seriously asking for my help, how about Sands and Company?"

"Anything you say, partner."

Chapter 9

Chairs
(Monday, April 29)

"Old man Koller had a will of course," said Joel after Trinidad and Anne had poured themselves coffee and found a seat around the lawyer's plush conference table in his Delta City office.

It was early on Monday morning and everyone had enjoyed a lavish company breakfast. Anne would have preferred tea, but she decided not to make a fuss.

"*I like these chairs*," Anne mused, her thoughts already formulating a plan to refurbish Trinidad's Spartan home office.

"And no doubt somebody's contesting the old man's will," said Trinidad, trying to focus his impetuous bride-to-be on the task at hand.

"A plethora of somebodies to be exact," Joel laughed. "So, I'm afraid that, as far as the will is concerned, *it'll be all over but the shouting*." When his guests didn't react to his attempted witticism, he added, "I'm sorry, that's a little lawyer joke we use to refer to the reading of a will."

Trinidad and Anne were silent.

"Because there is sometimes shouting, you see, when the will is read. Especially when the document contains surprises, which this baby definitely does."

"And how do you happen to know anything about the contents of Koller's will?" Trinidad asked.

"Oh, didn't I mention it? My brother-in-law, Sid, is the attorney for the Koller estate and he bent the rules a little to give me a heads-up that the old man made a recent change to his will—a change which is bound to upset his presumptive heirs, which is good news for me and my client."

"How so?" asked Anne.

"Well, a boatload of people are lining up to claim they're related to Koller, but my source guarantees that there are only a handful of legitimate contenders. And those contenders add up to three potentially upset heiresses plus two upset heirs, which means five brand new murder suspects for the cops to consider in addition to my client—or should I say *our* client."

"Ray Zumberto's mug shot has been all over the news," said Trinidad. "So, as far as the media and the public are concerned, the police have their man."

"Which is great for us," Joel grinned at Anne. "Now, can you tell me why it's great for us, madam detective?"

Anne smiled. She considered herself a quick learner and it was great being called upon, especially when she knew the answer, or thought she did.

"Because..." she began tentatively, "since our other five suspects are not in the limelight, they won't have their guard up—which will make it easier to check up on them."

"Your wife is one smart cookie," Joel beamed.

Trinidad grinned too. Their wedding plans were still vague, but he liked the sound of *your wife*.

"So," Joel continued, "You can probably guess why I've called this meeting. Since I can't share my suspicions with the cops until the contents of the will are officially revealed, I need the two of you to discreetly check into the alibis of Koller's soon-to-be-disappointed relations, only one of which—or so Andrew implies—is going to walk away a winner. I need you to help establish their whereabouts at the time of the so-called Eastertide Murder."

"The media are having a field-day with that catchy *Eastertide* title," said Trinidad. "And the headline might be more appropriate than the newshounds think. Because, as far as our investigation goes, my guess is we're dealing with a crime of passion," he suggested. "It seems to be a classic case of one or more of Koller's immediate relations discovering that they were being disinherited and stabbing the old man in a fit of rage. My take is that this was an irrational murder that satisfied an impulsive urge, even though killing Esau Koller didn't move the murderer one inch closer to an inheritance."

"A mighty fine working premise and so your husband it seems," Joel said to Anne, "is also a smart cookie."

It was Anne's turn to grin. She liked the sound of *your husband*."

Chapter 10

Lunch Is on Joel

Joel's brother-in-law had stopped short of revealing whom the famous Esau Koller had named as his sole heir. It was enough to know that there would be only one beneficiary. That fact made it possible to predict that any relative destined to miss out on the old man's fortune might be sufficiently irate to murder Esau. The disposition of the will would be made public just after Pentecost, which left about six weeks to track down and interview five suspects. So, it was time for the lawyer's newly hired investigators to get to work.

Both members of the recently expanded Sands Detective Agency had spent Monday morning conferring with Joel Signet. Then Joel had taken them for a leisurely lunch in downtown Delta City. After shopping at City Market, it was mid-afternoon before they drove home and passed beneath the archway leading to Lavender Hill Farm. Surveying the farm's broad fields which stretched on both sides of the narrow dirt road, Trinidad was pleased to see his neatly-spaced rows of drought-tolerant plants basking in the spring sunshine. When they reached the hill beyond the fields and descended to the farmstead below, Trinidad was not surprised to see a patrol car sitting in their driveway. Jack Treadway was on the radio, so Trinidad sat down in the porch swing and waited while Anne took their groceries inside.

"Have a seat," said Trinidad as the sheriff mounted the stairs.

"Hot for April," said Jack as he settled into the nearest wicker chair.

Small talk is good, Trinidad thought. Then he smiled and said aloud, "Ah, here's the lemonade."

Anne sat the tray down on the wrought iron table and handed the fresh lemonade around. Then she sat beside her fiancé on the porch swing and resisted the urge to set the thing swinging.

"Quite a shock this Koller business," said Jack. "Knife in the face. A nasty way to die."

"Actually I…" Trinidad began.

"And a great blow to his readin' public, of course. It makes me sad that his life was—you should forgive the expression—cut short before he finished his latest masterpiece. But I don't have to tell you all this. I'm sure you both know old man Koller wrote over a hundred books, if you can believe it. Prolific is… well it's just too small a word for that much work! It's a cryin' shame that no more will never see the light of day. Still, 108 published best-sellers in print must be some kinda record. And, believe it or not, I've read everything he ever wrote. Now, Miss Anne, I hear you like a good read, so I wonder if it ain't bein' too nosey, can I ask which one is your favorite?"

"*Hacksaw Fury*," both detectives said without skipping a beat.

"Hands down my absolute favorite," Anne added.

"Ha, mine too!" agreed the sheriff. "And did I ever tell you that I read *Hacksaw* from cover-to-cover durin' a cross-country trip? Not zoomin' up there in no airplane, mind you, but moseyin' along on an actual passenger train. And it was such a crackerjack story that—even though I was firmly planted in that earth-bound railroad car—I don't know how to put it, except to say that readin' it sorta gave me wings—wings. You understand what I mean?"

"Wings," Trinidad repeated as he remembered how he'd scattered a flock of doves by tossing Anne's copy of Koller's unnerving novel out their second-story window. "Yes, we understand completely."

Not sure what Trinidad meant but anxious to support him, Anne nodded and said, "Yes, I agree, it made me want to fly away for sure."

"Well," said Jack, "So we all agree that old man Koller was a great writer and meantime Denver is pretty sure they've got his killer in custody. Well, anyway *we* have him here in Delta County. And now I hear that our mutual friend, Joel Signet, has put you on his payroll."

So, thought Trinidad, *we've finally come around to the reason for the sheriff's unannounced visit.* "Is that a problem?" the detective asked aloud.

"I should ask you that," said the sheriff. "*Is* this gonna be a problem?"

"Not for us," said Trinidad and he took Anne's hand.

Jack raised an eyebrow as he followed Trinidad's motion and noticed the ring. "So, the rumors *is* true," Jack said. Then the sheriff grinned and continued, "And now I suppose I'll have to deal with a sleuthin' couple like that pair in the old-time movies—the ones with the little dog whose name keeps comin' up in crossword puzzles."

"You mean Asta," said Anne, "the little fox terrier from *The Thin Man*."

"Yeah," said Jack, "And you two are just like Asta's masters—that's kind of fun to say: 'Asta's masters.'"

"Maybe—except I'm no longer a hard-drinking detective," said Trinidad.

"And also, we don't have a dog," added Anne, "and I'm not a wealthy heiress."

"That we know of," corrected Jack. "In a few weeks, come Pentecost, when old man Koller's will is read out-loud, somebody around here is for sure gonna strike it rich and it might as well be you."

Chapter 11

Nightmare
(Tuesday, April 30)

The next morning, long before dawn, a nightmare forced Anne awake. Yesterday's visit from the sheriff had unsettled her. The last time she remembered a cop car making a house call, she was just a girl and they'd come to lead her father away in handcuffs.

She'd been dreaming she was a girl again in rural Arizona and alone in the family cabin while her mother was miles away tending to a sick neighbor. Anne was a teenager and old enough to drive—although not legally. With her mother away, it fell to young Anne to operate the old family truck to drive her father to work and pick him up when his shift ended at the Bisbee mine.

At first, she'd dreaded the prospect of spending time alone with her father, but to her surprise a week passed and her old man stopped drinking. He even shaved and bathed more regularly and he praised Anne's middling cooking and complimented her appearance.

She should have seen it coming. Why did she not see it coming?

"You awake?" Trinidad asked.

"Yes," she whispered in the dark.

"Good awake or bad awake?"

It was a chance to tell her present lover and future husband more about her troubled past. A little he already knew and some he'd guessed. They were, after all, sharing the same bed and this was not the first time a bad dream had shocked the sobbing woman awake.

"How much do you want to hear?" she said as tears began to cloud her eyes.

Trinidad reached over and pulled her close. "Tell me everything," he said.

Chapter 12

A Sizeable Package

"How do you want to do this?" Anne asked as she loaded the last of the Tuesday morning breakfast bowls into the dishwasher. A sizable package had arrived from Joel, sent by courier. It was her turn to cook, so she'd cleared away the breakfast dishes while Trinidad opened the bulky envelope and separated an assortment of photographs and dossiers into neat piles on the kitchen table.

"My initial reaction is to have you investigate the women and me the men," he said. "But that's not necessarily the best way. So, let's each take a suspect and read up on that person and take notes as we go. Then we'll each pick another file and read that one from front to back and so on until we've both read everything and have a better idea of the people we're dealing with. And let's create a discard pile where we can toss any documents that seem irrelevant to our case."

"Smart cookie," she teased.

"Focus," he chided.

Joel's efficient staff had done a thorough job of compiling background materials. It took the rest of the morning plus a working lunch and most of the afternoon to get through the files. Their diligent study included two hours spent digesting the thickest file—a bulky dossier dedicated to Isaac Koller, one of Esau's natural children and the only son.

By sunset, the two detectives had absorbed a general, though dated, biography of Esau Koller himself. Then came the backstories of the old man's two wives (both deceased); his twin brother; his natural son and daughter plus two step-daughters and a natural daughter who had died as a child. In all, the subjects amounted to three dead relations, two living heirs, and three living heiresses. When they were finished, they had a preliminary idea of the Koller clan, and—even though there were gaps in the information—it was not a pretty picture.

Anne seemed to sum up both their feelings when she said, "The wonder is not that one of these damaged people probably killed old man Koller. The wonder is that they didn't form a posse and do the murder as a group; or that he didn't kill them first; or that they didn't murder each other."

"Well, aside from this loathsome exercise making us both feel like we need a shower," said Trinidad, "I think it's safe to say that I should take son Isaac. With his prison record he's clearly the most dangerous of the bunch."

"Be my guest," said Anne. "And I'll take Jacob, the lecherous brother with a thing for younger women and girls. Given his predilections, I should be able to charm him into revealing something incriminating."

"I'm not exactly sure what 'predilection' means," said Trinidad. "But just be sure not to find yourself alone with old Jacob in a dark alley."

"Or any alley at any time of day for that matter," she agreed. "So, what about the females?"

"I'll take two and you take one," said Trinidad.

"Yeah, I get that," she said, "But which one?"

"Flip a coin?" Trinidad suggested.

The quarter came up heads which meant that Anne would interview the brother Jacob and Ruth the natural daughter.

"Anybody in this family have a name that's not from the Old Testament?" Anne asked as she examined their copy of the Koller family tree. "And what's with this lavender family crest and the falling leaf?"

"No idea about the crest," Trinidad admitted as he picked up two sheets from the discard pile. "His first wife's name was Chloe. But the deceased child was named Naomi, so the Old Testament theme was a Koller thing."

"At least he didn't impose the pattern on his second family," Anne observed. "Because the surviving step-daughters are named...give me a second." She consulted the lower level of the tree document. "Millie and Juliet and those two seem mostly normal. Millie, the youngest, is a student in Glenwood Springs and sister Juliet operates a restaurant on the other side of Grand Mesa, in the tiny metropolis of Collbran, population 700, so she should be a cinch to find. Meanwhile their mother, Koller's wife number two, was called... Hortense—which I think is a great name for a murder suspect. But I presume she's in our discard pile because she and the other wife and the baby girl are all dead."

"Naomi was an infant, drowned in a flash flood along with her mother. So, the baby and the two wives are dead and buried," said Trinidad. "And Hortense, the most recently deceased, was lavishly interred against the wishes of Koller's son who, when the time came and in the interest of economy, wanted his step-mother cremated."

"Instead of holding an expensive funeral which would've cost a fortune and reduced the estate," Anne guessed.

"Precisely—so already we see a motive for the son which takes the form of familial tension," said Trinidad referencing an entry in his notebook. He looked at Anne and saw her staring at her own notes. "What have you written down?" he asked.

"Almost nothing," she sighed. "And, until you mentioned it, I totally missed that son Isaac might be holding a grudge because of his step-mother's expensive funeral."

"It'll come to you as you get more experience," Trinidad assured her. "Was that too patronizing to say?"

"No," Anne smiled, "that was just about right and more than I deserved. Now, how about that cleansing shower? Join me. Save water."

Chapter 13

Ray's Story
(Wednesday, May 1)

Things were moving quickly. Within a day of sending the background materials to his detectives, Joel had arranged a Wednesday afternoon conference allowing his newly hired team to meet their client. He considered it vital that they hear Ray's story for themselves. The meeting was important for the repairman too. Ray was understandably nervous and Joel knew that it would ease his anxiety to know that he had three bright young people (Joel naturally included himself) working on his case.

"Well, that's about all I kin remember," Ray frowned as he glanced at the ubiquitous shadow of the deputy sheriff lingering just outside the conference room, fulfilling his role as guard. Ray's nose itched, something about the stiff fabric of the orange prisoner jumpsuit he was obliged to wear. He used both handcuffed hands to scratch it. He'd just finished repeating his memory of the events of Easter Sunday and the following Monday. "So, am I screwed? Beg pardon, ma'am, I don't mean no offense."

"No worries," Anne said and she gave the nervous man a smile. "And the answer is *no you're not*. Not with the three of us on your side—you'll be fine."

Ray seemed relieved to hear it and he visibly relaxed. "Okay," the repairman said. Then he took a deep breath, let it slowly out, and asked, "What now?"

"Let's go over your recollections about the elevator again," said Trinidad. He was being all business and Anne liked to see him taking charge.

"Well," said Ray, "it's like I said. I rode the elevator that first day, up and down, no problem. Then, when I comes back the other day, there's a sign—see?"

"And, again, are you able to remember now what the sign said?" asked Trinidad.

"Uh—let me try again—I think it was..." Ray stared at the ceiling as if the answer were written up there somewhere. "Temporary service inter...something."

"Might the word have been *interruption*?" Trinidad asked.

"That was the very animal," said Ray. "Temporary service interruption—that was it alright."

"And was this a proper sign or hand-printed?" Anne asked.

"Is that important?" asked Ray. "Not that I don't doubt you, ma'am."

"Yes," said Trinidad pleased with his fiancée's insight. "It's very important."

"Well, now that you mention it, the thing was hand-printed."

"On what sort of paper?" asked Joel. "On a regular 8 ½-by-11 piece of paper? A sheet of lined notebook paper? Or something else?"

"Well, it was writ out on one of them little teeny cards like you used to see in the library books," said Ray.

"A 3 by 5 card?" asked Joel as he rummaged in his briefcase. "A card like this?"

"About that size only more-smaller, like I said, and it really was a card like in the library," insisted Ray.

"Why do you say that?" asked Trinidad.

"On account of it had all them little bitty dates stamped on it. Like when the book is due back and such."

Anne and Trinidad were both taking notes and they looked up from their notebooks and exchanged a smile.

"Okay," said Trinidad, "Now we're getting somewhere. Did you try the elevator?"

"I don't get you," said Ray.

"He means," explained Anne, "did you press the ground-floor call button to summon the elevator car?"

"Oh no, ma'am," said Ray favoring the beautiful young woman with a toothsome grin. "I just believed that sign. And I remember thinkin' what a chore it'd be to fix the dang elevator and how glad I was it wasn't me that would have to fix it, and then I cusses and starts walkin' upstairs. Do you need to know the cuss words I used?"

"We can imagine you were perplexed," said Joel, struggling to suppress a laugh. "So, no need to give us the specifics, just skip what exactly you said and remind us again what happened in the stairwell."

"Well," said Ray, seeming to enjoy the attention of these earnest young people. "It's like I said, I hikes a-ways up and I sits down in-so-much as that typewriter machine is heavy, you know, and it's so hot and then all of a sudden I hears the elevator goin' down."

"Now, you are absolutely certain it was going down?" asked Trinidad.

"Absolutely," insisted Ray. "That's why I cussed it out when it passed me by. On account of I figured somebody was holdin' it upstairs and makin' me walk all the way up—all on account of they wouldn't let the dang thing come down."

"Ray," said Joel as he nodded to his partners, "I think we may just have saved your neck."

Chapter 14

Clock
(Evening)

Sitting at the kitchen table, the two detectives had been working non-stop, scrambling to skim through the latest information pertaining to the Koller case, when they heard the hall clock strike the hour. Trinidad glanced at his watch. It was not yet 9 p.m. on a rainy Wednesday. As soon as they were less busy, he'd lower the pendulum bob, an adjustment which would slow the clock down. Several more hours would be required to absorb all the new evidence which had landed in their laps. They were up against a tight deadline and the irascible timepiece's determination to hurry the passage of time was unhelpful. When Anne looked up from her reading, their eyes met and she guessed his thoughts.

"Go," she said as she reached across the table, grabbed Trinidad's papers, and added them to her own pile, "I'm about done with twenty-nine and I can finish Chapter 30. You go tinker with William."

Trinidad left the table and walked into the hallway to deal with the clock. It'd been Annie's idea to give the vintage grandfather clock a Christian name. She had an endearing, if puzzling, habit of naming certain inanimate objects, in particular those which had a tendency to malfunction. The undependable coffee grinder was *Grendel* (based on the unholy complaint it made when processing beans), the on-again/off-again garbage disposal was *Burt*, and the unpredictable toaster—naturally—was *Toasty*. It was all he could do to recall the pet-name of each device and so she'd assisted his memory by taping name tags to the devices in question.

"What's the idea?" he'd inquired.

"Everything works better when it's part of the family," was her cryptic reply.

Standing in the hallway recalling his fiancée's endearing foibles, he knelt down, opened the lower portion of the clock's glass case, stilled the pendulum, reached beneath the bob, and turned the adjustment nut to the left.

Left for lower and lower is slower, his thoughts recalled his father's instructions on the day he'd passed the family heirloom to his only son. Setting the pendulum swinging again, Trinidad closed the lower glass, stood erect and, opening the upper glass which guarded the clockface, he moved the minute hand back ten minutes. Watching to make certain the second hand was advancing, he closed the upper glass and headed back along the hallway in the direction of the kitchen where his fiancée was diligently plowing through Koller's rambling memoirs.

He didn't know exactly how Joel Signet had convinced the Denver metro police to release such a sheaf of evidence from the dead man's apartment. But he was pretty sure the lawyer's brother-in-law, who served as executor of the Koller estate, had pulled a few strings. Whatever working agreement Andrew and Joel and the Denver police had reached, a uniformed courier had arrived at Lavender Hill Farm a few hours ago, just before sundown, seeking the detective's signature. The courier was under strict instructions not to place the packet in Trinidad's hands until the detective signed a binding pledge promising to surrender the document when the man returned twelve hours later.

So, the clock was literally ticking.

The packet contained summaries of Denver police interviews with Koller's cook and housekeeper, whom Denver had cleared as suspects, and a file box containing 213 photocopied pages of a manuscript. The vast majority of manuscript pages were neatly typed and double-spaced. The final dozen were handwritten sheets on lined paper. Taken together, the pages appeared to represent a draft of Koller's unpublished memoirs—a work of some 60,000 words, about the length of his published novels. The first 200 pages were in coherent order. They began with a prologue describing how the old man had come to grips with his mortality. Next came thirty typewritten chapters divided into six distinct sections:

1) BIRTH AND CHILDHOOD: Chapters 1-5, describing an idyllic boyhood growing up in Carbondale, Colorado, as the favored son and the making of his family's fortune—first in silver and ultimately in potatoes;

2) EDUCATION: Chapters 6-10, his Ivy League college days;

3) MARRYING WELL: Chapters 11-15, his union to a wealthy heiress;

4) RISE TO PROMINENCE: Chapters 16-20, his subsequent relocation to Aspen as well as the lavish lifestyle supported by two vast inheritances;

5) TRAGEDY: Chapters 21-25, the tragic drowning of his first wife and infant daughter and his second marriage;

and 6) LEAVING ASPEN: Chapters 26-30, his decision to become a novelist, leave Aspen behind, and relocate to Denver to continue his lucrative writing career.

It was a passable tale but hardly epic.

"The rich get richer," Anne had said and her partner had agreed.

Having divided up the initial typewritten chapters as they separately searched for clues, the two detectives reached a gap which had intrigued the Denver investigators. This break in the memoirs' otherwise cohesive narrative came at the end of Chapter 30 and consisted of a seventh section which was incomplete. This seventh section was introduced by a single sheet with the typewritten heading "CONSEQUENCES" which had been scratched out and replaced with a handwritten substitute. The top of the page showed signs of alteration. The new heading, written in ink, was "REDEMPTION." The section sheet was followed by a single typewritten page and Koller's final handwritten sheets.

Entitled 'Chapter 31: Darling Daughters,' the page ended with an unfinished, typewritten sentence which seemed to dovetail with the opening line of the handwritten pages. Koller's prologue as well as each of the author's first thirty chapters were brief—averaging six double-spaced sheets. It seemed reasonable to presume that, once the handwritten pages were typed-out, the work would be complete.

Morton Blake, the capitol city's lead homicide investigator, had paper-clipped his business card to Chapter 31 with the suggestion "Call me" hand-written in ink next to the department's logo, along with what appeared to be a personal phone number. Anne suggested and Trinidad concurred that it was not too late to try calling Denver. The phone rang four times and was about to go to voicemail when the officer picked up.

"Division Chief Blake."

"Chief," said Trinidad, "This is Trinidad Sands of the Sands Detective Agency..."

"Yes, I see your name on my caller ID. I've been expecting to hear from you, but I figured it would be morning before you rang and I was about to call it a night," said Blake.

"Sorry. Should I call back tomorrow?"

"No worries. I've still got a few chores to do. I need to walk the dog and set up the coffeemaker before turning in. Anyway, you must be a speed reader. The delivery receipt on my end says you've only had that bulky package since seven or so. I figured it would take you much longer than a couple of hours to plow through the pile," said Blake.

"I had help," said Trinidad as he beamed at his fiancée. "Do you mind if I put this call on speaker phone?"

"Go ahead," Blake agreed. "Jack said there was a pair of you."

"Hello," said Anne, "This is Anne Scriptor..."

"Anne with an 'e,' Scriptor with an 'o' right?" said Blake.

"Yes. How did you...?"

"Jack again," said Blake. "And I have to tell you both that I was against this sharing business until Sheriff Treadway vouched for you two. Anyway, let's get to it before my little dog throws a fit."

Chief Blake reported that his squad had established a working theory that there were no missing pages.

"Everything is accounted for. The prologue and first thirty chapters were found on the bedside table, neatly stacked inside a wooden box and in numerical order. The prologue opens with the old guy pondering his death, but—aside from that exceptional beginning—the rest of the read-through on our end pegs the work as a typical autobiography. A narrative filled with self-aggrandizing recollections, tempered with a healthy dose of regrets."

"Was Chapter 31 in the box with the rest of the manuscript?" Trinidad asked.

"No. The opening page of Chapter 31—a single typewritten sheet—was found on the bedroom floor near the penthouse's side door and, before you ask, the handwritten ones were stuffed in one of the victim's pillow cases. They were apparently shoved in there alongside the pillow and in a hurry since—although you may not notice it on your copies—the lined papers are thoroughly wrinkled."

"Koller used his bedroom like an office," Trinidad speculated.

"Sort of. According to his Denver domestics, the victim did his typing on the old Remington at a butcherblock work desk in his den. That's the largest penthouse room with a huge bar and wide exterior windows overlooking the cityscape—you can see our office building from there. Anyway, the help said he did his typing in the den and most of his pen and paper writing in bed, propped up against a reading pillow and using a serving tray as a lap desk. Nice work if you can get it, I guess."

"Anything unusual about the murder scene?" Trinidad asked.

"Well, as I'm guessing you already know, we found our victim in the marble hallway near the side door, in his pajamas and his feet were bare. So, our working premise is that Koller was in bed writing away when somebody interrupted him and he felt compelled to hide what he was doing. Our idea has him halting his work and, for whatever reason, stuffing the handwritten pages into his pillowcase. We picture somebody ringing the penthouse door-bell, which caused Koller to stash his writing before leaving the bedroom and walking through the den to open the front door. Must've dropped the fountain pen, the one the help said he always used, on his way to answer the door and the missing pen must've landed someplace weird because we haven't been able to locate it. Finally, as for how he ended up in the side hall, we visualize something going south with the visitor in the front parlor which caused the old man to try escaping through the side door. Whatever went down on Easter Monday morning, it looks like he was overtaken and killed in the side hall."

"So, he opened the door to a visitor he knew?" Trinidad speculated as he looked at Anne, wondering why she wasn't asking questions, and saw that his helpful partner was busy taking notes. Smart cookie, he smiled to himself.

"Probably somebody he knew," Blake agreed. "Or at least somebody he expected. Which, to my way of thinking, leads us straight back to our repairman. We found an invoice on Zumberto for sixty-five hundred dollars plus tax. That's a tidy sum for fixing an ancient manual typewriter, which my people tell me might be worth ten bucks at a yard sale. Our best guess is the repair guy was running some kind of blackmail scheme, and Koller refused to pay, and the two had an argument over the bill."

Hearing this, Anne looked up from her notes, made a disapproving face, and seemed about to protest before her fiancé interrupted her potential rebellion with a question.

"Murder weapon?" Trinidad asked.

"Medical examiner figures it was an ice pick or maybe a knitting needle or another probe of some kind. Not the sort of thing your average citizen carries in their pocket. Anyway, no sign of the weapon. We suspect our killer carried it away or might have dropped whatever it was down the trash chute, which was handy. The chute runs from the top of the building all the way down to the basement. There's a trash opening at every floor and the penthouse receptacle was nearby, in the hallway wall, and just a hop, skip, and a jump from the crime scene. Unfortunately, the trash was picked up before we arrived. So, no chance of locating that particular needle in the haystack of our City and County of Denver landfill. Meanwhile, Koller's hired help had Easter Sunday and Monday off and they both reported that the old man had few visitors, so it seems the repair guy was the only thing on the Koller agenda that morning. So, he's probably our guy."

"I don't suppose Esau Koller kept an appointment calendar," Anne speculated, her tone betraying her growing irritation with the lawman's desire to pin the murder on Ray Zumberto.

"Good question and that would've been handy," said the chief. "But, alas, no written record of whether he was expecting more than one visitor that morning. You'll find vague references in the handwritten pages to the imminent return of a prodigal child, but that's a longshot because the notes don't say who or when or where this supposed reunion was to take place."

"Prints?" Trinidad asked while Anne continued to fidget in her chair.

"No extra prints on the loose pages or the boxed ones or the box or the tray or anywhere in the bedroom—only Koller's. Fingerprints elsewhere in the apartment belong to the old man as well as the housemaid and the cook, both of whom have air-tight alibies. But the lab boys hit the jackpot on the front door knobs. Inside and out what we have is a pristine set of our prime suspect's thumb and fingers."

There was a pause in the chief's explanation, suggesting he was weighing what more he could share with the detectives.

"Look," Blake continued, "I understand Jack is half-convinced that the repair guy's story holds water—his claim about somebody else in the elevator. And, on my favorite sheriff's say-so, I've agreed to leave our prime suspect in Delta County custody while you two check out Koller's relations. I'm all for a public/private partnership on this one since Jack's shop is stretched thin and my measly budget won't absorb sending my own people all the way to the Western Slope. But I have to tell you this: since nobody else noticed somebody joy-riding in the elevator that morning, Ray, the over-charging repairman, still looks good for this murder."

"Well, I believe Ray," said Anne with feeling. "He's a gentle soul and could no more stab someone to death than the man in the moon! So, I think you're wrong to suspect him and what's more we're going to prove..." she stopped talking because Trinidad was shaking his head as his face displayed a disapproving frown.

"Wow!" said the chief. "Jack told me your young Anne was a pistol. The repair guy's lucky to have such passion in his corner. Anyway, I was about to add that your Grand Junction lawyer sent us a transcript of your interview with Zumberto, so—based on that—I guess I'm willing to entertain the idea that he may not be our perp. Now, about the clipped page, I take it you haven't read it or the handwritten pages yet..."

"We stopped reading at the end of Chapter 30 and contacted you as soon as we saw your card and the note to call," said Trinidad.

"Nice," Blake said. "I only wish my own people paid as much attention to my instructions as you folks." Then he laughed and added, "Tell you what, I need to walk the dog, and after discussing the case with you two, I'm too jazzed to hit the hay, so why don't you look the rest over and call me back in about an hour?"

"Roger that," said Trinidad.

"Okay," said Blake. "Oh, by the way, we weren't able to detect anything special about that last typewritten page—just a fluke of some kind so far as my guys can tell. Our theory is the perpetrator was after the handwritten pages, maybe looking for something in particular, maybe trying to confiscate something incriminating. Maybe the killer was upset at not finding all of Chapter 31 and was in a hurry and dropped that single page. But no way of telling what the perp was after. There's no gap there since the handwritten pages match up. Anyway, I'll be interested to hear what you two have to say."

"Thanks for the summary," said Trinidad.

"Oh, a couple of more things before I forget," Blake added. "There were ink stains on the victim's hands from what looks to be a leaky fountain pen. The servants said Koller was a creature of habit and the housekeeper recalled that the old guy pitched a fit when she wrote him a note suggesting he have her buy a new fountain pen and toss the old one. Anyway, speaking of pitching a fit, my little spoiled-rotten Corgi's whining..."

"One more question," said Trinidad. "Any ink in the hallway?"

"None on the tile or walls," said Blake. "Just on the victim's hands and a little on his face too—probably from trying to protect his eyes—a natural-enough reflex given the repeated stabs. Gotta run now. Phone me later."

Ending the call, the couple realized they'd been so intent on studying their copy of the Koller manuscript that they hadn't eaten. While Trinidad rummaged in the refrigerator to pull together a late supper, Anne began reading the final typewritten page. The Denver investigators hadn't detected a pattern, but Anne only had to review the half-dozen paragraphs before she recognized one.

"Clear as a bell if you read between the lines," she noted while Trinidad handed her an extemporaneous sandwich. "Here's how I see it: the page opens with paragraphs describing each daughter—including Naomi the drowned infant—in glowing, paternal terms. Then the writing ends abruptly and just at the moment when he starts to wax poetic about his daughters. Listen to this incomplete thought at the bottom of number 201," she said as she read aloud the interrupted sentence which concluded the page: 'God forgive me, because I must admit that my darlings...'" Anne stopped then, stared at her partner, and—when he didn't respond—she added, "Isn't it obvious?"

Trinidad hazarded a guess. "Could be the opening sentence of a confession," he suggested.

"Has to be," she agreed. "And I'm guessing the handwritten pages expose the extent of Koller's affinity for his daughters—and not in a good way..."

Anne felt a catch in her throat as memories of her own father flooded back with such vivid clarity that she was compelled to tell herself to think about something else.

"I get what you're saying," said Trinidad as he pulled his chair near, sat beside Anne, and gently placed a supporting hand on her shoulder. "You okay, Annie?" he asked.

"Better now," she said. "Better with you here."

"So..." said Trinidad. He hesitated, sensing his partner was struggling to weather the unhappy memories which Koller's unfinished chapter stirred up.

"Go ahead..." Anne said, unable to find the words, hoping he could follow her lead.

"The killer guessed at the contents of the missing pages," Trinidad continued. "And maybe that person wanted to purge any mention of Koller's relations with his daughters..."

"And unfortunately, I can guess why," Anne added. Then she grew silent as a single tear slid down her cheek.

"Do you want to take a break?" Trinidad asked.

"I'm done here," she said as she got unsteadily to her feet.

"Do you want me to..." Trinidad began as he stood to follow her upstairs.

"No thanks," she said. "You stay here. Stick with it. I'll be okay."

Trinidad watched Anne go. The implications of the handwritten pages had proven too much for her, but he believed she was on the right track.

Trinidad could only guess at the details of Koller's confession. The insightful detective was sure his dear partner could fill in the blanks, but he had no intention of asking.

He'd drop the subject for now. With luck, further investigation would lead to other sources which would confirm his fiancée's suspicions. Either way, for the time being, Anne's insights had placed Koller's daughters squarely in the prime suspect column. Trinidad picked up the phone and dialed Denver.

"Smart cookie," Chief Blake agreed when the detective called to share Anne's discerning conclusions. "Leave it to me and my team of male lunkheads to miss the obvious. As soon as we hang up, I'm calling the squad together and expanding our group to include the fairer sex. We'll start working on leads on the daughters from this end and I'll keep Jack in the loop. Can I count on you to share what you find over there?"

"Absolutely," said Trinidad.

"Have you taken a look at the handwritten stuff yet?" Blake asked.

"Next on my list," said Trinidad.

"Remember, the reason those pages are rumpled is we found them stuffed inside a pillowcase. I'm thinking the killer missed them. And as for their content..." Blake began. "Well, let's wait until you and Miss Scriptor have had a look-see. I don't want to influence you one way or another. Call again when you have something. Good hunting."

Chapter 15

Coffee
(Thursday, May 2)

Trinidad was alone in the kitchen at Lavender Hill Farm and frowning while he brewed a pot of coffee. He'd meant to review the final twelve pages of Koller's memoirs hours ago, but he'd yet to accomplish the task of plowing through the photocopies of the old man's handwritten sheets. Hearing the hall clock strike 6 a.m., the weary detective had raised his head and glanced out the kitchen window. The first blush of dawn had already ignited the far horizon and he wondered if Thursday was going to be another warmer than average spring day.

Chief Blake had asked them to call back last night, but Anne had gone to bed and Trinidad had laid his head down on the kitchen table, like a kindergartener taking a nap, and instantly fallen asleep. No one had stayed awake to read the handwritten pages or call Denver again and what the chief would think was anybody's guess. During their telephone discussion last night, Trinidad had gained the distinct impression that Blake was a patient man. Probably he'd accept their follow-up call whenever the detectives got around to making it, so long as the manuscript itself was returned on time.

Whatever the new morning held in store, the night had passed and the veteran half of the Sands Detective Agency was awake now and brewing coffee as he fortified himself to tackle the handwritten pages. While Anne safely

slumbered upstairs, he'd study Koller's concluding pages and prepare a summary of the contents. And he'd word that summary carefully because he had
no wish to distress his bride-to-be. He'd soften his summation by devising
a multitude of euphemisms to describe the corruption he was certain he'd
discover there. Tact would be required because he had his own theory as to
what the handwritten pages contained and why they were untyped.

Putting himself in the old man's place, the detective surmised that, as
described by the author's biographers and confirmed by his hired help, Koller
had been following his habitual procedure of writing a first draft in longhand
before typing the finished manuscript on his vintage Remington. Koller's
prologue and the first thirty chapters of his memoirs had been neatly typed
with no evidence of a faulty "H" until he attempted to type Chapter 31.

If Trinidad had deduced the circumstances correctly, he had to agree
with the metro police that there were no missing pages—only an interrupted
process which had been truncated in the closing paragraphs of page 201,
when the old man's machine began to malfunction. The misalignment of
the eighth letter of the alphabet—Koller's precious "H"—on the incomplete
typewritten page meant one thing to the detective. Trinidad was certain
that the confession the old man had been in the process of typing-out didn't
end at the bottom of the page. He had to agree with his bride-to-be that the
incomplete narrative would resolve itself in the handwritten pages.

Certain that Koller's wickedness would be on full display in those closing
pages and feeling the need to steel himself for what he anticipated would be
an odious task, the detective poured himself a cup of coffee, returned to the
kitchen table, and reached for the handwritten sheets.

But no amount of caffeine could have prepared him for what he found.

Chapter 16

Last Words

Trinidad sat at Lavender Hill Farm's broad kitchen table as the rising sun ignited the farmhouse windows. The detective was figuratively and literally shaking his head. As surely as the morning banished the darkness, his expectations regarding the final pages of Esau Koller's unpublished manuscript were evaporating. To begin with, Koller's penmanship was flawless, a circumstance which made his final words all the more poignant. The detective had expected the handwriting to resemble a nearly-illegible scrawl, as if some feral animal had scratched out the letters. He'd expected those letters to form disgusting words that coagulated into vile sentences as the old man confessed his sordid past in lurid detail.

Instead, the author's handwritten pages ignored the past entirely and spoke instead of a recent epiphany which caused him to renounce his evil ways and chart a path toward redemption. The catalyst of this conversion seemed to be a much-anticipated reconciliation with his long-lost prodigal child—a reunion which Koller believed was to be achieved with an impending visit. The old man's apparently heartfelt declaration ended with a series of emotional sentences.

The sun is up, Koller wrote in his exquisite hand, *and this morning's apparition has come and gone. Now the street door chimes to proclaim that my angel is nigh. I must confess to being light-headed and giddy with anticipation, but the angel mustn't see these unrefined lines—words not yet fit for celestial eyes—not until I've polished them to perfection. Before my long-awaited guest arrives, I'll put these sheets aside and trust instead to the joy of our precious reunion which, in time, will make my finished creation all the sweeter and...*

The thought was apparently interrupted, for there had been no time to continue the line. Closing his eyes to concentrate, Trinidad put the pages aside and tried to envision what must have happened next.

Like most Denver urban high-rise condominiums, the Stevenson Building had a security system which consisted of an exterior call button positioned next to the outside entrance. What the old man intended by mentioning a morning apparition was unclear, but whatever ghost he'd seen, its appearance didn't diminish his enthusiasm. Clearly, he was expecting someone special. The author's mysterious visitor would have activated the call button to request admission and the signal sounding in the penthouse would account for the chimes Koller described. Before buzzing his visitor in by deactivating the main door's magnetic lock, the giddy old man would have taken time to rip a handful of sheets from his writing tablet and stuff them into his pillow case, with the intention of typing them up later in order to make them the final stanzas of his memoirs.

On the sidewalk far below, hearing the entry buzzer, the mystery visitor would have passed through the building's outer door. Koller believed he was admitting his estranged child, but unless there had been voice or video confirmation, the unseen arrival could've been anyone. Trinidad made a note to doublecheck the details of the Stevenson's security system, but he'd studied online images of the vintage building and had his doubts that the system featured anything as sophisticated as a voice intercom or video surveillance.

Imagining the scene in the Stevenson's plush lobby, Trinidad pictured the visitor traversing the unoccupied space, hanging a bogus 'out-of-order' sign, pressing the elevator call button on the ground floor, and beginning the ascent to the penthouse. Arriving there, the killer would have locked the elevator car at the top, crossed the marble hall, and rung the old man's front doorbell.

If Trinidad understood the timeline correctly, Koller's last handwritten words would have been composed on the morning of April 22 and shortly before the old man was killed. Moments after penning those optimistic lines, Koller's dream of a heavenly encounter with his prodigal child would have been shattered when someone confronted him on his threshold, wielded a sharp instrument, pursued him into the adjoining hallway, and extinguished his life.

Trinidad opened his eyes, stood up, crossed to the stove, poured himself another cup of coffee, and stared out the kitchen window. In the growing morning light, he could just make out the wrinkle of soil that marked the spot where, days ago, he'd buried his fiancée's spurned copy of Koller's *Hacksaw Fury*. The prolific horror author's own death had been a ghastly affair which would have fit well into his series of disturbing novels.

The detective had seen the autopsy photos—an experience he'd purposely spared Anne. Esau Koller's face had been virtually obliterated. Like his optimistic partner, he couldn't see Ray Zumberto doing anything of the sort. The killing had been horrific and—to the detective's way of thinking—highly personal. Such a methodical and vicious murder spoke of familial angst, so Trinidad had been convinced from the first that the perpetrator was a relative. Depending on which suspect was ultimately linked to the crime, the detective's working theory meant that one brother had slaughtered the other, or else a child—adopted or natural—had murdered a parent. For him, the Koller case boiled down to one scenario or the other. Either they were investigating an instance of brutal fratricide or one of merciless patricide.

Having completed his review of the Koller manuscript, Trinidad was sipping his fresh cup of coffee and contemplating the dawn when he heard the padding of delicate feet on the staircase and in the downstairs hallway. He turned to see his partner standing in the kitchen doorway wearing nothing but a pair of socks. Sporting an alluring grin, his fundamentally naked partner beckoned him forward with a single wag of her finger, and Anne didn't have to tell him twice to come to bed.

Chapter 17

In the Woods
(Friday, May 3)

It was lunchtime on Friday and Ray Zumberto's prospects were steadily improving. Jack had been able to confirm the story of the supposedly inoperable elevator by interviewing other tenants and revisiting the statement made by Leonard, the building maintenance man. However, Leonard had found nothing amiss with the elevator and, if there had been an out-of-order sign on the ground floor, no one but Ray remembered seeing it, so the repairman was not quite out of the woods.

But the work of Joel Signet, Esquire, and Sands and Company, coupled with new breakthroughs being pursued in Denver, had raised a growing crop of doubts. So, the Delta County district attorney had entered into a pact with Jack's office and the Denver investigators. The arrangement was to keep the repairman under wraps. The big city squad agreed to pursue leads along the Front Range of the Rockies while the Sands agency conducted its unofficial, but highly awaited, Western Slope inquiries. It was a lovefest of statewide and public/private cooperation that seemed to amaze everyone concerned—at least everybody but Jack.

"I put this whole thing down to your Annie," the sheriff told Trinidad as he and the detective stood side-by-side at the men's room urinals. "Plain and simple," Jack noted as he flushed, zipped up, and washed his hands at the sink. "That-there young lady's the wildcard you and me been missin' all these years, I reckon."

Trinidad managed a qualified smile to hear Jack's unsolicited praise of his beloved partner. Anne had been a catalyst all right, even though she'd paid for it dearly by having to wrestle with unpleasant girlhood memories and the persistent ghost of her abusive father. He wouldn't mention his fiancée's trials and tribulations to Jack, but he'd be absolutely certain to tell his intrepid Annie about Jack's lavish compliments the moment he got the chance. If his bride-to-be pressed him for details, which Trinidad was certain she would, he'd reprise the episode as best he could, although he'd gloss over certain details of the restroom setting.

Passing down the long station house corridor, the detective and the sheriff joined the young woman herself who was waiting in the conference room, along with Joel and Ray and Ray's jailhouse guard. Jack led the meeting, delivering the good news that, for once, no one had blabbed to the media. As a result, the case had five new suspects who were flying under the radar, unpursued by inquisitive journalists and unknown to a general public. The refreshing episode of Colorado cooperation had produced a handful of new possibilities, all of whom were likely to believe that Ray Zumberto was the sole focus of police attention. Even Ray seemed content with the arrangement when his team explained the implications.

"So," the earnest repairman realized, "looks like I stay put for now. Well, it ain't so bad. The food's pretty good in here and my nephews is runnin' the shop okay and two guys have been leavin' a ton of phone messages about them wantin' to write a book about me."

"And you can bet I'll be screening the intentions of those eager-beaver opportunists," said Joel. "Can't let some hack get a strangle hold on my client's exclusive story. I'll do whatever's necessary to protect Ray's publication and syndication rights from a pack of ghostwriters."

"I like when you call them guys ghostwriters," said Ray. "I ain't never met no real ghost."

"Consider yourself lucky," said Anne as her father's specter came to mind. *Think about something else*, she thought.

Leaving Joel and Ray and Ray's escort behind at the county jail, the two detectives walked toward the adjacent parking lot in silence. When they reached the Honda, Trinidad, who was steadily becoming attuned to his prospective mate's moods, came to a decision. Earlier that day, they'd dropped Anne's old Nissan truck off at the repair shop for an oil change and tune-up and, as they wheeled through town, he made a suggestion.

"You look tired, Annie. Why don't I drop you off at the shop? Then I'll get a line on Esau's wayward son. Isaac is supposed to be in Grand Junction somewhere, so I'll take the Honda over there and use my big city contacts to track the big hoodlum down. Meanwhile, you should drive your Nissan home and get some rest and wait until I get back. Then tomorrow we can go together to Carbondale and see the devious brother."

"Sounds okay, boss," she said.

He dropped her off at the Delta City dealership and headed for Grand Junction convinced that Anne would soon be on her way back to Lavender Hill Farm. He should have known better.

Chapter 18

Loggers

There seemed to be some kind of detour in force because Highway 133 was infested with log trucks, all heading northeast on a Friday afternoon and all apparently in a powerful hurry to get up and over McClure Pass in daylight. Tired of being followed too closely as she negotiated the narrow highway's tight curves, Anne pulled over to let yet another lead-footed trucker pass.

Since leaving Paonia Reservoir to climb toward the pass, she'd been trying to drive slowly enough to spot the turn-off she was seeking and that exploration had been made impossible by the tailgaters. This latest maniac had been following so close that a glance in her rearview mirror had enabled Anne to read the Kenworth logo on the truck's front grill.

Determined to let the speed-demon get well ahead of her, she pulled far over onto the shoulder, turned off the Nissan's engine, and rolled down both windows. Reaching into her leather case, she extracted the area map, pushed the door open, and got out to fill her coat pockets with four stones. Then she spread the Western Colorado topo-map across the truck's hood, using a stone to secure each corner. Despite Trinidad's insistence, she continued to resist using her Android as a navigation tool. She was no Luddite when it came to technology, but she still preferred a full-sized map to the tight parameters of a magnified screenshot.

She liked to see the context of a place, the more the better.

Running her finger along 133, she traced the highway down from McClure Pass. The spot she was seeking had to be somewhere between her present location above Paonia Reservoir and below the 8,700-foot pass that led to Redstone and eventually to Carbondale. Koller had described the place in his memoirs. But his information was vague—reflecting the confusion he must have felt years ago on the stormy night he left the highway and took the wrong road. A sequence of fateful actions which led to a series of unintended consequences which, as far as Anne was concerned, set in motion all the tragedies which followed. She looked up from her map and scanned the surrounding topography.

It would be a risky place to navigate at night and Koller's memory was probably faulty. Even in daylight, the capricious landscape was a hodgepodge of obstacles. The undulating hills bristled with menacing boulders and the slopes were thick with low-slung tangles of pinon and juniper, their scrubby expanses broken here and there by healthy stands of majestic spruce trees. The Koller tragedy had unfolded in August when the drab scenery would have been augmented by yellow buds of rabbitbrush and rust-colored knots of willows. Now the brush and willows were muted. But, whatever the season, the place remained a disorderly jumble and a hazard in the dark.

So, it all began somewhere near here, she thought. *Thunder, lightning, flooding, death, and betrayal, a cavalcade of disturbing climatology and emotional angst—enough drama to fuel an Italian opera.*

Extracting what she could from the old man's writing, Anne was searching for a particular riparian area. From her vantage point on the raised roadway, she could see likely spots marked by swatches of narrow-leaf cottonwood trees and her map denoted several likely streambeds adjacent to the highway, any of which might have played a role in the tragedy. The old man's inability to pinpoint the spot might be attributed to the darkness and the weather, but the fledgling detective was convinced that his supposedly faulty memory demonstrated a pattern of avoidance.

To Anne, the evidence was clear.

In his memoirs, Koller made a point of emphasizing that he'd never once returned to the scene in daylight. In fact, if his account of the twenty-odd years since the accident is to be believed, not only did Koller avoid revisiting the distressing location, he never again set foot on Highway 133, never again drove the so-called 'short-cut' to Carbondale. For Anne's money, this habit of avoiding the scenes of various travails and tragedies was a recurring theme throughout the old man's confession.

Anne allowed herself a sad smile.

All the men, including Joel and Trinidad and the metro cops and Jack and especially the late Esau Noah Koller, were fond of referring to the latter's unpublished manuscript as his memoirs. She preferred the term "confession" since, for her, the lion's share of the writing amounted to a declamation of the old man's many foibles and transgressions, including the tragic night in 1996 when his miscalculations killed his wife and infant daughter.

As for the apparent connection between Koller's typewritten and handwritten pages, Anne was certain something was missing. Her interpretation of the old man's final morning on Earth differed from Trinidad's. In Anne's version of events, the faulty "H" had not stopped Koller from typing the whole of Chapter 31. She envisioned the determined author forging ahead until every letter, every space, and every scattering of punctuation was complete. Given the length of the old man's preceding chapters, Anne was convinced that at least a dozen typewritten pages were missing and that the original content was a far cry from the poetry of parental pride and rosy recitation of a celestial reconciliation as described by Trinidad.

Anne had read those same handwritten pages and deduced that Koller's original manuscript—what he'd initially intended to write—had been exactly what his altered title said it was. Which meant Chapter 31 was a chronicle of "Consequences." If, by some miracle, these missing typed pages came to light, she was positive they'd contain a damning rendition of Koller's self-serving justifications for abusing his wives and daughters. The killer must have known the sordid details and such knowledge drove that person to commit murder.

With his handwritten addendum, Koller had been attempting to rewrite history and failed. His efforts to amend his self-aggrandizing and delusional recollections had proven futile. In the end, the old satyr's plan to revise his opus fell short because he'd hidden his newly penned pages. Unaware of the concealed pages, the killer never discovered the old man's final ironic hand-written paragraphs describing how he intended to reconcile with at least one child whom he'd wronged. Try as she might, Anne was unable to buy Koller's last-minute declaration of redemption, and she had to believe that whoever killed him felt the same way.

Earlier in the day, Trinidad had been under the gun to return the evidence packet to Denver, but Anne had taken the precaution of photocopying certain typewritten pages and the handwritten sheets and, for good measure, she'd also copied the entire chapter describing the accident which had claimed the life of his first wife and their infant daughter. Then she'd reduced the accumulated pages to a small four-up document which she cut apart and eventually stitched together into a pint-sized booklet. She'd made the copies surreptitiously while Trinidad was taking a leisurely shower. She didn't ask anyone's permission and she didn't tell her partner what she'd done. She'd concealed the miniature booklet in her pocket and, standing on the shoulder of Highway 133, she pulled the thing out and thumbed through the small pages until she found the passage she was looking for. The words were miniscule, barely readable, but her eyesight was perfect and so was her memory.

Describing the anticipated arrival of his visiting angel, the old man wrote in a clear hand which demonstrated his mastery of the lost art of long-hand cursive. Every letter was precise, a work of patience and training, which both confirmed and belied his advanced age. Anne re-read the passage.

> *Though I have possessed the precious objects no more than two weeks, Koller declared, I have nearly worn the heartfelt letter and much-loved photograph raw with my constant handling, my joy mingled with the staining moisture of my repentant tears. It will be a blessing to see my angel tomorrow, to hear that longed-for voice, and I doubt if I shall sleep a wink tonight as I anticipate the joy of our meeting and this unexpected chance at reconciliation.*

Anne studied the writing for a moment more, then sighed.

Either purposefully, or by happenstance, all of the old man's handwritten pages were worded in such a way that the gender of the anticipated angel

remained ambiguous. Perhaps the old man had been drunk or otherwise fix-
ated in the grip of a euphoric stupor. Whatever the source of the obscurity,
the particulars were unclear. The context seemed to suggest a female, which
kept the estranged daughters and step-daughters on the suspect list. But a
liberal interpretation might encompass his son Isaac and brother Jacob as
well since Koller and his male relations were decidedly on the outs. Plus, as
Trinidad wisely pointed out, Koller may well have been expecting the person described in his final chapter, but that didn't necessarily mean it was the
anticipated angel who rang the outside buzzer, ascended in the elevator, and
delivered the fatal cuts.

At breakfast that morning, Trinidad had summarized his suspicions.
"Regardless of who Koller was expecting," he'd said, emphasizing the strength
of his convictions by gesturing with his fork, "I'm still laboring under the
assumption that any one of his disaffected relations could have done it."

Anne had nodded, but, having studied Koller's ambivalent lines, she'd
found herself wishing the old man had invested a little less effort in produc-
ing self-serving prose and simply and unambiguously come out and named
the guest he was expecting. Because—although she'd been reluctant to con-
tradict her future husband—Anne believed that, whoever the old man's
anticipated Easter Monday visitor was, that person was most likely the killer.

Trinidad had his 'it could have been any of them' theory and even Joel
saw the matter differently. Only yesterday, the earnest lawyer had told Anne,
"I'll take what I can get." Then, prompted by her quizzical look, he added,
"It's true old man Koller didn't name names, but I'll tell you one thing..."

"Which is?" Anne prompted

"The fact that someone wrote to him to arrange a meeting amounts to
a legalistic windfall in the form of premeditation," Joel said, then flashed his
polished smile in Anne's direction.

How many juries, she wondered, *has our suave lawyer friend charmed with
that handsome visage and those perfect teeth*? Then, reminding herself that she
was practically a married woman, Anne refocused her thoughts on the Koller

confessional as she searched the pages of her munchkin book looking for the accident chapter. "Ah," she said aloud as she stretched out on the Nissan's fender and reviewed the pertinent passage.

On August 18, 1996, it had been raining hard all day, but the weather had cleared up by the time Esau Koller and his reluctant family began their summertime drive through the Colorado mountains. It wasn't a pleasure trip. They'd been in Delta City to pick up Koller's new automobile and were returning to Aspen to be with their infant son, Isaac. The boy was being cared for in the town's general hospital while he recovered from a bout of jaundice. Esau was driving a brand-new Lincoln Town Car—a luxury model and a heavier vehicle than he was used to. Twelve-year-old Ruth was sitting in the passenger seat, fuming over having been made to miss a friend's birthday party. Esau's first wife, Chloe Koller, was napping in the backseat, next to Isaac's twin sister Naomi who slumbered in her vintage car-carrier.

Their spontaneous road trip had been Esau's idea. Chloe had objected to leaving Isaac behind and dragging the ailing boy's sisters over McClure Pass and back again, complaining that it would be past midnight by the time they returned. Esau had offered to have his brother help, but Chloe flatly refused to let Isaac's black-sheep uncle anywhere near the children.

"Over my dead body," she reportedly told her willful husband.

"We're going," Esau said, insisting that he must have his precious automobile at once rather than waiting three whole days for some stranger to deadhead it over the pass and on up to the family's Aspen manor.

Esau packed his family into their not yet one-year-old Taurus sedan and drove 120 miles to trade a perfectly serviceable Ford for the newer Lincoln. Koller loved being rich and he coveted the trappings of wealth. He was the head of his household and lord of his manor. He wanted to make the trip and so the Ford was enlisted to transport the master, his wife, two children, and a screwdriver. The tool was needed to remove Esau's vanity license plate from his old vehicle and attach it to his new acquisition.

Except for a minor rain shower, their journey from Aspen to Delta City had been uneventful and they were on the return leg, heading north by east on Highway 133. At one in the morning, they were approaching the fringes of McClure Pass, when the rain returned with a vengeance, accompanied by wind, piercing lightning, and fearsome thunder.

Long story short, Esau was flummoxed by the downpour and he misread a highway sign pointing the way to Collbran as an alternative route to reach Carbondale. Becoming disoriented in a storm was a situation which Anne found all too familiar because—less than a year ago—she herself had taken a wrong turn. That had been a chance error which landed her in the village of Lavender and put her temporarily in danger. But it was also a blessed blunder which shoehorned her into Trinidad's life.

Regrettably for Koller, his erroneous turn didn't lead to anything resembling good fortune. At that early morning hour, in the clamorous darkness, he'd turned sharply left, gotten lost, and finally returned to the highway, where he made the mistake of becoming completely turned around and heading back south. Now totally disoriented, he turned left again onto a dirt road, got lost again, topped a rain-soaked hill, and lost control of the unwieldy vehicle. He cursed aloud and his adolescent daughter screamed as the Lincoln skidded and plummeted headlong into Lee Creek, ordinarily a dry arroyo, but swollen that night by a roiling flash flood. The speeding car jack-knifed over the edge of a cliff, flipped in the air, and crashed roof-first into the flow.

What happened next is a matter of conjecture.

The Denver detectives had obtained two separate accident reports, one from the Colorado Highway Patrol and another from the Gunnison County Sheriff's Office. Koller maintained he was knocked unconscious when the car careened into the water. Owing to not having fastened his seatbelt, he said he was thrown clear of the scene and only regained his senses when he'd been carried far downstream from the submerged Lincoln. The current was strong. He could see little in the darkness and heard nothing on account of the rushing stream and the cacophony of wind and thunder.

By Koller's account, as he stood waist-deep in the rushing current, something collided with his legs and nearly knocked him over. He reached down to fend off the obstruction and realized it was his daughter, Ruth. He pulled the girl ashore and administered CPR until she regained consciousness. She was in shock but otherwise unhurt, so he left her alone on the shore and stumbled upstream along the bank, until he found himself parallel with the submerged car. He was entering the stream, preparing to wade out to rescue his wife and baby, when the flow increased and a huge tree trunk swept downstream knocking him back and carrying the car away.

The bodies of his wife Chloe and infant daughter Naomi were recovered a day later in the muddy but otherwise empty creek bed. Both cadavers were inside the Lincoln which was still upside-down and lodged sideways in an oxbow of the meandering stream. Chloe's seatbelt was still fastened and Naomi had apparently drowned while strapped into her car seat. The car was visible from Highway 133 and—although the damaged vehicle was pinned to the bank by a pile of flood debris—there was no sign of the giant tree described by Esau.

Esau claimed he abandoned his efforts to rescue the rest of his family that night because, owing to the intervention of the marauding tree which carried the car away, he was unable to locate the vehicle in the disordered darkness. Also, he insisted that his main concern was to get his daughter Ruth to safety. Leaving the noise and chaos of the engorged stream behind, the two walked to the highway where a passing motorist drove them back to Paonia and authorities were called.

Anne had her own suspicions about Esau's behavior—a more sordid version which she presumed would come to light, if and when they managed to track Ruth down. As she visualized the potential outcome of the daughter's interview, Anne's thoughts mingled with unwelcome recollections of her own unhappy past. With effort, she suppressed her memories and pulled herself back to her mission and the busy highway.

Another log truck blew by, so near and at such a hurried pace that the gust generated by its passage dislodged the map from its stone anchors and sent the sheet flying. The runaway map danced through the air like an ungovernable kite. Drifting skyward, it floated away from the highway and tumbled toward a roadside ravine with Anne in hot pursuit.

With a final burst of speed, she managed to overtake the errant paper and snatch it just before it jumped a fence and fell into a gully below. Standing there at the margins of the highway, she refolded her map and was about to return to the Nissan when a flicker of movement caught her eye. She watched as a raven skimmed low through the gully, hugging the ground like a rural crop-duster before ascending smoothly skyward.

"No way," she said as she stuffed the folded map inside her shirt and ducked under two strands of barbed wire. "No freaking way," she repeated as she sidestepped down the bank to reach the dry bed of a roadside stream. She stood there among the pebbles and, judging the slope of the bed in order to look downstream, she spotted it at once. Twenty yards away was the beginning curve of a sharp oxbow turn and in that curve lay a broad and jumbled pile of bleached driftwood.

Walking toward the corner, she could see that the wood had accumulated in a haphazard pile which extended higher than her head. When she reached the corner, she was almost certain she'd chanced upon the place where the Koller Lincoln had come to rest in 1996. A few more details would confirm her speculation, so she turned, looked back upstream, and found the evidence she sought. There in the distance was the primitive bridge spanning the streambed which Koller had described in the accident report and there also was the dirt road and the hill up which he had so unwisely driven all those years ago.

Twenty-three years ago, Anne thought. *I was a baby then—no older than Naomi. How the infant must have screamed when the water...*

Imagining the child's terror, she took an involuntary step backward and nearly lost her footing when her boot heel collided with something unexpected. Looking down, she saw the obstacle. It was the upturned corner of a slim but sturdy object buried in a narrow spit of sandy soil. Picking up a driftwood limb, she knelt and dug into the streambed until she'd unearthed an elongated strip of metal.

"Sweet," she exhaled Trinidad's one-word tribute which succinctly expresses the serendipitous joy which attends a happy accident.

The smiling detective pulled the thing free just as a siren sounded and an unseen emergency vehicle roared past on the highway above. Anne smelled smoke, then she heard thunder rumble and looked northward where the sky was dark and menacing. A second vehicle passed, siren blaring, but that sound was immediately swallowed up by a cascade of proximate thunder. A chill ran through her as she scrambled to her feet. She was downstream from a growing storm which put her directly in the path of a potential flashflood.

Better move, Dumbo, Anne told herself as she sprinted toward a low spot in the bank. Lobbing her streamed prize skyward to clear the steep embankment, she heard it clatter onto the rocks above as she stretched to her full height and reached up to grapple with the roots of scrubby underbrush. With a desperate spurt of energy, she managed to climb up hand-over-hand until she'd pulled herself out of the gully. Then she stood on the bank and leaned forward, breathing raggedly. The exertion had left her panting and wondering, *am I that out of shape,* until she realized why the short run and frantic climb had been so exhausting. She'd been holding her breath the entire time she was sprinting across the streamed and clawing her way to safety.

Don't forget to breathe, her high school track coach had admonished her years ago when she was struggling to master the hurdles. Her fear of colliding with the wooden barriers had made her tense and the tension had shut down her breathing.

The thunder sounded again—this time much closer as a pulse of lightning snaked overhead. Following the sound, Anne looked aloft to discover a percolating sky, thick with a writhing expanse of indigo clouds.

"Dang it!" she shouted as she retrieved her find and rushed back toward the Nissan, ducking under the barbed wire and stumbling through roadside brambles. She reached the truck as the first dollops of rain bounced off the hood and she had just enough time to roll up the truck window before the deluge struck.

A dozen frantic minutes of intense pounding and it was over—a typical spring squall, rapidly hammering the ground as it rocketed past, then just as suddenly, vanished. In the brilliant sunshine which followed the hastening storm, Anne stepped out and used her phone camera to photograph a double rainbow. Then she retrieved the mud-caked license plate from the cab, posed it on the Nissan's fender, and took another picture.

"Exhibit A," she observed. If any question arose as to whether she'd discovered the genuine site of the Koller tragedy, this piece of unearthed evidence would remove all doubt. The thing was twisted and missing some of its green paint, but the embossed license plate was nevertheless decipherable.

"Tater," she read the word aloud.

Clearly, the old man had chosen to acknowledge the source of the Koller family wealth by choosing to display that particular word on his vanity plate. As for the plate's age, Anne had only to examine the plasticized renewal sticker which, owing to having been encased in a cocoon of mud, still clung to the battered metal. The renewal year—a bold "97" in black letters on a silvery-white background—was clearly visible. The number designating the renewal month, which had once resided in the left-hand corner, had been exposed to the elements and weathered away, but the renewal year was all she needed to confirm the plate was current in 1996. This telling sticker, when coupled with Pitkin County motor vehicle records, would be proof enough that the plate had belonged to Koller.

Confirming the site of the wreck and tying Esau to the plate may or may not influence their investigation, but Anne was convinced that understanding the victim's past would help solve his murder. Besides, she planned to present her prize to Trinidad with a flourish and invite him to marvel at her emerging detection abilities.

She placed the plate in the Nissan's lockbox and was climbing out of the truck bed when she heard distinct sounds of hissing and cracking coming from the direction of the streambed. She hesitated for an instant, then decided to chance it as she crossed once again to the wire and ducked under. Standing safely on the bank, she stared upstream and saw exactly what she expected to see.

Working its way downhill, a churning wall of mud, rocks, brush, and branches had burst beneath the bridge and was rapidly filling the gully from bank to bank. Cocking her head, she confirmed the advancing flood as the source of the hissing. It was a classic natural phenomenon and she had only to recall her university studies to understand the cause. The distinctive sound was generated as debris-laden water penetrated the parched streambed, forming and instantly bursting millions of tiny air bubbles. Until the rain, it had been a hot spring day and, the hotter the inundated sand, the louder the hissing.

As for the cracking, that was a result of rocks carried by the madly churning current, tumbling in the flood, colliding with one another, and clashing with stones in the bed. Few people who have witnessed the force of a flash-flood will forget not only the sight of the flow but also the ominous sound of water, rocks, and wood caught in the grip of gravity.

Feeling safe above the torrent, Anne continued to watch as the flood rolled past her until its accumulated power reached the oxbow and slammed into the corner, shooting water and debris in every direction.

Enough to carry a Lincoln? Anne asked herself. "You bet'cha," she said aloud and took a picture.

Returning to the Nissan, she was feeling something like empathy as she reconsidered Esau Koller's account of that fatal midnight flood of two decades ago. She scrambled inside, fished the map out of her shirt, started the truck, and resumed her journey toward McClure Pass. Traveling higher through the sunny afternoon, she continued onward until she encountered a line of traffic cones, which led to a flagman with a ponytail, who raised a hand to stop her.

"Emergency vehicles only," he told her.

Not wishing to turn back, she hastily handed the man one of Trinidad's business cards. She'd meant to add her name, just as she'd meant to contact a photographer, write up a draft of their engagement announcement, and email the picture and text to the Delta City Print Shop. A surge of guilt washed over her as she realized plans for their impending wedding seemed to be stuck in neutral.

"Detective," he noticed. "Impressive—rock on!" he waved her forward.

Just below the pass, she saw the problem. She drove past a line of smol-dering flares until she reached a knot of emergency vehicles and a platoon of men and women dressed in reflective coats. Uniformed workers and law officers of every description were clustered around two vehicles which, though far apart, gave every indication of having been involved in a brutal head-on collision. One car was blackened and also covered with a gelatinous layer of fire suppression foam. Looking beyond the wreck, she could see that the adjacent hillside was smoldering as a crew continued to aim water at the burn site.

That flare-up would account for the smoke I smelled, she thought and the scientist in her added a mental qualification. *Probably my nose had detected a combination of the roadside fire and the ozone spawned by an impending thunderstorm.*

Her thoughts were interrupted as she was stopped again and showed the card again, this time to a sheriff's deputy—a sergeant if she remembered her chevrons.

"Sands Detective Agency, huh?" the sergeant asked. "Would that be Trinidad Sands out of Lavender?"

"That's him," Anne confirmed.

"Hmm. Didn't know he had a partner."

She resisted the urge to show her ring and merely shrugged her shoulders and offered a smile.

"Okay," the sergeant said and then he continued in a collegial tone. "What's happened here is a mudslide which is blocking half the highway on the hill-side. No surprise that somebody seen the block too late and swerved into the oncoming lane and bang!" He pounded his fist into his open hand.

"Anyone hurt?" Anne asked.

"One dead in the downhill car. Two others hauled back to Carbondale. They'll live, I guess. We're close to the county line here—more than one county line in fact—and no one ain't sure where the lines are which accounts for this crowd," he waved his arm toward the gaggle of first responder vehicles, then he leaned on the Nissan's window and gave Anne a broad smile.

Damn, she thought, *this guy is flirting with me.*

"So how long are you in town for?" he asked as he leaned even further forward, presumably intent on making certain Anne had a waist and two legs.

"Drake!" a voice reached them from the nearest squad car. "Leave that filly alone and get back to work!"

"Roger that!" he shouted back as he stood erect, but then leaned down again and handed a calling card through the window.

"Listen," he whispered, "Here's my number. If you need anything at all—anything—call the station and ask for Officer Smiley..."

Anne could not control her reaction and her laugh just slipped out. "Sorry," she said.

"No apologies necessary," he said. "I get it. I work in the schools with kids, see. I'm our K-9 handler, so the teachers introduce me as Officer Smiley."

"It suits you," Anne agreed.

"Thanks."

"Drake! Come and call your mutt! She's pissing everybody off!"

"Come, Cozy!" the sergeant bellowed and a gun-metal gray German shepherd bounded toward the Nissan. "This side," the sergeant instructed. "Up!"

The obedient dog stood on its hind legs, rested its front paws on the base of the Nissan's open window, and balanced there with a look of profound intelligence on her earnest face.

"Cozy, meet—uh," the sergeant hesitated.

"I'm Anne," she said. "Pleased to meet you, Cozy," she added as she shook a paw. "How old is she?"

"Two and a half," said Sergeant Drake as he beamed at the animal with obvious pride.

"Drake! For crap sakes! Leave that gal alone and get to work!" the voice demanded.

"Well," said the deputy with obvious reluctance, "better go, I guess. Cozy, off—sit, girl. You have yourself a nice day and drive careful," he saluted as he and Cozy turned their attention to the next vehicle in line.

Anne steered slowly, weaving through the accident scene as she followed the hand signals of a chorus line of hunky officers. And, after she passed each man, she silently chastised herself for looking in the rear-view mirror to check out the seemingly endless parade of well-proportioned butts.

Look, but don't touch, she thought. *But a girl's gotta look. I may be engaged to be married, but I ain't dead.*

Chapter 19

The Scenic Route

Anne's drive from Delta City to Carbondale took more than four hours and not because the Nissan acted up. The mechanics had worked wonders and her old truck ran fine and she might have made it sooner, but she'd decided to take the scenic route over McClure Pass. Her progress had been delayed by her detour at the gully and an accident scene and then further interrupted while watching road graders and county trucks haul rocks. She should have known better than to drive that way since portions of Colorado 133 were often tied up with rock-fall mitigation.

She'd blown the better part of Thursday afternoon before she reached the outskirts of Carbondale, a modest community which lay north of the glitter and glamour of Aspen. After getting gas, she paused at the station's convenience store, and frowned at her map. The Western Colorado counties of Delta, Mesa, Garfield, and Pitkin all somehow figured in the Koller saga and the borderlines of this cartographic foursome overlapped awkwardly like rough-cut pieces of an unlovely jigsaw puzzle.

As counties go, the four were relative youngsters which had been formed by slicing up the tracts of larger and older counties. This geographic surgery had been performed shortly after 1876 when the Territory of Colorado was admitted as a state to the growing American union. To reach Carbondale, she'd completed a veritable trifecta by driving roughly north along Highway

133 from Delta County and passing through a tip of Gunnison County to reach her destination which lay just over the line in Garfield County.

Meanwhile, the ancestral Koller lair—which the old man had christened White Quail Manor—lay further away in yet another county. Esau's memoirs and Joel's supplementary documents revealed that the palatial manor house was once situated on four hundred acres—surrounded by an untamed forest the size of New York City's Central Park. Just after Esau abandoned the alpine showplace, the expensive edifice had been reduced by fire to an unsightly pile of rubble. Nothing to see there and besides the burn site was situated in Pitkin County and she had neither the desire nor the time to wrestle with Aspen traffic. For the time being, her mission was focused on the smaller and more sedate town of Carbondale.

For an instant she wondered what Trinidad would say when he learned that she'd set out on her own, following her instincts to track down leads she'd gleaned from her study of the case files and the incomplete Koller memoirs.

Isn't it, she reasoned, *more efficient for each detective partner to work their own hunches?* To be an equal partner, she needed to pull her own weight and today's adventure would be the beginning of that strategy.

Something in the file on Juliet had stuck with Anne and piqued the fledgling detective's interest. Juliet Koller was Esau's adopted daughter who had apparently run away from the Aspen manor as a teen. Through a series of misadventures, Juliet had ended up in Collbran, a tiny town on the fringes of Grand Mesa where she married a local man and began operating an out-of-the-way café. A rather ordinary story, although a notation in Juliet's sketchy biography suggested that she had kept a journal and that the journal might possibly be stashed somewhere in the collection of the Carbondale Public Library. Meanwhile, Jacob Koller, the dead novelist's twin brother, was also in Carbondale and she was anxious to track the old rascal down and the library was on the way.

Efficient, she commended herself for her initiative, *first the library and then a daring foray into the lion's den.*

She'd anticipated a quick trip, but it took her twenty minutes to locate the library because someone had been screwing around with the way-finder signs. After several wrong turns, she eventually found the place. The journey was a marathon, but moments after parking and stepping inside, she'd been pleasantly surprised when the librarian on duty was instantly able to locate Juliet's supposedly missing journal. It took some persuading, along with her signature on an agreement and payment of a sizeable deposit, but Anne was miraculously allowed to take the unbound journal with her.

"This, combined with the license plate, will set Mr. Sands on his ear," she said aloud as she carefully added the journal to the truck lockbox. When she arrived back home, she'd present her sleuthing prize to her amazed fiancé with a flourish, but in the meantime, she'd wait until they could read it together. Momentarily distracted by visions of her triumphant return to Lavender Hill Farm, she shook off that image and pulled herself back to the present. Glancing at her watch, she realized that the day was advancing and she'd yet to contact Jacob Koller.

Relying on intelligence gained from Joel's files, she'd gathered some props to facilitate her encounter. She wheeled confidently across town, convinced that Jacob Koller would be an easy man to find and also a cinch to interview. Trusting the information, she was certain that every weekday afternoon the old man could be found on his knees in the Carbondale community garden lavishing attention and fertilizer on his prize roses. It was warm for April and Joel's information had convinced her that Jacob would be working in his garden plot, anxiously racing with the calendar to stabilize his new bushes before the waning days of springtime pulled a fast one and galloped into summer.

The younger of the Koller twins was currently enamored with a particularly delicate rose that went by the provocative name of High House Hybrid. Apparently, Esau wasn't the only brother obsessed with the letter "H."

Arriving at the garden, she spotted Jacob's vintage Volvo—accurately described in Joel's background materials. Parking a discrete distance away, she noticed one more vehicle, an ancient truck more battered than her own. Anne hadn't counted on witnesses, but, donning a sunhat and elbow-high gardeners' gloves, she decided to go ahead with her performance. She slipped kneepads over her durable jeans, took one last look at her costume, and set out to insinuate her way into Jacob's afternoon.

Reaching the front gate, she found it locked and was relieved to encounter a bearded man in overalls who was on the point of leaving. Seeing Anne's attire and assuming she was a garden regular, he politely held the gate open for her. When he was about to lock it, she lied that she'd forgotten her key and convinced the man to leave the gate unsecured.

"I promise to lock it up tight as a tick when I leave," she said, adopting a southern accent which, in her experience, men of all ages found irresistible.

"Sure enough, honey-child," the man said in an authentic Dixie accent and, even as his grin exhibited a handful of missing teeth, she was sincerely embarrassed to be manipulating the old fellow.

Exuding a contrite politeness which she genuinely felt, she thanked him profusely, asked directions, and learned that Jacob was indeed on-site and working his plot. Anne watched the man drive away, waving enthusiastically and hoping he wouldn't sound his horn, a parting shot which might alert her quarry. To her relief, the man merely waved back, after which she made her way to a far corner of the garden.

Settling onto a patch of ground adjacent to Jacob's rosebushes, Anne got down on her hands and knees. She positioned her body strategically and pretended to pluck weeds from someone's carrot patch, while also giving the old satyr next door an unobstructed view of her butt. In a matter of moments, she made contact.

"Ahem." A voice sounded behind her. It was a raspy sound, like an insistent but decidedly ancient foghorn.

"Hello," said Anne, slightly turning her head but remaining on her knees with what Trinidad seemed to think was one of her best features on full display.

"Koller is the name," said Jacob and the lust apparent in his voice made it obvious that he was addressing his remarks to a young woman's firm buttocks. "And I don't believe we've been introduced."

"Alice," said Anne without looking up. *Take it slow*, she thought.

"Charmed. You—uh—look as though you could use a break. I have some tea in my thermos. And perhaps..." his voice trailed off.

Anne did not respond but continued pulling weeds, tilling her crop like a good little farmer. Not for nothing had she watched Trinidad prune his lavender plants. She was being industrious and coy, but her pigeon might be losing interest. It was time to strike.

"You've planted High Houses I see," she said as she got to her feet and offered her prey a full view of three more of Trinidad's favorite features: her winning smile and her perfectly perky breasts.

"Oh, my word, yes," said Jacob. "Yes," he repeated unnecessarily as his eyes covered every inch of the attractive young stranger standing before him. "Do you know the hybrid?"

It was Anne's turn to say yes twice and in as dulcet a tone as she could muster. "Yes—yes of course. It's a hybrid tea as I recall. And speaking of tea..." Saying this she actually batted her eyelashes. At least she assumed she was batting them. She'd seldom consciously attempted that particular maneuver. But whatever she was doing with her eyes, it seemed to work.

"A capital idea. Won't you join me?"

Was it her imagination or was her fellow American trying to fake an English accent? Well, that only seemed fair since she herself—a died in the wool westerner—was feigning a southern drawl.

With Jacob smoothly taking her arm, they moved casually through the garden which, with the departure of Anne's naïve guide, was now deserted. As they walked, she surreptitiously padded her front pocket where she'd meant to place a small cannister of pepper spray. The pocket was empty of course. In her haste to don her costume, she'd forgotten the spray.

Too late to add to your arsenal now, she chastised herself. Then, her thoughts subconsciously falling under the influence of Jacob's faux-British accent, she told herself, *Stiff upper lip—full steam ahead.*

A weathered wooden picnic table squatted beneath the overarching canopy of the garden's enormous horse chestnut tree. Slipping into the welcome shade, the two of them settled in on opposite sides—Anne slipping in as limber as a schoolgirl and Jacob climbing stiffly aboard. The old man, his fox-like eyes betraying his accumulating desire, continued talking roses and nonsense as he poured the tea. His thermos was a deluxe model, a sleek black cylinder topped by two cups nestled inside one another.

The old seducer comes prepared, I'll give him that, Anne thought.

She smiled and nodded and interjected enough jargon into their conversation to suggest that she knew a bit about roses. But she soon ran out of chit-chat and was relieved when the topic switched to the weather. Twice the old fox mentioned how warm it was for May and suggested that they adjourn to his lair for lemonade and scones—he'd said "apartment" but in her mind she'd definitely heard the word "lair." Despite his deliberate efforts to steer her behind closed doors, Anne demurred and said that she was not dressed for formal dining. And all the while she was thinking that her being dressed one way or the other was undoubtedly the last thing which horny old Jacob had on his dirty mind.

Eventually even the weather began to lag as a topic of conversation and Anne saw her opening.

"Koller?" she asked. "Is that with a 'K?' And are you any relation to the famous writer?"

If the community garden's spacious grounds had not consisted of tilled soil and sprawling groundcover which would absorb the sound of a falling pin, you could have heard one drop as Jacob's sardonic witticisms and sparkling repartee evaporated like spit on a griddle. For several minutes while Anne dutifully sipped her tea, the old man remained silent and scowling and she was just beginning to think that she was out of her depth when Jacob spoke.

"My brother," was all he said at first, his tone dripping with venom.

"You're the brother of Esau?"

"Yes," he admitted. "And tell me, young lady, do you know your Bible?"

Anne did not want to go there. "I know my Bible," she said aloud as she inwardly thought, *but I'm a New Testament gal, which leaves me a bit shaky on the Old Testament parts.*

"Well—we're twins, you know?"

She did know. She'd studied Jacob's file and, not only that, but she'd also seen Esau's book jacket. *And,* she thought, *this Jacob is—you should forgive the expression—a dead ringer for his late brother.* "No kidding," she said aloud.

"I kid you not," said Jacob.

Gone was the British accent she noted. The old man's vernacular was back where it belonged, modulated with a regional twang of good old-fashioned

East Coast Yiddish. This shifting of accents seemed to verify what Anne had read in the bitter brother's file. While Jacob paused, drumming his fingers on the picnic table and staring into space as he apparently wrestled with his anger, Anne recalled the details.

At the tender age of twelve, a sad and bewildered Jacob had been sent east to live with his father's no-account cousins. In an action which seemed deliberately calculated, young Jacob's father had essentially banished his youngest son to a mediocre life in the squalid tenements of Newark, New Jersey. Meanwhile, Esau remained in Colorado, ensconced in the family fold, basking in his role as favorite son, and cementing his eventual emergence as sole heir to the vast Koller fortune. In Anne's opinion, such a cruel paternal slight constituted a classic motive for murder. It was a tentative notion, but one which was bolstered by a decade of exposure to standard movie plots. And she might have spent the afternoon musing about Jacob's role as the prime suspect in the slaughter of his privileged brother, but her thoughts were interrupted as the old man returned to his narration.

"In the Bible..." said Jacob and he paused. She could see his demeanor shifting as rising anger began to color the old man's waxy complexion. He seemed to struggle with his thoughts before he continued. "In the Bible that lucky bastard Esau came out first and baby Jacob followed after, clinging to his elder brother's heel—or so it is written."

Jacob paused, glanced at his tea, scowled, and took a sip. So apparent was his anger that Anne was amazed that the liquid did not emit steam when it touched his fuming lips.

"*My brother...*" Jacob continued, enunciating both words as if they were vile, toxic things. "Let us consider 1931, when the Koller twins were born. Esau came first and I was destined to be the second son. And, mark my words, I entered this world unassisted! I had no need of my brother's help to enter the land of the living and, besides, it would've been a neat trick to locate, let alone grip, his slippery heel since my eyes had yet to focus and my dexterity was questionable." The sarcasm in the old man's voice rose steadily as he forged on. "Still, I should have seen it coming because all our lives, my brother, my damn brother, came first—always damnably first."

There was yet another pause during which Anne heard the old man growling just beneath his breath while he seemed to be rehearsing some long-suppressed declaration.

"My consummate weasel of a brother has been hailed as such a great storyteller, but I'll amend the Bible story with a parable of my own," Jacob began. "Let me add, if you will, an embittered footnote," he continued, the rising volume of his baritone voice projecting his growing anger. "In my story, the moment—the very instant—my esteemed brother emerged from the womb and found himself on firm territory, the little imp asserted his deplorable birthright by spinning cruelly on his famous heel and kicking me right in the balls. Right smack-dab in my unsuspecting balls and, from that day forward and until the very day he died, the first-born little devil kept kicking and kicking and kicking and cruelly and endlessly kicking!"

A pin would have thundered in the silence that followed this outburst.

"I don't want to talk anymore about my asshole brother," said Jacob and, after delivering what might be the understatement of the year, he seemed to lose interest in either continuing the conversation or seducing Anne.

"Well," she said as she stood up, "it's been real and it's been fun." But she thought to herself, *it hasn't been real fun.* "Good luck with your roses."

She left Jacob brooding at the picnic table and made her way out of the garden, mulling over the old man's rambling diatribe. It certainly spoke to motive and, if uttered before competent and sober witnesses in a television episode of "Perry Mason," such a soliloquy would be nothing less than a show-stopping confession. Trying to commit the gist of Jacob's harangue to memory as she returned to her truck, Anne passed through the entrance and was just re-fastening the garden gate when someone grabbed her arm.

"You don't belong here," the man said, "so you'd better shut your mouth and come with me."

And so, Anne went along in silence. As if she had any choice with the huge bulk of the wayward son, Isaac Koller, firmly gripping her arm with one beefy hand while he shoved the muzzle of a pistol into her ribs with the other.

Chapter 20

Shed

It was nearly dusk as Isaac, the late Esau Koller's jailbird son and Jacob's nephew, forced Anne toward a shed that lay just outside the high deer fence surrounding the Carbondale community garden. He was a huge man with a lengthy police record and a nasty reputation whose hulking mass dwarfed his prisoner. As they neared the shed, Anne secretly stripped off both gloves and let them fall one at a time to the ground. She was leaving—she hoped—a trail for someone to follow but, like Hansel and Gretel's breadcrumbs dropped in the forest, she suspected doing so was an act of desperation. When they reached the rustic structure, the powerful kidnapper kicked the door open and pushed his struggling captive inside.

There were no windows in the cramped shed. The interior was dark and the place smelled of manure. A potting shed, she imagined. As Isaac turned to latch the door, she pressed her back against the nearest wall, and was encouraged to feel something solid poking her. There would be a rake or a hoe or a shovel hanging there if she needed a weapon—if she could reach it in time.

"Start talkin'," Isaac growled, "and I better hear some answers I like, or else."

"What should I talk about?"

Her eyes had adjusted to the darkness and she could see the large man raise his open hand, presumably to strike her, but she was too quick for him. Seeking to fend off the ex-con, she reached back to grip something tightly.

She swung the object forward and hit the lurching man hard. Isaac howled and fell back, giving up enough ground to allow the desperate woman to slip past. Anne lunged for the unlatched door and shouldered it open. Bursting clear of the shed, she ran full speed toward her Nissan.

Keys! she thought to herself as she fumbled in her pockets without breaking stride. Reaching the truck, she scrambled inside and started the Nissan. Hitting reverse, then first gear, and peppering the shed and the garden fence with gravel, she peeled out of the parking lot.

She didn't check the rearview mirror and she wasn't listening to anything except the hum of the Nissan's engine. She didn't want to know if Isaac had tumbled out of the potting shed covered in horse-crap and fired wildly in her direction. She'd check for bullet holes later. For the time being she had no plans to stop until she was safely through the crazy quilt of counties, over McClure Pass, and back to the safety of Lavender Hill Farm.

Chapter 21

Paradise

It was midnight on Friday and there was trouble in paradise. Anne and Trinidad were in the kitchen having a family talk, or it might have been a staff meeting, either way they were sitting across the table from one another and fuming.

"I thought we agreed you'd take a rest," said Trinidad.

"I didn't have time to agree. You'd already agreed for me," said Anne.

"Fine," said Trinidad.

"Fine," said Anne.

"Is this how it's going to be?" he asked, his voice tense with emotion. "We decide something and then you just go off on your own? I love you, but sometimes I just—don't you realize this isn't a game? You might have been hurt! Didn't I say the guy was dangerous? Didn't I...?"

"Wait," Anne interrupted as she stood up. "Go back a bit."

"What do you mean *go back*?"

"Go back to the part where you said you love me."

They were silent for a moment and then Trinidad too stood up. "Annie, all I'm saying is your getting killed would definitely have ruined our wedding. So, just promise me this: no more commando tactics. No more suicide missions. No more going off on your own without telling me what you're doing. Promise me."

"That goes for you too," she said. "And, yes, I promise."

"I promise too," he said. "Now, for pity sakes, tell me that you got something out of the horny uncle and his homicidal nephew."

"Take notes," she said.

The couple sat back down as Trinidad pulled out his pocket notebook while Anne related Jacob's venomous dislike of his seconds-older twin and the shock of Isaac's sudden appearance. She was tempted to mention that she'd also discovered Esau's buried license plate and Juliet's missing journal, but decided to wait until emotions were less agitated.

"The little bastard must have been following you," said Trinidad.

"No kidding, Sherlock," said Anne. "And I wouldn't call that gorilla little if I were you. And, by the way, weren't *you* supposed to be following *him*?"

"You're right. Sorry. I got distracted," he admitted.

"Distracted by...?" she prompted.

"By the sister," he blushed.

"Which one?"

Trinidad was silent.

"Let me guess," Anne speculated as she laughed out loud. "The redhead, right?"

"Yeah, Ruth, the redhead. Before I left Delta City, I checked in with Joel and apparently Ruth Koller called the office earlier in the day, agreed to take part in a Skype interview, and then somehow got his secretary Erik to spill the beans about our involvement."

"Somehow you say," said Anne. "She *somehow* got to Erik? You men are really something. *Somehow*? I know exactly how she did it. Don't forget I've seen her picture in the stuff Joel sent us—I've seen the largely unobstructed view of her fabulous cleavage—and I can just imagine the sultry voice that goes with that rack. I'm remembering how she led with her chest in that steamy nearly pornographic photo. Alabaster skin, fiery red hair, pouty lips, and headlight breasts—my gosh if I weren't a flaming heterosexual, I'd go for her myself."

"You finished?"

"Yeah. Yeah, I'm done," she laughed. "And that felt good. I think I'm getting the hang of this detective banter."

"Great. I'm glad you're entertained," said Trinidad as he tried to reinforce his mock displeasure with a disapproving scowl. "So now it's time for you to learn some more detective banter."

"I'm all ears, master."

"Okay, see if you can follow this," he said. "Take this phone. Got it?"

"I'm with you so far," she said as she held the landline expectantly.

"Now see all these numbers here? Take those lovely fingers of yours and punch in 9-1-1. Then, when the dispatcher answers, tell her you want to report an assault. We'll have Jack work with the Carbondale police to pick the big bastard up and then we'll see how our amateur ambusher, a big ape who's been foolish enough to flash his unauthorized weapon, likes dealing with a parole violation."

Chapter 22

Room A
(Good Shepherd Sunday)

Regretting the necessity of missing Father Tom's after-Easter sermon at Delta City Episcopal, Sheriff Jack Treadway walked reluctantly down the county's empty institutional hallway. Every year, Father Tom gave the same talk, but it was a corker about Simon Peter's decision to go fishing. Jack loved that story, not only because he loved the Lord, but also because the sermon rang absolutely true. Peter and the others went fishing alright and the Bible says they caught nothing.

What could be truer than that? Jack wondered. It was a beautiful spring day outside and the unhappy sheriff paused at one of the county's exterior windows and cranked the transom open to breathe in the aroma of new buds floating on the warm air. *Ahh*, he thought. *Here's the lusty month of May beckonin' and me stuck inside. Back to work I reckon.*

He reached into his pocket, fired up his smartphone, and examined an image. A tip from Joel had inspired the authorities to conduct a secondary search of the lobby of Esau Koller's hotel and that reexamination had turned up a crumbled bit of pasteboard.

"Is that what I think it is?" he'd asked when Deputy Madge Oxford texted him.

"I found this wadded up in a wastebasket in the lobby of the Stevenson Building," said Madge.

Jack reached out and used his fingers to enlarge the image.

"Pretty fancy writing," he said.

"Fancy for sure," said Madge. "And not only fancy but left-handed fancy."

"And Ray Zumberto's a righty," said Jack.

"Bingo," said Madge.

The sheriff pocketed his smartphone, took one last look out the window, and left the idyllic scene behind. He traversed the deserted hallway and rapped on the blank metal entrance to Interview Room A.

A buzzer sounded as the door clicked open. Nodding to the deputy who was standing guard in the dim interior of the musty room, Jack dismissed the man, closed the door behind him, and regarded his prisoner. Instead of contemplating the joys of post-Easter reflection, duty compelled him to spend the morning confronting this muscular fellow who met the sheriff's arrival with a defiant glare.

Sitting down across from the giant, Jack was thankful that Isaac Koller was securely handcuffed to the interrogation table. At six-five with broad shoulders and a solid physique which belied his forty-plus years, Jack was no shrinking violet. But Esau Koller's natural son sported a solid frame of muscle and bone—as if one of the massive characters in Michael Short's larger-than-life, bronze-cast public sculptures had suddenly come alive, escaped from the streets of Montrose, and traveled twenty-one miles north to plant itself in Room A. In any event, it was going to take a combination of strength and cunning to interview this particular over-sized jailbird.

"Ok, tough guy," Jack began with a measured tone, then paused as he opened the dense binder that filled the space between the two men. It was an overstuffed file folder, thick as a crosscut slab of freshly-cut lumber and brimming with documents. "Let's do the math. You've got a juvenile record stretchin' back to age sixteen. Then you grew up and got arrested for grand larceny and assault, which got you tried as an adult and earned you a five-year felony rap, except you lucked out and got three years' probation. Then you managed to keep off the radar for two years while doin' odd jobs for your uncle until Thursday when you fell off the wagon and violated your parole by wavin' a pistol around. So, what you're looking at now..." Jack made a show of pretending to figure a sum on the notepad in front of him. "Let's see, carry the two, and we're back to the original five years. So that wasn't very smart was it?"

"I want a lawyer," said Isaac with a taciturn growl.

"Wrong," said Jack. "Slow down and take a deep breath. You're gettin' ahead of yourself. You need to wait until I read you your rights."

"Somebody already did that two years ago," said Isaac. "So, I still want a lawyer."

"You must be pretty sure you did something wrong since you keep askin' for a lawyer."

"Maybe I wanna make out a will," snarled Isaac and then he stopped talking, perhaps realizing he'd said too much.

"Okay," said Jack, "let's start over. As far as gettin' your rights read to you, do you have any idea who Ernesto Miranda was?"

"Do I get my lawyer or not?"

"Now see you're still confused," said Jack. "I'm the one askin' the questions here. Your job is to either answer them or not answer them. Is that clear?"

"Yeah, I guess."

"Okay. So apparently you don't know who Miranda was. Well, he was a bad dude—much worse than you. He stole $8 in Arizona, but when they arrested him, he confessed to a boatload of other crimes—pretty much everythin' but the Lindberg kidnappin.'"

Isaac stared blankly and Jack guessed that the young moron had no idea who Lindberg was.

"In any event, the Supreme Court of these United States threw out Miranda's convictions on the grounds that he wasn't informed of his right to avoid self-incrimination. Is any of this sinkin' in?"

"Jeez-us," said Isaac, "That's what I get for askin' for a got'damn lawyer. Did anybody ever tell you that you sound exactly like some ice-hole shyster?"

Jack was silent for a moment and then he looked Isaac straight in the eyes and said, in an official tone that suggested his prisoner needed to pay attention. "Listen, my friend. If you take the Lord's name in vain, or utter one more cuss word in this room, I'll recommend they push that five years to ten. Do we understand each other?"

"I guess."

"Good. Now, as far as the Miranda warnin', most people think if the police forget to read you your rights, you're free to go. But it don't work that way. All that happens if you don't get your rights read to you is this: we can't use anythin' you say against you in court. So, as long as I don't read you your rights, you can tell me anythin' you want. Do you follow me?"

"Is this some kind of bullsh...I mean lawyer-trickster trick? To get me to say somethin' I don't wanna say?"

"Probably. But remember, I haven't read you your rights, so whatever you say to me right now can't be used against you in court. Look, tell you what, let's try somethin'. I'm gonna ask you three questions and you're gonna answer them honestly and, if I like your answers, we might make this probation beef disappear."

"Disappear? Like—disappear?"

"Yes, ready for my questions?" asked Jack.

"Okay, but if I don't like where this goes, you gotta read me my rights and I'm done talkin' to anybody but a lawyer."

"That sounds fair," said Jack. "So, let's begin. Question number one is really a written question. Take this pad and this pen and write what I say. Ready? Begin. Write these three words: Temporary—Service—Interruption."

"What was them words again?"

"Never mind. I see you're right-handed."

"What of it? Do you want me to write them words or not?"

"Not necessary. Hand the tools back please."

"Tools? What tools?"

"The paper and the pen please," said the sheriff. "Thank you. Now, on to question two: can you tell me your whereabouts on the morning of Monday, April 22?"

"The day after Easter you mean? When my father was offed?"

"That is precisely what I mean."

"That's an easy one..." Isaac began, but Jack interrupted.

"You're going to tell me that you were with your parole officer in Junction," the sheriff suggested.

"Got that right," smiled Isaac and he attempted to assume a smug pose by crossing his arms, but the handcuffs prevented the gesture.

"Is that your story?"

"Damn straight it is," Isaac assured the sheriff.

"You're certain?" Jack asked.

"Yup."

The sheriff pressed a buzzer beneath the table and a voice sounded over speakers in the ceiling of the dim room.

"April 16th," said the voice.

"Hey, is that..." Isaac protested.

"Yes, that's your parole officer, who's right outside. And he seems to remember the date differently. How do you explain that?"

"Musta got it wrong," said Isaac quietly.

"Pardon?"

"I said I musta got the date wrong..." the criminal's voice trailed off.

"Now, do you want to tell me where you actually were on the morning of April 22nd?"

"It's gonna sound bad to say it," said Isaac in a tone that was part apologetic and part resignation.

"Humor me," said Jack. "It may not sound as bad as you think. Tell me the truth."

"I was in the basement of the Stevenson Building," Isaac whispered.

"And that would be the same Stevenson Building on Welton Street in Denver where your late father was killed?"

"That's the place all right."

"And what were you up to down in the basement, I wonder?"

"I was un-cratin' books."

"I see. Were these your father's books?"

"Yeah."

"Signed editions?"

"Yeah."

The men were both silent.

"See, what it was," Isaac continued, "I figured the old geezer would live forever—who knew? And he weren't no saint like the papers say. You just ask my maw—may she rest in peace. Or better yet ask my sisters—step and otherwise. Anyways, I figured this: I figured he's got all them books in storage, see? And I had no idea what crap like that was worth until my girlfriend, she looked it up on eBay. Chri...I mean cripes one book with his moniker in it was sellin' for five hundred bucks to some idiot in Nebraska! Can you believe it? Five C-notes just for writin' your fuc...friggin' name? I figured I could use a piece of that action."

"So, you were stealin' your father's autographed books with the intention of sellin' them."

"Yeah."

"While someone else was upstairs murderin' your old man?"

"Looks that way since it sure wasn't me did it because I couldn't get outa the crap-suckin' basement because the crap-suckin' elevator wouldn't... Sorry—you ain't gonna count them cuss words agin me are you?"

Jack was almost sympathetic as he said, "No, I won't count 'em. Clearly you were upset about being trapped in the basement at the time of the murder."

"So, you believe me?"

"Yes. Feels good to tell the truth doesn't it?"

"I guess. What now?"

"I think your probation officer and I can come to an agreement. You've helped us out with our investigation. You've cooperated by answerin' my questions. So, how does four weeks of house arrest with a monitorin' ankle bracelet sound to you?"

"Better than five years in the joint, I guess," muttered Isaac.

"I'm afraid it'll mean you'll miss hearin' your father's will read out."

"Don't think I'll be missin' much," Isaac frowned. "Everybody knows the old man cut me off years ago."

"Well just in case, we'll have that lawyer of yours attend in your place," said Jack.

"Do I got a lawyer?"

"Oh yes," said Jack and he hit the button again. "Allow me to introduce your appointed counsel."

The buzzer sounded and the interrogation room door clicked open and three figures entered. One was the stern-faced deputy who unlocked Isaac's handcuffs. Another was a portly, pasty-faced individual whom Isaac recognized as his long-suffering parole officer. And the third was an energetic figure in a trim grey suit who handed Isaac a business card.

"Joel Signet, Esquire, attorney extraordinaire and all-around champion of the oppressed. Pleased to meet you. So, I'm going to have you sign a proxy. Do you understand what a proxy is? It's a..."

The lawyer was explaining his tactics and escorting Isaac, his parole officer, and the shepherding deputy out of the room when the confused criminal stopped dead in his tracks.

"Hey," he turned and addressed the sheriff, "wait a minute. You said three questions. What's the third one?"

"Well," said Jack, "I was goin' to ask you how you got all them cuts and scrapes on your hands and forearms but since you was trapped in the basement and we have evidence that somebody broke out one of the lower level windows and opened the transom from the inside and he must have been a big guy considerin' all the trouble he had squeezin' through that jagged openin'," Jack paused to take a breath. "And with all that evidence already in hand, I just have to figure that your story holds together."

The deputy chortled and Isaac mumbled a profanity. As the others departed, Joel lingered behind.

"Jack," the lawyer whispered, "If you ever want to give up this law enforcement gig, I think there's a future for you in writing mystery stories. But a word of advice—you need to work on your punctuation."

Chapter 23

The Case
(Monday, May 6)

It was Monday night and just warm enough to start the crickets chirping in the blossoming meadow surrounding Lavender Hill Farm.

"Now, my love," said Anne, "let's see where we are."

"We're in our bed, of course," said Trinidad as he kissed her neck.

"With the case I mean."

"Oh, that old thing," Trinidad joked.

It was late and the two of them were snuggled in the upstairs bedroom with papers and photographs and notebooks and pens scattered haphazardly on the bedspread. Earlier that day, they'd elected to clear up their work and return the kitchen table to its rightful purpose with the idea of working in Trinidad's office. But that cramped space had proven unsatisfactory and they'd decided to move upstairs to try spreading things out on the bed. Then one thing had led to another and one more afternoon delight was recorded in the sensual pages of their hypothetical lover's logbook.

"That was so great that I think we'll be able to skip the honeymoon, sweetheart," said Anne after they were both spent and lying in each other's arms.

"You had better be kidding," he said and frowned. "I've already booked our flight to Ireland like I promised."

"Great," said Anne. "We have a honeymoon scheduled, but not a wedding yet. Talk about putting the horse before the cart." Then, before her fiancé could protest, she added, "Yes, I'm kidding. So, now—let's see if we can keep our hands to ourselves as we review the case."

Though Isaac had seemed a good suspect, Jack had telephoned to say that the ex-con's alibi looked solid. The wayward son's prints were all over the basement and the broken window was caked with his blood type and DNA. Plus, he'd even left his monogrammed crowbar behind, so it seemed likely that the bumbling giant had been stuck below ground when his father was murdered.

"Who the heck has a monogrammed crowbar anyway?" Trinidad asked.

"Focus, dear," Anne chided as she took over the summation.

Whoever the murderer was, Anne noted, he or she must have arrived just after Isaac rode the elevator to the basement. Then the unknown killer must have placed the out-of-order sign on the first floor, commandeered the elevator, ascended to the penthouse, and used a fire service key to freeze it upstairs.

"Hmm—isn't it illegal to own a fireman's key?" Anne asked.

"Possessing the key isn't illegal per se," Trinidad answered. "But it's quite another matter to use it to commit a crime."

"A crime like stabbing someone sixteen times in the face, for example?"

"Yeah," said Trinidad. "My turn to do some speculating. Hand me those notes."

"Say please," she teased.

"Please," he said as he paused to plant a kiss on her forehead before continuing. "The way I see it, the murderer was keeping the elevator off-line during those frantic moments when Isaac had been unable to summon the car. And the perpetrator continued to hold it at the penthouse level when Ray arrived to deliver the typewriter. The old man was probably already dead when the murderer buzzed Ray inside. The bogus out-of-order sign sent Ray to the stairwell and, soon after Ray started upstairs, the murderer stranded the cursing repairman on the stairs as he descended to the ground floor and he escaped."

"He or she," Anne corrected.

"Right," Trinidad agreed. "So, Isaac the son had no way to use the elevator to get out of the basement, let alone ascend to the penthouse, and he's also right-handed—whereas Jack tells us the out-of-order sign was written by a lefty. So, we can safely eliminate your favorite ex-con as a suspect. All of which brings us to Esau's brother." Trinidad stopped to check his notes and then continued. "You documented Jacob's hatred for his older brother. But Jack asked the Carbondale police to question Jacob and our friendly neighborhood sheriff also asked them to interview members of the community garden. Jacob's fellow gardeners confirmed the old fox's whereabouts at an Easter Monday gathering in Carbondale which lasted long enough to cover the time of his brother's murder. So, the bitter brother is also off our suspect list."

"And good riddance to those two," said Anne. "A right-handed ape and an aging lothario—a fine pair of scoundrels. So, I guess that leaves the women —and my money's on the redhead."

"You may be right," Trinidad grinned. "That woman and her amazing breasts are at the top of my list."

"Keep that list and everything else in your pants, joy-boy," said Anne as she gave her lover a playful tap on the noggin. "I'm expecting you to focus this fabulous brain of yours on the task at hand. So, stop fantasizing about redheads and start doing some serious sleuthing. The reading of the will is right around the corner and we still don't have a line on who killed old Esau Koller."

"So, we'll do a line-up. Where's the masking tape?" asked Trinidad as he jumped up and pulled on his trousers.

"Again, with the pants," she laughed. "You sure know how to show a gal a good time."

"And you should put your robe on at least," he insisted. "Or we'll never get through this. Ah—here's the tape in the closet, right where you moved it to after I put it where I always put it..."

"In the dresser drawer," they said in unison.

"Jeepers," she exclaimed. "How long have we been a couple anyway?"

"Long enough to already start sounding like my parents, who I promise you'll meet at the wedding," said Trinidad as he worked to tape the dossier photographs to the bedroom wall.

"If there ever is a wedding," Anne suggested.

"No worries, my love," he assured her. "We'll get our ducks in a row. Meanwhile, here's a row of pigeons, so come take a look."

Anne slipped on her robe and joined her industrious fiancé at the wall where he'd arranged photos of the three remaining suspects in a more-or-less straight row. For some minutes the two of them stared at the photographs.

"I've never liked this wallpaper," Anne said. "Can we change it?"

"First chance I get," Trinidad promised. "*After* we've solved this case. Now without considering any other facts, except these three faces..."

"You mean these two regular faces and this one particular face attached to an outlandishly fantastic breast-fest of a torso," corrected Anne.

"Okay have it your way," he laughed. "So here we have face number one and face two and face three plus its fantastic torso. Who looks likely to you?"

"It can't be that easy," she protested.

"Come on—take a chance—play a hunch. Who looks guilty to you?"

"The torso..." Anne began.

"Forget the torso," said Trinidad.

"I will if you will," she suggested.

"Come on," he said. "Be serious for five seconds and, leaving the torso aside, look at the faces and tell me who you think did it."

"Door number one," she said.

"Number one?" he asked.

"Absolutely," she declared.

"Funny," he said. "I was just going to say the same thing."

And so, with daylight beginning to fade, they both moved in for a closer look. Their target was wearing a wedding dress. The black and white image was not only the best photo they had of the woman—it was the only one.

"I've gotta say I love that dress," said Anne.

"This coming week," said Trinidad as he tapped the photo, "once we've cleared things with Joel and Jack, we'll drive over Grand Mesa and break this suspect's alibi."

"Oh boy, Mrs. Juliet Sturgis," said Anne as she addressed the photo, "I wouldn't be in your shoes next week—no way—not for all the tea in China."

"Come to bed," said Trinidad as he picked up his fiancée and carried her back across the room.

"Careful," she said when he started to deposit her in the middle of the cluttered quilt. "Put me down. You'll wrinkle everything. Let me get all this crap out of the way."

"I love it when you talk dirty," he said. "And, by the way, just so you know..."

"Know what?" she giggled as she pushed the case files to the floor, flung off her robe, and slipped under the covers.

"What you said earlier..." he whispered as he wriggled out of his jeans and nestled in beside her.

"What I said..." she breathed.

"About China..." he reminded her.

"What about China?" she asked as his kisses caused her toes to curl.

"No matter how you spell it..." he whispered. "...*there ain't no 'T' in China.*"

They lay together for a moment, their naked bodies entwined in silence, until Anne burst out laughing while her humorous fiancé worked his lover's magic.

Chapter 24

Awake

(Tuesday, May 7)

Five minutes after midnight, Anne sat abruptly up in bed. Being careful not to wake Trinidad, she slipped from beneath the covers, put on her robe, and went downstairs. Freeing her fiancé's heavy Loki coat from the hall-tree, she also pulled on a pair of oversized galoshes and ventured out into the cold spring night.

The May moon was riding high and she glanced up at the slim outline, a silver arc, no wider than a fingernail. The garish pink blush of last month's April moon was a distant memory. Absently recalling her one and only university botany class, she seemed to remember that the reddish April moon tended to appear around the same time as a variety of wild phlox flowers—an early springtime blossom and also pink. By contrast, tonight's moon was modest, although its elegant curve reminded her of her engagement ring and she held her hand aloft, positioning her ringed finger just below the distant crescent.

"Pretty," she said and an owl, hidden deep in the globe willows that encircled the farmyard, seemed to question her pronouncement. "*Who?*" she answered the unseen bird. "The moon is *who.*"

Hiking up Trinidad's huge jacket, which was far too long for her, she climbed up into the bed of her Nissan and opened the truck's lockbox.

Days ago, she'd placed Koller's vanity plate in there, then added Juliet's journal, and pushed both pieces of evidence out of her mind as she interviewed Jacob in the Carbondale community garden and ran for her life from the treacherous Isaac. After those incidents, she and Trinidad had argued—*more of a discussion, really,* she told herself—and in all the excitement she'd completely forgotten the plate and the journal.

She left the plate where it was. That hunk of aluminum would keep for another day. For the present, since she and her partner had reconciled and mutually settled on Juliet as their new prime suspect, it would not be too soon for the young detective to study the step-daughter's journal.

Chapter 25

Juliet

Returning to the farmhouse in time to hear the hall clock strike 1 a.m., Anne made coffee. Then, while Trinidad slept upstairs, she sat at the kitchen table fingering the manila envelope containing the pages of Juliet's journal. Having read Juliet's dossier, the fledgling detective anticipated that the step-daughter's journal would prove to be a poignant chronicle of unhappy details—details which were likely to kindle unwelcome echoes of Anne's own hidden memories.

She tasted her coffee reflectively, then sat the cup aside, opened the clasp, removed the contents, and placed the trussed-up journal on the kitchen table. Steeling her resolve, she took a final sip of coffee before untying the crisscross of strings which held the loose pages in place. She squared her shoulders and began to read. It only took a glance to recognize that Juliet's handwriting bore a distinct similarity to her step-father's impeccable cursive. Anne fingered the page, as she recalled the history of the elegant writing.

Earlier in the week, Anne and Trinidad had been sitting side-by-side on the farmhouse's comfortable sofa as the two of them conducted a conference call. The unseen participants were the servants who'd worked for the Koller family years ago at White Quail Manor. During the interview, the hired help had revealed that—despite residing within commuting distance of the well-respected Aspen public schools—the girls of the Koller household were homeschooled. The old man had insisted on keeping his daughters at home and mandating that—among other subjects—they master cursive, even as that skill was being phased out in regular classrooms.

"Grueling it was—them writing exercises," the manor cook had reported. "Them poor tykes was forced to labor away on endless swirls and sweeps and other such while banished all the time with me in the kitchen. Sittin' at the butcherblock table they were and ordered by their pa to get their writing perfect before the old fox would let them go to the proper dining table and eat. First Miss Ruth did the writin' over and over again and then it was the step-girls laborin' away. Poor little Miss Millie tried her best, but could no more master the writin' than the man in the moon. And it was like that at every meal—perfect penmanship or nothing to eat. If I hadn't slipped the girl a scrap now and then, well I don't doubt that she'd have starved to death."

The lessons, however inhumane, seemed to have taken root, because Juliet's clear and crisp letters were exceptionally rendered. An unblemished flow of flawless curves and slants and connectors created lines which were themselves things of beauty. But the words formed by those perfectly fashioned letters were heartbreaking.

Struggling to read Juliet's opening page, Anne soon recognized that the step-daughter's story confirmed her worst fears. Juliet spoke of things only hinted at in the servants' recollections of life at the Aspen manor. Anne had already guessed that Esau had been abusing his daughters in more ways than one and that supposition was now verified by the testimony of one of his victims.

Anne sighed and looked away—unable to continue. Ordinarily, in the early morning darkness, it would be impossible to deal with her own raw memories. *How,* she wondered, *will I be able to stomach someone else's graphic tale of woe?*

She tried to begin again, but stopped reading as tears clouded her vision while her fingers grasped the sheet, seemingly frozen in place. Anne sat there, incapable of movement and unable to turn to the next page. Despite the journal being an original—and therefore irreplaceable—source document, the agonized detective was sorely tempted to crumple up the entire sheaf of handwritten pages and fling them out the nearest window.

Days ago, she'd begged Trinidad to throw Esau's horrifying novel out the farmhouse window. Tossing the journal away would be one way to avoid the writing, which pulsated with the mistreated girl's accounts of corruption. Anne had been repelled by *Hacksaw Fury*. Faced with the stark reality of Juliet's chronicle, her feelings of revulsion were parallel. But the detective suspected that, where horror was concerned, Juliet's straightforward story would far outweigh her step-father's fiction.

"Coffee," she said aloud as she stood up and crossed to the stove to prepare another pot. Refilling the vintage percolator, she turned the burner on.

The sound and smell of the budding beverage fortified her tenacity. Returning to the table with a fresh cup in hand, Anne sat resolutely down, intent on tackling the journal. The caffeine helped and she reminded herself that Trinidad was just upstairs. The combination of the proximate beverage and her nearby lover gave her courage to continue. She'd reach out for Trinidad if needed, but in the meantime, she'd soldier on.

Which is precisely what she did.

Literally fighting to suppress memories of her own abusive father, the determined detective went to war. Battling through each of Juliet's succinct sentences, she reacted not only to the implicit meaning of the writer's statements, but also to the habitual nuances which every abused child learns to master in order to avoid the pain of remembering. She understood Juliet's anguish. She'd been there, dancing around the memories, trying to suppress the truth—striving to think about something else—anything else.

Anne literally put her head down and read on until, at last, on page sixteen, it happened. Having unburdened herself of darkest memories, Juliet left her past behind and emerged strong and resolute.

"I've done it," Juliet wrote. "I've found my voice. I've slipped my bonds. I'm free!"

Sitting alone in the farmhouse kitchen with William, the ancient grandfather clock, measuring the passing hours, Anne pressed onward. As she feared, Juliet's journal absolutely authenticated Esau's predatory behavior, but it also celebrated the abused woman's triumphant endurance.

Using her iPad, Anne took notes as she read. She imagined the intrepid author carrying the journal with her everywhere, safeguarding it and her fountain pen, so that—whenever she found a spare moment to express her thoughts and document her recollections—her writing would be consistently crisp and uniform. Juliet's words, so disheartening at the start, blossomed into objects of beauty, ceased to be barriers, and became guideposts.

Juliet's writing might confirm that the step-daughter had an indisputable motive for killing old man Koller, but for Anne her journal was also a testament to the woman's survival. Juliet had survived Esau Koller. She had lived, she had married, and built a new life for herself. The prolific author had put it all down on paper from her girlhood recollections and her odyssey across America, to her redemption and her hidden life in Collbran. Everything had tumbled out, every betrayal, every disappointment, every hurt, every prayer—and, in the end, Juliet had endured.

Anne stopped reading and fingered her engagement ring. She herself was on the cusp of overcoming her own unhappy childhood and about to embark upon a relationship with a man whom she loved with every fiber of her being. The inquisitive detective had reached a tipping point. Her investigation had evolved from an odious task into a mission.

Returning to the journal, Anne warmed to her work, empathizing with Juliet's trials, catching glimpses of the writer's girlish determination and her wry sense of humor, sensing the woman's indomitable spirit and looking forward to meeting her.

In the days to come, she and Trinidad would arrive on Juliet's doorstep with investigative intentions which might lead to her arrest. But Anne decided that, despite Juliet's probable guilt, at least one member of the Sands Detective Agency would be willing to shake the courageous woman's hand.

Anne reviewed her notes. She wanted—in an odd role reversal—to spare Trinidad from having to read the compelling journal without a measure of context. Without the benefit of Anne's insights, she suspected her intrepid partner would be inclined to fixate on Juliet's sad life and, like most men, he'd want to solve her problems for her. Anne could just imagine her valiant hero wanting to take action. He'd wish to go back in time to rescue Juliet from the dragon's lair at White Quail while eviscerating her abusive step-father for good measure. Her fearless husband-to-be would puff-up his righteous manhood and conjure up a superhuman desire to make it all go away, like it never happened, even though it did. And, doing so, he'd entirely miss the point that—yes, it had been a rough life—but Juliet had emerged from it and moved on to create a satisfying future.

The morning birds were singing outside the kitchen window. Anne looked up from the writing, stretched, and listened. The sun was rising and she'd already accomplished a great deal. As an empathetic survivor, Anne was moved by Juliet's story which chronicled how a durable spirit can rise above the most heinous betrayal. As a questing detective, she was gratified that the journal also shed much needed light on Esau's transgressions. Summarized in Anne's faithful notes, Juliet's recollections painted, from a step-daughter's perspective, a revealing portrait of Koller as a totally manipulative and profoundly unlikeable man.

Anne set the journal aside and reviewed her notes. One of Juliet's early journal entries established the theme.

Thinking back to her girlhood days, Juliet wrote about the fateful morning she'd first set foot in White Quail Manor in the company of her mother and her younger sister. Hortense Hapsen had been Esau's second wife, but she treasured the memory of her first husband and young Juliet and her sister Millie also wanted to honor their natural father. The three had planned to manifest their affection for Hiram Hapsen by adopting the hyphenated name of Hapsen-Koller. And, when the widow and her children came to live with Koller in his sprawling manor in the foothills of Aspen, they said so.

But that request didn't sit well with Esau Koller. Moments after his new wife and her two young daughters arrived at the manor, Esau hustled them inside and assembled his nascent family, along with his household servants, in the drawing room of his palatial manor.

"Here's the way it is," the old devil said, pointing emphatically at his new wife. "I'll be *screwing* this woman," he shouted. "And as long as I am *screwing* this woman at my leisure, she will use the name *Koller*. So, my dear," he told his sobbing wife, "we'll have no more mention of this hyphenated crap!" Then he turned his scornful attention to his two step-daughters who were weeping and clinging to their mother. "Now understand this, you two little tarts: *I am screwing your mother*," he allegedly told eleven-year-old Juliet and nine-year old Millie. "So, young ladies, that means that she and both of you will honor the Koller name. So, forget the damnable Hapsen-hyphen and that is the end of this particular time-wasting discussion."

Eight years later in the dead of winter at the stroke of midnight, Juliet's journal recorded that she'd resisted Esau's unwelcome amorous advances and, despite a freezing night, rushed outside. Shivering and raging, she'd stood barefoot in the snow, shouting obscenities at her step-father's bedroom window three floors above. She shouted despite knowing that, as was his habit, Esau had probably turned off his hearing aid upon retiring. She shouted and the live-in servants definitely got an earful. When the enraged girl had put a rock through a downstairs window, she walked away from White Quail Manor with nothing but a sore throat and the clothes on her back.

Cold and shaking, Juliet reported that she managed to reach the highway where the freezing girl hitchhiked north as far as the outskirts of Carbondale. Her last ride turned out to be a kindly truck driver who bundled her in his coat and drove her into town. Seeing her weakened condition, he delivered her first to St. Joseph's where they turned the girl away because she had no crucifix or wallet, and finally he carried her limp body to the general hospital where he made an unholy scene before they reluctantly took her in.

"What next?" asked the incredulous truck driver. "Put her in the damn stable maybe?"

Reading this account of the truck driver's actions, Anne thought to herself, *Now here is a man—a good man—who should be nominated for sainthood for resisting the temptation to rape the vulnerable teenager.*

Juliet spent weeks in the Carbondale hospital, fighting double pneumonia and racking up astronomical bills. She gave a false name because she didn't want anyone to find her. She had an uncle in town, but she had no desire to contact Jacob. The last person she wanted to see was her step-father's twin. No one visited her. She should have reached out to her mother, but she blamed Hortense for marrying a monster and dragging her and her sister into the demon's lair. Juliet should have thought of her sister Millie, left alone in the sprawling manor with her wicked step-father, but she was too depressed to care about anyone—even herself. In many respects, Juliet was a typical teenager, but one who'd been robbed of the opportunity to experience the roller coaster that typified the ups and downs of a normal adolescence.

For Juliet there were no ups. For Juliet it had been all downhill.

Hours before Juliet fled from the manor, Esau had burst into his step-daughter's room intending to rape her, but the willful girl had fought him off. Concerned that the other occupants of White Quail Manor had heard the turmoil, Esau fired everyone except his manservant. The cook, the chauffeur, the groundskeeper, and the housekeeper were all given their walking papers and, by next morning, Juliet too was gone.

As for what occurred in Aspen after Juliet abandoned the manor, hints of the Koller saga had been revealed when she and Trinidad interviewed the Aspen servants, who recounted things which the fleeing girl couldn't have known. At that time, Trinidad had been dutifully taking notes while Anne orchestrated the conference call which brought together individuals who were scattered throughout the nation. Most of the hired help had been dismissed within hours of hearing a thundering argument between Esau and his step-daughter. They'd also heard her plaintive cries in the night.

"Was a terrible brouhaha," the housekeeper remembered.

"Things was broke," the cook declared.

"I shoulda done something," the chauffeur recalled.

"A window was put out," the groundskeeper testified.

Phillip, Esau's loyal manservant, who was also part of the conference call, had yet to say a word. One-by-one the witnesses recounted the battle waged in young Juliet's upstairs bedroom and the winter evening filled with deranged screaming and cursing in the dark, followed by a haunting silence.

"Such cursing I never hope to hear from a sailor," the housekeeper said.

"An avalanche of profanity," the cook said.

"Like to break your heart," said the groundskeeper.

"Shoulda done something," the chauffeur repeated.

According to the talkative servants, they thought Juliet had come back inside after her tirade in the snow. But they hadn't had a chance to check on the girl, because everyone except Phillip had been cashiered the following morning. Whatever the servants supposed, by noon, the over-sized manor with three sprawling stories and more than two-dozen rooms had been reduced to four occupants: the doting manservant, Esau, his youngest step-daughter, and his distraught wife.

Hearing that the mother had been present but had done nothing to protect Juliet, Trinidad had passed a note to Anne, nominating Hortense Koller for mother-of-the-year. For her part, Anne recalled her own mother's inability to mitigate the abuse inflicted by Hendrix McDougal on her younger self, his only daughter. Her mother was also a victim of abuse and Anne had already forgiven her inaction. So, she crumpled Trinidad's note, shook her head, frowned at her fiancé, and mouthed the words, "Not funny."

When a pause in the conference call conversation signaled that the participants had exhausted their recollections, Trinidad thanked them and was about to sever the connection when Anne stayed his hand. Anything which happened after the others were sacked was a mystery to everybody but Phillip. It was a circumstance which compelled Anne to make a request.

"I'll ask Phillip to remain on the line please," she'd said. Then she'd addressed the others, saying goodbye to each in turn and thanking them for their assistance. And, the moment the final subject had rung off, she turned her attention to Phillip who, to her ever-loving relief and consummate surprise, didn't hang up. "We'll need your help from this point forward," she said, hoping the taciturn man would cooperate.

"I will help if I can," came the measured reply, enfolded in the auditory embrace of a perfect British accent.

"That will be splendid," Anne had gushed. "And if you were here in person, I'd offer you tea, but, of course, you'd have to serve it."

"Hmm," the stiff reply told Anne that her lame attempt at humor hadn't been appreciated.

"Sorry," she'd offered. "Just a little attempt at Yankee humor. Trying to break the ice."

"Don't," Phillip had retorted.

"Of course. Sorry," she'd repeated with a furtive glance at her fiancé whom she hoped would join in the interrogation. But Trinidad just mouthed the word "apologize" and gave her an unhelpful thumb's up. Taking the hint, she continued. "And I humbly apologize for my ill manners."

"Accepted," he'd said and his tone suggested he'd indeed comprehended, if not actually enjoyed, her attempted witticism about who'd be expected to serve the tea.

Love those British, she'd thought.

"Ask your questions as you will," Phillip said and she'd pictured him settling in for a fireside chat.

"First, can you collaborate what the others said?"

"Their recollections are essentially correct."

"No rebuttal?"

"None."

"Mind if I keep my recorder going?"

"Hunky-dory."

"So, what can you add?" she'd asked.

"Only this..." Phillip began and—as Anne hurriedly checked to make certain the battery on her smartphone recorder had sufficient juice—the previously silent man launched into a rich narrative. It was an unexpected avalanche of information, which made the fledgling detective glad she'd kept the manservant after school.

According to Phillip's detailed recollections, after Juliet vanished, the scene at the manor continued to deteriorate. Within days, her mother, distraught with worry over her missing daughter and unable—even with Phillip's help—to manage the household, had a nervous breakdown. After two weeks, during which Hortense refused to copulate, Esau reacted by dispatching the poor woman to a convalescent home.

"The Master would not go and Miss Millie was to be spared the journey, so I alone accompanied my Mistress to that unhappy place," Phillip recalled in a tone that, even mitigated by the phone connection, conveyed an aura of sincere regret. "And I consider my complicity in Mrs. Koller's incarceration to be one of the most shameful episodes of my life."

The disappearance of Juliet and the old man's decision to institutionalize his second wife meant Esau was running out of women. Only one female remained in his sphere and Phillip believed that the old satyr must have been sorely tempted to continue his pattern of molestation.

"He had treated Miss Ruth most shabbily," Phillip confessed. "And he had tried the same with Miss Juliet and now I feared that he would turn to Miss Millie. I..." the man seemed to lose his voice and both Anne and Trinidad sensed that the conflicted manservant was sobbing on his end.

"Would you like to...?" Trinidad began.

"No, no," said Phillip. "By all means let's continue. It's a relief to unburden myself if you'll tolerate a bit more."

"Go on," Anne encouraged.

Isolated in the rambling manor with only, as Phillip labeled himself, "a dithering manservant" to shield her from her rapacious father, Millie was virtually unprotected. Phillip knew of Esau's abuse of Ruth and, when he learned of the dust-up between Juliet and her step-father, it was easy to guess the cause.

"First Miss Ruth and now Miss Juliet," he recalled. "If only..." but he didn't finish his speculation.

Given Phillip's knowledge of his master's appetite for daughters, he grew to fear that Esau might well act to make his youngest step-daughter his newest conquest. Instead, quite unexpectedly, the old manservant declared that a miracle occurred. Recalling that earlier phone conversation and Phillip's contention of having witnessed a miracle, Anne set Juliet's journal aside and rummaged through another stack of papers. She was searching for the transcript of their interview with the manservant who'd managed the Aspen and Denver households. She'd revisit Phillip's quotation—the exact words he'd used when describing this so-called miracle. Re-reading the quote, Anne could still remember the voice recording and the last time she'd reacted to Phillip's claim.

In the wake of their earlier conference call with the White Quail Manor workers, Anne had been operating her smartphone while Trinidad sat at his laptop, rapidly and accurately typing the words. They'd finished transcribing the recollections of the other servants and were several minutes into reviewing Phillip's recorded testimony when, abruptly, both partners had paused and exchanged a glance.

"Play that again," Trinidad had requested.

Both had reacted to a certain point in the recording which had captured a voice taut with emotion as the aging manservant testified to his master's unexpected change of heart. According to Phillip, within days of being left alone with his youngest step-daughter, Esau Koller had undergone a sudden transformation. Anne cued-up the recording and replayed the excerpt.

"You might say that overnight the master grew a conscience," Phillip declared. "And, therefore, considering all that he might have done to Miss Millie, I prefer to think of his remarkably changed behavior as a miracle."

Never mind that the two detectives had previously learned from Joel's treasure trove of documents that the date of the old reprobate's alleged epiphany handily coincided with his cancer diagnosis. Considering the timing, it was the joint opinion of the Sands Detective Agency that a chilling medical verdict was the true source of Esau's abrupt metamorphosis. The news, documented in Esau's medical records, had been a two-fold blow. Not only was the patient compelled to contemplate his mortality, he also had to simultaneously absorb the reality that an operation to resolve his testicular cancer meant he would be cursed with permanent and irreversible erectile dysfunction. Given a choice between death and sex, there seemed little question which diagnosis had most distressed the old satyr.

Listening to Phillip's glowing report of his master's rapturous conversion from an incestuous pig to a Lamb of God, the two detectives had exchanged a glance and rolled their collective eyes.

Some miracle, Anne thought. *For my money, the thing falls far short of marvelous. The righteous conversion which Phillip describes was nothing more than an old sinner's faded libido masquerading as miraculous. I wonder what else our reticent manservant glossed over. What else didn't he tell us?*

"Good morning, dear." Trinidad's voice pulled Anne back to the present. "What have you been up to?"

Chapter 26

Daughters
(Jubilate Sunday)

Preparing for their Collbran trip, the intrepid members of the Sands Detective Agency had invested all week in reviewing the stories of Esau's daughter and step-daughters. By Sunday morning, drawing from a variety of resources, they'd assembled a clear picture, with Juliet's journal filling in the gaps.

"Good background," Trinidad said as he finished reading Anne's notes and reached out to pat his lover's hand. "This must have been a tough read."

The journal turned out to be a particularly valuable piece of evidence. Proud of her discovery, Anne explained she'd been fortunate to obtain the unpublished work from the Carbondale Public Library an hour before her interview with Jacob and run-in with his threatening nephew.

"You ought to send that librarian a thank you note," Trinidad suggested.

"We might need a librarian to organize this mountain of stuff," Anne grumbled as she surveyed the stack of papers, photographs, and recording devices arrayed on their living room coffee table. "So much for the glamourous life of a working detective."

"Yeah, boy," Trinidad agreed. "I better put the coffee on."

In addition to reviewing Juliet's journal and Koller's memoirs, the couple had recorded phone interviews with the Aspen manor servants. Trinidad had also made preliminary contact with Esau's publisher and CPA. Both men lived in California and both were willing to cooperate. Trinidad planned to reconnect with them eventually. In the meantime, the efficient detective also worked the phones to conduct follow-up interviews with Esau's most recent set of hired helpers, the cook and housekeeper who looked after the author's Denver penthouse. Given the old man's hermit-like behavior, the Denver servants had little to add to the statements they'd already given to the Denver Metro police, except to confirm that their employer communicated with them by written note. Unfortunately, neither could recall anything in writing, or any change in Koller's routine, which might shed light on whom the old man had been planning to meet on the day he died.

"Mr. Koller never went out," they'd both confirmed in separate but nearly verbatim statements. "And he never had visitors."

Anne found this revelation particularly significant since, in the final two days of Esau's life, the aloof old man had opened his door to not one but two visitors: Ray the repairman and the person who ultimately stabbed and killed the unsociable hermit.

"Years of isolation," she noted, "and then suddenly the place is Grand Central Station."

With this background material in mind and, in anticipation of receiving the go-ahead from the lawyer and the sheriff to interview Juliet Sturgis, the two detectives settled down in the farmhouse's spacious living room. Their aim on this sunny Sunday morning was to sit together and review one final piece of evidence. Anne was bubbling with anticipation because, in addition to interviewing a host of supporting characters, Trinidad had managed to corner one of the Koller drama's leading ladies—the elusive Ruth Koller. The contents of her interview were explosive and he'd been waiting for the right moment to share his findings.

"You okay with this?" he asked for the fourth time.

"Like I said," she responded, "better late than never. Go ahead."

As Anne listened with rapt attention, Trinidad proceeded to share the transcript and audio recording of a Skype interview he'd conducted with Esau's natural daughter. When Trinidad reported this encounter, Anne had been tempted to protest. She was miffed because—based on their original plan to divide up the suspects—the striking redhead was supposed to be her quarry. But she'd let that pass. She decided not to mention it since Trinidad's interview with Esau's steamy daughter had been conducted on the very same day when Anne herself had tangled with members of the Koller clan while nosing around Carbondale.

"Go on, honey," she said. "I'm all ears."

According to Trinidad, Ruth seemed eager to communicate, quickly taking charge of the interview and talking nearly nonstop during their twenty-minute encounter. Speaking from an undisclosed location, Ruth began by disputing her father's version of key events. Trinidad's carefully phrased question about the circumstances surrounding the deaths of her mother and younger sister, drew a particularly irritated response.

Esau's memoirs presented a self-serving account of his actions following the tragic events which led to the drowning of his first wife and infant daughter. In her Skype interview with Trinidad, Ruth—who, along with her father, had survived the tragedy—told a decidedly different tale. She maintained the so-called raging flash flood was more of a steady trickle, leaving the old man every opportunity to save her mother and sister. Instead, Ruth alleged, her father abandoned them in favor of saving the unlucky daughter whom he'd intended all along to groom as his lover.

"Picture this," Ruth had told Trinidad. "I woke up, lying on my back on the stream bank with my own father kissing me and fondling my chest. And that was the beginning of it."

Hearing the daughter's words, Anne briefly wondered if Ruth may have mistaken her father's attempts to administer CPR as sexual. Then she immediately dismissed the idea in favor of a belief that Esau, aroused by intimate contact with his under-aged daughter, had been tempted to forego efforts to rescue his wife and infant. Her logical mind told her that both perceptions might be valid since the reality of a given situation, especially a trauma from the dim past, was open to interpretation.

But, in her heart, she was inclined to believe the daughter.

There was power in Ruth's testimony and her memories were supported by the contents of Juliet's journal. Esau's manuscript had much to say about his own accomplishments, but touched little on his family life. For Anne, his victimized daughters represented the most reliable informants to fill in the blanks. Juliet's writing had provided a bitter foretaste of Esau's relations with his daughters and Anne only needed a hint of the Skype encounter to guess that Ruth's testimony would verify the worst. Given these parallel accounts, Anne had every expectation that Ruth's story of a natural daughter abused and cast out would mirror Juliet's tale told from the point of view of a step-daughter. In fact, as she listened to Ruth's testimony, she was struck by the fact that the two women used nearly identical words to describe their miserable experiences.

Immediately after recounting her memory of the drowning incident, Ruth noticeably altered her attitude. In an almost wistful tone of voice, she seemed to temper her anger by claiming that she and her father had always been close. Then, almost as suddenly, her speech devolving into something feral, she added, "A little too close."

According to Ruth, immediately after her mother's funeral, Esau seemed to instantly forget his first wife and infant daughter—a cold-hearted indifference which also applied to his son. On the Monday following the weekend burials, he instructed Ruth to remain in her room while he picked up the telephone. The girl listened on the extension as her father, with a single call, made clandestine arrangements to farm the boy out to the care of a nearby foundling home. Moments later, she stood at her window to watch and listen as Esau ordered his hirelings to incinerate the boy's toys and extra clothing and enlisted his manservant to bundle Isaac up and carry the squalling infant to the manor's front gate. Then, the moment the van carrying Isaac away had disappeared from sight, the old man took his under-aged daughter by the hand and led her into the manor's spacious garage where he kept a little-used station wagon. Opening the passenger door for her, he took special care to fasten her seatbelt before starting the engine and backing out. Phillip, along with a half-dozen household workers, stood in a disciplined line near the front door—stiff and unmoving, like a rank of soldiers. Ruth waved as they started down the long driveway and found it odd that no one in the group waved back.

Inviting his daughter to sing a round of "Row, Row, Row Your Boat" as they wheeled through the sprawling grounds, Esau steered out through the manor's wrought-iron gateway. Driving along isolated roads, the old man turned onto a narrow track and into a space beside an isolated cabin where he comforted the grieving girl by allowing her to share a bottle of wine. An hour later, when the twelve-year-old was sufficiently drunk, he stretched her out on the plush davenport and pulled her pants down. Working feverishly like a man possessed, the old satyr stripped the girl naked and, when she complained of being cold, he carried her into another room, tucked her into a narrow bed, and crawled in beside her.

"To this day, hearing the song 'Row Your Boat' makes me want to puke and I can still hear the bed springs beneath that old camp mattress squeaking and squeaking and squeaking and..." Ruth might have continued this recollection indefinitely had Trinidad not cleared his throat.

"Anyway," she said, "let's just say he rowed the living girlhood out of me."

From that moment on, Esau slept with the girl for three weeks running. The two of them remained in the cabin while the manor's household servants, unaware of the goings-on in the sordid love nest, delivered regular doses of food and water and liquor. Eventually abandoning the cabin, the old man and his daughter returned to the family manor—a sprawling abode which he'd inherited from his wealthy parents. Arriving there, Esau conveniently forgot he had a son and set up house with Ruth.

Steadily gaining the bewildered girl's trust, he convinced her it was perfectly proper and logical that she should take her mother's place and the shameless manipulator proceeded to instruct her in the mechanics of servicing him in every way possible. Confused by her father's advances, Ruth was initially ashamed, then flattered, and finally captivated.

Trinidad paused his review of Ruth's testimony and looked intently at Anne.

"You okay hearing this?" he asked, knowing Esau's incestuous behavior must be touching a nerve with Anne.

"Give me a moment," she said, grateful for a chance to leave the room. She calmly walked to the bathroom, closed the door, and turned on the tap, hoping Trinidad would believe she was getting a drink of water. Then she sat on the floor, straddling the commode, and vomited until her throat was raw with reflux and her eyes stung.

Trinidad tapped lightly on the door.

"You okay?" he asked.

"Bring me some honey?" she requested, her voice hoarse with emotion.

Trinidad sat on the edge of the bathtub while Anne spooned honey onto her raw throat and swallowed hard. When the jar was empty, he helped her up, carried her to their bed, and was about to leave her there, gently sobbing, when she reached up and grabbed his sleeve.

"Stay with me," she whispered.

He sat on the bed and let her snuggle into his lap until she fell asleep. As she lay there gently snoring, a text pinged onto Trinidad's cell phone. It was Jack giving the detectives the final go-ahead for a Thursday confrontation with Juliet Sturgis.

As his exhausted fiancée slept, Trinidad reviewed the remainder of Ruth's story in his mind, thankful that Anne wasn't awake to hear the rest of the sordid details.

Ruth had testified that Esau continued to abuse her, telling the naïve girl that his affection for her was natural, promising that he loved her, promising that everything would be all right. Meanwhile, Esau dealt with Isaac by calling in some Pitkin County favors, having the boy declared an orphan, and sending the unclaimed infant to the Front Range to languish in a Denver orphans' asylum.

Trinidad paused. Jack had reported that tough-guy Isaac blubbered like a frightened child when left alone in the dark in his county cell. Deputy Madge

Oxford had drawn the duty that night and had been obliged to sing the forlorn prisoner to sleep.

"Couldn't help myself," Madge had confessed. "And in the morning, the story of his days at the orphanage just come tumblin' out of the big ape—like an avalanche of hurt."

According to Deputy Oxford's notes, when Isaac had reached age sixteen and was legally free to do so, he'd walked away from the urban institution to which his father had banished him. By then, the orphan's asylum had morphed into the Denver Children's Home. He'd been treated well there, the giant man said, and he was on his way to learning a trade when he had an unexpected visit from somebody—he couldn't recall who. Some guy with a British accent, he claimed. For years after the unusual encounter, Isaac imagined the visitor had been his own father.

"But that woulda been impossible," Isaac concluded. "Since the old fart never ever said as much as 'boo' to me, ever."

In any event, that enigmatic somebody gave Isaac a wad of cash and informed the dumbfounded lad that he was the forgotten son of Esau Koller. The money was intended to keep the boy happy and far away from Aspen and the Koller manor. The sum had its intended effect as the confused youngster fled from the Denver institution and spent the cash all in a single night of non-stop drinking, at the close of which he was arrested. Escaping incarceration, young Isaac fled west to lie about his age and join the Coast Guard. Isaac's story and Ruth's overlapped as Trinidad remembered the unhappy woman's claim that her brother was reduced to a distant memory when her father took charge of her life, her body, and her education. She recalled being coerced into learning cursive.

"A curse of cursive you might say," she'd joked during their Skype interview.

A year passed and their father-daughter bond grew even stronger—much too strong as it happens. The blossoming girl's sensuous red hair, pouty lips, steadily maturing breasts, and smooth freckled skin seemed to drive her father wild. Esau ravaged her over and over again like a rapacious hound in heat. She protested that he was hurting her, but her pleas to stop only inspired him to plow her more vigorously.

He used a condom during intercourse and, although the pills made her nauseous and caused her to gain weight, he forced his daughter to use birth control. For a full year—during which time he convinced local school officials that he was "home-schooling" his daughter—he lay with Ruth and manipulated the impressionable girl into thinking they were inseparable lovers. He paid the servants well with the tacit understanding that they keep their suspicions to themselves and look the other way. His wanton abuse continued until the girl turned thirteen, a milestone which he celebrated by getting roaring drunk and inadvertently impregnating her. The more she began to show, the more he tired of her.

"You're about as appealing as screwing a walrus," he declared.

One cold December morning, without warning, Esau pushed Ruth out of bed and ordered her to pack a suitcase. Though the distraught girl wept and pleaded to stay, he sent her away.

"I haven't seen or spoken to the old weasel since 1998," Ruth had said. Then the audio and video of her Skype connection began to fade and she closed her mouth.

Throughout the transmission, Trinidad had been unable to pick up anything from Ruth's facial expressions and only a little from her voice. Both her Skype image and the accompanying audio were distorted. However, he'd been able to recognize that she wore a scanty halter top which left little to the imagination and he'd assumed the sensual outfit had been chosen for his benefit. Furthermore, in insisting on this method of communication, Ruth— who volunteered no information about where and in what capacity she was employed—had claimed to be vacationing in Hawaii. But she could have been anywhere.

"And again, your whereabouts on April 22nd?" he'd asked, repeating once again the same question he'd asked at the outset of the interview.

"We'll have to get back to you on that one," she'd said and ended the transmission without clarifying her unexpected use of the first-person plural pronoun generally reserved for royalty.

Chapter 27

Countdown to Collbran
(Monday, May 13)

It was a rainy Monday.

A few days ago, with undisguised cynicism, Anne had summarily dismissed Esau's miraculous conversion from satyr to saint as a function of the aged man's wrinkled libido. Her judgmental skepticism hadn't surprised Trinidad, but it definitely reinforced for him how deeply his dearest friend had herself been wounded.

This morning, Anne had stayed in their bedroom with the door locked. He'd left her a breakfast tray and cleared it all away uneaten. Then he'd carried up lunch and again collected the untouched dishes.

At twilight, he was only slightly relieved when at last he heard her descending the stairs and found her in a strangely animated mood, which suggested she was trying—but not succeeding—to put on a brave front.

"What'd I miss?" she quipped.

Ever since the detective had known Anne, she'd been striving to suppress her girlhood traumas by varnishing painful memories with the mantra to think about something else. Now he sensed that the Koller case had cracked that veneer wide open. He wondered if she and he were strong enough to weather the tornado of emotions which were about to cascade out of her agonized past and into their present relationship.

For one thing, it did not escape his notice that Anne seemed to have lost interest in planning their wedding. But at least her appetite had returned because, after asking what she might have missed, she didn't wait for a response. Instead, she flittered past her fiancé and made a beeline for the refrigerator. Returning to the living room, she balanced a plate of cold chicken on her lap and proceeded to devour the impromptu meal.

"What?" she asked when Trinidad shot her a bemused glance.

In a few days, the detectives would pursue their confrontation with Esau's oldest step-daughter, Juliet Sturgis. On Thursday morning, they planned to drive together up and over Grand Mesa to reach the tiny town of Collbran. They'd be coming unannounced.

"Maybe," Trinidad suggested.

"Small town, big ears," Anne agreed.

"If Mrs. Sturgis suspects we're coming," asked Trinidad, "do you think she'll run?"

"If she's even a fraction like her journal," Anne said, "she doesn't seem the type to turn tail."

"Who'd warn her anyway?" he wondered.

"Nobody knows we're even interested, unless..." Anne bit her lip.

"Unless?" he prompted.

"Well," Anne admitted. "There's the Carbondale librarian—the one who helped me find and borrow the journal. She knows I'm interested."

"So, who would she tell?"

"Nobody probably," Anne decided. "Do you think our redhead might alert her step-sister?"

"There's a chance Ruth could spread the word that we're nosing around," Trinidad speculated. "Seems a possibility, since my Skype interview rattled her cage, although I have a distinct feeling the two women haven't kept in touch."

"Not exactly a close family," Anne observed.

"Understatement of the year," said Trinidad. "So, now, what do you think, should we review the background stuff one more time?"

Anne shook her head. Feeling adequately prepared for Thursday's encounter, she refused to read or listen to any more evidence.

"It's all in the vault," she sighed as she tapped her weary head. "I admit I haven't waded through the whole transcript of your interview with Ruth. But I've absorbed enough to keep the elusive redhead high on my suspect list. And, before you go defending her, I've also decided to take a more charitable view of the well-endowed woman. Meanwhile, this fledgling detective has developed a bit too much empathy for Juliet, which'll make it a challenge to remain objective on Thursday."

"Objectivity is over-rated," Trinidad assured her.

After all the dishes had been cleared away, the couple sprawled at opposite ends of the oversized couch in the farmhouse's broad living room with the fireplace crackling as they listened to the jazz guitar of Paul Lucas. They were, separately and jointly, glad for a break after days of dissecting the trials and tribulations, delusions and faults, of the Koller clan. As the hall clock struck eight, Trinidad glanced at his fiancée who seemed lost in thought. Her silence worried him.

"Let's review the manservant's audio one more time while the conversation's still fresh in our minds," he suggested. "Or I can do it, if you're tired."

"Okay," she sighed as she rolled to her feet and went upstairs to bed.

Trinidad watched her go.

"Call me if you need me," he shouted after her.

"Okay," came her muffled reply from the upstairs hallway.

When he heard her latching and bolting the upstairs bedroom door, he sighed, then inserted earbuds and cued up Phillip's interview. Fast-forwarding to the pertinent passage, he began at the point where the old servant's recorded voice quaked with emotion.

"Whatever motivated the master," Phillip testified, "his changed nature proved to be Miss Millie's salvation, because all indications are that he never laid a finger on the girl. Instead, he did what any responsible and very rich parent would have done. The very moment Miss Millie completed her high school equivalency examination, he enrolled her in an expensive private college."

With Millie safely away at school, Phillip recalled events moving in rapid and surprising succession. First, Koller closed up White Quail Manor. Next, after extracting from Phillip a solemn promise to join him in Denver, the old man reluctantly granted his servant a brief leave to tend to his dying mother.

Then, Esau said farewell to the mountains, immigrated to Denver, and kicked his already prodigious writing career into high gear.

White Quail sat vacant for a year before an unknown arsonist torched the place and burned it to the ground. What the flames didn't destroy, person or persons unknown thoroughly looted until nothing was left except a charred concrete foundation. Musing on the manor's destruction, Phillip recalled having experienced, at the time, a feeling of profound relief and, where the devastation was concerned, old man Koller was similarly indifferent in his memoirs.

"Ashes to ashes, too bad the woods didn't go up as well," was all Esau had written regarding the destruction of his ancestral home.

Given these peculiar reactions, Trinidad had the impression that the manor's final residents viewed the place's fiery end as incidental and inescapable. Both seemed elated with the prospect of never having to return there. Phillip had never liked the country and Koller rapidly adapted to Denver's urban environment. If the rural Aspen property hadn't been inherited, it seems unlikely that the old man would've chosen to live there. Looking back, despite the beauty of the surrounding forest and mountains, both men had dismissed the manor's secluded location as unappealing.

On the surface, Koller's objections to remaining in the manor were vague and driven in part, Trinidad suspected, by guilt over his conduct within its isolated walls. Phillip's concerns seemed more practical and appeared to center on the difficulties involved in procuring goods and services to keep a luxurious household operating in the middle of nowhere. The manservant had apparently been unimpressed with the opulent manor.

"A scenic place to be sure, but did the family *really* need five fireplaces?" Phillip had wondered aloud during the course of his telephone interview.

And Esau had once told a reporter that the place was "drafty as a crumbling castle and damp as a well-digger's armpit."

Still, there was more to their dislike for the setting. In separate statements, they confided that the remote spot evoked a visceral apprehension.

Esau seldom ventured beyond the well-manicured grounds, assigning to the surrounding timberland a malevolent aura. In the end, both were happy to be quit of the place because neither man could shake the eerie feeling that, as Phillip put it, "the forest was forever watching."

Trinidad stopped the tape, located Phillip's use of the phrase in his notebook, and underlined the words. Then he switched the recorder off.

When he extracted his earbuds, the house was utterly still until the clock struck half-past eight. Hopefully, Anne would remain sound asleep while Trinidad turned his attention to reviewing other sources.

If Esau was distressed by the destruction of the Aspen manor, Trinidad could find no evidence of that emotion in their copy of the memoirs or in the handfuls of complementary materials. Thumbing through clippings of author profiles and critical reviews, all of which had been included in Joel's packet, the detective found what he expected. There was no further mention of the fire and only the slightest reference to Koller's Aspen days. These were glaring omissions which reinforced the detective's deduction. Clearly, the old man had thrown all his energy into living and working in Denver while reducing Aspen and the manor he'd occupied there to distant memories.

If Anne was downstairs, she'd probably repeat her cynical theory that Koller himself had the place destroyed in a guilt-ridden attempt to purge the scene of his lechery. For his part, Trinidad had to agree that Koller's apathy regarding the ruined manor fit a pattern of selective memory. Whether institutionalizing his wife, ignoring his younger brother, banishing his infant son, or displaying callous indifference toward his victimized, then cast-off daughters, Koller's apathy was staggering. For the old man it was definitely a question of out of sight, out of mind.

If his biographers are to be believed, once removed from the mountains to the metropolis, Esau forgot the past and put his head down as he wrote and wrote and wrote. Lionized as a prolific novelist, he repressed his history while cultivating a public image as a doting father who began dedicating his finished novels to Millie. It was as if, in deciding not to reduce the final female in his life to an object of unwholesome desire, the old fox had transformed her into his muse.

Reminded of Esau's habit of acknowledging his step-daughter in print, Trinidad checked his watch and decided it was not too late to reach Koller's West Coast publisher. Apparently playing a hunch that a murder investigation would be good for sales, the opportunistic man had agreed to be on-call. So, the detective dialed the publisher's home phone number and found the L.A. maven more than willing to talk.

"Mind if I record this?" the detective asked.

"By all means and send me a copy," said the enthusiastic publisher, whose name was William Budweiser, although he insisted that Trinidad call him Bud.

Chatting freely in a rich and contrived California baritone, the loquacious Bud shared his opinion that Koller was not only a prolific author, but also a devoted parent. According to his publisher, in addition to working on his novels as promised, the old man had invested hours writing fatherly letters to his youngest step-daughter, who was away at school. Each of Esau's missives asked after Millie's health and happiness and ended with the same parting lines imploring her to visit him in Denver.

"It was pitiful, you know," said Bud. "My heart went out to the old guy."

Bud knew the details of Esau's one-way correspondence because he'd read it all. It seems the old man was concerned that he wouldn't be able to manage a weekly letter while laboring to meet his fiction-writing deadlines. So, he'd given his publisher a box of sealed letters with instructions to mail them to Millie at precise intervals. Not quite sure what the old satyr was up to, Bud had steamed each envelope open to review the contents.

"Can't be too careful these days," Bud asserted. "I was cognizant of rumors concerning E.K.'s infatuation with Ruth, his estranged natural daughter, and Juliet, his oldest step-daughter, both of whom seem to have disappeared. Well, anyhow, let me say this, E.K. was spooky enough with his odd-ball family and his hermit act. So, a sordid daughter-daddy scandal would be, you understand, bad for business...although..." Bud paused and then added, in a mental note to himself which he might not have intended to say aloud. "Although now that I think about it..."

Cutting his sordid thinking short, Bud went on to explain that the dad-to-daughter letters he'd examined contained nothing incriminating. Instead, each one was a sincere expression of fatherly affection from a loving parent with the usual gentle hints that a letter or call or visit from his beloved Millie would be most appreciated.

"Who'd of thought such an old curmudgeon would turn out to be such a sentimental softy?" Bud asked.

"A prince of a guy," Trinidad suggested.

"Hardly," Bud corrected. "More like Vlad the Impaler, if Vlad the Impaler could now and then magically transmogrify into Mr. Rogers."

While the man droned on, the detective watched the undulating peaks and valleys of Bud's voice print, as the pulsating line danced across the screen of Anne's smartphone. The pattern reminded him of Phillip's interview and the old retainer's observation that Koller—though a rotter in many respects—nevertheless exhibited uncharacteristically doting behavior where his youngest step-daughter was concerned. In fact, the publisher and the manservant both agreed that the old man had used his royalties to shower Millie with gifts and regular infusions of cash and that the girl was consistently unresponsive.

"We get all the mail here and sort it before sending it on," said the publisher. "Not one note from the little brat...not an iota."

Trinidad was only half-listening to Bud's palaver when his attention was piqued as the publisher divulged an interesting tidbit. The detectives and the police knew that Esau had been working on an autobiography and, apparently, Bud had also guessed as much.

"A publisher senses these things. E.K. had no idea that I'd ferreted out his little secret, but I suspected all along that he was squirreling away time here and there to work on his memoirs—it's a thing all our aging authors indulge in eventually. And now a little bird tells me that the authorities have run across the piece and I'd absolutely adore having that manuscript released from police evidence," confided the publisher. "I don't suppose you have any pull in Denver."

"I'll see what I can do," Trinidad lied. "Thanks for your candid assistance." The detective rang off and immediately composed and sent a text to Jack, asking whether the sheriff could intervene to get the Denver PD to re-release the copy of the Koller manuscript. But he had no intention of transporting the pages to the publisher. Instead, he wanted to have the entire document returned to Lavender Hill Farm so he and Anne could study it once more. He had a nagging feeling they'd missed something in their initial hurried review. Seconds later, Jack's text reply came in the form of a blue 'thumbs-up' icon.

"*Sweet*," Trinidad told himself.

Continuing to work the West Coast phones, the persistent detective made a second call—this time to the San Francisco-based certified public accountant handling Koller's finances. Reached on his home number, the seasoned accountant, like the overanxious publisher, was only too happy to help. Speculating on motives and drawing on his own experience in interviewing a certain class of witnesses, Trinidad thought he understood the accountant's willingness to cooperate. Probably the buttoned-down man was motivated by the novelty of being contacted by a genuine detective and asked to do something mildly mischievous or at least out of the ordinary.

The thrill of telling tales out of school, Trinidad speculated.

"Happy to help," the accommodating man said. "Let me just double-check my records." His name was Leon Mumford of Mumford and Company, CPA, Ltd, and he didn't offer a nickname. "Yes, here it is. Aloe College—an expensive private school—a liberal arts outfit run by some obscure charity in Glenwood Springs, Colorado—your neck of the woods it appears. Any-who, this Aloe joint regularly sends tuition bills directly to us and Esau instructed our firm to pay everything without question. Guess that's over now...pending...whatever..."

Trinidad allowed Mumford to collect his thoughts, sensing that the man was mentally calculating the lost revenue if and when his Koller enterprise dried up.

Getting back on track, the CPA explained that, for the first two semesters, Esau had financed Millie's stay in a high-priced residence hall and, when the girl moved off-campus at the onset of her sophomore year, the billing followed suit. Soon a Glenwood landlord and a handful of city utility companies were sending invoices—piling up financial obligations which, under orders from the old man, the firm consistently paid. Department stores and the grocers and the dentist and the eye doctor and gynecologist sent bills and Esau paid for it all. Periodically, when the girl's checking account dipped below $2,000, the bank notified Mumford's firm which was under orders to instantly deposit several thousand more.

"We're talking tens of thousands of dollars here," the accountant assured the detective. "He must have really loved that kid."

After requesting copies of pertinent documents, Trinidad ended the call and poured himself a glass of milk. Taken together, all the sources uncovered by the sleuthing of Sands and Company had agreed on one thing: after Esau sent the young woman away to college, the old man never saw or heard from Millie again. There was no evidence that she ever came to Denver—not even for holidays. In fact, the records indicate that Esau paid for her to spend term breaks in Hawaii and summers abroad. There was no indication that she ever wrote and, apparently, she never called. Meanwhile, by all accounts, it appears that the more Millie broke his heart, the more Esau indulged her.

Could this coddled co-ed with a heart of stone be the "angel" the old man was expecting on Easter Monday?

Trinidad considered Millie's behavior, until, as if summoned by his thoughts, the detective's cell phone began to vibrate and a text message added another mystery to the young student's conduct. While his bride-to-be remained upstairs and wrestling with her demons, word came from Jack that this same pampered Millie—the ungrateful recipient of her step-father's overindulgent largess—had finished her term at Aloe and then, abruptly and unaccountably, gone missing.

Chapter 28

Pretty Country
(Tuesday, May 14)

By the next day, bright and early on Tuesday morning, Esau's unfinished memoirs arrived once again, borne by the same uniformed courier.

"Not necessary to sign your life away this time," the courier quipped. "Just need your initials. Says here, this is your copy to keep."

"Thanks," said Trinidad. "Sorry to make you drive all this way twice."

"No problem," the courier assured him as he pocketed his receipt. "The city's a drag and I don't mind the drive through this pretty country."

When the courier left, Trinidad lingered on the front porch swing, admiring the view. It was indeed pretty country. The stand of globe willows surrounding the farmhouse stirred languidly in the morning breeze. The risen sun hugged the skyline, infusing the surrounding hills with a mantle of gold. The dark outline of Grand Mesa stretched across the horizon—its broad crest marbled with streaks of late-spring snow. The sky was clear and impossibly blue. All that was missing was the halo of lavender which, at harvest time each year, brightened the rim of the steep hill which formed the border between the fields above and the farmyard below.

The detective looked fondly at that incline, remembering the day, months ago, when he'd sprinted uphill in pursuit of Anne, then his fleeing suspect, now his future bride.

The plants up there looked dormant now, but soon Lavender Hill Farm's sprawling fields would come to life with this season's bumper crop. The seemingly lifeless plants had been trimmed and pruned and the bindweed—which always seemed to find a way to insinuate itself—had been, if not tamed, then at least discouraged.

Soon the fields would yield the hardy riot of aroma and color which he looked forward to every year. This year those blossoms would take on new meaning. If he had anything to say about it, the glory of his harvest would decorate the altar and the aisles of the nearby wedding chapel. In his mind, he envisioned a lavish and wholly lavender wedding. He'd planted well, pruned judiciously, and, ultimately, the harvest would come and, like his bride-to-be, it would be spectacular and well-worth the waiting.

As the detective gazed tenderly at the rural beauty surrounding him, the front door screen creaked and he was joined by Anne who'd padded downstairs to see who'd come calling so early. She sat beside her partner, rested her head on his shoulder, and used her bare feet to set the porch swing gliding.

"This is pretty country," Trinidad said.

"Uh huh," she agreed as she noticed the package. "Is that what I think it is?"

"We are now the proud owners of our own personal photocopy of the Koller autobiography, holes and all. Jack's influence is so omnipotent and all-powerful that the manuscript, once confiscated and held by Denver detectives, has been forwarded to us not once, but twice."

"Let's get on it," she said with such enthusiasm that her husband-to-be glanced her way to be rewarded with a pleasing view of Anne's winning smile and rosy cheeks. "I'll review this hot mess," she decided, "while you, my handsome love slave, gather the eggs, slaughter the pigs, grind the coffee beans, thresh the grain, and mix the pancake batter to start our breakfast."

As Trinidad prepared their morning meal, Anne tackled the now-familiar manuscript and a second glance through the pages confirmed what she'd supposed.

"This pile of typewritten papers representing old man Koller's prologue and first thirty chapters," she told her hard-working fiancé as he tinkered at the kitchen stove, "as well as the partially-typed chapter which follows, were all created on his vintage Remington. Certain capital letters, especially those arrayed along the upper row of the manual keyboard, are slightly higher than the surrounding text. This pattern indicates that the typist was inefficient in going through the repetitious and laborious process of manually pushing down the shift key while also striking the chosen letter key."

"Tell me more, oh wonderful wizard," Trinidad beamed as he blended their morning omelets in a mixing bowl. He had a pretty good idea what Anne was going to say, but he'd let her have her own Sherlock Holmes' moment.

"Well," she continued, "most typists create a signature as they labor away on a manual keyboard. Koller had apparently struggled to capitalize letters using keys immediately above the home row—including and especially two capitals which required the use of his pinky fingers. As a result, both the capitalized 'P' and 'Q' float ever so slightly above the horizontal line of type. This struggle might have been the result of a physical deformity, but it's unlikely that both pinkies were of the irregular variety. Of course, we know from his medical files that the old man struggled with bouts of arthritis. On the other hand, so to speak, it was just as likely to have been caused by careless technique."

Observing the floating capitals, Anne recalled her own misadventures in a remedial keyboarding class taken in college. It had been a desperate attempt to compensate for a childhood without access to a typewriter or personal computer. Owing to such a late start, her typing remained a hunt-and-peck adventure, whereas Trinidad was a whiz on the keyboard. He was a natural and—having completed her University of Arizona coursework—Anne had every intention of taking full advantage of his skills—if she ever got around to finishing her thesis. Thinking about her interrupted master's program, Anne sighed. She'd return to Tucson to earn her archaeology degree one of these days. Right now, she was content with her Colorado life.

"A penny for your thoughts," said Trinidad as he crossed to the kitchen table and poured her another cup of coffee.

"Thanks, honey," she said. Then, in response to his comment, she added, "I was thinking about my unfinished degree."

"Just say the word," he declared, "and, after the wedding, I'll farm out the farm and we can be together in the desert by nightfall. I think I'd enjoy seeing you in your natural habitat."

"Maybe," she laughed. "And is it proper to say 'farm out the farm?' And what would the village of Lavender do without its leading citizen? And where is the money coming from to support my idle husband and his penniless grad-student spouse?"

"Details," he said as he kissed the top of her head and returned to the stove.

Sitting alone at the kitchen table, Anne watched her fiancé's graceful movements and admired his tempting physique. Even clad in an incongruous apron, his firm torso aroused her ardor. Maybe there would be time this morning for one last roll in the hay.

"You want to fool around after breakfast?" she asked.

"I'm your huckleberry," he answered as he poured one omelet into a sizzling skillet and loaded the neighboring griddle with his famous pancake mix.

Turning her attention to her task while Trinidad fixed breakfast, Anne re-read Esau's typewritten prologue, the introduction to his memoirs entitled "Death's Knell." In that revealing opening, the old man reported that—having run the gauntlet of physicians and specialists—he'd been forced to accept their unanimous verdict. His cancer had been in remission, but the relentless disease had returned with a vengeance and put down roots this time, so there'd be no discouraging it. Quoting from his medical records, Esau related the terminal tale.

"Everything came to a head in February," he wrote. "As I stood staring out an icy window while snow drifted down, I was informed that I had ninety days left—maybe a few more or less—the doctors couldn't be absolutely sure. The only thing they were willing to guarantee was that I was likely to be unconscious when the end came. And, just before I lost contact with the world, they promised to pump me full of enough medication to anesthetize a horse."

'You'll go to sleep and the good news is you'll be feeling no pain,' his pull-no-punches primary care physician had told him in a hand-written note which

Esau reproduced in typewritten form. 'And of course,' the doctor added, 'you'll be dying alone.'

The doomed man must have considered this idea of a lonesome death to be an interesting notion, but, based on Esau's answer, not a particularly unnerving one.

"Big deal," the old man reportedly said. "*Everybody* dies alone."

"The moment the doctors put a number on how long I had to live," Esau wrote, "I began compiling my memoirs. I outlined the sections, developed the chapters, used my pen for each first draft, and relied on my trusty Remington to polish the work. I was obliged to keep up appearances by working on my upcoming novel and there were times when I had little hope of finishing my privately personal story before I died. Nevertheless, I worked tirelessly on this, my final opus."

According to his prologue, upon hearing the news of his imminent demise, Esau had initially devoted two days to obsessing over his death sentence, and then he'd stopped thinking about it. He could do no more.

"I'm an asshole," he admitted, "and tired of playing that particular role, but it's too late to audition for another."

His chief regret, he lamented, was that no one would credit his final acts of charity toward his step-daughter, Millie, and probably not even the girl herself would appreciate his good works. He decided he could live with that because, in a flurry of writing which may or may not have been motivated by his so-called conversion, he ended his prologue by declaring he would "tell all" in subsequent chapters.

Given this intention, the old outlaw seemed poised to chronicle his sins. Everything from Koller's prologue through Chapter 30 seemed to reflect this confessional theme. The sole exception was his final chapter which overflowed with handwritten clichés about his fatherly affection for his daughters. Anne was convinced that his paternal platitudes were bald-faced lies. To her, Esau's final words, despite their flawless penmanship, were nothing more than dishonest substitutes for typewritten pages which had documented his depravity. She was certain pages were missing and, when others suggested such pages didn't exist, she was undeterred.

Though Anne remained the lone subscriber to the notion, she held fast to her belief that there were lost pages and she was betting it was old man Koller himself who'd destroyed them. What better way to purge one's soul than to type it all out and then, like a surgeon removing an offending tumor, excise it all away as if it never happened. She imagined the old satyr's thinking might have gone something like this:

> *I'm about to welcome my prodigal back into my life. Unable to foresee such an unexpected reunion, I'd written everything down, confessed the depths of my corruption. But the eve of this unhoped-for reconciliation is no time to risk reminding the child of my former sins. No sense memorializing my transgressions in 12-point type. Better to remove those offending pages, take up my expunging pen, and rewrite the ending.*

If this was true, she challenged her pondering mind, *where was the evidence? Where were the missing pages?*

She hadn't quite worked it out yet, but that oversight failed to dilute her conviction that the author of the missing confessional paragraphs was also their eradicator. She was convinced that Koller himself had destroyed his typed confession and substituted a handwritten proclamation that he was a shoe-in for father of the year.

Dismissing the typewritten portion of Koller's self-serving narrative, Anne decided to test her theory of the missing pages. Pushing the prologue and the first 200 pages aside, she grasped the photocopy of page 201 and centered the single typewritten sheet on the table before her, placing it in easy reach, as if it was an 8 ½ x 11 dinner plate. Then she plucked the topmost of Koller's handwritten sheets and placed it beside the typewritten page.

Dinner and dessert, she thought as she followed the lead of others in an effort to link the two pages. The belief that Koller's final typewritten line and his first handwritten line blended together to create an exact continuity was strong. That deduction had been sufficient to convince the Denver PD to eliminate the Koller daughters as murder suspects. Viewed through a male lens, it seemed a logical conclusion, but Anne had other ideas.

The top of the typewritten page had been amended in Koller's impeccable hand. The section title was changed and the date had been revised to April 21, 2019. Anne considered the significance of this latter revision. If the date was accurate, the handwritten pages which followed represented the old man's last words.

Adjusting her reading glasses, the questing detective scanned down the typed page until she reached the final, and ostensibly unfinished, sentence. Then Anne reviewed the first handwritten paragraph, attempting to link the final typewritten words with the first line of the handcrafted sheet. The Denver PD had noted that the sentence began on one page and then appeared to flow seamlessly to the next. Anne had her doubts.

"God forgive me, I must admit that my darlings…" Esau had typed these nine words at the bottom of page 201. Everyone else seemed to believe that the old man had continued that thought in his flawless cursive so that, moving from one page to the next, the combined sentence could be interpreted to read: "*God forgive me, I must admit that my darlings* wherever they have roamed, be they living or dead, are and were more precious to me than I deserve."

Reading this, Anne emitted an audible syllable and the scoffing sound caused Trinidad to look up from his cooking. "You okay?" he asked.

"Diving in," Anne said as she continued reading the remainder of Koller's handwritten paragraph. "Liar," she muttered under her breath.

Rising as they did from the grave, the old man's parting words might strike some as an unassailable fountain of truth. To Anne, the finely crafted letters were a frail mist, a calculated façade which evaporated in the penetrating light of day. She was unmoved by the writing, even though the author seemed to be pouring his heart onto the page.

"I've been a scoundrel all my life," Koller wrote. "I am not a religious man so I have no hope of redemption. For now, all I can do is write my books, rake in the money, and spend barrels of it on my beloved daughter. My affection for her knows no bounds…"

Anne could stomach no more and stopped reading. Instead, even though her efficient fiancé seemed on the cusp of announcing the advent of a piping hot breakfast, she decided to take a fresh approach to the memoirs by physically partitioning the manuscript. No sense plowing again through the autobiographical fluff which amounted to an ordinary and eminently forgettable story of an already rich guy who falls ass-backwards into fame and even more fortune. Better to chop the thing into manageable segments, separating the prologue from the typewritten sections, and to further isolate each section. And she was just arranging the photocopies into separate piles when she noticed it.

Old man Koller had opened each section with the date of the work's composition and a subtitle which previewed the contents of chapters in that particular segment. His prologue described a regimented writing schedule. Seeking to confirm his process, she walked around the kitchen table which was now completely covered with eight piles of paper, one for the prologue and one for each of the seven succeeding sections. Reading the date on each pile, she quickly verified the pattern.

"Holy crap," she said aloud as she rushed to the kitchen's wall calendar and flipped back through the past months until she came to February. Snatching the calendar from its nail, she returned to the table to find Trinidad standing there, balancing two full plates, intent on serving breakfast. Though reluctant to discourage her fiancé, Anne was equally anxious to pursue her theory.

"Are you..." he began, but she interrupted.

"A moment my little iron chef," she insisted. "I'm about to experience a breakthrough."

"I'd rather you'd experience a break-fast," he chided. "And where am I supposed to put everything?"

"Listen to this," she said, as she ignored his question, gently nudged him aside, and excitedly circled the kitchen table. Carrying the calendar along for reference, she proceeded to compare dates with Koller's title pages. "Prologue, February 15, a Friday, check. Section 1, February 22, a Friday, check. Section 2, Friday, March 1, check..."

Finishing her inspection, she announced that each section was typed a week apart and always on Friday. Apparently, Esau spent the week writing out each rough chapter in longhand, then devoted the final weekday to polishing the entire section at his typewriter.

Section 3 was dated March 8 and Sections 4-6, March 15-29—all Fridays—all one week apart. The exception, the sole exception, was Section 7 which should have been dated April 5.

"But," Anne declared, "that typewritten date was crossed out and changed, in Koller's handwriting, to Sunday, April 21, in other words, Easter."

"So?" asked Trinidad as he reluctantly carried his lavishly-prepared breakfast back to the stove and covered the dishes in a valiant attempt to keep the meal warm.

"So," Anne explained, "Koller was a creature of habit with a strict work ethic. Beginning right after he got his fatal cancer diagnosis in February, the old bastard wrote all week and typed up a new section every Friday. Meaning he must have been done typing the entire manuscript on April 5. So, what happened to the original Section 7, where's the original Chapter 31, and what the hell was he doing from April 6 to April 21?"

Not waiting for her confused partner to respond, she dropped the calendar on the kitchen floor and dug through the photocopies of Koller's handwritten pages.

"Gotta be here," she told herself aloud, her tone sounding frantic. "Gotta be here. Gotta be here."

With a sense of growing alarm, Trinidad returned to the table, "Annie, I..."

"Here it is!" she proclaimed and, before her confused fiancé could interrupt, she declared, "Listen to this!"

Nearly breathless, Anne held the page in her trembling hand and re-read a key passage inscribed in Koller's handwriting:

> *Though I have possessed the precious objects no more than two weeks, I have nearly worn the heartfelt letter and much-loved photograph raw with my constant handling, my joy mingled with the staining moisture of my repentant tears. It will be a blessing to see my angel, to hear that longed-for voice, and I doubt if I shall sleep a wink as I anticipate the joy of our meeting and this unexpected chance at reconciliation.*

"That," Anne declared, slapping the photocopy back onto the table, "explains everything!"

"Or," Trinidad observed as he stood behind his fiancée and wrapped his arms around her, "in my case—nothing. Care to fill me in, genius?"

"Look," she said as she wriggled free and sprinted to the old chalkboard on the kitchen wall.

When giving her a tour months ago, Trinidad had explained that the farmer who owned the original house had nailed the old school blackboard up there to help drill his young children on their spelling words during meals. Now the well-worn surface sported a variety of information: love notes from her to him and vice versa; a shopping list; the odd telephone number; and so on. She erased it all and took up the chalk.

"The dates," she said as she wrote them in descending sequence. "The sections," she said, writing (P) for prologue next to February 15 and then the numbers 1 through 7 next to each corresponding date. "The section subtitles..." She started to write these, then stopped, and exclaimed, "Damn!"

"Now what?" Trinidad asked, unable to follow Anne's rapid-fire logic while his curiosity was about to burst.

"Seven sections..." she explained. "Section 1 with a theme of envy telling how he was the favored son; Section 2 with a prideful account of his Ivy League education; Section 3 chronicling his greed manifested by inheriting a train-load of money and marrying well; Section 4 documenting the slothful decadence of his years in his Aspen manor; Section 5 telling of his anger at God for letting his first wife and infant daughter die; and Section 6 detailing his gluttonous and over-blown writing career. So, what's missing, partner?"

Trinidad joined her at the blackboard, a sense of recognition beginning to dawn on his face as he pointed to each of the numbered sections and said, in turn, "Envy, pride, greed, sloth, wrath, gluttony..." He paused then, his hand hovering over the final section.

"Six of the seven," she agreed. "Go on, say it..."

"Lust," he said as he banged his open palm against the blackboard, raising a cloud of chalk dust. "The Seven Deadly Sins—all neatly packaged in Koller's memoirs—intentional or coincidental?"

"Gotta be on purpose," Anne said with certainty. "The critics agree that Esau Koller never wrote anything without an agenda. So, I'm one-hundred-and-ten-percent sure he wasn't merely chronicling his achievements for posterity," said Anne. "Just as he said in his prologue, he was confessing right and left, burning his way through his misspent life like an avenging prairie fire."

"All the way up to Section 7 where the pattern fades," noted Trinidad.

"Oh," said Anne, "there was a confessional section containing the sordid details of his lustful behavior all right—all typed up and ready for the printer. But, in anticipation of his unexpected reunion with this so-called angel, he must have destroyed the offending pages. Probably pitched the sordid sheets down the Stevenson Building's garbage chute and was in the process of reworking his concluding chapter when the Remington gave out. So, he turned to his pen but was unable to finish before one of his victims arrived and ended his career."

"If you're right..." Trinidad began, then halted as he sensed his fiancée was about to protest, and started again. "Lower case 'i' and lower case 'f'." If you're right, this puts everything that went before in sharper perspective. So, the disagreement you and I had, and the difference between our divergent views and the interpretation of the Denver detectives—all those misunderstandings about the missing pages suddenly make sense. There's probably merit to more than one theory about Koller's final words, but if you're right, they all have a common denominator..."

"Again, with the 'if'..." Anne began.

"Easy, honey," Trinidad protested. "I'm coming around to your way of thinking—I think. Give me a moment..."

"The floor is yours," Anne said. "Literally, it's your floor, so press on. Don't mind me."

"Okay," Trinidad agreed. "But what's mine is already yours, or soon will be. So, technically it's *our* floor."

"Get to the point," Anne complained. "Preferably while we're young."

"As you wish, Buttercup," Trinidad laughed. "But how about a pause in the action while we eat breakfast?"

"Sold," said Anne as she reshuffled papers to make room for their meal.

Chapter 29

Dishes
(Late Afternoon)

Clearing away the breakfast things, the detectives skipped lunch to take a well-earned nap in the living room. Refreshed but hungry, they ate an early supper and Trinidad attempted to load the dishwasher.

Critiquing his technique from across the room, Anne mused to herself: *How long does it take a man to properly load a dishwasher?* Then she answered her own question by adding: *No one knows—it's never been done.*

Unaware of his bride-to-be's silent evaluation, Trinidad returned to the kitchen table, took a chair, and picked up where he'd left off earlier that day.

"So," he said, "given old man Koller's propensity for finishing his works in exactly thirty-one chapters, maybe—just maybe—he originally typed up closing remarks with the intention of confessing his incestuous behavior and finished that work on schedule on Friday, April 5. If you're right, sometime between then and Easter he changed his mind about the contents, ditched the previous version and used his famous—and now missing—fountain pen to compose a new chapter in long-hand in which he proclaimed himself a changed man. But he was unable to type the final draft without getting the Remington repaired, and so on. Any idea what he was doing in the days leading up to Easter?"

"My turn?" Anne asked.

"Your turn," Trinidad nodded.

"Okay," she said. "Try this on for size: the motivation for his change of mind—regardless of whether that change was genuine or contrived—was the thing monopolizing his attention prior to Easter. It's obvious from his writing that everything revolves around a letter and photograph from his long-lost angel expressing his or her—probably her—desire for reconciliation..."

"Let me stop you there," said Trinidad. "Koller's publisher mentioned no such letter and his office monitored all the old man's mail..."

"Who says the angel in question used the post office?" Anne pointed out.

"Touché," Trinidad admitted. "Continue."

"In my deduced chronology of events," Anne said, "the missive with enclosed photo was probably delivered secretly and by hand. That letter inspired Koller's last-minute change of heart. And, as for the whereabouts of the letter, obviously the killer retrieved it, but his epiphany—whether genuine or fake—came much too late to suit the avenging angel. In the end, it doesn't matter what Koller admitted to in his typewritten pages or how he attempted to paper-over the past in his handwritten version. And no matter whether he or someone else destroyed the typed pages—the old fox wasn't killed for what he had or hadn't written in his memoirs but for his former sins. Somebody knew the truth and that somebody has to be our killer."

"Probably," Trinidad agreed. "Which once again places the daughters squarely in our sights as likely suspects. So, let's review what the memoirs tell us. Your sleuthing convinces me that Koller himself and his lazy pinky fingers typed everything we have before us and I'm convinced the rest is in the old man's handwriting. The stilted and perfect cursive matches the notes he left his servants. Just to be certain, I faxed copies to his publisher and Bud confirmed the writing was Koller's and—to support his belief—he faxed back a sample of a Koller letter."

"So, it's *Bud* now, is it?" Anne teased. "And also, who the heck has a fax machine these days, let alone having one on both the sending and receiving ends?"

"Just the fax, ma'am," Trinidad quipped.

"Television trivia, mister *Dragnet* fan," Anne said with a wry laugh. "So, how about devoting as much time to adopting my cinema mania as you do toward your habit of quoting from vintage TV?"

"Would you accept *Dial 'M' for Murder*?" Trinidad ventured as he recalled the title of a classic Hitchcock thriller.

"Well-remembered," his partner agreed, "but not even a remote match to our present case. However, keep that title in your back pocket for a future investigation."

"I'll file it away, along with a tantalizing quote which I'm hoping to work into future circumstances."

"Which is," asked Anne with sincere interest.

"The stuff that dreams are made of," said Trinidad doing a passable Humphrey Bogart impression.

"I love you, Mr. Sands," she cooed.

"And I'm awfully fond of you, Mrs. Sands-to-be," he said as he planted an affectionate kiss on the top of her head.

"I appreciate the sentiment," she said, "even though it reminds me how far behind we are on making wedding plans."

"Speak for yourself," Trinidad declared as he pulled his bride-to-be to her feet to give her a proper hug and kiss. "I've already dispatched Cruz to pick up the proofs of our wedding invitations."

"No fair," she protested, although she did nothing to escape from the folds of his warm embrace. "It's unsporting to have an army of workers helping you."

"As if you couldn't use that pretty face of yours to make Cruz and the rest of the lavender crew do your bidding."

"I'd never..." Anne began as Trinidad swept her off her feet and began to carry her upstairs. "And where, may I ask, are we going and what precisely are your intentions?" She pretended to protest.

"Upstairs with you, my pet," Trinidad informed her. "And as for my intentions..."

"Shush," she said. They were halfway up the staircase as she placed a finger to his lips and announced, "I'd rather you surprised me."

Chapter 30

Dreaming
(Midnight)

Anne stirred in her sleep as visions invaded her slumbering mind. She was exhausted by the effort of preparing for their journey to Collbran to interview Juliet Sturgis. Now, deep in the night, her imagination caused her to re-live the marathon of research that had so recently occupied her waking hours.

The Sands Detective Agency had learned of Juliet's trials, Millie's miraculous escape from abuse, and much of the Koller saga through a combination of sources. Their references included the recollections of Esau's publisher and his accountant as well as his long-suffering servants, not to mention Ruth's chilling Skype interview. Much of what they learned contradicted the old man's belated attempts to prune pages that confessed his abuse and amend his memoirs with a final handwritten chapter.

But when it came to the detectives' efforts to theorize the identity of Esau's killer, all other resources paled in comparison to Juliet's journal. Anne had been fortunate to discover the document and her dreaming mind recalled that fateful afternoon at the Carbondale Public Library.

Somehow Juliet's hand-written journal had been cataloged for inclusion in the local authors' section of the county library, but the unbound manuscript never made it out of the archives. Possibly it had been considered too graphic for public consumption. When Anne had run across the document, she'd been searching for background on the Koller family. Guessing that the journal might be in Carbondale, but without much hope of unearthing it, the fledgling detective had been surprised when she and the Carbondale librarian discovered the pages in a storage area. The unbound journal entries were still in a manila envelope, the battered face of which was covered with a blanket of three-cent stamps and postmarked from Collbran.

"That's funny," said the librarian who'd helped Anne track down the elusive journal. "They never do that."

"Do what?" Anne asked, surprised that the taciturn librarian, who had said little thus far, seemed to come alive the moment they discovered the envelope.

"Postmark it that way," said the librarian. "It must have been hand-canceled by someone. Otherwise, what comes out of Collbran is postmarked Grand Junction."

"Somebody must have taken a special effort," said Anne.

"Must have," the librarian agreed. "Well, I don't imagine anyone is going to miss this, so sign here please and I'll need that viewer's deposit in cash if you don't mind."

Anne had to fork over $200 to borrow the manuscript, so she had every intention of treating the artifact with care. She'd carefully wrapped it in a blanket and locked it in the Nissan's truck box and forgotten it as she ran for her life at the community garden. Then came the argument with Trinidad and she'd nearly overlooked the document until days ago when she'd trundled out into the darkness to retrieve it.

That morning, she'd put on a pot of coffee, sat down at the kitchen table, and slid the journal from its protective envelope. Forcing her way through the opening pages, she'd been captivated by Juliet's story and—though she struggled with the memories which the writing stirred in her—she'd nevertheless stayed awake all that night reading as much of the document as she could bear.

Days later, while Anne slept and as the hour set aside for their Collbran trip drew ever nearer, snippets of Juliet's narrative returned to haunt her.

Permeating her subconscious, the step-daughter's stirring words conjured up vivid images that flitted through the detective's slumbering mind. As her dream deepened, Anne was pulled into a nightmare in which she recalled every detail of Juliet's writing.

Juliet's tale began shortly after the runaway teenager left the Carbondale hospital and it started as a retrospective. Anne pictured the troubled girl, caught up in horrific circumstances—homeless, motherless, with no idea of a future. But somehow Juliet had managed to ignore her immediate plight and find a measure of solace in the cathartic act of chronicling what had gone before.

Thus, the early pages of Juliet's journal were devoted to a remembrance of her troubled childhood and tragic adolescence. Eventually—after devoting considerable space to the past—her writing fell into a 'real-time' diary as she documented her wandering life after the hospital. For a few years, bill collectors sought to recover her medical debt by hounding her from one low-wage job to another until she decided to disappear.

Her once-faithful daily written record ceased for over a year until she surfaced in San Diego, where she recounted cutting her hair, binding her breasts, and hiring onto a fishing boat. Her disguise worked for a time until the vessel's widowed captain discovered she was not a lad and took her to his bed and then, unexpectedly, to the altar. He was sixty-two and she was eighteen.

At the wedding, a civil ceremony held in the dank confines of the old sailors' memorial hall, Juliet mouthed her vows in the company of a ragged crowd of witnesses who stank of brine and fish. After the ceremony, the crew of *The Forlorn Hope*, her new husband's third-rate fishing trawler, sang a hideous recital of a cappella sea shanties that would have made a manatee blush. Then the intoxicated captain fell asleep and the crew wiled the night away taking liberties with the young bride.

Juliet didn't cry out. She just laid there and took it.

The next morning, still clad in her blood-streaked wedding dress, the ruined bride tried to commit suicide by walking into the sea, but instead she merely floated like a cork until a miraculous wave deposited her back on shore. So, she turned inland and walked for two days and nights until she came to a railroad where she stood in the dark in the middle of the tracks waiting for a train to come and kill her. When no train came, she took it as a sign and went to the nearest church and turned herself in.

She tried convent life for six months, but that ended badly when a visiting priest convinced her to let him crawl under her novice habit to sanctify her breasts. She knifed the man in his sleep and served time in a Nevada penitentiary for attempted homicide until she was granted trustee status. She worked in the prison laundry, supervising the arrival and departure of delivery trucks, which allowed her sufficient privileges to take advantage of the system and walk away.

Since her squalid marriage, she'd been living for three years as the estranged wife of the late Captain Bogart Faraday. That was the surname inked on her underwear and memorialized on her prison record.

Alone and penniless in Las Vegas and faced with a choice of embarking on a lengthy journey to return to the sea or fleeing to nearby Arizona, she chose the desert. After living for a time on the streets of Phoenix, she fled north to the open spaces of the Navajo Reservation. She might have been content to live and die there as Mrs. Juliet Faraday had she not encountered a stray canine who seemed to beckon her to follow. Trailing after the yellow dog, she found herself in a little town called Page near the shores of Lake Powell. It was after midnight and she was desperately trying to steal quarters by using the sharp edge of a purloined license plate to pry open the change box on a Maytag commercial dryer.

It didn't work.

Juliet sat on the floor of a 24-hour laundromat on the outskirts of town and bawled like a lost lamb until she found she could muster no more tears. She stood up then and went looking for someplace to blow her nose. Ignoring the admonition that restrooms were for customers only, she searched both the men's room and the women's lavatory. But she discovered no toilet paper and there were no paper towels. Returning to the main laundry, she opened all the machines—washers and dryers—in search of any scrap of cloth.

She refused to wipe her nose on her sleeve—she hadn't sunk that low— not yet. And she was just about to block off one nostril and jettison a nugget of phlegm onto the laundromat's already filthy floor when her eye landed upon the book. Someone had crammed a paperback novel into the space between two dryers, presumably to keep the unbalanced machines from knocking together.

Juliet pushed her chest against the machines, leaned over, and stared fixedly at the paperback. She hadn't read a book since—well, she couldn't remember the last time. But, thinking of books and her days at White Quail Manor, she managed to recall her vengeful habit of defacing the vintage hardbacks in her step-father's prized library.

The library door was always bolted, but picking locks came easy to her, so she came and went as she pleased. As for being discovered, only the servants took notice and they had informed her step-father just once. Esau had used a riding crop to whip Juliet and, seeing her so severely punished, the maids, the cook, and even the fastidious butler took pity on the child. From that moment on she was indulged by the help and never again did anyone inform on her movements.

Juliet soon had the run of the sprawling manor. Left alone in the library, she pursued her girlish crime wave. As months passed, the young vandal used an ink pen to draw lewd satirical cartoons on the blank end-papers in the front and back of Koller's precious books. Her favorite theme was a duck with a giant penis.

Whether her step-father ever noticed her graffiti, Juliet couldn't say. But she was gratified to learn much later in life that the mutilations she inflicted on the manor's books had consequences. It was very likely that her scribbles greatly diminished the value of an otherwise collectible work by Dickens or Tolstoy or Twain. So be it. Eventually Esau would send Juliet's mother away and he'd try to rape her and God only knew what he intended to do to her younger sister. So, she was satisfied with whatever revenge had come her way.

As thoughts of her girlhood rebellion tumbled back to her, Juliet laughed out loud in the Arizona night and the echo of that laugh reverberated in the unoccupied laundromat. She was alone as she regaled in her memories and after a moment more of reflection, she threaded her thin arm down between the machines, seized the paperback, tore out the first page, and enthusiastically blew her nose. It was then that she noticed the cover. The title was laughable, but the author's name struck her like a penetrating salvo of forked lightning. The room seemed to swirl and she felt faint as her vision clouded and her ears began to ring.

Could there be more than one Esau Noah Koller?

That seemed unlikely. Juliet turned to the back cover and there, along with a self-aggrandizing blurb, she saw the old devil's photograph. A place! A place! Where was the old bastard hiding out these days? How long would it take to reach that hideout? And what could she pick up along the way that was long enough and pointy enough to shove up her step-father's ass and simultaneously pierce his wizened heart?

As the Arizona sun rose, patrons began arriving to launder their mountains of husband work overalls and underwear and their heaps of baby clothes. Juliet ignored them and continued to frantically search through the paperback until she found the author's acknowledgments. "I wish to thank…" she read. "If not for the…" she read. And then she found the prize she was seeking: "The author lives alone in a cozy penthouse in the heart of metropolitan Denver."

"Not for long," she said aloud as she stuffed the paperback into her tattered jacket, pulled her filthy sock-cap over her ears, and ventured out into the rain. "Not for long."

Anne opened her eyes. The vivid dream had shattered her slumber and rekindled a memory. Slipping quietly out of bed, she donned her robe and padded downstairs in her bare feet. The metro police packet was still sitting on the coffee table. She turned on the reading lamp, sat on the couch, opened the package, and pulled out the crime scene photos from old man Koller's penthouse. When the mountain of evidence had first arrived, she'd only given the images a cursory glance, but even then, she'd noticed something which until now hadn't registered.

She sifted through the photographs until she found the image of Koller's bookcase. Carrying the picture to the kitchen, she switched on the overhead light and rummaged through the utility drawer in search of Trinidad's magnifying lens. Centering the photo on the kitchen table, she took a seat, and put the lens to her eye.

"Bingo," she said.

There it was, as plain as day on the spine of each of old man Koller's novels, the evidence that confirmed Juliet's guilt. Someone had taken an ink pen and altered the "o" in the writer's last name, blackening in the circle and adding a dot. In a crude act of graffiti, the author's name on every book in Esau's horror series had intentionally been altered to read "Killer."

Anne breathed a heavy sigh. Leaving the photograph on the table, she walked upstairs and woke Trinidad.

"I think we have our murderer," she told him.

Chapter 31

Review
(Wednesday, Noon)

The next day Anne stood in the kitchen surveying the contents of the refrigerator. The Sands Detective Agency had taken the morning off in favor of an early hike in the still icy tundra of Grand Mesa. They'd arrived back at the farmhouse tired and happy and hungry.

"Leftovers," she sighed.

"Order a pizza?" Trinidad suggested.

"Great idea, Slick," she said.

Seated at the kitchen table, the two partners ate their delivery pizza in contented silence before loading the dishwasher and moving to the living room where piles of photocopies occupied the coffee table. Shifting through a mountain of material, they'd come to a decision point. With their interview of Juliet Sturgis set for the following morning, they had to narrow their focus.

"So how do you want to do this, Slick?" Anne asked.

It was the second time today his bride-to-be had called Trinidad by the nickname which Jack bestowed on him years ago. Grinning from ear-to-ear, the love-lost detective couldn't help but notice that his loins, which had never stirred when the sheriff said "Slick," reacted amorously whenever Anne said the word.

"Hello," Anne said, playfully tapping her lover on his noggin.

"Thinking about something else," said Trinidad.

"I know that look," said Anne. "So, keep your pants on and pay attention."

"Yes, ma'am," he said as they locked eyes, both grinning like school kids.

Those eyes, Anne thought as she recalled the day, months ago, when they'd first met at the Jiffy-Spiffy Car Wash in beautiful downtown Lavender. Not the most romantic setting, but...

"Hello," said Trinidad, repeating the gesture of gently knocking on his partner's lovely skull.

"Sorry," she said. "I was miles and months away."

"I hope I was there too," he said.

"Always," she said and before he could lean forward to kiss her, she changed the subject. "Back to the Koller case," she insisted.

"Okay," he agreed. "Given our plan to confront Juliet Sturgis in the morning, we need to take a final look at her journal..."

"But first," Anne interrupted, "let's settle our argument from this morning. Do we go with the old man's version of events or side with the daughters? Do we go with the memoirs, or the Skype interview and the journal?"

"A tough choice," Trinidad suggested. "Like I said this morning, who's more credible? Esau, the fiction writer, or his victims?"

"You know my vote," Anne said.

"I have to admit I was a skeptic when we started uphill this morning, but you wore me down on the way back to the trailhead and now I'm inclined to agree with you," Trinidad decided. "So, we'll go with the daughters. And, if we place the daughters' stories in sequence, Ruth's report of Esau's abusive behavior forms the preamble to Juliet's recollections. Esau's pattern of abuse was well-established by the time he remarried and ushered in a new crop of daughters. And, once we locate Millie, my guess is she'll validate her sisters' experiences. Suppose we assume Millie will back up her sisters. Why not fine-tune our investigation by melding the essence of Ruth's testimony with Juliet's story to create a single point-of-view?"

"Agreed," said Anne, "and I don't think we'll be missing much because the two sisters have used virtually the same language to describe their ordeals. So, are you ready for this?"

"Ready," Trinidad assured her as he reached for the memoirs.

"Remember what we talked about on the trail this morning," Anne reminded her partner. "Your mission is to objectively review Koller's prologue and sections 1 through 6. We're looking for clues that he invested decades in abusing his matrimonial, natural, and adopted kin. It'd be an easier search if we had this document in an electronic format and could use 'control-find,' but we ain't got that luxury."

"No, we ain't," said Trinidad. "But I'm equal to the task. I'll skim for the victims' names and double-check for Koller's sins of omission."

"Smart cookie," she said. "As for me, I'll comb through the handwritten pages once more in search of anything which might shed light on the identity of Koller's visiting angel."

"Roger that," Trinidad said as he tried once more to kiss her.

"Get to work, cowboy," she chided. "I'd better carry my assignment to the kitchen table or we'll never get anything done."

Trinidad sighed as he watched her go, then got to work.

His close reading of his assigned chapters revealed instances where Koller had sanitized any overt mention of his abusive habits. Among his approaches was his use of the phrase "quit the place," as in saying that his natural daughter and eldest step-daughter had "quit the place," rather than confessing that his lustful abuses had driven them away. He offered no further explanation or apology. Once the detective looked closely, there were innumerable instances where the old man white-washed the truth. In composing his prologue and first six sections, Esau Koller was, the detective decided, willing to confess a variety of other sins but unwilling to own up to his predatory nature.

The detectives were nearing the end of their respective searches and Anne was still in the kitchen, studying Koller's handwritten pages, when the phone rang and Trinidad picked up the landline.

"Where you at?" Jack asked. "I ain't heard a peep since I persuaded Denver to send the Sands Detective Agency its own personal copy of the Koller memoirs. What's the latest?"

"I just finished reviewing all the opening pages," Trinidad whispered into the receiver. "Looks like Koller admitted to a boatload of deadly sins but took pains to cover his tracks in the lust department. Re-reading the memoirs with Annie's insights in mind, I can see the old guy using elusive language to gloss over his abusive behavior. And I agree with my partner that the old bastard typed up a version of 'Darling Daughters' which amounted to a confession. But, in the end, he thought better of telling the unvarnished truth. Our guess is he destroyed the tell-tale pages, and—while waiting for his trusty Remington to be repaired—spent the closing minutes of his life penning a revision. But, even in the final written words of his life, he couldn't quite bring himself to compose a true *mea culpa*. He must have been afraid that his readers would think less of him if they knew he was a child molester." Trinidad told all this to the sheriff, but confessed he was reluctant to use the latter term with Anne.

"Your Annie ain't no China doll," the sheriff advised. "And secrets, however well-intended, got no place in a marriage. Besides it's no good keepin' stuff from your partner—I know you know what I'm talkin' about."

"Okay," said Trinidad as he rang off, thinking to himself that Jack was right about secrets. Years ago, the struggling detective's effort to conceal the trials and tribulations of his battle to remain clean and sober had nearly scuttled his relationship with Jack. The sheriff was right. Partnerships, be they professional or personal, required the participants to be truthful. It wasn't healthy to pull his punches when it came to sharing findings with his present partner and future bride.

Re-cradling the phone, Trinidad walked to the kitchen where he rescued the sun tea jar from the window pane and pulled an ice cube tray from the freezer. Pouring two glasses over ice, he sat down at the kitchen table, and waited patiently while Anne studied the pages before her. She was using a magnifying glass to compare the handwriting in Koller's final chapter with a faxed sample of the old man's correspondence. If his publisher was to be believed, it was one of hundreds of letters Esau had written to Millie during the time she was away at college.

"Gotta be his writing," she concluded as she took a sip of tea. "Even though good old Bud's fax leaves much to be desired in the way of resolution, I'm convinced that Esau Koller wrote the letters to Millie and the final pages of his memoirs using the identical fountain pen and tablet and..." She stood up and carried two sheets of paper to the living room window where she laid one over the other as she continued her analysis. "Bingo. When I compare the word *affection* from pages A and B, the two cursive words overlap. So, the handwriting is Esau's—no question. Unfortunately, still no solid clues about the visitor—although I'm pretty sure it was a daughter—step or otherwise. Now what should I know about the pages you reviewed?"

"The old weasel used a carload of platitudes and a self-delusional festival of tortured euphemisms for bad behavior," Trinidad said. "Including, in order of frequency, such golden-oldie phrases as: 'my behavior wasn't up to scratch, my reaction left much to be desired, my decision may have been question-able,' and the like. Anything to keep from admitting or confessing guilt."

Trinidad paused, realizing that he himself was dancing around the elephant in the room, still reluctant—despite Jack's advice—to use anything approaching the phrase "child molester."

"So, everything suggests he was a died-in-the-wool pervert, right?" she clarified.

"Yes," Trinidad confirmed. "And, re-reading those pages through your eyes, I'm sorry you had to wade through those contrived chapters. I know it's savage stuff," he apologized.

"No more savage than Juliet's journal," she countered, "which I need to have another go at while Koller's versions of events are still fresh in my mind. I want to look for similarities and differences between both sources—search-ing for comparisons which might influence our interview with Juliet in the morning."

Retrieving the packet from the kitchen shelf, she opened the over-sized manila envelope she'd discovered in the Carbondale library. She extracted Juliet's bulky journal, then looked at her partner and motioned to him.

"Come sit with me," she requested. Juliet's journal was savage indeed and she'd be glad to have her partner nearby. Taking Anne's outstretched hand, Trinidad let her lead him into the living room.

So, as the farmhouse clock measured the passing hours, the two of them sat side-by-side on the sofa and spent the afternoon working their way once again through the old man's life story. It was a thorough review which compared Esau's self-serving narration with parallel events as reported by his cast-out step-daughter.

As needed, Trinidad rose briefly to traipse into the kitchen, returning with apples and chips and sandwiches and coffee. He also served as go-fer, retrieving notes which summarized the recollections of other observers, including Esau's CPA, his publisher, and his servants. Finally, to fully represent the daughters' point of view, he fetched the transcript of Ruth's Skype interview.

Ideally, a comprehensive review would have included testimony from the male Kollers—the aggressive son and the surly twin brother. But son Isaac wasn't talking. Joel Signet had acted honorably, and in his client's best interest, by advising the unschooled ex-con to clam-up. As for Jacob, his alibi seemed airtight. Moreover, the two brothers had been alienated for decades, so it was uncertain whether Jacob could add anything of substance to the case.

Juliet's journal seemed to offer the most undiluted source of information about Esau's true nature. But the journal had its limitations. In particular, they wondered how Esau's exiled step-daughter could possibly have known details which she herself hadn't witnessed. Juliet had roamed far afield after she fled from the family's Aspen manor. One way to explain certain entries was to conclude she must have managed somehow to speak to her mother and sister as well as the servants. The only other explanation was one which Anne was reluctant to accept, which was that Juliet had manufactured some of her stories out of whole cloth.

By whatever means Juliet acquired the information, the dates recorded in her journal tracked closely with the chronology of Koller's chapters, with one glaring difference. Where the old man omitted the details of his iniquities, Juliet revealed their sordid depth. Accepting Juliet as the family's most reliable narrator required a leap of faith, but the detectives had little choice.

The surviving Koller men were off the table, Ruth's whereabouts were unknown and Millie was also missing, whereas their sister was nearby. When it came to understanding Esau's murder, Juliet's journal represented required reading for a pair of detectives who had to get up bright and early next morning and drive twenty-five miles to interview Juliet herself.

"I feel like I'm back in college, staying up late to cram for a test," said Anne. "Although it's Juliet who'll be taking the test."

"Another hour," said Trinidad, "then we call it quits."

So, they examined the journal, accepting Juliet's accounts at face value, even though some of her reports strained credulity. According to Juliet's December 2011 journal entries, Hortense fell to brooding over her runaway daughter to such a morbid extent that she ceased to interest Esau sexually. When this happened, the old reprobate heartlessly sent her away. While his distraught wife languished in a nursing home, he had the helpless woman declared incompetent. Without missing a beat, he officially transferred her considerable fortune, which she'd intended to pass on to her daughters, to his name. Ultimately, the abject woman died in her sleep of a self-administered drug overdose. Testimony from Phillip, the Aspen manservant, had verified all this, but how could the runaway herself had known such details?

By whatever means she learned of the happenings at White Quail Manor, Juliet corroborated Phillip's belief that, shortly after acquiring his wife's fortune, Koller abstained from abusing his last remaining step-daughter and instead sent Millie away to college. In his version of events, Phillip reported that the old man had experienced an epiphany. Anne insisted this change fell far short of a miracle, believing Esau's shrinking libido was the cause.

In his memoirs covering the same period, Koller said little on the subject only noting that he moved to Denver to enhance his writing career. His mercurial rise in the publishing industry seemed to have no prelude. One moment he was a thoroughly pedestrian man—although a wealthy one—but with no apparent literary talents and the next he'd somehow transformed into a legendary novelist. It seemed an unlikely evolution.

Anne had her own theory on this subject.

"Isn't it obvious," she asked, "that the old pervert sold his soul to the Devil?"

Whatever bargains Esau made, his success was a matter of public record and his publisher had filled in the details. Trinidad played the audio file to refresh their memory.

"More-or-less overnight our rising star was turning out a dozen books a year and critics were gushing that his villains were not only believable but also deliciously irredeemable," the publisher declared. "And every reviewer agreed on one thing. They all wrote that what made his novels so marketable were his enduring villains."

When Trinidad closed the file, Anne was silent for a moment until she summed up her impression of the publisher's testimony. "Writing villains must have been a cinch for old Esau," she said. "For inspiration he only had to look in the mirror."

"My sentiments exactly," said Trinidad as he reached up to switch off the living room lamp. "Early morning tomorrow. Let's call it a night."

Chapter 32

Kindred Spirit
(Thursday, May 16)

Trinidad had been driving in the dark through the late spring snow and up across the summit of Grand Mesa. He and Anne had reached the Collbran cutoff just as the sun rose. They were on their way to confront Juliet, now going by Sturgis, who'd made a new life for herself in a remote western town.

Having spent an hour bombarding her sleepy fiancé with excerpts from the sad tale of Juliet's life, Anne was beginning to have second-thoughts. Much of the unfortunate girl's story struck chords which were far too familiar.

"Maybe I'm wrong," she told Trinidad. "Maybe we should just leave her alone."

"We've got to do this, Annie," he said. "And we're almost there, so remind me again of the rest."

Anne sighed, consulted her notes, and continued her recitation of the trials and tribulations of a wronged step-daughter.

In the final installments of her journal, Juliet told of leaving Page with murder in her heart. The wanderer traveled further across the Reservation and up through the San Juan Mountains where she stopped and sat by an alpine stream until it began to rain. Then she prayed and let Nature wash her clean. She seemed to lose track of time but, when she emerged from the mountains, her heart had begun to soften. She went looking for further peace and—journeying still further north—she found it high on Grand Mesa on a windswept trail called Crag Crest. It was summer and, despite the mosquitoes, she slept there in the open under the stars.

She drifted onward, relishing the trees and lakes and vistas of Grand Mesa and followed her heart along a narrow stretch of pavement until she arrived in Collbran. There she met Preston Sturgis and there she stayed. When Preston broke both legs in a rodeo collision, she nursed him. And when his pie-in-the-sky Wolf Island gold claim petered out, she took a job in town as a waitress and he became a cook.

After closing hours, they earned extra money singing as a duo called "Rockfall Danger," a name they appropriated from a highway department sign which warned mountain motorists to be on the lookout for rocks on the road. And when their boss died without a living heir, they discovered that he'd left the restaurant to his employees who were Mr. and Mrs. Preston Sturgis of Ball Creek.

She had married well. It was her wedding picture that Anne had picked out from Trinidad's spontaneous line-up and which she now held in her hand.

"Maybe we should just..." she tried again to express her misgivings as she replaced the photo and closed Juliet's file folder.

"The best thing we can do for Mrs. Sturgis," said Trinidad as he guided the Honda along the road to Collbran, "is cross her off our list. And for that to happen, she's going to need an air-tight alibi."

"But you said we're coming here to break her alibi."

"Better to test it now than in a courtroom," said Trinidad. "From what you say, Juliet may have had good reasons to kill her step-father, but whatever she's suffered, it's not our call to give her a free pass. Look, I know about getting involved with a target. It comes with the territory. A detective sees few people at their best. Mostly we see people at their absolute worst on the worst day of their lives and during the positively worse fifteen minutes of that horrible day."

"Maybe I'm not cut out to be a detective," she frowned. "At least in archaeology if someone has a bad day it happened an eon ago and no one is the wiser."

"With any luck," said Trinidad, "Our next case will involve a missing person with an ancient last known address—one that's so obscure that we'll have to dig through three thousand years of stratum to find it."

"I'm impressed, my love, that you know what *stratum* means," Anne smiled.

"Hold that thought," said Trinidad, "We're here."

Chapter 33

Don't Order the Meatloaf
(Morning)

Chauncey's Diner occupied a 19th century stone building in the con-
stricted city block that passed for downtown Collbran. Under the same
name, it had once been a tavern and brothel. According to local legend, a
tunnel once ran from the basement of Chauncey's, under the street, and three
doors down to the old billiards hall. This secret underground passage allowed
men to tell their wives they were going to play billiards with the boys when
they actually intended to traverse the tunnel and spend the evening drinking
and whoring.

This same legend held that a miner's wife got wind of the subterfuge and
collected dynamite dust from her husband's cuffs and boots until she had
amassed sufficient material to fill a sausage case. Then, one winter's night,
the intersection of Short Street and Main erupted in a fiery blast and a ton
of surface cobblestones collapsed to close off the tunnel. Unfortunately, the
explosion also killed twenty head of cattle that one of the town fathers had
been billeting below the brothel to protect them from the freeze.

Some say the tunnel never existed. Some say it was re-bored during
Prohibition and is still in use today. And some say the legend is as good a
reason as any to not order the meatloaf.

There was no one in Chauncey's when Anne and Trinidad entered. The anemic warning bell over the door announced their arrival and, as they slid into a booth, a man passed through a split curtain to bring coffee and take their order.

"Pancakes," said Trinidad without looking at the menu.

"And you, Miss?"

"Pancakes," said Anne.

"A good choice," the man smiled. "I make 'em myself from scratch."

"You working alone today?" asked Trinidad.

The man was silent for a moment and then he said, "You two ain't lookin' for work maybe?"

"No thanks," said Trinidad. "Just wondered how you manage a big place like this all on your own."

The conversation was interrupted by the sound of a baby crying. The sound seemed to come from the kitchen.

"Excuse me," said the man and he rushed away.

"What the...?" Anne exchanged a glance with Trinidad.

"No idea," her fiancé shrugged.

The baby continued crying. Then the poor soul began wailing as though its heart would break and Anne was on her feet.

"I gotta go help that poor guy," she said and Trinidad didn't try to stop her.

Anne was gone for fifteen minutes during which time the baby transitioned from wailing to snuffling and from snuffling to cooing. When the cooing stopped, Anne emerged from the kitchen carrying a tiny sleeping newborn. She sat down opposite him.

"Hold on to your hat," she said. "Or maybe I should say get out your handkerchief."

"What's up, partner?"

"Well..." she said and she began to cry. "We—we can cross Juliet off our list. On..." She couldn't continue.

Trinidad got to his feet and slid in beside her. "What is it?" he asked.

Anne held the infant close, put her head on his shoulder, and tried to compose herself. At last, she sat up again and continued in a halting voice.

"On April 22, Juliet was in—was in the hospital at Glenwood Springs. And Preston—that was him that waited on us—he was with her. And—and—and she died there giving birth. She died there more than two hours before her step-father was killed in Denver. And, oh my God—it's—just—so—damn—sad."

Anne continued to weep and Trinidad put his arm around her and the three of them—the detective, his love, and little baby Hortense—sat in Chauncey's Diner waiting for their pancakes.

Chapter 34

The Road Home
(Noon)

After leaving Collbran, Anne and Trinidad rode in silence for the first twelve miles. When they reached Highway 65, Trinidad turned left and headed for the summit of Grand Mesa.

"There's a coffee shop up ahead," he said. "I think we could both use a cup before we start for the top."

The parking lot was filled with green and white forest service trucks and inside a gaggle of young people in khaki-colored uniforms occupied the few inside chairs.

"Sorry for the commotion," said the counter person. "Trail crew's taking a break. There's seats outside on the back porch if you want."

"The porch will be fine," said Trinidad.

When he and Anne were seated outside, a raven landed on the railing and considered the couple. Then it flew away.

"You haven't said a word since we left Collbran," he said.

"Can't think of anything to say," she said.

"Do you...?" he began.

"I don't think I can do this anymore," she interrupted.

"Okay."

"No, I mean it," she said.

"I get it," he said.

Another raven landed, followed by two more.

"They want something," Trinidad observed.

"Everybody wants something," she said.

For a moment they sipped their coffees in silence.

"You know," she said. "It's one thing to read about murders and investigations and criminals and car chases and mysterious clues and hacksaws. It's another thing to experience death and its aftershocks in person. And it's way too personal for me."

"Let me show you something," Trinidad said. He pulled out his wallet, extracted a well-worn photograph, and handed it to Anne.

"This is you as a teenager," she said. "I've seen this picture before."

"Look closer," he said.

"Well," she said, "there's you holding a tennis racket, that's sweet and—wait—that can't be you."

"Because..." he prompted.

"Unless I'm mistaken, that sweater has a couple of lumps I never noticed before." Anne looked up and studied Trinidad's torso to confirm her observation. "This photo definitely shows a pair of breasts, small but unmistakable, so this can't be you."

"It's my twin sister."

"How come I never..."

"She disappeared at birth. Someone snatched her from the newborn wing. One minute she was there beside me, the next minute gone without a trace. So, you see I know all about how personal a mystery can become."

"Then how...?

"My parents kept it from me. I learned the truth when I was doing a genealogy unit in third grade. I went to the courthouse to get a copy of my birth certificate. All the other kids were showing around their certificates and baby footprints and bronzed baby shoes and I didn't want to be left out. My parents had originally nixed the idea, but I went behind their backs and got an older neighbor kid to pose as my father. We even made him a fake mustache—my first attempt at creating a disguise. Anyway, I didn't think it would work, but lo-and-behold, we pulled it off. We paid a dollar and the clerk handed the stuff to me in a manila envelope. I also paid my fake dad a dollar and that was when dollars were hard to come by. Anyway, I didn't open the envelope until I was all the way back home and, even then, I hid under my blanket and used a flashlight. It was..." Trinidad faltered and seemed about to cry.

"Okay," Anne smiled and patted his hand.

"Anyway—anyway there were two names on the certificate. I was confused and then I was angry because it looked like I'd gone to a lot of trouble and paid two dollars for the wrong damn paperwork. Meanwhile, the nosy courthouse clerk did some snooping and ended up calling my parents and then the ceiling fell in. My mother cried and my father lectured me about bearing false witness, but eventually they told me the truth and gave me a bundle of newspaper clippings. In those days, we were watching *Perry Mason* re-runs on television and I wished that Paul Drake, you know, Perry's private investigator, could look into my case. I even wrote him a letter care of our local station asking for his help. I never heard back, of course, he was just an actor and I was just a kid. So anyway, I started my own investigation. I rode my bike to the Mount San Rafael Hospital in Trinidad and snooped around trying to pick up the trail at the newborn nursery. I was looking for clues, but had no clue what I was looking for, of course."

"No clue," said Anne.

"Time passed. I grew up and, as they say, I put aside childish things. But I'd been bitten by the investigative bug, so after high school, as you know, I tried majoring in pre-law, but washed out of Boulder and hit the road to work the summer at Grand Lake—which is a whole other story. Anyway, I eventually went back home and studied criminal justice at Trinidad State JC. Among other things, I learned about cold case techniques and, when it came time to do a class project, I couldn't think of anything colder than a 20-year-old baby snatching. So, with my professor's help I started making inquiries by mail and through the internet."

"Go on," Anne said.

"I'm talking too much. Are you sure you want to hear this?" he asked.

"Tell me everything," she said.

Trinidad continued his story. Hoping that twin siblings would share facial characteristics, he included with his written inquiries two mug shots of himself. The images consisted of a full-face and profile, courtesy of his JC course in forensic photography. He sent the photos, never thinking that this institutional combination might suggest "mug-shot" to his correspondents.

"I was a young, dumb, broke college kid," he sighed.

"Well at least you're not broke anymore," she said. "So, then what?"

Trinidad said that his inquiries must have struck a nerve somewhere because the photograph of his twin sister arrived in the mail with no return address and no accompanying explanation. Nothing but the photo and a mysterious sequence of letters and numbers typewritten on the back—then the trail went cold again.

Trinidad wrote his project paper entitled *The Road Home*, got an "A" for his effort, graduated with honors, went to work, and filed everything in a folder labeled *River*.

"Why River?" Anne asked.

"It's the name my mother intended to give my sister. They would call me Trinidad and her name would be River. We were named for a special spot along the river that flowed through my hometown. I later came to realize that this so-called *spot* was probably the place where the two of us were conceived."

"And the less we know about that the better," Anne interjected.

"Agreed," he said.

"Wait a minute," Anne said. "Remember when you and me were watching that old Liberty Valance movie last week on *Turner Classics* and John Wayne said what's-his-name was the 'toughest hombre south of the Picketwire' and you laughed and said that was the name of the river where your parents met?"

"I remember. But how would you like it if I was named *Picketwire?*"

"Or don't you mean Purgatorie?" The nearby voice startled them.

"Pardon?" said Trinidad.

"You was talkin' about the Picketwire," said a large man who had joined them on the porch. He stood a few feet away dressed for bad weather in a cowboy hat and full-length rain slicker. Engrossed in conversation, the detectives had failed to notice his arrival. "I know the town," the man continued—

his deep Texas drawl perfectly complimenting his western outfit, "and I know that Picketwire is another name for the Purgatorie River which runs through town—most times a trickle and sometimes a flood. And I know that there ain't no such Colorado water as is called the Trinidad River."

Anne was peeved that this over-dressed cowboy was horning in on their private conversation, so she sneered at his rain slicker and asked, "And do you also know that it ain't raining today?"

"Not yet it ain't," was the man's reply. "Well, anyhow, Heckleson is my name—Fingers Heckleson. And you," he pointed at Trinidad, "you'd be Carl and Emma Sands' boy I reckon."

Trinidad stared at the man and the man stared back. Neither one blinked.

My God, thought Anne, *good thing it isn't 1872 and these boys aren't armed or somebody would be pulling iron about now.*

"But where's my manners?" Heckleson laughed. "No, children, this ain't no *Twilight Zone* episode. I was sent to fetch you by the Delta sheriff. Well, not fetch exactly, I guess. I was askin' after you and he said you was headed to Collbran and I woulda caught you up earlier but I helped to stop some people change a flat tire. Anyway, I was told what you was drivin' and I was on your trail when I spotted your rig. So here I am."

"And what brings you to our neck of the woods?" asked Trinidad.

"Why, son," he said, "I come bearin' good news. Ain't you heard? We done found your sister."

Chapter 35

Reunion Delayed
(Friday Morning, May 17)

It was Friday when the couple learned that the reading of the Koller will, originally set for the week following Pentecost, had been moved forward to Saturday afternoon. That left less than twenty-four hours to pursue the case.

Overwhelmed by news of his sister, Trinidad was understandably distracted. He and Anne and the others were sitting around a conference table in the sheriff's tiny briefing room.

"Sorry to spring Ranger Heckleson on you," apologized Jack. "I tried to call and give you a head's up that old Fingers was on his way, but no cell service on that side of the Mesa."

Trinidad and Anne were sitting side by side. Jack was at the head of the table. And Joel was sitting across from them fiddling with his chair.

"Can't get used to these old-fashioned seats," Joel complained. "What the hell is the use of these arm rests?"

"We don't have anything like your budget, counselor," said Jack. "Next time we'll meet at your up-scale place. I understand that, on a clear day, you can see the San Juan's from there."

"And the Walmart parking lot," Joel added.

"So where are we with all this?" the sheriff asked.

Trinidad seemed not to hear the question, so Anne opened her notebook and reported their findings. "We've confirmed the alibis of three suspects," she said. "The brother, the son, and one step-daughter are in the clear. In fact, the step-daughter in question is deceased. That leaves Millie, the other step-daughter, and Ruth..."

"The redhead," said Jack and Joel at the same instant.

"Yes," said Anne. "Ruth, the frigging redhead."

"Continue," said Jack. He looked at Trinidad who seemed to awaken from a nap.

"Millie is MIA," said Trinidad. "No sign of her since she left Aloe College in Glenwood Springs a month ago. Wherever she went, presumably she isn't using the name Millie Koller. She didn't enroll for the next term and she hasn't been back to her apartment. She doesn't drive, so no DMV. No criminal record. No credit records. Nothing."

"And no alibi," said Jack.

"Obviously, no alibi," said Trinidad. "As for Ruth Koller, I finally pinned her down last night and..."

Both Jack and Joel squirmed in their seats and cleared their throats.

"Go ahead," Anne said, then couldn't help smiling. "You pinned the redhead down and..."

Trinidad blushed then continued, "Anyway I got Miss Koller on the phone and—contrary to what she said in her Skype interview—she went on and on about what a great guy her father was and then she trotted out her brother as her alibi. But, as we all know, brother Isaac was trapped in the Stevenson basement at the time of his father's murder."

"So, Ruth moves to the head of the list," said Joel.

"She and her missing sister," said Trinidad. "Missing sister," he repeated unnecessarily.

"Okay," Joel said, "I think we can take things from here. I've cleared the way for myself and our two detectives to attend the reading of the will on Saturday. I'll be there representing Isaac's interests. So, Anne and..."

"Trinidad's not going," Anne interrupted.

"Not going?" asked Joel.

"I think our friend has better things to do. Am I right?" asked Jack.

"I'm leaving for Colorado Springs tonight," Trinidad explained. "I'm trying to arrange a commuter flight to meet my parents at the Broadmoor—and maybe my sister..." His voice trailed off.

"So, it'll be Joel and Anne at the reading of the will," said Jack. "And I'm sure that'll be fine. So, let's go, cowboy, Madge'll have to use the siren or you'll miss your jet."

"My jet?" asked Trinidad.

"Yup," said the sheriff. "No way am I lettin' my favorite detective wallow around on standby. I've got a jet waitin' in Montrose, courtesy of my pal Thad Cloud in the Springs—he's CSPD—he's the one who worked your sister's cold case with Ranger Heckleson. And don't worry, Cloud'll meet your plane but hang around just for the handoff, then he'll leave you and your family alone."

Outside the meeting room, Jack pulled Anne aside as Trinidad was busy transferring his luggage from the Nissan to Madge's patrol car.

"If things go bad with this business in the Springs," he whispered, "Sergeant Cloud will call me and I'll call you."

"Bad?" Anne whispered back. "What could possibly go wrong?"

"You never know," said Jack. "Good luck tomorrow."

Chapter 36

Sing Along
(Friday Night)

Yesterday afternoon, when she and Trinidad had stopped for coffee on the way home after visiting Chauncey's Diner, Anne left Trinidad alone with Ranger Heckleson. While her husband-to-be and the rainy-day cowpoke compared notes, she strolled through the coffee shop. Browsing among the t-shirts and postcards, she'd discovered and purchased a Rockfall Danger CD. She'd figured it was the least she could do to support the grieving husband and motherless baby. If Anne hadn't done all those things in that exact order, she might never have popped the disc into Trinidad's ancient Walkman, plugged in his prehistoric headphones, and listened to the Rockfall's cover of *In the Baggage Coach Ahead.*

"Son of a bitch!" Anne shouted. It was growing late and she'd just finished stripping the bed and was sitting on the mattress in the upstairs bedroom. Her hands shaking, she pulled off the headphones and dialed Trinidad's cell phone, knowing he was far away, winging his way toward a reunion with his long-lost sister. "Pick up. Pick up. Pick up." She repeated as the ringing continued.

"Trinidad Sands at your service," the message said. "Well, not really, so talk to me after the beep."

Anne left a partially incoherent message, talking too fast and too loudly, and she hung up certain that her frantic voice was echoing across the miles.

Unable to stand waiting for Trinidad's return call, but terrified she might miss it, she ran downstairs to get a root beer, then rushed back upstairs taking two steps at a time. She was wearing her gym socks and skidded across the bedroom's hardwood floor just as her cell phone rang.

"What's up?" Trinidad asked.

"Where are you?" Anne asked.

"Up in the air somewhere," he explained. "This side of Colorado Springs, I guess. Are you calling from home? I'm amazed at the signal clarity."

"Let's hope it lasts. Listen to this," Anne demanded as she pressed the earphones against her smartphone, experimenting with the position, not quite certain where the input conduit was. "Can you hear anything?"

"Just barely," said Trinidad. "What are you trying to do?"

"Oh, never mind, hold on, I've got another idea," she said as she put the headphones on again and struggled to cue the disc to the opening cut. "Can you still hear me?"

"Yes, and tell me what's up," said Trinidad. "I can't see what you're doing and you're beginning to scare me."

"Sorry, I'm just trying to think through the logistics, but I'll keep talking," she said. "So, here's the thing: remember that CD that I bought at the Mesa coffee shop?"

"Yeah," said Trinidad in a tone that suggested he had no idea where this conversation was going.

"Well...okay...I've almost got it. There!" She tapped the video conference icon and instantly images of both her and her distant lover popped onto her smartphone screen. "Can you see me? I can see you."

"Okay," said Trinidad. "You're in a big box and looking lovely and I'm in a smaller box and looking perplexed."

"I see just the opposite in sizes and I absolutely wanted to see your face—perplexed though it may be at the moment—because I'm about to enlighten you and the only way I can do that is to cue up the Rockfall Danger CD on your prehistoric Walkman and sing the song out loud as I listen to it through the earphones."

"Have I mentioned that I love the fact that sometimes you sound positively nuts?" he asked. "So, what you're saying is you set up this earth-to-sky video chat so I can watch you doing Karaoke in our bedroom?"

"That's the basic idea, I guess. Now okay," she said, "get ready, I think I've got it—listen."

Haltingly, she began trying to mimic the Rockfall Danger song on the fly and watched as her mate's video face progressed from confusion to attention to realization. "Sound familiar?" she asked.

"Damn," he said. "Have you got the lyrics handy? Send me a screenshot."

Encouraged by Trinidad's request, Anne grabbed the CD jewel case, extracted the compact sheet bearing the lyrics, focused on the offending song, took a picture, and sent it to him as an email attachment.

"The lyrics are on the way," she reported. "Check your email."

There was a momentary delay as Trinidad put his head down, fired up his tablet, and opened his email. He read for a moment, then asked Anne to reverse the camera and scan the photos on the far bedroom wall.

"Time to revisit our line-up," he said.

"You got it, Slick," she said, as one-by-one she centered the daughter's photos and held the image long enough for Trinidad to get a good look.

"Next," he said. "Okay, next one, and now a close-up of our tricky little redhead."

"Anytime now," Anne scolded when he seemed intent on lingering over Ruth's come-hither portrait.

"Got it," he said with a laugh. "Now see if you can put them into the order I'm visualizing. Put your phone down for a bit and get up there and rearrange our rogues' gallery while I do an internet search for that goofy song."

"You don't like my singing," she pouted.

"I love your voice," he said. "You know that. But..."

"I'm kidding," she said. "I know I must sound like the soundtrack of a badly dubbed Japanese movie. So, you go ahead and do your music search and I'll take a crack at rearranging the photos. And I'll be right back."

As Anne worked, she guessed that her husband-to-be had successfully located the song. She could hear the unmistakable beat of the Rockfall

Danger song coming from Trinidad's end, although the words were barely audible through her tinny Android speaker. After trying different combinations, she reordered the photos, but wasn't sure that she and Trinidad were on the same wave length.

"Can you guess what we missed the first time?" Anne asked.

"Is that a rhetorical question?" Trinidad asked.

"What does rhetorical even mean?" she wondered aloud.

"Well, rhetorical or not, the answer was right in front of our noses all the time," he said. "Run those pictures by me again."

Once again, she slowly swept the phone camera across the photo array, moving from left to right.

"Not quite yet," he said.

"I don't get it," she said. "Can you...?"

A strident amplified voice interrupted their conversation.

"Gotta ring off," said Trinidad. "We're about to land and I've got to extinguish my devices. I'll catch up with you when we're on the ground."

Chapter 37

Picture Perfect
(9 p.m.)

For twenty agonizing minutes, Anne paced back and forth in the farm-house bedroom, drinking a second root beer, until she had an overpowering urge to pee. She rushed to the upstairs bathroom, cursed herself for not replacing the empty toilet paper roll, did her duty, and searched in vain for the hand towel.

"Laundry day," she told herself as her smartphone warbled and she sprinted back to the bedroom, drying her hands on her overalls.

"I'm going to start the darn song again from my end," said Trinidad. "And loop it to repeat." He cued up the cut and turned up the volume. The Rockfall Danger song played on as she and Trinidad looked at one another's video images. *Ahead in the Baggage Car* was a classic 1920's tear-jerker with several verses and a maudlin chorus about a young father, his crying baby, and a dead wife.

"On a dark stormy night," the Rockfalls sang, "as the train rattled on, all the passengers had gone to bed. Except one young man with a babe in his arms, who sat there with bowed-down head. The innocent one began crying just then, as though its poor heart would break. One angry man said, *Make that child stop its noise, for it's keeping all of us awake!*"

The theme of the song and the poignant scene at Chauncey's Diner were too similar to be discounted as coincidence.

"One of us needs to make a call," said Trinidad.

"I'll do it," said Anne. "You keep thinking about our wall of shame."

When she returned from using the farmhouse landline to alert Jack and Joel to the Chauncey Diner façade, Anne found that her loving fiancé wanted her to rearrange the sisters' images in a particular order. She was off one photo and, when she switched them around, a figurative light bulb snapped on in her brain.

"Dang," she said aloud.

When compared side by side, the reordered photographs of the sisters revealed something which both detectives had missed. The fashion in Ruth's photograph was contemporary. Juliet's pose in her wedding dress could have been taken anytime, but she was young and the date was clearly visible in the lower right-hand corner where the photographer had embossed his logo. And the photograph of Millie bore a sticker with the year of her high school graduation.

"Dang it!" said Anne as she left the phone on the chest of drawers and rushed back to the bed, lifted the dust ruffle, and crawled underneath. "Crap!" Anne's feet were sticking out and, though Trinidad couldn't see her ankles and stocking feet pivoting to-and-fro, he could hear her muffled voice as she repeated the uncharacteristic profanity. "Crap!"

"What's happening?" his voice inquired across the miles.

"Ouch!" shouted Anne. "Got it!"

Anne emerged holding the photograph of the late Hortense Koller which, since the time of their initial examination of suspect documents, had languished in their discard pile. The young detective carried the black and white image across the room, pausing only long enough to secure a fresh piece of masking tape.

Frustrated by her silence, Trinidad again asked what was going on.

"Patience, Grasshopper," Anne cooed. "There! Take a look at Hortense."

She slowly scanned the new arrangement, then reversed the screen to study Trinidad's face. As she hoped, his enlightened expression suggested that her placement of Hortense's photo represented what they both were belatedly beginning to recognize as the missing piece of the puzzle.

"I put her next to Juliet," she said. "In order to complete the calendar."

And so, it did. Positioned to the left of the daughters' pictures, Hortense's photograph was a black and white image of a woman in a frumpy dressing gown with wild hair and a vacant look in her eyes. The notation on the margin read "Mama's birthday March 23, 2008." Moving from left to right, the embossed stamp on Juliet's black and white wedding photo read "2015." Next was the sticker on Millie's teenaged photo, also black and white, which said "2016—Year of the Rabbit!" A contemporary photo of Ruth in stunning color completed the series.

Efforts to obtain more recent photographs of Hortense and the younger girls had been unsuccessful. It was as if Ruth had moved forward, while her mother and sisters were frozen in time.

The song continued to infect the bedroom with its relentless tale as more train passengers began to complain about the wailing baby:

"*Where is its mother? Go take it to her*, this a lady then softly said. *I wish that I could*, was the man's sad reply. *But she's dead in the coach ahead.*"

"Better let Jesse rob this train!" said Anne.

Trinidad was silent. The fact that his bride-to-be had unconsciously lapsed into using one of Ranger Heckleson's colorful Texas sayings was evidence of her dismay. Otherwise, she'd never have blurted out something akin to telling herself, "Step aside, girl, you're doing it wrong."

"How could I have been so gullible?" Anne asked.

"It happens," said Trinidad. "Thanks to you, Jack will have contacted the Collbran marshal."

"And child protective services," Anne insisted.

"Them too definitely," he agreed. "I'll follow up with the Collbran issue. I can do that by phone and email. And I'm guessing you'll be wanting to take a trip to Glenwood just to make sure. So, while you're at it, don't forget to check out that calypso band we talked about. They should still be at the hotel."

"I'll go," she said wondering to herself just how she was going to work auditioning a wedding band into the busy itinerary she was compiling in her head. "I'll go as soon as the will is read," she repeated, "and I'll need this." Anne removed Ruth's photograph from the wall and showed it to Trinidad. "Even money I won't need the other pictures tomorrow," she speculated.

"Even money," said Trinidad as he ended the call.

Chapter 38

A Stranger
(10:30 p.m.)

"Jeeves will take your wraps," said Joel as he greeted his guests and invited them out of the evening rain and into the plush interior of Signet Manor. "Come meet Kip Greeley."

Deputy Madge Oxford, who was a return visitor, declined to surrender her cap to Jeeves and followed Joel down the broad hallway. Anne lingered at the threshold, taking it all in and wishing Trinidad, who was far away in Colorado Springs, was by her side. Joel's call had come through on the farmhouse landline, minutes after she ended her musical ground-to-air conversation with her fiancé.

"You need to come over," Joel told her. "Madge will pick you up. I need you here right away. Don't dawdle." Whatever the lawyer had in mind Anne was pretty sure it was going to throw yet another curve into their investigation. Nevertheless, she couldn't help being impressed with Joel's lavish home.

"This is some place," she gushed as she traversed the broad hallway.

"Indeed," Joel's man intoned as he led the way.

"Say," Anne whispered, "is your name really Jeeves?"

"It's Topper," the butler whispered back, seeming to enjoy the prospect of a private conversation with the Manor's attractive young visitor. "Jeeves is a small joke between myself and Master Signet."

"So, he's your master," Anne wondered aloud.

"Force of habit," said Topper with a conspiratorial wink. "I've known my employer, man-and-boy, having served the family for years, beginning as a stable hand with Master Signet's grandfather and working my way up. You might say Master Signet and I grew up together. And here we are Miss, if you'd be so kind."

"Oh," said Anne as she handed her hat and scarf to the patient man, "quite a spell of weather we're having."

"Indeed," Topper agreed as he turned to go.

"Say," Anne whispered.

"Yes, Miss?"

"We've got a problem you might be able to help with," Anne confided.

"A *detective* problem?" asked Topper with obvious interest.

"Exactly," said Anne. "But right now, they'll be missing me. So, we'll talk later, okay?"

"As you wish, Miss," said Topper. "I look forward to our renewed conversation with the utmost interest."

"Thanks," said Anne warmly. "Ta-ta."

"Ta-ta," Topper responded in kind.

"I really like that guy," said Anne as she backed into Joel's well-appointed den. "Oh!"

Turning to face the others, Anne was momentarily shocked to see what appeared to be a tramp sitting cross-legged on the plush carpet, rocking in place, and softly chanting.

"Meditating," whispered Madge as she motioned the detective toward one of the room's overstuffed chairs.

"So, I see," said Anne as she took a seat beside the deputy. "What gives?"

"Om—om—om," the tramp intoned. Then the man—assuming the long-haired creature clad in a body-obscuring sarape was a man—stood up and began filling a china plate from a lavish smorgasbord laid out on a sideboard. When his plate was piled high, he sat once again on the floor and began eating with wolfish gusto.

Now what? Anne wondered.

"Mr. Greeley has only just arrived," Joel said in an offhand remark which Anne supposed the lawyer thought explained everything. She'd been so enamored with the vision of the disheveled apparition that she'd failed to notice the master of Signet Manor sitting nearby.

"I wast hoe-less," said the tramp, not bothering to swallow before speaking.

"Homeless indeed," said Joel, pressing his fingers together as if in prayer. "And that circumstance explains why it took the authorities so long to locate our elusive guest."

"Will somebody please..." Anne began.

"Of course," Joel responded in anticipation of her inquiry.

How does he do that? Anne wondered. *They must teach anticipatory interrogatories in law school—or am I thinking of written questions?*

"I know what you're thinking," Joel continued, causing Anne to blush.

"Do you?" she asked aloud before she could stop herself.

"Yes," Joel said and grinned. "You're thinking this fellow can't possibly be the young reporter whom Esau Koller threw out all those years ago, refusing to be interviewed—a traumatic incident which cost the young man his job, which drove him to drink, which led him to the streets of Denver."

"Littleton," Greeley corrected.

"I stand corrected," said Joel. "How many homeless in Denver, Kip?"

"3,245 in 2014," said Kip as he constructed another sandwich using crackers, salami, and cheese.

"And how many camping ban citations issued in beautiful downtown Boulder between 2010 and 2014?" Joel asked.

"1,766...no...67," said Greeley.

"Once a reporter, always a reporter," Joel explained. "Mr. Greeley knows the statistics contained in the University of Denver's 2016 study on the cost of criminalizing homelessness in Colorado. We were just discussing the volume when you rang the front doorbell. He knows the thing chapter and verse..."

"Not only do I know it," Greeley corrected, "I used the appendix to stuff in my pants for insulation last winter."

"Well," said Joel, apparently feeling that it was time to steer his prize pupil in another direction, "let's get down to brass tacks. Kip here has a warrant hanging over his head—not literally," he added when Greeley bowed his neck and glanced nervously aloft as if expecting a blow from above.

Clearly the man's not all there, Anne thought as she cast a more sympathetic eye on the destitute stranger.

"Sorry," said Joel, and his tone suggested he regretted getting carried away with his role as ringmaster exhibiting a trained bear. "Kip showed up on my doorstep, asking for help, and I'm happy to do so. I've made arrangements for a colleague to take his case pro bono..."

"His case?" Anne interrupted.

"Yes," said Joel. "Didn't I tell you? Kip Greeley is the latest suspect in the murder of Esau Koller."

Chapter 39

The Shouting
(Saturday, May 18, 7 a.m.)

Anne was barely awake and wishing she had another cup of coffee as she sat in the vast conference room at the firm of Keystone, Stucky, and Lacey. The place was packed. It looked like half the population of Grand Junction had turned out to hear the reading of the Koller will.

Last night had been a busy time. In addition to dissecting Juliet's Collbran deception, Anne had to absorb the unexpected phenomenon of Kip Greeley. Late last night, the homeless ex-reporter had surrendered docilely to Madge Oxford and the efficient deputy had handcuffed, transported, and booked the fellow in record time. When Anne next saw Greeley, around midnight, she'd hardly recognized the man who, despite being in custody, had somehow managed to obtain a shave and a haircut. Joel's doing, she imagined.

"Case closed," Madge had beamed in the wee hours of the morning as she drove Anne back to Lavender Hill Farm.

Anne wasn't so sure. Something was bugging her and she'd spent a sleepless night trying to puzzle it out. Hence her need this morning for coffee, but, looking around, she could see that this formal occasion lacked the amenities of a catered affair.

Joel's brother-in-law, the Keystone portion of the firm, was presiding and after the doors opened at 6 a.m. attendance had quickly ballooned to a standing-room-only crowd. For a widower, Esau Koller seemed to have acquired an unseemly gaggle of relations and also quite a media following. Joel pointed out reporters from all three Denver networks and 11-News and Channel 8 and the *Post* and *Sentinel* and *Independent*, plus there were a few new faces that he guessed must be cable journalists.

"I'm cousin Dell," a passerby leaned down and introduced himself to Joel. "You must be a cousin too. And hello to your lovely wife," he grinned at Anne. "Are you mother's or father's side?"

"I'm not certain," said Joel.

"I think he favors old Mrs. Koller," Anne declared.

"You know," said Dell, "I see the resemblance. Well, anyway, a pleasure to meet you both. Let's keep in touch."

"Mrs. Koller?" Joel whispered.

"You definitely have her eyes, dear," Anne smiled. "I'm kidding, but I sincerely hope our kid won't grow up to be a kiss-ass like old cousin Dell."

"Shh—they're about to begin." hissed a stranger sitting next to them—presumably yet another cousin.

Despite their neighbor's condescending forecast, the proceedings did not begin. Instead, Joel's brother-in-law and two other lawyers entered into a sidebar discussion that looked intense enough to eat up another twenty minutes. While the lawyers conferred, Anne took time to study the room and she was amused to see that Joel was doing the same.

We'll make a detective of him yet, she thought.

"Any courtroom dramas spring to mind from that cinematic memory bank of yours?" Joel asked with a smile.

"Stokes monkey trial—from *Inherit the Wind*—maybe," Anne answered distractedly as she concentrated on the crowd.

Looking from face to face she concluded that absolutely none of the people in the board room resembled one another in any way, shape, or form—let alone did they bear any resemblance to her vision of Esau Koller. And that included everybody's favorite redhead, Ruth Koller. As one of four living members of the deceased's immediate family, Ruth had made a dramatic entrance and taken pains to acquire a seat in the front row—a neat trick in the crowded room which required several men to jump to their feet and move aside to offer their chair to the vivacious late-comer. Ms. Koller was far away and Anne could only see the woman's shoulders and the back of her head, but she could see that Ruth was dressed to the nines.

Just look at that hat she's wearing.

As for other members of the clan, Jacob Koller had arrived at the same time as Anne and Joel. The old satyr had scrupulously avoided eye-contact with the detective and the lawyer as he purposely slinked to the far side of the room. The mutinous brother had placed himself far from the action—skulking and swearing under his breath. Isaac Koller was missing, of course. The discarded son was under house arrest and—even though no one believed Isaac was in line to receive one red cent of his father's fortune—Joel was acting as his proxy. And somewhere in the crowd might be the ephemeral Millie.

The photograph they had of the missing coed was an old one, but Anne had done her best to memorize the face and she'd employed her imagination to visualize how the apple-cheeked girl in the picture might have aged. Millie would be about twenty-one now, but there seemed to be no recent image of her, so they were stuck with what amounted to her high school graduation photograph, taken on the occasion of a ceremony celebrating her GED diploma.

Thinking of Millie's changed visage, Anne thought of Trinidad and wondered what might have gone through his mind as he winged his way to the 'Springs last night. Probably he too had been trying to visualize the current appearance of his birth twin. There had been no call from Jack or anyone else saying things had gone amiss, so she had to assume that all was well at the Broadmoor. She prayed this was so—actually prayed because she recognized how fantastically important this unexpected reunion was to the man she loved.

Pray if you must, she thought. *But it's even better if you force yourself to think about something else*, she told herself.

Abandoning her survey of the crowd, Anne looked again at the knot of lawyers. The proceedings were still bogged down. Joel's brother-in-law—she remembered that his first name was Andrew—was conferring with two other men. It had all the ear-marks of a lengthy conversation because one man was shaking his head "no" and the other two were nodding "yes."

Returning her attention to the room, Anne was struck with a whimsical impression. She couldn't shake the notion that she and Joel had happened upon a movie set, or—more precisely—had wandered backstage at a live theater rehearsal where a group of dissimilar extras had assembled in obedience to a casting call. Try as she might, she couldn't override the feeling that none of these people were genuine relations of the deceased but were instead auditioning for the part. She exchanged a glance with Joel and she had the distinct impression that he was entertaining the same belief.

Who the hell are all these people?

At last, the debating lawyers reached consensus and the event commenced. Stepping to a podium at the head of the room, Andrew Keystone welcomed the audience to this solemn occasion and tendered his condolences to family and friends of the deceased.

"If any," Joel whispered, his face alight with a mischievous expression.

Someone coughed.

Anne could hear the large wall clock ticking at the far end of the room. Outside, on the street two floors below, a car honked. Then silence reigned. Inside, in the crowded room, Andrew cleared his throat and droned on about "whereas this" and "whereas that" until Anne was compelled to excuse herself to use the restroom. She fully intended to leave Joel to sort out the reading and the crowd, but she immediately resumed her seat when she heard Joel's brother-in-law mention a familiar name.

"And to my loving daughter, Millie Alice Koller, I leave the disposition of my royalties for all works published in first-printing and all subsequent printings from the onset of my career to the present date as well as subsequent residuals, syndication rights, and any and all compensations due my estate whatsoever."

A collective gasp rippled through the crowd as unnamed cousin after unnamed cousin leapt to their feet and put in their two-cents worth.

"The very idea."

"That's the cream."

"Who the hell does this Millie character think she is?"

"She ain't even here!"

"Well, I never."

"And to think I sent the old stinker a Christmas card every year."

"What am I—chopped liver?"

Andrew Keystone paused, got eye-contact with Joel, and mouthed the words "all but the shouting." The gesture appeared to be lost on the disenchanted heirs and heiresses who remained on their feet and continued protesting and muttering while the presiding lawyer attempted to move on to other matters.

For his part, Joel settled back and enjoyed the show. What if all the money had been left to the missing girl? He'd heard stranger things. This was the thirty-sixth reading of a last will and testament that Joel had attended and he'd presided over twenty-five of those. The first one was six years ago and he'd been present as a junior partner. He'd just passed the bar exam after seven tries in three years which he realized might be some kind of record. Someday he'd write his memoirs including an account of the agony of those lost years—someday.

It had all begun in 2013 with the last will and testament of Serge Prescott. On the eve of the reading, Joel had been summoned by his mentor, Lou Edgerton. Lou was a crazy red-headed Irishman, his firm's lead partner, and the only man willing to hire a young attorney who had so conspicuously struggled to pass the bar examination. Lou's intention was to give his young charge a pep-talk.

"Don't fret about your exam history," Lou told young Joel. "Anybody who don't believe in second chances never played baseball. In baseball, you can be a bum and strikeout through eight innings, but it only takes one shot over the fences and all is forgiven."

Sometimes Lou's baseball analogies were a bit contrived, but Joel understood what the senior lawyer meant. So, the youngster had gratefully taken on the assignment of sitting in on the reading of old man Prescott's will with every intention of hitting one out of the park but without a clue as to how he would manage to do so.

Joel's assignment was deceptively simple. Lou suspected that something was amiss with Prescott's will and he wanted his young colleague to observe the reactions of the old man's surviving relations. Joel was instructed to study the family when the presiding lawyer announced that the deceased had left his entire fortune, not to any of them, but rather to the Los Angeles chapter of the St. Ignacio Infirmary.

Prescott had died suddenly and the reading of the will was postponed for over a year while the police investigated. Prescott had been found dead in the billiard room of his sprawling mansion on the outskirts of Boulder. No signs of a struggle and no burglary. Allegedly, he'd fallen and suffered a fatal blow to the back of his neck.

When Lou related the details of the alleged crime to Joel, visions of the board game *Clue* suddenly jumped into the young lawyer's head. As Lou spoke, all Joel could think was, "Colonel Mustard in the poolroom with a lead pipe."

When the cops ruled the untimely passing an accident, his ex-wife remained suspicious. A decade before Prescott's death she'd made out like gangbusters in an amicable divorce settlement, meaning she had no axe to grind, and anyway she still loved the old guy. The ex- was convinced that one of the nieces had done him in. So, she retained Lou to investigate and, while the older lawyer worked the phones to pursue leads in California, Lou had dispatched Joel to ride herd on the formal reading of Prescott's will.

As a result, Joel had been on hand six years ago to observe the behaviors of the heirs and heiresses. Choosing a good vantage point, he was poised to record what happened when relatives learned that their dear old dad, or doddering uncle as the case may be, had left his vast fortune to a free clinic designed to extend aid to West Coast sex workers and exotic dancers. Like any good lawyer, Lou had anticipated a certain amount of shouting in the wake of that shocking announcement.

And it so happened that, when the beneficiaries of the will were revealed, almost everybody pitched a royal fit. One son even tried to jump out a window, a gesture which was made no less dramatic by the fact that the lawyer's office was on the ground floor. However, the suspected niece showed no emotion whatsoever.

Anxious to make good on his assignment, Joel was determined to document the range of reactions that greeted the outrageous terms of the old man's will. He took copious notes on everything that occurred, including the nearly imperceptible conduct of one Mary Fisher, the niece who was on Lou's watch list. Later that same day, Joel handed Lou a handful of 3x5 cards on which he had summarized his findings.

"This is crap," Lou said after reading the first card. Then he proceeded to dispense a rapid-fire series of evaluations. "Card number two: crap. Number three: crap. Four: crap. Five: bull-crap. Six: extreme double bull-crap." The old lawyer continued pronouncing judgment on each of Joel's cards until he reached card number thirteen when he shouted, "Bingo!" Lou held the final card aloft.

"Our young Mary has sealed her fate. Your card tells it all. It neatly summarizes the fact that, of all the presumptive heirs and heiresses present, only she did not react when the old man's preposterous wishes were made known. Now, can you tell me why?"

Joel thought for a moment and then he ventured a tentative answer, "Because she already knew the contents of the will?"

"Yes, she already knew because..." Lou prompted.

"Because before he died, her unconventional uncle had privately revealed the contents to her."

"Yes, to her and her alone, and can you guess the circumstances of this revelation?"

"It would have been just the two of them in the old man's billiard room," Joel speculated and he was elated to discover that, as he spoke, he could clearly visualize the scene. "And the instant she learned she was going to inherit nothing, she lost all composure and reached for a handy weapon—there would have been plenty of billiard balls at hand. Unaware of her diabolical intentions, Prescott continued his game. When he leaned over the table to make a shot, his annoyed niece had only to pick up a ball, balance it in her open hand, and strike the old man in the back of the neck."

"That would certainly have done it," agreed Lou. "And that would also account for the fatal injury. The coroner found that a blow to the base of the cerebellum killed him. A single hand-held billiard ball would fit nicely into the nape of the neck don't you think? At his age, an accidental fall might have accounted for the deadly injury, but you and I know that Lou's Law of Gravity applies in this case. And what is that infallible law?"

Joel grinned as he obediently recited one of his mentor's many maxims, "Lou's Law of Gravity holds that fainting kids fall back, adults tip sideways, and senior citizens fall forward."

"With 97% predictability," said Lou as, without a tinge of irony, he tilted back in his luxurious office chair. "If I had a nickel for every instance in which I disproved a so-called accidental death by using my law of gravity, I'd be able to retire in style."

"That would be an option assuming you ever get around to retiring," said Joel.

"You have me there. I'll probably still be working long after I'm dead," said Lou. "Anyway, I think we have enough to go with murder on this one. We'll let the law work out the details. For one thing, they'll need to go back and dust all those balls for fingerprints. There's a joke in there, but I can't use it."

As the intense crowd reaction spawned by the contents of Koller's will descended further into chaos, Joel's attention was elsewhere. The young lawyer's ability to juggle multiple stimuli was legendary. It was a handy skill, but also a trait which contributed to his inability to concentrate his full attention on passing the bar exam. Even now, Joel's thoughts were simultaneously focused on the past and the present. On the one hand, he was mulling over Lou Edgerton's insightful "Law of Gravity." On the other he was mentally applying that maxim to the Koller case. Lou's law was pertinent in that it highlighted an anomaly.

"Senior citizens fall forward," the maxim declared. Given that notion, it followed that Esau's death was no accident. Someone younger and stronger had put the old scoundrel on his back and held him down, not to mention obliterating his face with repeated stabs. Joel shuddered as he recalled the gruesome autopsy photos and he jumped when Anne elbowed him.

"Earth to Joel," she said.

Chapter 40

Comparing Notes
(Morning)

If not for Anne's persistent nudging, Joel's thoughts might have remained in the past. Inside the chaotic confines of the Keystone conference room, the uproar continued while Anne tried again to get the lawyer's attention.

"Earth to Joel," she repeated.

"Sorry," said Joel as his attention returned to the present. "You were saying..."

"I said, *what a zoo*," she repeated.

Joel surveyed the room.

"It's a zoo alright," he agreed.

"Speak up," she yelled.

"Come with me," Joel said as he took her arm and pulled her out of the line of fire.

The two passed through noisy clusters of upset relations until they reached a point of relative calm near the front of the room, whereupon Joel invited Anne to study the crowd.

"Notice anything?" he whispered.

"Everybody is on their feet and going nuts," answered Anne.

"Not everybody."

She followed Joel's gaze. "Son of a bitch," she whispered.

"Well," Joel smiled, "a bitch anyway."

Ruth remained in her front-row seat, smiling sedately and immobile as a marble statue, while the rest of the conference room pulsated with distraught energy. Only after order was restored and the crowd began to shuffle out did Ruth stand and take her leave.

Anne and Joel could see Deputy Madge Oxford waiting at the exit door. Anticipating an arrest, they wanted to move closer, but their progress was blocked behind a phalanx of reporters who were trying to detain and interview everyone in reach. So, they were obliged to watch from a distance as Madge stepped aside and let Ruth Koller pass.

"Now what?" asked Anne.

"The cops have their man," said Joel with a shrug.

"But..." Anne began.

"Greeley was seen entering the building on Easter Monday and a search of his pup-tent turned up a handful of typewritten pages which the techs connect to Koller —in other words, Kip was caught with your missing chapter. I'll admit our redhead has a shaky alibi and, as for her failing to react to the reading of her father's will, we've got evidence that she knew what was coming long before my brother-in-law made it public. But—and you didn't hear this from me—young Greeley remains the likely culprit. Come up to Andrew's private office," said Joel as they finally made their way past the cameras and reporters. "We'll explain."

They left the conference room behind and climbed a marble staircase.

"You can see Book Cliffs from up here," said Joel. "And acres of lavender fields. It's the best view in town," he added as they topped the stairs.

Admiring panoramic vistas of the Grand Valley, bathed in mid-morning light and framed in a broad expanse of floor to ceiling windows, they walked along the highly-polished floor until they reached a handsome mahogany door. Joel was about to knock when the door opened and Deputy Phil Ellis emerged carrying a file box.

"Counselor," he nodded. "Miss Scriptor. Excuse us please."

Two more deputies followed Phil into the hallway. All of them were carrying file boxes and Anne watched as they headed for the elevator.

"Crap," said Phil and the trio passed the elevator and started down the stairs.

"Out of order, I guess," said Joel.

"There's a lot of that going around," said Anne.

"Here's Andy," said Joel and he escorted Anne inside his brother-in-law's palatial office.

Clearly, I should have gone to law school, Anne thought as the ostentatious door clicked shut behind them.

"Have a seat, Miss Scriptor," said Andrew. "So nice to meet you at last. Joel has been unswerving in his praise of your work and that of Mr. Sands. Do have a seat, please. Anyone need a beverage?"

"Coffee for me," said Joel.

"Herbal tea?" Anne asked tentatively.

"Of course," said Andrew as he pressed a buzzer beneath the lip of his massive conference table.

"Yes sir," a door opened and a smartly dressed young man appeared.

"Two coffees—black and bring hot water and the tea basket please," instructed Andrew. "And some scones I think."

When everyone was settled around the broad conference table with their drinks and scones at hand, Andrew began his summation.

"Our law enforcement colleagues have taken all the pertinent files, but I of course have total recall of the details. And Joel believes you may have questions. Do you have questions?"

"I absolutely have questions," said Anne, "but I'm uncertain how to begin."

"I find it is best," said Andrew as he brought his fingertips together to form a tent, "to start at the beginning. *Begin at the beginning, the King said gravely, and go on till you come to the end: then stop.*"

The quotation made Anne smile. Moments ago, as the reading of Koller's will had erupted into chaos and a likely suspect hadn't been arrested, she felt as if she'd fallen down a rabbit hole. But now—as she listened to Andrew reciting a well-remembered passage from *Alice in Wonderland*—she was once again in familiar territory.

"In the beginning," she said, "there were six suspects—five relations and one stranger. Ray the repairman eliminated himself by explaining the elevator situation—hmmm..." She paused.

"What is it?" asked Joel.

"Nothing, only it's strange just now when the deputies were leaving with the boxes. They saw the sign on the elevator, but they never even tried the button."

"Meaning...?" asked Joel.

"Nothing I guess," said Anne. "Anyway, with Ray eliminated as a suspect, we turned to the family. Jacob, the angry brother, had an alibi for the time of the murder and so did Isaac, the inept son who was floundering in the basement. That left the daughters, step- and otherwise: Ruth, Juliet, and Millie. Juliet allegedly died in Glenwood Springs in the early hours of April 22—but that scenario doesn't hold water. Which leaves all three women and wait a minute..." Anne opened her notebook and flipped through the pages.

Joel and Andrew exchanged a glance and Andrew mouthed the words 'What now?'

Anne continued to look through her notebook. "Where—where is it? Where—ah here it is. Listen to this from our notebooks: R. (that's Ruth) primary residence Aspen, but her whereabouts unknown for the year 2015 were as follows: September 25 to December 10. For year 2016 it was January 3 to March 10; then March 25 to June 2; then September 27 to December 9; and then the pattern repeats for 2017; and same again this year, except she came back to Aspen on March 17."

"I don't get it," said Joel.

"Spring break," said Anne.

Joel and Andrew looked at each other.

"Look, Aloe College is an expensive private school and it's on the quarter system. This pattern of dates, the dates when Ruth was and was not in Aspen, that's a college girl's schedule. Fall, Winter, and Spring Quarters—holiday breaks—summers off. That's a schedule Millie should be following, not her older sister." Anne paused and let her information sink in.

"What does that mean...?" Joel began.

"Look," said Anne as she stood up and crossed to the whiteboard. "The cops haven't arrested Ruth for killing her father. But, suppose they did—what would be their evidence?"

"Deposit box records, surveillance tapes," Andrew began. "Circumstantial evidence that she used her charms to insinuate herself into the bank's secure areas and got an unauthorized look at Esau's will."

"She didn't stand up when the will was read..." Joel added.

"Well, guys, I'm no lawyer—you should see my office, I use a bedspread for a desk—but never mind that..." she paused and blushed. "Now, what would you say are the odds that, if Ruth Koller is arrested, she walks? What are the chances that, based on the evidence the cops think they have, a judge would let her post bail?"

"Fifty-fifty," said Andrew.

"Maybe more like seventy-thirty," said Joel.

"I knew it. I knew it. I could feel in my bones that the cops missed it." Before either man could respond, Anne was drawing an illustration on the board. "Look, this is Colorado." She drew a lop-sided rectangle. "Here's Aspen. And the crazy counties—scratch that—they're too crazy to draw—so let's concentrate on the towns. Here's Denver. Here's us in Grand Junction. Here's Collbran. Here's Carbondale. Here's Glenwood Springs. That looks about right. Now I'll add our suspects." She switched from a black marker to a red one. "Here's R.—we all know who that is—let's put her in Aspen for the time being. Then here's Koller's brother Jacob in Carbondale and his idiot son Isaac in Delta City—he's still under arrest, right? Then let's put Juliet—our little schemer—in Collbran. And for good measure we'll put repairman Ray in Delta City too—he says the jail food agrees with him. So, there's your picture."

"Wait a minute," said Joel. "Where's Millie?"

"That, my friends," said Anne, "is what you might call the 64,000-dollar question."

Chapter 41

Interstate 70
(Noon)

The moment Anne left the lawyers behind, she set off to drive from Grand Junction to Glenwood Springs in record time and she figured she had just the car to do it.

Forsaking her old Nissan truck, she'd rented a brand-new highway-appropriate vehicle (it was made in Korea, she noted) and (consistent with her agreement with her husband-to-be) she'd used the Hyundai's Bluetooth connection to call Trinidad and tell him precisely where she was going.

In short, she was on a mission.

So, she'd opted for the rapid pace of Interstate 70 although, as usual, she marveled that she was the only one adhering to the 75-mph speed limit.

"Where's a cop when you need one?" she said out loud.

"Speaker phone." She jumped to hear Trinidad's voice. "You have the speaker phone on," he said—his voice emanating from the general direction of the Hyundai's stereo array.

"No way," she insisted.

"Way," he laughed.

"How long have I—don't tell me you were listening to me singing!"

"I admit that I was."

"Well…?"

"Not bad," he said, "I like your voice when you sing along with the radio. I groove on the harmony."

Groove, she thought, *I suppose that could have been a verb—back in 1996—* but aloud she said, "Thanks, but I turned the radio off because I needed to concentrate. And hearing your voice is way too distracting—you know why. And I see a knot of semi-trucks ahead and it looks like these big boys have formed an impregnable convoy. So..."

"So okay. You'd better sign off," Trinidad said. "Be careful and watch the road."

"Okay," she said.

"And don't do anything stupid."

"Yes, dear," she said. "Just one question."

"What?"

"How the hell do I turn the frigging phone feature off?"

It took Anne three tries to deactivate the function. During the ordeal she accidentally triggered the windshield wipers, activated the dome light, and restarted the radio.

I'll be glad to get back into the Nissan, she thought. *Fewer bells and whistles and an ordinary stick shift—who could ask for more?*

As she drove eastward through the small interstate towns of Parachute, then Rifle, Silt, and New Castle, she was making good time before traffic suddenly ground to a halt. She allowed the rental car to idle for a half-hour before she turned off the ignition and joined other drivers who'd gotten out to stretch their legs.

"Accident up ahead," she overheard someone say.

"How long?" one frustrated motorist asked another.

"No idea," was the reply.

Anne sighed, returned to her vehicle, rolled down the windows, and thought through her Glenwood itinerary. Assuming the accident cleared up in time, she might still make her 2:30 appointment with Stacy Musgrave and Kat Francis. The two Aloe College juniors had been classmates of Millie Koller and were, reportedly, the last two people to see Millie before she unaccountably disappeared. At four, Anne was scheduled for a session with

Millie's college counselor on the Aloe campus. At 5:30 she would meet with the hospital staff to lay the legend of Juliet and Preston Sturgis to rest. It was a brisk agenda, but she'd programmed all the addresses into the Hyundai's navigator, so she was certain she could manage. When she was done, she'd treat herself to a soak in a hot springs and a good night's sleep in a luxury hotel.

Another errand was nibbling at her memory, but she couldn't recall what. Something important, she imagined, but—if it was truly important—she figured it would come to her.

Anne was checking her watch when the movements of her fellow motorists suggested that the accident had cleared. She fired up the Hyundai. Ten minutes later she was back on schedule.

Arriving in Glenwood, she coasted to the first address, parked, and met with Stacy and Kat in the cozy common room of the lavish condo they shared with three other women. The two coeds sat on a plush sofa and Anne settled into an overstuffed easy chair. Nice digs, she thought to herself, as she remembered the cramped freshman dormitory room she'd endured at The University of Arizona.

Sitting side-by-side, their shoulders touching in a charming show of mutual support, the youngsters told Anne their story.

On the night before Millie fell off everyone's radar, the three coeds had been clubbing downtown—drinking and dancing. When they parted ways, Millie was last seen walking toward the Grand Avenue pedestrian bridge. Stacy and Kat hadn't been ready to call it a night and Millie had looked tired they recalled.

"We should have gone with, I guess," said Kat.

"As if we would know she was about to vanish," Stacy said.

"What can you tell me about Millie as a person?" Anne asked. The two women spent twenty minutes talking about what a diligent student Millie was and how she took her studies seriously. The two of them were exceedingly pretty and impossibly young. *Was I ever that pretty? Was I ever so young?* Anne wondered. The women were diffident and reluctant to say anything uncomplimentary about their missing friend. Anne knew the drill, the old sorority side-shuffle, if you can't say something nice about a person... After a lengthy silence, Anne was about to end the interview when Stacy let out a lingering and audible sigh.

"Well, since you asked, Mill was kinda quiet," began Stacy.

"Sometimes..." Kat added.

"Yeah, sometimes," Stacy agreed.

"And at other times she was...? Anne prompted.

"Well," said Stacy, "she could be—what should we say?" She looked to Kat. Clearly, they were struggling to find the right words.

"Play-acting," said Kat.

"Pretending to be playing a part," Stacy clarified.

"Like in a play," Kat added unnecessarily.

"Do you mean like a character in a play?" Anne asked.

"Sort of, but not exactly that," said Kat and she bit her lower lip.

"It was more like she was just a different version of herself," said Stacy. "A different person but also the same—sometimes her voice would—it's difficult to explain exactly."

"So, it was like this," said Kat. "One day she was Mill—the person we all knew. And then a day later she would show up pretending to be someone else. Usually, it was entertaining and funny."

"Until it wasn't," said Stacy.

Then both women grew silent.

"I understand this is difficult to talk about," said Anne. "How often did she pretend?"

"Maybe once or twice a quarter," said Stacy and the two coeds nodded to one another.

"Or more often if she was drunk," said Kat.

"Well, that's true—a couple of drinks and this entirely different person would pop up."

"She would pretend to be other people when she was drunk?" asked Anne.

"That's right—at least the drunk part is right," said Kat.

"How do you mean?" asked Anne.

"Well Mill would be drunk all right, but sometimes I got a feeling..."

"What sort of feeling?" Anne asked.

"It felt like she wasn't pretending."

Anne closed her notebook and thanked the women for their coopera-tion. "I'll need that back," the detective said.

When Anne first arrived, she'd handed the photograph to Kat, who passed it to Stacy, who continued to hold it throughout the interview—unwilling, it seemed, to surrender the image of their missing roommate.

"Okay," Stacy said. The young woman sighed, took a final look at the picture, and handed it over.

Anne resisted asking whether Millie, drunk or sober and in the throes of her personality shifts, went so far as to ask others to address her by a differ-ent name. She thought she knew the answer, but even if Millie's friends had noticed such behavior, Joel or any lawyer worth his salt, would dismiss such observations as hearsay. Anne needed an expert opinion from someone with credentials—an opinion which she hoped to obtain at the college.

Aloe College was named for its founder Alphonse Aloe, not the medic-inal plant. Parking near the campus was an adventure, but Anne finally located a visitor's lot. Consulting a kiosk containing a "you-are-here" map, she found Alphonse Hall. The brick building was home to the college's student services complex, if three small cubicles crammed together in a tiny alcove can be labeled a complex.

Each cubicle housed a desk—one desk for admissions, one for financial aid, and one for counseling. Anne was feeling sardonic as she imagined that their collective motto might be something like: "We get you in, we get you money, and—when you screw up—we're here to help."

The counselor on duty was J. J. Casey, a latent hippie with hair, beard, tie-dyed shirt, and sandals to match. Dr. Casey was the one and only staff member. If—God forbid—the entirety of Aloe's enrollment had a crisis at the same exact moment, the man's caseload would be 1,200.

For some, such an overwhelming client-to-counselor ratio might be a source of anxiety, but Dr. Casey's relaxed and jovial manner revealed no signs of stress. Anne respected his profession and she was familiar with the challenges and benefits of therapy. In her first two years at The University of Arizona, she'd made frequent use of the counseling center and she suspected she probably still held the campus record for most tissues used in a single semester.

She knew the drill: acknowledge that you have a problem; accept responsibility; build a fence...

Think about something else, she told herself.

Dr. Casey offered tea, which Anne gratefully accepted. There was a wide desk and an overflowing bookcase in the tiny cubicle, but somehow the counselor had managed to squeeze in two comfy easy chairs without making the space seem cramped. However, she had no idea how he managed to brew tea there without setting the place on fire.

"So, Detective," he examined Anne's newly printed business card and sported a broad grin. "You must be aware that information about a specific student is privileged communication and, even though there are ways around that verboten, my guess is you don't have a warrant. So, other than offering you another cup of tea and discussing the weather, I'm not sure how I can help."

"Can you maybe entertain a hypothetical?" Anne ventured.

"That might be an interesting dance," said Dr. Casey. "And it might work, but only if you lead."

"Glad to," said Anne. "Now suppose—hypothetically—that instead of a specific student named Millie Koller, you've been counseling a group of, let us say, two clients."

"Go on..." said the counselor.

"And suppose instead of using two file folders," Anne continued, "you found it possible to keep all your notes in a single folder."

"We're dancing pretty close for our first time around the floor," he cautioned.

"Well," said Anne, "the lights are low, so maybe no one will notice."

"Hmm," he said. "As it happens, I can neither confirm nor deny your hypothetical scenario, but I will tell you this: if I were counseling this alleged client, I wouldn't be foregoing two file folders in favor of using one. In the case I'm thinking of, I'd say the ratio was more like four to one."

Anne raised an eyebrow. It was a reaction which, Dr. Casey, who was skilled in assessing nonverbal cues, could hardly misinterpret.

"As many as that?" she asked.

"That we know of," he added.

Chapter 42

Valley Vista
(Late Afternoon)

Anne hustled across town to make her final appointment. It was near closing time and the traffic on 19th Street was brutal, so she was running late. She'd called Valley Vista Hospital this morning and asked a simple question, but no one had been willing to talk to her over the phone.

Although she arrived on time, the chief of nursing had been called away to deal with a trauma emergency. Anne had to wait an hour and a half to talk to the woman. After reading the same magazine three times, she rummaged through her handbag.

"Miss Scriptor?" The nurse interrupted her thoughts. "This way, please." Anne followed, gathering her patience and glancing at her wristwatch. Seated in the nurse's office, it only took a moment for Anne to ask her question and receive the answer she expected.

Not a single soul had died at the hospital on the morning of April 22. There was no record of ever admitting a middle-aged woman named Juliet Sturgis, let alone any new mother who had subsequently expired giving birth to a premature infant.

For Anne, those facts settled the matter, but it took another hour to convince the hospital that she was satisfied and wasn't going to make trouble.

"This is clearly a case of mistaken identity on my part," she assured the nurse more than once. "I must have gotten my story wrong."

It was well after 8:30 by the time Anne entered the hospital's parking structure. As she climbed the dark stairs to retrieve her car, she passed a security guard coming down.

"Your Hyundai?" he asked.

"Yes," she said. "Is there a problem?"

"You tell me," he said.

Someone had used white shoe polish to write the word "STOP" in capital letters across her windshield. The security guard took Anne's name and license number, then the two of them stood there in the darkness, staring at her car, until his gruff manner dissolved.

"Can't drive like that," he said. "Wait here."

Moments later, he returned, carrying a length of hose. He found a spigot, used a master key to unlock it, and hosed off the windshield.

"Not perfect," he said.

"It's much better," she said. "Thank you."

"Welcome," he said. "Lucky it's pretty fresh, so it comes off easy. This ain't typical of our town, so I'm sorry."

"No worries," said Anne. "And thanks for your help."

She sat in the car watching the guard disconnect and re-roll the hose. She was about to start the Hyundai and head for the pool when he tapped on her window.

"Drive slow," he said. "And I'll walk you down and punch you out. No way are you payin' for parkin' today."

"Thanks again," Anne smiled as she guided the Hyundai down the structure ramps and passed beneath the up-raised barrier arm. It was dark and she was glad to have his company. *Stir a hornet's nest*, she thought, *and see what happens.*

Once clear of the parking structure, she began to relax. It was a relief to think of ending her extremely long day with a dip in one of Glenwood's famous hot springs pools, followed by a good night's sleep far above the train tracks at the Hotel Colorado. When Trinidad had suggested these amenities, she'd objected on the grounds of extravagance.

"No worries," Trinidad had told her. "The pool is only a ten-buck admission after nine in the p.m. and, as for spending the night in luxury, the hundred and a half room charge won't break the bank. Besides, nothing is too good for someone who aspires to be the future Mrs. T.B. Sands."

"Keep throwing cash my way," she grinned. "And see what happens."

"One can only pitch and hope," he laughed.

By the time she finished up at the hospital and drove across town to the pool, it was five past nine. In less than an hour, everything would shut down, so she paid her ten dollars, picked up a company towel and padlock, and hurried to the locker room. Wearing her bathing suit as underwear had been a stroke of genius. In a matter of moments, she crammed her cellphone into her pants pocket, hung her street clothes in a locker, and pinned the key to her towel. Donning her swim cap, she draped the towel over one shoulder, slipped on her water sandals, hurried to the pool door, and stepped into the night.

It was springtime in the Rocky Mountains, but the evening was chilly and clouds of steam rose from the broad pool and small therapy basin. The skier crowd was gone and the summer tourists had not yet arrived in droves so the place was absolutely deserted. She padded across the cold bricks to reach the nearest entry point. Placing her towel on a dry spot, she slipped out of her sandals, grasped the handrail, climbed down the submerged stairsteps, and eased into the thermal oasis.

The water temperature had to be over 100 degrees. Crouching down, Anne settled into the soothing water until her chin rested on the surface. Feeling buoyant, she bounced her feet along the shallow bottom until she reached the nearest water jet. She punched the power button and spun around to fold her tired body into a molded seat while a hot vortex of pulsating water and wafting steam enveloped her.

Invigorating, she told herself. *Or should I say enraptured? Yes, that's it.*

Sighing, she surrendered to the whirlpool's embrace. Every inch of her body, from the neck down at least, was caressed and celebrated. As for her head, though it was exposed to the night air, it was occupied with searching for memories of the last time she'd felt so thoroughly saturated with bliss.

"That was easy," she said aloud. She had only to think of the many mornings she'd been awakened by Trinidad's gentle kisses. Anne closed her eyes. She was winding down from a busy day of sleuthing. The bubbling water jets spawned a relaxing cascade of white noise and soon her mind was drifting.

So, she thought, *Ruth Koller is a vessel of multiple personalities.*

That would explain much. Disowned by her father, Ruth had somehow been free to impersonate her sister Millie and had attended Aloe College in the younger woman's place with no one the wiser. Who was to say when she showed up for orientation with sufficient documentation that she was not Mildred Alice Koller? Probably nobody there had ever met the real Millie. Her father, believing he was supporting his youngest step-daughter, had asked no questions of college officials and, best of all, he'd continued to send barrels of money.

At last, disparate tidbits of information gleaned by Anne's study of the Koller family were beginning to fall into place. Unlike her sisters, Millie had been an indifferent student who hadn't mastered her cursive lessons. Anne reasoned that Ruth couldn't have risked exposing her distinctive handwriting by responding to the old man's letters, let alone answering his periodic phone calls. But ignoring him had only seemed to make him more diligent in his support. In snubbing her father, Ruth was probably acting in her own self-interest, but she must somehow have also sensed that even the virtuous Millie would have adopted a standoffish posture once she was free of her step-father's influence.

As for Millie's fate, Anne had no doubt that Ruth would have done whatever was necessary to make the substitution work. She might, at first, have tried to persuade her step-sister to cooperate, but in the end, there was only one way Ruth could be assured of taking Millie's place. Of all the questions

Anne might ask herself, the question of when Millie was forced from the world seemed the easiest to answer.

The doomed girl would have been murdered between the time she left the Aspen manor and the start of freshman orientation in Glenwood Springs. It was only a question of how Ruth had done it, whether anyone had helped her, and where the body was. There were plenty of places between Aspen and Glenwood where a body could be hidden, but one place in particular kept occurring to Anne and she couldn't shake the thought, even though she counseled herself to think about something else.

What secrets, the maturing detective wondered, *might an inquisitive digger discover in old Jacob's rose bed?*

Anne was convinced that, through malice and murder, Ruth had become Millie. And it wasn't a major leap to believe Jacob was somehow involved. So, Ruth was Millie, but her psychosis ran deep and that unholy masquerade may not have been enough. Juliet too may have fallen victim to the intrigues of her step-sister and uncle. Even before she talked with officials at the Valley Vista Hospital, Anne had discovered that Juliet's fairy tale of woe wasn't all it seemed. As a result, she was unsurprised to learn that no one had died at the hospital on the morning of April 22, nor did a premature infant enter the world that day.

No death, no birth, she thought.

How and where the very convincing Collbran "husband" had obtained the infant whom Anne had quieted a few days ago, she didn't like to think. But it'd only taken one phone call to Jack and the baby was with protective services and the man was under arrest for child endangerment and criminal impersonation. There would probably be more charges.

Anne hadn't quite worked out how long Ruth had been playing her dual roles as both Millie and Juliet, but her best guess was the latter substitution had taken place shortly after Juliet walked away from White Quail Manor. Just like Millie's disappearance, the manor was the pivotal point, the hinge on the garden gate of Koller intrigues. It was the fulcrum—the key. Everything that happened to the ill-fated sisters had begun on the Aspen end.

The questing detective surmised that, although Ruth had been cast out by her father, the banished girl must have kept watch over White Quail. Anne had seen photographs of the sprawling grounds. The place couldn't be any more isolated and there would be plenty of places for a determined and resourceful and vengeful person to hide and watch—especially a discarded woman. No wonder Phillip and Esau had felt that the forest was watching. Anne had come to see Ruth as manifestly persistent—a determined individual who was completely capable of initiating and maintaining a prolonged surveillance—absolutely crazy, but also undeniably capable.

So, Anne mused as she lounged in the steaming water, *Ruth as Millie makes sense. Millie is missing and Ruth has taken her place.*

It had been a bit harder to imagine Ruth as Juliet until Anne hit upon a notion. On a hunch, the fledgling detective had decided to test the idea. Delayed at Valley Vista earlier that afternoon, she'd searched through her handbag for a sheet of Aloe College class notes, supposedly recorded by Millie and obtained from her friend Kat. Sitting in the hospital waiting room, she'd had time to compare Millie's notes with a page photocopied from Juliet's handwritten journal. It had only taken a moment to confirm that Millie's notes and Juliet's journal had been written by the same person, so that Millie was Ruth and Ruth was also Juliet. And that had to mean there was yet another body out there somewhere.

As Anne's mind steadily relaxed, more clues slipped into focus. Lounging in the calming clutches of the healing waters, she gained a rising sense of context and guessed what must have happened.

On the night Juliet marched into the snow and lambasted the manor and cursed her step-father, Ruth must have been hovering nearby. As Juliet fled, Ruth would have followed her sister, maybe even made a show of comforting the distraught girl.

Could Juliet's death have been an accident?

If Anne's deductions were valid, there was a chance that Juliet had died in her step-sister's arms, her young life cut short by the cold and a broken heart. That was a romantic notion and, moreover, such a distressing trauma might have been what caused Ruth to snap.

There in the mountain snow, was Ruth somehow compelled to trade places with her dead sister? Did Ruth become Juliet on that fateful night—put on her sister's sodden dress, take off her own shoes, and wander into the night to be found by the hero truck driver?

If it happened that way, Juliet's entire journey, everything chronicled in her heartfelt notebook had really been Ruth's adventure—the hospital, the seaside wedding, the gang-rape, the railroad tracks, the nunnery, the prison, and all the rest.

How many years would it have taken for those things to happen?

Too many—therefore Anne found herself forced to accept that Ruth, writing in the journal as Juliet, had simply made much of it up.

The stories of Juliet's library malfeasance and her having been severely punished—those were at least partially true. But those things may have happened to Ruth, not Juliet. Who was to say that Juliet's tale of fending off her step-father's advances was not merely a fantasy of wishful thinking on the part of a damaged Ruth who'd been unable to escape her father's lust?

Both girls had suffered similar fates at the hands of their appalling father. It would have been natural enough to transfer such distressed feelings and just as easy to blend those raw emotions into a single, albeit mercurial personality. If Anne substituted Ruth for Juliet, the story of finding the Koller novel in Page and making her way across Grand Mesa to Collbran, that part was probably true for Ruth masquerading as Juliet. It would explain how a conniving multiple personality managed to invent a wedding and lure or seduce the Sturgis character into staging that baby show at Chauncey's Diner. Maybe Preston Sturgis really was somebody's husband. Maybe he didn't know Ruth was not the true Juliet. Hopefully CPS and the Mesa County sheriff could sort things out and, if Preston was an innocent bystander, maybe he'd skate.

Even though she was sinking further into a relaxed state as the warm water soothed her, Anne was still nursing a grudge about Collbran and Preston and the baby. And she was also wrestling with a recurring and nagging feeling that, although portions of her thinking were resolving into crystal clarity, she'd nevertheless forgotten something important.

What the hell was it?

Chapter 43

Comfort Zone
(Evening)

Relaxing in the hot springs pool, Anne revisited her "to-do" list. She'd followed-up on the Rockfall Danger song. She'd talked to the coeds and the hospital nurse, and she'd danced with Dr. Casey.

What was missing?

As she'd done with the two coeds, she'd shown Ruth's photograph to the counselor whose audible sigh suggested a spark of familiarity—or maybe, like every other man, he was merely feeling the stirrings of an erection. She'd made the rounds with the sultry photo and, just as she suspected, everyone agreed that the stunning redhead was Millie. The coeds had recognized her. So had the counselor, although he'd implied that it took at least four folders to hold Millie's story. Assuming he was counting Millie as one, Juliet as two, and Ruth as three—that still left one personality unaccounted for.

Anne was continuing to ponder these things even as her unconscious mind seemed to prod her with the nagging feeling that she'd forgotten one of her errands. She closed her eyes and sought to clear her mind.

It was late and she was the sole occupant of the sprawling mountain complex. The main pool, where on a less hurried day she'd once swum laps, was about half a block long. Although the open water was reputed to be maintained at a constant 100 degrees Fahrenheit, the night air had grown chilly.

As a result, both the main pool and the smaller, and much warmer, therapy basin were becoming steadily obscured by an ever-increasing bank of steam and fog.

Languishing in the heat and mist, she allowed the water jets to caress her. In fifteen minutes, it would be 10 o'clock—closing time—and she was certain the staff would be glad to be rid of their final customer. Suddenly, Anne gulped and shook her head as she remembered the calypso band.

"Damn," she said aloud.

She should be making wedding plans. But, instead of choosing a band and a venue, compiling a guest list, and planning a reception, her thoughts kept returning to the fantastic events of the past few weeks. The case was troubling. Old man Koller's murder was still unsolved and the investigation had turned up a pair of scoundrels, a dead mother, two daughters missing, and a heavenly body possessed by a Devilishly splintered personality.

How deep does this sordid tale go? she asked herself.

She was lost in speculation until a nearby voice jolted her back to the present.

"My daughter needs your help." The voice came from the deck above her.

"Pardon," Anne said as she reached back to turn off the jets.

"She needs your help," the voice repeated.

Anne pushed away from the pool wall and pivoted in the shallow water until she could make out the figure of a woman standing on the deck. The woman was covered from neck to ankles in a full-length robe. Her hair was obscured by a swim cap and she wore tinted horn-rimmed glasses. Anne tried to study the face, but the lenses were fogged over and she couldn't read the features.

"Mrs. Koller?" Anne ventured the name of the woman she knew to be dead.

"I prefer Mrs. Hapsen," the woman said. Her voice was husky.

"Of course," said Anne. "How can I help, Mrs. Hapsen?"

"It's not me who needs you," the woman intoned, as though the act of speaking made her weary. She remained totally motionless as if rooted to the deck. "It's my daughter."

"Which one?" asked Anne as she stole a quick glance in the direction of the bathhouse hoping to see somebody else, anyone else, coming out to take a late-night soak.

"All of them," came the reply—not husky this time, but also not womanly. It was a deep sound, almost animal in tone.

"And how do you suggest I go about helping...?" Anne nearly added "the dead," but she caught herself and let the truncated question stand.

"You need to stop," the woman said.

"Stop?" Anne asked.

"Stop what you're doing," said the woman as the night wind shifted and steam began to envelop her.

Must be getting colder, Anne thought but aloud she inadvertently said, "Must be getting closer."

"Too close," the woman declared.

In the silence which followed, Anne pivoted and swam further away, feeling the need to put distance between her and this apparition. When she reached a cooler portion of the pool, the detective turned and treaded water. The steam had overwhelmed the therapy basin and the deck was also obscured. If the woman was still there, Anne couldn't see her.

"Mrs. Hapsen?" she asked. "Hortense," she shouted, but there was no reply.

Perplexed by the silence and unable to perceive the figure, Anne looked beyond the steam and focused on the distant bathhouse doorway. To reach the public lockers, the woman would have to walk back across the bricked deck and open the door. The door itself was featureless and dark, but its margins were clearly outlined by light from the changing rooms beyond. Anne stared at the door. By all rights, she should hear something and see a flash of light when it opened and the woman went inside.

But there was no sound and the door remained motionless. Whatever path the woman had followed to arrive at poolside and depart again, the route was neither apparent nor typical. For all intents and purposes, the mysterious visitor had vanished. A misty rain began to fall and, although the temperature in the pool remained sufficiently hot to generate healthy columns of steam, Anne felt a sudden chill and her teeth were beginning the chatter as she swam back toward the stairs.

"File folder number four," she said aloud as she emerged into the cold air, slipped on her water sandals, and began to towel off. Walking briskly back to the bathhouse, she became aware of something clinging to the sole of her foot. She stopped, took off her left sandal, and extracted a bit of pasteboard. She replaced the sandal and, gripping the pasteboard tightly, rushed toward the bathhouse door.

Inside, she sat on a damp bench and examined the pasteboard. It was a blue rectangle, slightly smaller than a 3x5 card, with blanks on top for author and title, and three columns underneath chronicling the date due, borrower name, and date returned.

Anne stared a moment more at the library book card, then she hurriedly opened her locker and grabbed her cell phone. Trinidad might already be on his way home, but he was more likely to be 200 miles away, not to mention 35,000 feet in the air, so her text to Jack was succinct: "Carbondale Library ASAP. Search warrant. Arrest warrant Ruth Koller. Leaving G. Springs now. Call me. Meet u there."

Chapter 44

Roaring Fork
(Midnight)

Anne activated the speaker phone and filled Jack in as she drove to Carbondale.

The detective was leaving behind a king-sized bed at the Hotel Colorado. There'd be no luxurious shower surrounded by body jets, no lavish buffet breakfast. Instead, she was driving through the dark and talking in the direction of the car radio as she wheeled the compact Korean car up Highway 82. It was a good road which paralleled the Roaring Fork River and the river's current was audible at times, but invisible in the dark.

Anne was traveling thirteen horizontal miles and seven-tenths of a mile vertically up into the Colorado night and those numbers were important because, in her haste to leave Glenwood, she'd failed to fill the gas tank.

The low-fuel indicator blinked to life the moment she was beyond the urban lights of Glenwood. It was a persistent amber icon—a little miniature glowing gas pump that seemed to mock her as she talked with Jack.

She'd left the intermittent rain behind, but it was still cold outside. The sky was crystal clear and the full moon illuminated the summit of Mount Sopris. Topped by a frosty mantle of springtime snow, the peak shone with a pearly white luster and so brightly that it seemed to float like a gigantic kite above the dark horizon.

"I'm gonna need more to go on to get them warrants," said Jack. "Judge Smyth is leanin' in our direction, but he finds your logic a bit sketchy. What's our probable cause?"

"I guess a dead woman taking the air at a hot springs pool sounds kind of fishy, huh?" Anne suggested.

"You might say so," said Jack.

"Is this Judge Smyth we're talking about?" Anne asked. "Judge Purdy Smyth from Delta City?"

"The same," said Jack.

"Heck," she addressed her unseen colleague who was taking part in the tenuous conference call that faded in and out as Anne wound her way toward Carbondale. "Ain't that our judge?"

"That's him all right," said Jack.

"So, we need help from Judge Smyth—the same one who'll be marrying Trinidad and me, if and when we ever get out from under this Koller case and get the wedding planned. Can we get him on this line?" asked Anne.

"Kinda irregular," said Jack. "But maybe so. Hold on."

"Heck," said Anne as she thought aloud, "I'll bet I can charm the old fox into granting us a..."

"You know he's already connected," warned Jack.

"Oh, hello," said Anne.

"Old fox speaking," said Judge Smyth. "Who's this on the line?"

"Sorry," said Anne. "It's Anne Scriptor."

"The better half of the Sands couple," said the judge. "The pair that wants me to travel up on top of Grand Mesa during mosquito time to solemnize their vows."

"That's us," said Anne.

"Hmm," said the judge. "And now I hear you want our sheriff to convince the Carbondale authorities to execute my warrants."

"Yes, sir," said Anne and Jack simultaneously—both were on the road to Carbondale, Anne driving south and Jack traveling east with Deputy Oxford at the wheel of their patrol car.

"Tell me, young people," the judge continued, "is anyone within the sound of my voice talking on a phone while operating a motor vehicle?"

"Not me, your honor," said Jack.

Anne was silent.

"Pull over," said the judge. "Then we'll talk."

"I'm on the shoulder, your honor," said Anne.

"Good," said the judge. "Now, although I like to think at my age that I'm somewhat immune from the charms of Miss Scriptor, I'm nevertheless inclined to issue both the arrest warrant and the search warrant. In fact, my unhappy clerk is standing at my door as we speak, with his traveling clothes fitted over his pajamas, with instructions to transmit the same electronically. I just want to make certain I understand this request of yours to search the Carbondale Branch Library. They'd be closed now, I reckon. Can't this wait until daylight?"

"We have reason to believe that the subject of the arrest warrant is on the premises," said Jack.

"After hours?" asked the judge.

"We believe so, your honor," said Jack.

"Well," said Judge Smyth, "belief is a powerful mechanism, not to mention a motivator of action. For example, I believe that if I am compelled to ascend to the top of Grand Mesa before the middle of July, I will be eaten alive by mosquitoes. Do you catch my drift, Miss Scriptor?"

"Yes, sir, your honor," said Anne.

"Good—just so we understand one another." There was a pause and then the judge returned to the line. "My signatures are in place. The ink is dry and the clerk has mounted his steed, which I believe is a mellow-sounding four-cylinder Aprilia Shiver 900 by the sound of it. He'll be off in a moment and traveling as fast as two wheels can carry him. Now, can I do anything else for you folks before I go back to bed?"

"No thank you, your honor," said Jack.

"Goodnight," said Anne.

Chapter 45

Overdue
(Cantate Sunday)

The sound of someone playing the piano reached the officers surrounding the Carbondale Branch of the Garfield County Public Libraries. The place was dark inside and the flashing lights of police vehicles, which encircled the building on all sides, seemed unable to penetrate the front windows. Reflecting back a constant stream of pulsating illumination, the site shimmered with animated light, setting the building's towering array of ribbed channel glass ablaze with ricochets of red and blue.

The officers on the perimeter were tense. Lieutenant Sanchez, the Carbondale officer in charge, stood beside his colleague, Delta County Sheriff Jack Treadway, as the two brother officers stared down the empty expanse of Sopris Avenue.

"Where's this Scriptor chick?" asked the lieutenant. It was the third time he'd made the identical inquiry.

"On her way," said the sheriff.

"Out of gas?" Sanchez smirked. "How is that even possible in this century?"

"She'll be here soon," Jack responded.

Five minutes later, a delivery van arrived with the tardy detective in the passenger seat.

"Sorry everyone," Anne said as a female officer fitted her with a ballistic vest of tactical body armor.

"I still don't like this idea," said Sanchez.

"We're convinced the suspect ain't armed," said Jack.

"Based on..." the lieutenant prompted.

"The metal detectors at the entryway," said Jack. "I was first on the scene. When I pulled up, our suspect was on the way in. She spotted me, I challenged her, and she rushed inside."

"You sure those detectors are on?" asked the lieutenant.

In answer, Jack made a radio call to his deputy Madge, who was crouched in riot gear near the front door. "Check it again," the sheriff said.

"Roger that," Madge answered and she pushed the barrel of her carbine toward the margins of the walk-through metal detector. The flickering overhead light testified that the detector was still working.

"No light or sound when the suspect passed through twenty minutes ago. We disabled the annoying beeper," said Jack, "but we kept the light just in case."

"They're closed, so why the hell did the damn library bitch have it on in the first place?" a patrolman asked.

"As you were," growled the lieutenant. "And watch your language. She obviously had it on just so she wouldn't be surprised by an unexpected visitor. Especially one carrying a service revolver—am I right?"

"Bingo," said Jack and then he turned to Anne. "Kiddo, we wouldn't risk this if there was any other way to defuse this situation. She hasn't threatened us, but she did promise to do herself harm if we try to break in. We got her to answer the phone inside and tried to get her to speak to the police negotiator, but she said she'd only talk to you."

"Picking up the conversation where we left off, I guess," said Anne, recalling her poolside visitor.

"You sure about this?" the lieutenant asked. "Deputy Oxford volunteered to go in your place."

"The woman inside knows me by sight," said Anne. "And nobody has to die today, including me, so I'll be careful."

Jack leaned in close for a moment and whispered in Anne's ear, "Glad you don't wear that body armor all the time. I can't get a grip on you to practice my steps and I still plan to dance at your wedding, so for God's sake be careful."

"Intend to," she whispered. "And I'll save you a dance."

The lieutenant tried the telephone again. When there was no answer inside, he picked up a bullhorn and signaled the technicians to fire up the generator and switch on the tower lights.

"Dang!" said Anne. "You sure that's bright enough?"

"We can turn on another bank if you want," the lieutenant said, and the brilliant illumination highlighted his sarcastic smile.

"No thanks," she said. "I can already see every chink in the wall and every grain of concrete as it is."

"Attention, library," said the lieutenant, and the echo from his amplified voice seemed to permeate the night. "Anne Scriptor is here as you requested and she's coming in alone."

There was no verbal response from the dark building, but the piano playing paused for a perceptible beat and then resumed.

"That might be my cue," said Anne, and she started slowly forward holding both hands up to show whoever might be watching that she was carrying no weapon. Without incident, she passed by Madge who knelt next to the detector. Madge gave her a thumbs up, then pressed a finger to her lips and inclined her head toward the main door. Looking closer, Anne could see Officer Friendly and Cozy positioned on opposite sides of the entrance. Cozy perked up her ears as Anne reached the front door and pushed it open.

"Twenty minutes," the lieutenant's amplified voice washed over Anne with a message apparently aimed at the woman closeted inside. "Twenty— and our man comes out again. No exceptions."

Great, thought Anne, *I'm going in a woman, but coming out a man.*

Inside, Anne followed the sound of the piano as she weaved cautiously through the stacks and down a hallway. Reaching a set of double doors, she pushed inside and found herself in a large carpeted room. The surface underfoot was soft and springy, probably a place where kids sprawled on the floor for story time.

Who'd believe tonight's story? she asked herself.

Moving cautiously forward, the resolute detective wrestled with two odd sensations. She was naturally intimidated by the prospect of walking alone into an empty library to face an unstable and possibly homicidal woman. On the other hand, she was equally troubled by the notion of having to explain all this to her disapproving fiancé.

At the far end of the spacious room was a grand piano and at the piano sat the suspect, her red hair cascading across her shoulders. As Anne moved closer, the woman continued playing, seemingly concentrating all her attention on the keyboard. She was a talented performer. She was focused. She was gifted. And she was absolutely naked.

Anne stopped walking and waited. The detective seemed to recognize the piece and reckoned the crescendo was near, but before the performer reached the end, her playing abruptly ceased.

"You came," the nude woman said as she folded a folio of sheet music, then regarded her visitor.

"You asked—I came," said Anne.

"So simple—if only life were so simple." The woman sighed, then whispered, "I'm quite mad, you know?"

"It's a mad world," said Anne, unable to think of anything else to say.

"Too true—so very true," came the reply. "I'm going to stop talking now."

The silence stretched out and Anne was aware of a large clock ticking in the room, unseen on the dark wall.

"Would you mind if I turned on a light?" Anne asked.

"Yes, I'd mind that very much. You think I want to light up this body for a sniper?"

"I don't think anyone wants to shoot you..." Anne began.

"And why ever not? I'm a criminal ain't I? Ain't I a menace to society?"

"Are you?"

"No—not to society writ large. Just to members of my so-called family. To them I'm a menace. Not many of us left now. Just the men. Just Jacob and Isaac—absurdly jealous Jacob, whose envy of his brother reached toxic levels years ago. And poor muddle-headed Isaac, with a classical physique, but a brain the size of a walnut. And, pray tell, what do you think of my brain?" She suddenly flung the question at Anne.

"Your brain?"

"Yes, my brain. As I'm certain you can understand—most people—men in particular—look only at this body." She stood up. "Observe this beautiful façade, these tips, these lits—sorry I've had a bit to drink—I meant to say 'tits and lips,' but you understand. You yourself are quite a beauty, in a girlish sort of way. Men dig that, I hear. Oh, I've been watching you ever since that day you arrived here with your little notepad and your detective calling card."

"That was you? The librarian?" asked Anne, trying to remember the mousy thing who'd led her beyond the stacks to search for Juliet's journal.

"Quite a disguise if I do say so myself," the woman laughed, then paused, and Anne could see that she was drinking from a bottle. "Amazing what impression a gal can create if she's willing to don a cheap wig and forgo make-up and bind these," she cupped her free hand under a breast and took another pull from her bottle. "Simply amazing what a few changes will do and then, of course, there's the expectations of your audience."

"People see what they expect to see," ventured Anne.

"Precisely! I knew you'd understand. I can see you're the right person to talk to. Yes, people expect to see a Plain Jane at the library and so it only takes a few alterations on my part to meet those expectations. Now, my dear, since you're a detective—albeit a fledgling one I understand—and since we have only a few moments remaining—I need you to do something for me. Please recite what you've detected so far and I will instantly evaluate your findings. You may stand if you wish or there's a chair somewhere there against the wall."

"I'll stand I think," said Anne as she glanced briefly behind her, making sure of the exit.

"Very well. Begin please."

"Where...?" Anne asked.

"Don't make me quote Alice in Wonderland—I understand you're familiar with that quotation."

"So," said Anne, "I'll begin at the beginning—at your beginning that is."

"You can't mean my birth? Surely we don't have time to start with that."

"Please don't take this the wrong way," said Anne, "but I'm guessing your actual birth is less relevant than your other—shall we say—your other beginnings?"

"A smart cookie. They said you were a smart cookie. Please continue."

"One beginning for you was Easter 1999—your step-mother's sixty-seventh birthday," Anne suggested. "Seeing her there in the nursing home must have been a shock. You never really knew your own mother and Hortense must have been kind..."

"Kind?" the reply bristled with disgust. "Kind? That woman was a genuine saint—a sacrificial saint who was harnessed to the Devil incarnate."

"Hortense killed herself that summer," said Anne, hoping she correctly remembered the details of the police report chronicling the second Mrs. Koller's suicide.

"Yes," the woman agreed in a voice that suddenly sounded insubstantial in the large room.

"And you were there. You witnessed her death," Anne speculated.

"Yes."

"And so—then you—well I'm a bit unclear on the sequence here..." Anne began, but stopped, uncertain how to proceed.

"Let me help you," said the woman. "Three years passed..." she prompted.

"Three years passed..." Anne contemplated the clue. *How does a mad-woman's mind work? Where will this line of inquiry lead?* The detective decided to guess. "Three years passed before Juliet's wedding in 2002. And honestly, I'm not sure where you were between your step-mother's death and your step-sister's wedding."

"Perfectly okay to drop the step- and refer to Juliet as my sister and are you truly stumped?"

"I'm afraid so," Anne admitted.

"Why, during that time I was doing what I do best, dear," the reply came in fits and starts while the speaker began to twirl around the room. "I—was—dancing."

"Ah," said Anne.

"Ah, indeed—and point and spin and point and spin and point," the twirling woman agreed as she briefly halted in front of Anne and leaned forward so their noses were nearly touching. "Don't you see it?" she asked. "You *must* see it."

Anne wasn't at all certain what she was meant to see, but—as the woman continued circling the room—she didn't take her eyes off the twirling nude.

"You must see and point and spin. You must see and point and spin," the words repeated as the woman danced to the far side of the room and back again, then stopped a few feet away and dropped like a rag doll. First, she went down on her knees and then leaned forward with her arms outstretched in a prostrate prayer position.

Anne knew a bit about ballet from a disastrous summer spent struggling with other hopeless eleven-year-olds trying in vain to master the five basic positions. And she knew something of yoga from a series of adult classes that she somehow never found the time to continue. But her scant knowledge of dance and movement didn't include the antics of a naked maniac who may or may not be suffering from dissociative identity disorder.

Earlier that same day Dr. Casey had spoken in generalities, perhaps hoping that Anne would draw her own conclusions.

"Don't you see it?" he'd asked. "How can I make it clearer? Try this: we don't use the term 'multiple personality' anymore," the counselor told her. "We don't even say 'split personality' for that matter. Those terms are imprecise labels for a rare condition, sometimes brought on by adult trauma such as war, but more often caused by childhood suffering, particularly abuse."

Think about something else, Anne had told herself, but the counselor's office was much too small to escape from the topic at hand. Her expression or her posture must have revealed her feelings because Dr. Casey had asked, "Are you okay?"

"Can we take a break?" the detective suggested.

"Of course," he said rising from his chair. "In fact, believe it or not, I have a back door somewhere between these bookcases. My own private exit, leading to a set of steps which will deposit us onto a lovely grassy quad. We can walk and talk in the open air if you like."

"That would be splendid," said Anne.

The quad had indeed been lovely—a broad expanse of impossibly green grass bordered on all four sides by stately trees. It was an intentional design which contrasted the unusually vibrant lawn with bordering rows of red-bricked campus buildings. Anne had felt that she could breathe out there and, before she asked the counselor to continue his exposition, she leaned down to pluck a blade of grass.

"It's Bermuda, so they tell me," Dr. Casey said. "Some people think it's a weed, but this warm spring weather has caused our little campus to have the greenest lawn in town. So, to continue with our hypothetical discussion, without naming names, here's the thing about a dissociation disorder: you can think of it as an intense form of daydreaming. If a person builds an alternative reality and takes it to the extreme, such fantasizing can lead to a belief that the present world is not real. A person experiencing dissociation disorder can suffer a loss of memory or, more correctly, can invent memories and attribute them to a separate identity. Such thinking creates a self-fulfilling loop with the assumption of other identities becoming a way to escape reality."

"Would such a disorder make a person prone to violence?" Anne asked.

"Not necessarily," said the counselor. "However, the untreated disorder can be, let us say, warped and tilted toward violence if the dissociative individual happens to be taking psychoactive drugs."

"Such as...?

"You name it—cocaine, meth, LSD, cannabis, opioids, even some over the counter stuff, including alcohol. Anything which scrambles the brain can cause an already dissociative person to experience severe mood swings, distorted perceptions, and behavioral abnormalities."

"Behavior abnormalities," Anne said, "such as repeatedly stabbing someone in the face with a nine-inch filleting knife, for example?"

"From your mouth to God's ear," said Casey as he stopped walking. With renewed interest, the counselor turned to consider the seemingly-normal young woman who walked beside him across the campus lawn. The chilling example she'd articulated was out of step with Anne's calm demeanor and the bucolic setting. It took him a moment to absorb the contrast.

"Dr. Casey?" Anne inquired.

"Well, my young friend," Casey sighed, "as a guy who reads the newspaper every day and also watches Fox News and listens to NPR just to make things fair and balanced, I like to think I'm keeping up with events. So, I have to ask, does your interest in our missing student have anything to do with the murder of Esau Koller, the novelist?"

"I can't say," said Anne.

"A succinct, though not particularly useful answer," the counselor frowned. "So, do you mean you don't know? Or do you mean you won't say?"

"Can I level with you?" the detective asked.

"Not sure," said Casey. "Will it get one of us into trouble?"

"Probably me," she admitted.

"Then by all means *don't* level with me," he said and his hearty laughter seemed to fill the empty quad. "Take what little I've given you and do what you must, but spare me the details. I've already said too much and you must see it now."

Dr. Casey had given her plenty to gnaw on and his final words rang in her ears as she stared at the odd woman genuflecting on the carpet. The motionless figure lay before her, face down and seemingly frozen in an utterly submissive pose, like a worshipper praying toward Mecca.

The counselor had told her that she must see it and the now-silent woman had said much the same thing.

What are they trying to tell me? Her thoughts swirled. *What must I see? The woman and I were inches apart a moment ago and I—I—what was it?*

The two had locked eyes for a protracted instant. Anne had stared back, expecting to see a middle-aged redhead, still beautiful but with unmistakable signs of maturity. At that close range, the face would reveal telltale wrinkles, a slight relaxation of once-firm youthful skin, the subtle etching of crows-feet and laugh-lines, things a man would miss, but a woman would notice. Instead, even in the diminished light, Anne had been face-to-face with a far younger woman.

"Who are you?" Anne asked.

And, though the room was dark, Anne sensed, rather than saw, the change in demeanor as the tension seemed to drain from the prostrate form before her.

"Who indeed," Anne repeated, but it was not a question. There was no reply and the young detective abruptly ceased her musing because the woman seemed a bit too still.

Was she breathing?

The carpet might be more forgiving than a hardwood floor, but Anne doubted that its ply and backing were designed to support vigorous dancing and full extension poses. She was on the verge of checking for a pulse when the woman suddenly spoke.

"Can you help me?" the voice was small—almost childlike.

"I think so," said Anne. "What do you need?"

"I don't have no shoes."

"I see," said Anne.

"And it's cold and I got no coat and no place to go and I want to run—I want to run far away. But I'm so cold..."

Anne felt a wave of compassion as she sensed she was no longer communicating with the piano player. The troubled woman was channeling another personality, probably Juliet, because the creature on the floor seemed to be re-living an ill-fated flight through the winter snow to escape from White Quail Manor. The wise-cracking woman had transformed into a forlorn girl and that girl was literally freezing. The silent figure maintained her pose as Anne wriggled out of her body armor, let it fall to the carpet, took off her jacket, and walked tentatively forward.

"Here," Anne said as she extended the jacket. "This isn't much but..."

"Fooled you!" shouted the woman as she deftly sprang to her feet and lunged at Anne with such force that she knocked the startled detective off balance. Anne lost her footing and fell onto her back as the woman pounced to hold her down. Her attacker was incredibly strong and quickly had Anne pinned to the floor. "Should let her go," the woman growled. "Never—she dies. It's not him. Kill only him. Shut up, all of you!" The woman's heaving voice lurched from one short sentence to the other until this internal dialogue ended with a piercing scream.

Anne was uncertain where the weapon came from, but she saw something flash and wondered how light managed to penetrate this dark room at the rear of the library. Instinctively, she glanced behind and saw the hallway door swinging open. She heard a low growl and became aware that a crouching shape had entered the room. Her assailant heard the growl too as she scrambled to her feet, raised her weapon, and turned to face the intruder.

Anne heard strident barking and glimpsed a blur of motion as the on-rushing dog sprang forward. In that same instant, she heard shattering glass and the thud of a rifle shot. Then Anne watched in horror as the madwoman slumped sideways and let her weapon fall. For an instant, the thing rotated in the air, then tumbled point-down toward the floor and the young detective had less than a second to turn aside and cringe as she felt something slide past her ear.

Chapter 46

Pas de Deux
(Three Days Later: Wednesday, May 22)

"In ballet," said Anne as she fingered her bandaged cheekbone and the shank of hair that had been pruned by Ruth's falling weapon, "a dance for two is called a pas de deux. The French is roughly pronounced like the nonsensical English sentence: 'Potty due.'"

She heard herself talking, but suspected she wasn't fully awake. She slurred her words, felt a dollop of drool forming in the side of her mouth, and rolled her head to one side in a vain attempt to focus her vision.

The coming dawn caused the unfamiliar elongated curtains on the unusually tall windows to glow like sheets of phosphorescent gold. Her meds were kicking in and—in her muddled state—she'd been reduced to reciting snatches of dance trivia she'd retained from her dreary weeks as a fledgling ballerina. The supine detective paused and, with some effort, lifted her head and surveyed the hospital room through half-closed eyelids. Sensing that others were near, and convinced that her audience wasn't going anywhere, she laid back and continued her recitation.

"Usually, a man and woman dance together—think sugarplum fairy and prince—but on other occasions—especially in dance classes for eleven-year-olds when there aren't any boys to be had—two women may dance a duet. Two women... That seems familiar. Is my medication working? Am I rambling?"

"No, my love," said Trinidad and he caressed her fingers with care so as not to dislodge the intravenous drip protruding from the back of her hand.

"My ring," said Anne in a sudden panic. "Oh, there it is. Silly me—wrong hand. Am I feeling sleepy? Oh, the nurse, she said to count backwards, but how can I do that when I can't even get up out of bed to turn around so..."

"She's under," said the nurse. "You can stay if you like. The sedative is just a precaution. I understand she's had a shock."

"Yeah," said Trinidad. "She was wrestling with four women and one of them was armed with a fountain pen. It was touch and go."

The nurse raised an eyebrow. "Oh," she said, "you're that smart-aleck detective we've been warned about. They say you and your partner are a regular comedy team—like Abbott and Costello. By the way, where is this partner of yours?"

"Right here," Trinidad said and he offered the nurse a broad grin. "She's right here."

Chapter 47

A Lavender Wedding
(June 9, Pentecost)

As with all weddings, what could go wrong did go wrong.

The original date had to be postponed a week when the chapel and surrounding grounds were booked for a classic car show and square dance clinic. The postponement placed the ceremony on a holy day, a situation which was resolved by moving the starting time to 3 p.m.

Then five dozen sheathes of lavender—which were gathered to decorate the church and which had been carefully harvested, lovingly bundled, and stored in the tool shed at Lavender Hill Farm—were discovered by neighborhood goats and reduced to toothpicks.

"Huh," said the owner when he came to retrieve the wandering herd. "Never known 'em to eat them particular plants. Probably they was after the ribbons."

The wedding rings were lost, then found, then lost again until Trinidad drove two nails into the kitchen wall and hung them there for safe-keeping. The bride's custom-made luminously lavender gown went in for alterations and instantly disappeared. All seemed lost until searchers combed through the cavernous back room of Delta City's Tip-Top Cleaners and discovered the errant gown misfiled on a rack of unclaimed garments due to be recycled to the local thrift shop.

Meanwhile, the groom's stylish cummerbund, which had been ordered online from a Wisconsin supplier, got crossed up with a shipment of turkey calls meant to go to a hunter in Wyoming.

"Don't even think about it," Anne had said as she watched Trinidad finger one of the jet-black shafts of fluted rubber, then try to see if it would stretch enough to encompass his waist.

The wedding invitations were printed on time, but the enterprising printer had taken it upon himself to alter the spelling of "Lavender" by replacing the "e" in the final syllable with an unwelcome "a." The reprint meant that most of the invitations had to be hand-delivered. But, in the tiny village that was no problem and, moreover, the recipients considered the personal touch to be charming.

Trinidad's newly-found sister was unable to attend and his parents got lost and nearly missed the ceremony. The original singer came down with laryngitis and the last-minute substitute challenged the harpist to discover an entirely different key. And so on.

And, as with all weddings, every obstacle was overcome and all eyes were on the bride.

Anne had wanted to be married in the open on Grand Mesa, but Judge Purdy Smyth had forced her to trade away that option. So, the couple pledged their vows in the presence of one hundred competent and soon to be un-sober witnesses assembled in the mosquito-free interior of Lavender's picturesque Chapel of the Cross. The ceremony went splendidly—however the wedding gremlins were not quite finished. An outdoor reception was planned. But, as the newlyweds walked down the aisle, thunder boomed and the Colorado sky erupted in a spectacular downpour.

The pounding cloudburst obliged everyone to remain inside. An intrepid crew of friends braved the storm to rescue the cake and wine and everyone seemed content to spend the afternoon nestled snuggly beneath the dependable roof of the historic chapel.

Toasts were drunk, punch was spilled, and a short-lived fistfight was settled by a local pastor who firmly escorted the combatants out the side door.

"Roll around in the mud, my brave boys," he suggested as he latched and bolted the door.

"Wow," Trinidad whispered to his giggling bride. "I've never seen a church bouncer in action before."

"Pastor Paul used to be a soccer referee," Anne reminded her grinning husband. "So, I imagine he's seen it all."

As they stood together accepting congratulatory comments and shaking hands, one final surprise came calling. The chapel door burst open emitting wind, rain, and a tall man with a battered umbrella. All eyes turned toward the entrance as the man shook and folded his umbrella, then started down the aisle toward the altar.

"Trinidad Sands? Anne Sands?" he inquired.

"Yes," the couple exchanged a puzzled look before answering in unison.

"You've been served," the man said as he handed them two rain-soaked subpoenas.

Chapter 48

The Butler Did It
(Tuesday, June 11)

With their testimony required in an upcoming series of trials, Anne and Trinidad were forced to postpone their honeymoon. Instead of taking a plane to Ireland, the couple rolled up their sleeves to review the Koller case, including one particular piece of last-minute evidence.

Anne's spontaneous recruitment of Joel's butler, the unflappable Topper, had paid unexpected dividends. Their arrangement had been reached hours before she made her fateful journey to Glenwood Springs. As a result, while the detective made her intuitive dash southward to the Carbondale Public Library to confront Koller's killer, Topper had remained behind to embark upon his particular mission. Anne suspected that Phillip had withheld vital details and she guessed correctly that Topper was just the bloke to get his countryman talking.

The butler-to-butler interview had taken place and—as Anne hoped—Topper had managed to extract a wealth of material. Thanks to Anne's hunch and Topper's gentle persuasion, Phillip revealed much. It was a marathon encounter, which Topper lubricated by sharing a vintage bottle of 53-year-old scotch whiskey.

At Anne's request, the diligent Topper had recorded the entire conversation on a borrowed smartphone and, after some delay while he wrestled with the technology, managed at last to forward the audio file to the questing detective. The information arrived late in the game, but it was a rich bonanza which filled in several gaps in the Koller saga.

Fortified by liquor, Phillip poured out his heart. In the course of a day-long conversation, the old manservant disclosed that, over the years, he'd been acting as guardian angel to Esau's discarded children.

"I did as I could and yet I should have done much more," Phillip admitted as he concluded the recording which chronicled his interventions.

Sitting spellbound at the farmhouse kitchen table, Anne had just finished listening to the eight-hour marathon of recorded recollections. She looked up to see Trinidad arriving home after a day spent laboring in the lavender field. The kitchen door swung open and her industrious husband stomped into the kitchen, deposited his soiled boots on the mud-mat, and paused to hang his Stetson on the wall hook.

"Better hang onto your hat, cowboy," Anne warned her detective partner. "Topper's recording has arrived at last and it'll knock your socks off."

"Other than mixing up your clothing metaphors," Trinidad smiled, "what have you got for me?"

Re-cuing the audio, Anne played the sprawling interview in its entirety while Trinidad, his hat and socks firmly intact but his mind spinning, listened with rapt attention as piece after missing piece of the Koller puzzle fell into place.

Beginning at the beginning, Phillip laid it all out.

Phillip had begun his covert work in 1998, on the December day Esau Koller threw his unfortunate daughter out of their Aspen manor house. As one of several newly hired staff, the manservant had only been in harness for a month when a decidedly pregnant Ruth was sent packing by her abusive father. Informed of the incident, Phillip slipped away and sought to locate and help the distraught girl.

It was Phillip who followed Ruth's meandering tracks toward the isolated cabin where the girl had first been seduced by Esau. The portly manservant was still several yards away, floundering in the deep snow, when he heard an infant crying. Rushing to the cabin, he found Ruth hanging from the rafters. Beneath her lifeless body, on the icy floor next to an upturned wooden chair, lay a squalling newborn baby girl.

Anne paused the recording.

"R-2," she said and, when Trinidad gave her a puzzled look, she added, "Ruth's daughter—I glimpsed the resemblance when we fought in the library. I failed to process what I was seeing that night, but my eyes are open now and I've christened her R-2 to keep the two women straight."

"But..." Trinidad began.

"Don't look so surprised. Phillip will explain," she said as she restarted the audio and Phillip's testimony resumed.

"It was a coffin birth," Phillip sighed. "Decidedly rare, of course, but not unprecedented. A miracle child born of a dying mother. What to do?" he asked rhetorically. "What to do?" he repeated.

"A shocking dilemma," Topper agreed, his voice sounding clear and gentle on the audio file. "However, it seems you rose to the occasion." Throughout the recording, Topper continued to prompt his subject, seeming to sound just the right tone whenever Phillip's account began to falter.

"Indeed," Phillip agreed as he recounted his conduct. He spoke modestly, without dwelling on the resourceful coolness which characterized this, the first of many selfless actions he undertook to right the wrongs perpetrated by his employer.

On that winter's day two decades ago, the old manservant quickly removed his overcoat and knelt on the frosty floor. Fighting back his own tears, he rocked on his heels as he sought to warm and comfort the distressed infant. When the baby calmed, he gathered up the placenta, tucked it inside the overcoat, and placed it and the sleeping child on a dilapidated couch.

"Naturally, I refrained from cutting the umbilical," Phillip assured his audience of one.

"Quite right," agreed Topper and Anne pictured the two well-informed bachelors exchanging an approving glance.

Balancing precariously on the rickety chair, Phillip unknotted the rope and eased Ruth's limp body down. He offered a prayer for the dead mother, then turned his attention to the newborn.

Calling in favors from his close-knit network of fellow domestics, he used his vintage flip-phone to convince the custodian at an Aspen funeral home to drive to the cabin and bring along a little-used showroom casket. It was an outdated model which had been languishing in a storeroom and which the mortician was unlikely to miss. With Ruth gently tucked inside and the coffin secured in the rear of the custodian's station wagon, Phillip and the baby were transported to the outskirts of Aspen. It was nearly midnight when they arrived at the Roselia Foundling Home where yet another servant, whose name Phillip refused to divulge, took the infant in. Then Phillip and the unnamed custodian drove to Aspen's historic Ute Cemetery where anonymous hands operated a backhoe in the dead of night to bury the dead mother's body in an unmarked grave.

There was, Phillip maintained, no question of reporting any of his actions to Esau Koller.

"Lord only knows," Phillip said, "what the old man might have done. Miss Ruth was beyond his reach and so, I determined, must the baby be."

Purposely, or out of a sense of urgency, when entrusting the infant girl to the care of his confidant at the foundling home, Phillip had left the impression that the baby's name was also Ruth.

Hearing this, Trinidad signaled for Anne to pause the audio file.

"R-2?" he asked.

"Yes," Anne said. "And you're about to suggest we contact Isaac and let him know his sister's dead and also inform him that he's an uncle," Anne guessed. "I already did that."

"Good, but..." Trinidad began

"And, furthermore, you're about to ask how the Ruth you interviewed on Skype, believing her to be Koller's natural daughter, could possibly have—in fact—been Koller's illegitimate granddaughter," Anne speculated.

"Bingo," Trinidad responded. "However, I can answer my own question. The Skype image was imperfect. All I actually saw was the vague outline of a well-endowed redhead who might have been in her thirties or her twenties. I see now that R-2 is the spitting image of her mother which must have been how she convinced Esau Koller to open his front door. As for Aloe College, the granddaughter looked the part of a coed and everyone there presumed she was Millie because she said she was. Meanwhile, no one had laid eyes on anyone named Ruth Koller since 1998 when her father banished her."

"Except Phillip, as you'll soon learn when I restart the interview," Anne corrected. "And me, of course, but my sightings were incidental and out of context. Sighting one," she began, ticking each incident off on her fingers, "I encounter granddaughter Ruth—let's continue calling her Ruth-2 for clarity—I encounter R-2 at the Carbondale Public Library, tricked out in a mousy disguise with her hair up and no makeup and tinted horn-rimmed glasses—looking just like I'd expect for a stereotypical librarian. Sighting two: I glimpse her at the will reading, from a distance and from behind, but she quickly vanishes in the crowded confusion at the conclusion of the reading. Sighting three: she visits me at the hot springs pool, obscured by a swim cap and funky bathrobe and sunglasses not to mention a healthy swirling of nighttime fog. Sighting four...well..." She paused then, fingering her cheek.

"You okay to continue?" Trinidad asked, his voice tense with concern.

"Water over the dam," Anne responded as she restarted the audio file.

Phillip's continuing testimony revealed that he'd been a busy boy, cleaning up Koller messes right and left. He'd been at it for years. At first, he kept tabs on Isaac until the boy was sent to far-away Denver. Later, chastising himself for not protecting Ruth and, in the wake of her tragic suicide, he regularly returned to the foundling home to visit R-2. Eventually he grew close to the growing girl and felt compelled to tell her about her mother's fate and her grandfather's indiscretions.

"It was like striking a puppy," Phillip admitted, "but I couldn't help myself. When she earnestly inquired about her origins, I found myself unable to lie. I wanted to spare her the sordid details, but little-by-little the truth came tumbling out. Then the master remarried and I was obliged to look after a new crop of daughters, so I curtailed my visits. By the time I returned to the foundling home, the girl would have been nearly twelve. After a period of unwise neglect, I went there to see her, bringing flowers and chocolates, only to learn that young Ruth had vanished. Therefore, sadly, for a time, I lost track of her and so I turned my attention back to her unfortunate brother."

It was Phillip who, on Esau's orders, had carried the infant Isaac to the foundling home. But it was also Phillip who sought to blunt Esau's attempts to warehouse his abandoned son in various institutions. Phillip kept tabs on the boy and he eventually made contact with sixteen-year-old Isaac. At Phillip's request, the earnest manservant and the discarded youth met briefly one autumn day in 2012 beneath a sheltering oak tree on the grounds of the Denver Children's Home. Pressed for time, the older man gave the bewildered lad a wad of cash, counseled him to steer clear of his vengeful father, and disappeared.

Within days of Phillip's visit, as if following suit, Isaac himself vanished—only to resurface four years later, and a thousand miles away on the Oregon coast, in the summer of 2016. It was an inopportune time and Phillip was hard pressed to help. Having closed up his Aspen manor, Esau insisted that Phillip join him in his urban penthouse, but the cagey manservant invented a pretext.

"I asked for permission to tend to my dying mother," Phillip told Topper. "But I lied, for there was no mother, dying or otherwise."

Phillip, it turns out, was himself an abandoned orphan—a survivor of the same foundling home where Esau had banished Isaac and where the manservant had placed Ruth's infant daughter, only to lose her again. Far from a visit to his mother's death-bed, the old retainer's requested furlough turned out to be an excuse to continue his clandestine work of tying up loose ends.

Which is why he asked for permission to delay his journey to Denver. Esau was closing up the Aspen manor house with the intention of relocating to the urban metropolis. The fate of his banished son was the furthest thing from the old man's mind. But the moment Phillip was out of Esau's sight, the old retainer made a beeline for the Pacific Northwest. Enlisting the aid of a confidential Portland lawyer, Phillip anonymously made certain that Isaac—now a hardened criminal at twenty and due to be released on probation—had sufficient cash to make his life as an ex-con more palatable.

But the lawyer connection made Isaac uneasy and the wary young man refused the proffered funds. Instead of starting a new life far from Colorado, as Phillip hoped the lad would do, Isaac hitchhiked east with no firmer plan than a burning desire to stalk and, at the very least, haunt his hated father. Despite Phillip's efforts, he learned that Isaac had reached Colorado without friends or prospects and that his enmity for his father had led him to form an unhealthy alliance with his Uncle Jacob. Much to Phillip's dismay, he discovered that Jacob had hired his naïve nephew as an underpaid errand-boy and informal bodyguard.

"Once again, I had failed both children," Phillip sighed, his voice rigid with emotion. "It seems that my unfortunate pattern of ineptitude was destined to continue—this business of being, as the Americans say, 'a day late and a dollar short.' Can we take a recess, I wonder?"

There were sounds of fumbling on the audio file as Topper endeavored to stop, then re-start the recording. In the process, some of Phillip's testimony may have been garbled, but the detectives concluded that Topper had taken pains to ensure the narrative was faithfully amended.

"You were saying, over tea," Topper began when the recording recommenced, "that you lamented your inability to influence Isaac's future and—although you failed to reunite with young Ruth—you nevertheless suspected she remained nearby. Remind me how that came to pass."

"Certainly," Phillip responded warmly—his hearty voice suggesting his demeanor had been refreshed by sharing tea with his benevolent inquisitor.

"While doing my best to keep Miss Juliet and Miss Millie safe, I learned from their mother that the two girls had begun to speak of an imaginary playmate whom—they maintained—lived in the nearby woods and regularly joined in their girlish games of tag, lawn tennis, croquet, and other such outdoor pastimes. Mrs. Hapsen, that is to say the late Mrs. Koller, had never seen this person nor had anyone else at the manor house. And she added to her odd report by noting the curious fact that at no time did this alleged playmate join a single indoor game, but remained—or so her girls testified—a creature of the out-of-doors. And, though I admit it sounds incredible, to this day I can't help wondering whether the old man's missing granddaughter might not be the source of these childhood stories. Might she have returned to haunt the manor house, living as a wild thing in the surrounding forest? It gives one pause..."

"Indeed," Topper agreed after the audio file had cycled through a lengthy silence of dead air. "Did you endeavor to locate the elusive child?"

"I must confess that I searched," Phillip reported. "Once when the master was away for a fortnight, I trod through the woods calling her name, but, if she heard, she did not show herself. I even searched the old cabin and thought I detected signs of habitation."

"Most curious," Topper commented.

"Indeed," Phillip agreed.

"And as to the fate of Miss Juliet?" Topper prompted.

"Another sad affair," Phillip sighed. "One winter's evening there came a terrible argument reported by my fellow servants. I was away that evening and by the time I returned, the others had been dismissed and Miss Juliet had flown from the manor house never to be seen again. Then came her mother's breakdown and my unholy part in that poor woman's removal from the manor. And I believe you know the rest."

"Detective Anne has informed me that Miss Millie left for college unmolested whereupon, soon after, the manor was vacated," Topper said. "And, with the exception of your trip to Oregon to help Esau's son, your contention is that you never again interacted with any of the offspring."

"Yes. From that point forward, it was down to the master and myself, until he severed that relationship. And as for our diligent detective," Phillip noted with a wry chuckle, "she is quite beautiful they say, though I've only heard her voice—a dulcet voice to be sure."

"To be sure," Topper agreed. "And I myself have had the distinct pleasure of meeting the young woman and I can enthusiastically and accurately testify to her unparalleled beauty."

As these compliments rolled out, Trinidad glanced at Anne who was blushing like a schoolgirl.

"To be sure," Trinidad whispered.

"*Shush*," Anne said as she paused the audio. "They're nearly finished and I don't want you to miss this part."

"Okay, boss," Trinidad said as Anne re-started the file.

"...young woman herself," Topper's voice repeated.

"Let us hope our conversation will be of assistance to her and her dashing husband," Phillip concluded.

"Dashing he may be," said Topper, his tone carrying a hint of levity, "but, in my humble opinion, he is not, as they say, at all within her league."

"Ha!" said Anne and, though it made her injured cheek smart, she held her grin until Trinidad took off his hat and swept her up in a playful embrace.

Chapter 49

Crime and Punishment
(June 14, Flag Day)

Her shoulder wound healed nicely and the accused murderer known as Ruth Koller stood trial wearing her well-toned arm in a color-coordinated sling. The seemingly cool and collected woman sat erect, her perfect posture and charming smile never wavering, even when Deputy Madge Oxford took the stand to testify that she had to wing the defendant to keep her from stabbing Anne Scriptor.

Ruth's lawyer, Joel Signet, did an outstanding job of untangling a complex case. It took some time, and constant reminders, for the court to grasp the notion that the defendant was not in fact the original natural daughter of Esau Koller, but rather the illegitimate offspring of that unfortunate woman and the incestuous old novelist.

"Let's go over this again" the judge suggested after requesting a recess and assembling the lawyers and the defendant in his chambers. Her trial was entering its final stages. Jacob, her wicked uncle, had just finished his testimony and the judge sensed that the jury needed a break in the wake of the brother's bitter remarks.

"So," the judge continued, "you're telling me that this Ruth Koller isn't the original Ruth Koller?

"Yes, your honor," Joel repeated.

"Well, she's the spitting image of her mother," the judge noted as he compared the photograph of Ruth Rachel Koller with the flesh-and-blood defendant sitting demurely before him.

"Everyone seems to think so," Joel agreed.

"And the prosecution accepts the notion that this young woman is the granddaughter of Esau Noah Koller?"

"Yes, your honor," the district attorney answered.

"And she stands accused of killing her grandfather who's also her father? Don't answer that—I meant it to be rhetorical and... counselor..." the judge addressed Joel with an urgent tone.

"Your honor?"

"What in Heaven's name is your client humming?" The judge sounded exasperated.

"The tune, your honor?" Joel asked. "I believe it's *Row, Row, Row Your Boat.*"

"Can you make her stop? Such peculiar behavior's certain to prejudice the jury and I don't relish a mistrial!"

"Ruth," Joel whispered, but the humming continued. "Millie... Mrs. Hapsen... Juliet...?"

"Yes," she answered in a wistful voice, as if waking from a dream.

"The judge wants you to stop humming," Joel told his client.

"Sorry," she said in a small apologetic voice. "I didn't know I was doing it. I do that sometimes. I'm very, very sorry if I disturbed you, sir."

"That's quite all right," said the judge in a softened tone which suggested he felt he was addressing a child. "Just please don't do it when we're in the big room again."

"I'll be good," she promised.

As the district attorney exited and the bailiff arrived to escort the defendant back to the courtroom, the judge pulled Joel aside.

"*Ex parte,*" the judge whispered, "do we know the fate of this poor woman's mother or her missing sisters?"

"We have Jacob Koller's statement and more details will be sorted out at his trial," Joel revealed. "Our investigation indicates the mother has been dead for years. And, as for one of the sisters, we'll learn more soon. As you know, I'll be showing the court a video that'll clarify things. Meanwhile, when she's done here, my client's due to testify in Grand Junction and that eventuality seems to have inspired the brother to come forward in exchange for a possible sentencing reduction. We'll see what impact Ruth has in federal court and what her old fox of an uncle has to say when she testifies there."

"Jacob Koller seems to be cut from the same cloth as his unholy brother, so maybe he'll get what's coming to him, and you didn't hear any of that from me," the judge cautioned.

"Didn't hear what?" Joel asked.

When the judge reconvened the trial, Trinidad and Anne testified, then the former reporter Kip Greeley, was called to the stand.

Months ago, Kip had been detained on a vagrancy charge. Before authorities could connect him to the murder, the itinerant man had been released, only to be sought again in a metro-Denver manhunt when a search of his homeless hovel revealed several of the missing typewritten pages from Esau Koller's unfinished memoirs. On the run, Kip happened across a newspaper article which told of Joel Signet's role as defense attorney for Ray Zumberto, the Denver repairman who was also a murder suspect. With nowhere else to turn, the fugitive hitchhiked over the Continental Divide and turned himself in at the home of the Delta City lawyer. The exhausted but philosophical vagrant was taken into custody, transported back to Denver, and placed in a line-up. Whereupon residents of the Stevenson Building identified him as the stranger they'd seen loitering around the main entrance on Easter Sunday and Monday. The unlucky man was instantly arrested as a prime suspect, then reduced to a material witness when Ruth Koller became the primary accused.

Questioned by the district attorney, Kip testified that he had indeed been haunting the Stevenson Building, hoping to accost the famous author whose petulance years earlier had cost him his job. Being fired, he felt, had led to the downward spiral of his existence. He blamed Esau Koller for his dire circumstances, but had no plan to harm the old man.

"I just wanted him to see what he'd done," said Kip.

Since surrendering to Joel, who'd avoided a conflict by steering the homeless man to another barrister, Kip Greeley had started to turn his life around. Well-groomed and handsomely dressed at his court appearance, he spoke in a clear voice as he described his actions on the morning of Easter Monday.

"I waited for my chance, noticing that, whenever a particular rotund individual was buzzed inside, his girth forced the vintage door to open wide and the stressed hinges temporarily seized up, leaving the door uncharacteristically ajar for several seconds. So, I kept to my post and bided my time, waiting for the fat man."

Upon hearing this testimony, all eyes in the courtroom turned to the rear seats of the gallery to study the torso of Milton Weedle, brother of a resident of the Stevenson Building, a regular visitor, and the fat man in question. Sensing the attention, Milton squirmed nervously in a hopeless attempt to vanish from sight. As a murmur swept through the courtroom, the judge banged his gavel and called for order.

"Anyway," Kip continued when he resumed his testimony, "the expected man came just after dawn. I rushed in behind, and—while his back was turned waiting for the elevator—I slipped into the stairwell and started up. There are 264 steps leading up to the lair of Esau Koller, and I climbed them all. Emerging into the penthouse hallway whom should I encounter than the old man himself standing there in his bathrobe holding a sheaf of papers. I had a sudden recollection of the scene years ago when he unceremoniously threw me out and I was overcome by a sense of continuation. I had the impression that I had traveled back in time and interrupted him on his way to the trash chute, intent—or so I imagined—on throwing away my interview notes.

"*Those are mine*, I said. Then I pulled the pages from the hands of the astonished man, turned on my heel, and rushed back down the stairs. He was obviously confused, but also very much alive when I left him. I reached the ground floor, sprinted across the lobby, burst through the door into the dawning morning, and nearly collided with that one as she was coming inside."

"Let the record reflect that the witness has indicated the defendant," the district attorney instructed. "Your witness."

"No questions," said Joel.

"Defense?" the judge inquired, sounding decidedly hopeful. Though he sought to project an air of impartiality, his tone seemed to suggest that he'd fallen under the seductive spell of the redhead's legendary beauty. Or maybe he'd been charmed by the defendant's humble demeanor as she shifted personalities to channel young Juliet.

"If it please the court," said Joel, "We have only one thing to add in the form of a video deposition."

"Consistent with my pre-trial ruling, I'm going to allow this. But once more, I'll ask the prosecution to go on record as concurring with this unusual request," the judge said. "The jury should be aware that the deposed individual is a vital witness. She's appearing in this highly unusual manner to protect her anonymity."

"The prosecution waives any objection to the admission of this video deposition," the district attorney replied.

"Noted," said the judge. "With those understandings, let's proceed."

Instructing the bailiff to dim the courtroom lights, the judge ignored the defendant's gleeful outburst as the image of Millie Koller materialized on a large-screen video.

"Hi, Mill!" she shouted.

"I understand you're looking for me," Millie's pre-recorded voice seemed to acknowledge the hello. "I'm right here in Oregon. Have been all the time. Sorry if my taking off caused trouble for anybody. Seemed like a good idea at the time."

For twenty minutes, the vivacious woman sat on her sofa in a rural farmhouse with a baby on each knee and explained how, years ago, she and the defendant had voluntarily exchanged places.

"Never wanted college," she said. "And getting as far away as possible from 'the dragon' seemed like a good idea to me. She was itching to go to school, so we switched. Simple as that. Hope this helps her in her troubles. We're all rooting for you here abouts. Take care, dear one, and all my love to you. Wave goodbye," she instructed the babies and both children obeyed as the screen went black.

"The defense rests," said Joel.

Rising to address the court, the district attorney succinctly summarized the state's case. The murder weapon—a vintage fountain pen belonging to the victim—had been found in the defendant's possession when she was arrested at the Carbondale library. The defendant had confessed to the murder of Esau Koller and her statement had been placed in evidence without objection from Joel.

Regarding that statement, the district attorney reminded the jury that the defendant had admitted to meticulously planning the murder. She'd begun by impersonating her mother and writing a letter to Esau Koller promising reconciliation in order to gain access to the Stevenson Building.

Once inside, she'd used a library book card, a discarded bit of pasteboard obtained from her place of employment, to hang a misleading out-of-order notice on the elevator. She then ascended to the penthouse level where she used a fireman's key to place the car off-line. At the entry door, she'd confronted her victim, revealed her true identity, and pursued the startled old man into the penthouse hallway. When he slipped and fell backward, she pounced on him, seized the fountain pen from his hand, and repeatedly stabbed him in the face.

Her motive, she stated, was to revenge the abuse and deaths of a host of family members including her mother, her grandmother Chloe, her grandmother Hortense, her Aunt Juliet, and her Aunt Naomi. At one point while dictating her confession, she grew quiet and asked to be excused to use the bathroom.

When she returned, she refused to answer to the name Ruth and cycled through various personalities before settling-in as Juliet, whereupon she accused Esau Koller of killing her mother, raping one step-sister and drowning another, and abandoning her step-brother. Fourteen times, she interrupted herself to change personalities and amend her charges. In the end, her speech devolved to a growl and the interrogators ended the session.

Reminding the jury of this dramatic confession, and, even though her tone seemed to lack conviction, District Attorney Donna Marie Forest closed by suggesting that the defendant's deliberate and calculated actions amounted to premeditation and that the woman's supposed mental incapacity was a subterfuge.

In his summation, Joel reminded the jury that his client's confession spoke for itself and that a host of psychiatric experts had testified that her mental condition was genuine. He maintained that the poor woman had already suffered greatly at the hands of her progenitor. In closing, he asked the jury to look into their hearts when rendering their verdicts. The prosecution offered no rebuttal.

The defendant was escorted away, the judge vacated his bench, the jury filed out, and the members of the court and spectators cleared the room.

"Now we wait," Joel informed Anne and Trinidad as the three of them stood in the courthouse hallway. "Supper's on me."

The jury deliberated for six hours, mulling over multiple counts. At ten o'clock, a violent rainstorm spawned a windy microburst which knocked out power. The foreman took this as a sign and called it a night. The sequestered jurors agreed to start fresh the next morning.

At the beginning of the trial, the defendant had faced indictments for the murders of Juliet and Millie as well as the extortion and killing of Esau Noah Koller. The district attorney had wanted to add the charge of assaulting Anne Scriptor, but Anne refused to press charges and neither the grand jury nor the trial jury took up that matter.

Addressing each count in turn, by eight in the morning the five men and seven women found the striking redhead not guilty of the murder of Juliet, whose death they were convinced had been tragic but accidental. The deciding factor for the jury was the testimony of Jacob Koller. Clad in a prison jump-suit, Jacob had testified in Delta City even though he was busy defending himself in Grand Junction where he was being tried on federal charges. The fact-finding leading up to the Delta City trial had exposed evidence which led a federal grand jury to indict Esau's disgruntled twin. Things looked bad for the old man, so Jacob's defense had pulled out all the stops.

Jacob's Grand Junction lawyers may have been hoping for a miracle when they agreed to let the old man appear at his grandniece's trial. It was a calculated risk to have Esau's twin brother go on the record regarding Juliet's death. No one knew the details of Juliet's fate until Jacob told his tale. Recalling a cold winter's night long ago, he claimed he'd intended to rescue Juliet, but arrived too late and found the girl dead in the snow. The old fox suggested that the defendant had also been present on that fateful night and had ensnared him in a conspiracy to hide Juliet's corpse beneath his rose beds in the Carbondale Community Garden.

Somehow in the dead of winter, the old uncle and his young co-conspirator were alleged to have buried Juliet's body deep enough to avoid its being disturbed by rototilling and other gardening activities. The entire incident might have gone unreported had Jacob's lawyer not convinced his client to broach the subject in an effort to shift blame elsewhere.

But this strategy backfired.

Jacob claimed not to remember the year that Juliet died and a delayed coroner's examination was unable to shed light on the precise timing of the girl's death. But whichever way the old weasel tried to parse the coroner's estimate, his alleged co-conspirator still came out a minor. So, despite Jacob's contention that his grandniece had instigated everything, her skeptical jury placed the blame squarely on Jacob's shoulders.

Regarding the idea of exchanging places with Millie in order to defraud Esau, the unhappy brother did all he could to deny his guilt, portraying himself as an innocent while insisting that the scheme had been entirely the idea of his conniving grandniece.

As for holding Ruth's daughter accountable for Millie's murder, the jurors readily accepted the reality that Millie was alive and well and living under an assumed name in a tiny unincorporated town in rural Oregon.

The extortion charge had been hotly debated. The jury recognized that the troubled defendant had impersonated Millie in order to extract money from Esau. But they'd been unable to reach consensus regarding her intentions until Jacob's self-serving testimony convinced them that the oily uncle had authored the blackmail scheme.

Regarding the killing of old man Koller, a handful of jurors advocated a verdict of one count of first-degree murder, but deliberations deadlocked.

At last, the foreman asked the judge for clarification and the judge's response assured the jurors that the burden was on the prosecution to prove that the defendant was sufficiently sane to be held responsible for her actions.

Proving that turned out to be an uphill battle.

Expert witnesses for the defense included none other than the Aloe College counselor, Dr. J. J. Casey, who'd added his two-cents to the million-dollar testimony of a veritable who's-who of psychiatric specialists. Ultimately, the jury found the defendant not guilty by reason of insanity and the judge concurred that she should be committed indefinitely to the state mental hospital.

When the judge pronounced sentence, the troubled woman beamed and said, "Thanks."

Two days later, far to the north in Grand Junction, the jealous younger brother of Esau Koller learned his fate. Jacob's jury found him guilty of a string of crimes, ranging from the misdemeanor failure to report a death to the felonious behavior of contributing to the delinquency of a minor. For good measure, he was found guilty of mail and wire transfer fraud for conspiring to have his grandniece pose as Millie in order to bilk money out of Esau Koller.

The bitter old man was named an accessory after the fact for his role in aiding and abetting a scheme to hide Juliet's body and keep Millie's disappearance a secret. The indictment alleged that both of these ploys were perpetrated in order to defraud Esau. Jacob was also nailed on tax evasion for his failure to report his share of the money intended for Millie, a small portion of which the crafty brother had channeled to Ruth's daughter to insure her cooperation and silence.

Jacob's protestations that his young co-conspirator had employed her feminine wiles to seduce and manipulate him fell on deaf ears—especially once his federal jury heard testimony from the woman herself. Fresh from her own conviction in Delta City, Ruth's daughter was ushered into the Grand Junction courtroom. Her entry was greeted by hushed silence which made all the more audible Jacob's unhappy groans as he watched her take the stand. Clad in an unflattering smock, with her hair pulled back in a tight bun, and her face unadorned with make-up, the woman had seemed every inch the mousy Carbondale librarian who'd deceived detective Anne Scriptor.

The legal machinery had churned for months as Jacob's attorneys wrangled with the federal prosecutor's sentencing recommendation. Ultimately, Jacob received the maximum on all counts with the stipulation that his multi-year prison terms be served consecutively. It was an outcome which guaranteed the octogenarian would die in prison. Cornered by an enterprising reporter on his way to the federal lock-up, Jacob had only one comment.

"And so, it goes," the younger Koller brother declared.

Chapter 50

Post Mortem
(June 21, Solstice)

Joel Signet was holding an invitation-only get together in his newly refurbished Delta City conference room. Anne and Trinidad were sitting side-by-side, their knees pressed together beneath the highly polished table. Trinidad was beaming at his bride. Anne was sipping tea and absently fingering the thin scar that had taken up permanent residence on her otherwise flawless cheekbone.

Jack stood in the corner of the room with his back to the others, staring out the high windows, seemingly lost in thought. Joel's secretary, Erik, was fidgeting at the room's elaborate service bar, tentatively inserting a pod into the office's newly-installed coffee machine and hoping he was doing it correctly.

"Word has reached me that our new federal convict, Jacob Koller, has been assigned to grow ordinary geraniums in the prison greenhouse," said Joel as he stood up and crossed the room to assist Erik. "There...you have it exactly! Good job," he assured the nervous secretary. "We can manage now. You take a break."

As Erik departed, Trinidad commented, "Old Jacob's new job is quite a comedown from his former avocation of breeding prize roses. I suppose the guards can't trust him with the thorns."

"More than likely that's the case," Joel confirmed. "So, now that we've discussed the Koller trials, let's take a moment to review the situation of my rags-to-riches client."

"Which one?" Anne couldn't resist joking. "Do you mean Ray-Ray, the best-selling author, nee repairman. Or is it Isaac K, the potting shed assassin who inherited an obscene crap-load of money? Or are you referring to Kip Greeley, the nation's newest internet sensation?"

"Well, as you know, Kip Greeley's not my actual client, but I get your drift. So, let's discuss them in numerical order, starting with the richest first," suggested Joel.

"Isaac K then," said Jack as he joined the others at the table. "I guess he's goin' with that name officially, or so I hear."

"You hear correctly," Joel confirmed. "I filed the paperwork myself. The tabloids are still having a field day with old man Koller's sensational and sadistic past. And they're leaving no stone unturned in their search for the elusive Millie. But they'll never find her, because Isaac and I have whisked her away to an undisclosed location where... Well, let's just say that, thanks to her generous brother, she and her family are now living in style in a temperate spot where the sun shines considerably more than in rainy Oregon."

"So, the elusive Millie is out there somewhere working on her tan as we speak," Anne suggested.

"No doubt," answered Joel. "Meanwhile, Isaac is staying put in Colorado and he's set me up with a generous retainer as he and I and his PR people opt for rebranding."

"I take it back," Anne interjected.

"Take what back?" Joel asked.

"For a second or two, having been dazzled by the palatial set-up here in your new office and even more dazzled by the sumptuous digs which your brother-in-law occupies in Junction, I considered becoming a lawyer. But now that I hear your plan to put lipstick on our muscle-bound swine, I take it all back."

"Isaac's not a bad sort once you get to know him," assured Joel. "Considering that he could have written Millie off financially and saved money by consigning his sisters to unmarked graves and abandoned his institutionalized niece, he's chosen to do right by all four."

Anne had to admit that Isaac had been uncommonly generous.

The shouting which had accompanied the announcement that Millie Koller was to inherit her step-father's fortune, lock-stock-and-barrel, had been but a whisper compared to the clamor which arose when the unpredictable woman refused the inheritance. Acting through intermediaries, the youngest surviving Koller signed a disclaimer waiving all rights to her step-father's fortune, an unexpected action which temporarily threw the Koller estate into the murky realm of intestate.

But Joel and his brother-in-law soon hammered together a solution. Wading through the whereases of Colorado's rambling intestate statutes was probably child's play to the counselors. Anne and Trinidad had tried to make sense of the law, but soon abandoned the effort.

"I think my eyes may be permanently crossed," Anne had complained as she and her partner re-shelved the Delta County Libraries' hulking copy of *Colorado Revised Statutes 15-10-101 through 15-10-122*.

"I defer to Joel on this one," Trinidad agreed. "I'd guess that the money goes to Isaac, but my brain is fried."

"Ditto," said Anne.

In the end, Trinidad was correct. Millie's withdrawal might have thrown the disposition of the estate into a pitched battle between Jacob, the old man's surviving sibling, and Isaac, his forgotten son. But Jacob's felony convictions instantly quashed his claim, which should have left the field clear for Isaac to inherit everything, except Isaac was also a convicted felon.

"Vive la difference," Joel reminded his conference room audience. "Jacob was convicted of extorting money from his brother, which tied his felonious actions to the intestate decedent. Whereas Isaac's infractions were accumulated when he was a minor and involved circumstances outside the family." Joel paused and surveyed the group gathered around his broad meeting table, trying to judge whether he should continue holding court.

"Don't let us stop you," Jack said. "It looks like you're about to burst with wanting to heap more praise on our reformed convict."

Thus encouraged, Joel warmed to his subject as he launched into a litany of Isaac's good deeds.

"Having inherited the entire estate, Isaac has proven to be a good steward of the family fortune. He's no financial wizard, but he's got a big heart and he immediately drew upon his familial instincts to fulfill Millie's desire for continued anonymity. He's relocated her entire family to a secret spot and made arrangements to sustain the whole bunch in perpetuity with a generous monthly stipend. With Millie safely installed far from prying eyes, Isaac turned his attention to rectifying other wrongs.

"He's repurposed the rural Colorado site which once encompassed the grounds of White Quail Manor and landscaped the abandoned acres into a combination public park and cemetery where the region's unknown dead can be interred with dignity. He did this in memory of Ruth, his missing sister, whose once-lost remains—thanks to an anonymous source—have been found and laid to rest next to her mother and baby sister. He also returned to Aspen where he sought out the grave of Hortense Hapsen and erected a tasteful monument marking her final resting place and restoring her former married name.

"As for Juliet, Jacob testified that the girl died years ago, having frozen to death in the December snow after walking away from White Quail Manor. The old weasel admitted to discovering the body, denied taking Juliet's life, but nevertheless confessed to unceremoniously stashing the dead girl beneath his prize roses. When questioned why he'd taken such a macabre action, he could offer no better reason than a vague notion that the corpse might someday be used to injure his hated brother.

"Appalled by the callous indifference of his father and uncle, Isaac continues to gather up the remnants of his discarded family. He had Juliet's body retrieved and laid his step-sister to rest beside her mother. Then he disinterred and relocated the remains of Chloe Koller and his twin sister, Naomi, and reunited them with Ruth on the grounds of the family manor. The three are now enshrined in a miniature Taj Mahal with its own reflecting pool.

He even found it in his heart to purchase a shared headstone and double-plot for his father with space for the irascible Jacob when his time comes.

"As for his niece, the woman convicted of murder and placed in psychiatric custody, Isaac is sparing no expense to make certain she's cared for. In fact, the prodigal uncle has taken up residence in Southern Colorado in order to be near and visit her often."

Joel paused then, once again gauging his audience. He found almost everyone nodding in approval—almost. Anne alone sat frowning with her arms crossed.

"And let me add," Joel said as he caught Anne's eye and favored her with his patented smile, "regarding his little run-in with my favorite detective in the potting shed, Isaac forgives her for knocking him unconscious with that zucchini."

"Is that what I used?" Anne said as she returned Joel's smile. "Well, I'm pleased and proud to be the first person to discover a practical use for such a ubiquitous and profoundly misunderstood vegetable."

"I'm not sure we're accomplishing as much here as we might," Trinidad complained, "I..."

But his critique was interrupted by a knock on the conference room door.

Chapter 51

The Lieutenant, the Sister, and the Dog
(Noon)

Following a respectful pause, Trinidad's sister swept into the room, her open honest face beautifully framed in black and white. Her winkle was crisp and her habit billowed, creating the impression that she was floating, rather than taking ordinary steps, to advance across the room.

Everyone stood up.

"I do wish people wouldn't do that," she said as a blush colored her already rosy cheeks. "It makes humility all the more difficult to maintain."

"Hi, sis," said Trinidad as he gave her a peck on the cheek.

"Humility," she said with a merry smile and a single index finger which she raised in mock admonition. "You'll spoil me with your attentions. Good morning, dear brother. Good morning, dear sister. Good morning, dear Joel and dear Jack."

"Good morning, Sister Tina Mary," the four of them responded in unison, like good Catholic children greeting their teacher.

"Sit please, for the sake of Heaven, sit," she said as she examined the bar. "Is there tea?"

Anne shared the contents of the teapot with Tina Mary. Then the industrious detective started more water boiling on Joel's state-of-the-art induction cooking pad.

"You're able to boil water on that thin ceramic wafer?" Sister Tina Mary exclaimed. "Why it looks no more substantial than a square of dark chocolate. What won't they think of next? I declare. Sit here, brother and you beside me, Annie. My time is short and I want you both near."

"Must you go back so soon?" Anne asked as she entwined her fingers around Tina Mary's warm left hand while Trinidad held his sister's right.

"What you mean is can the state of New Mexico manage without me?" Tina Mary asked and laughed at the thought. "I'm certain that no one in our Land of Enchantment will suffer harm before I return. It's the place where I belong—where I've been since arriving there as a baby. You, dear brother, should understand my profound attachment to Our Lady of the River."

"If you are attached to a place," said Trinidad, his voice rich with emotion, "then it must be a very good place."

"It is and I am fortunate to serve as the River's humble Prioress at such a tender age—our shared tender age," she added squeezing her brother's hand. "It is a weighty responsibility and I love it so—our work—our service to the poor is a constant source of joy."

The three were silent for a time, Trinidad and Anne gazing lovingly at their new-found but soon to be departing sister, and Tina Mary smiling first at one of her loved ones and then the other.

"Picture?" Joel suggested as he unlocked his Android and centered the scene. "Say 'cheese' or whatever it is you say in New Mexico."

"Chili peppers," Sister Tina Mary said as her angelic face formed effortlessly into a smile which Joel correctly interpreted as encompassing a pleasing combination of virtue and mischief.

Another knock and Deputy Madge Oxford entered.

"This a private party or can another badge enter?" Madge joked.

"Some of my favorite people are badges," said Joel. "Come on in." He pressed a button under the lip of the conference table and Erik appeared. "As you can see, our party is evolving. Please break out the croissant sandwiches and vegetable tray."

"Yes, sir," said Erik and, no sooner had he departed, than Joel sounded the buzzer to summon him back.

"And the sticky buns," the lawyer added. "Don't forget the sticky buns."

With Erik dispatched to assemble refreshments, Trinidad gave Joel a quizzical look.

"Andrew has a buzzer," Joel blushed but was unapologetic. "No reason I shouldn't have one too."

"Hell, even I've got a buzzer," said Jack. "Beggin' your pardon, ma'am," he added with an embarrassed nod to the visiting nun.

"No apologies necessary," she said with a laugh. "Without Hades and the Devil, we'd have little to do at the monastery but sing hymns and crochet doilies."

"And dig wells," Trinidad added. "And erect windmills. And deliver meals to shut-ins. And..."

"Humility," Tina Mary cautioned.

"Humble is as humble does," said her brother.

The refreshments arrived and, by acclamation, the morning's remaining agenda was tabled. More coffee and tea were brewed and everyone began to chatter at once.

"Tell me," said Madge when she'd gotten Tina Mary's attention, "with you now, is it like on *M.A.S.H.*?"

"I'm sorry," said Tina Mary with a puzzled look. "How do you mean?"

"Do you know the old TV show called *M.A.S.H.*? I think it stands for 'Mobile Army Surgery Hospital,' or something like that. Anyhow, the show took place in Korea. Do you know Alan Alda? Hot Lips Hoolihan? Frank Burns...?"

"Forgive me for interrupting," said Tina Mary. "I know the program, of course, but I'm not sure what you're asking."

"Well, in the show the Army priest, Father Mulcahy, has a sister who's also a nun, so he refers to her as 'his sister the sister.' So, is it like that with you and Trinidad?"

"Oh, I see," said Tina Mary. "Well, to tell the truth, it came as quite a shock that I had a brother at all, let alone a handsome twin. And I'm certain he's feeling much the same about the newness of our unexpected family reunion. Not to mention that I now have two loving parents, whom I only just met and whom I must visit soon and who would be justified in describing me as 'our daughter the sister.' So, you see that, frankly, it's a bit overwhelming. You understand?"

"Absolutely," agreed Madge, "I just wondered is all."

"Well," said Tina Mary, "my sister the sister is certainly a clever turn of phrase and I love wordplay and I adore puns and crosswords and Scrabble and..."

"No kidding?" interrupted Madge. "Me also. I positively *love* Scrabble."

"We must play sometime."

"It's a date!"

"Good," said Tina Mary. "Now, I must ask you something."

"Shoot," said Madge.

"I understand you are the one who saved our dear Annie's life."

"Well," said Madge, "Cozy did most of the work and I had the shot is all and I took the shot. The dog oughta get the credit for separating my mark from young Anne and giving me a standing target which I could hardly miss."

"Hardly miss from so far away and in the dark? Well, I accept that the noble dog did her part in following Anne into that danger zone and protecting her. Still, I believe you're being much too modest, Deputy, because everyone tells me that it was not merely a shot, but a spectacular one with little margin for error."

"It was tricky, that's for sure, in the dark, through a giant plate glass window and all."

"Well, I think it's one of the most splendid things a person who is sworn to protect and serve can do—to send a bullet flashing through the air and save three lives with a single shot."

"My golly," said Madge, "I didn't think of it that'a way."

"Well, that's the truth isn't it? A single shot saved our intrepid detective as well as brave Cozy and, I daresay, it also saved that poor troubled woman. And so," she nodded to her sister-in-law, "here's our beloved Annie, alive and well, and the dog is somewhere basking in the admiration of her colleagues, and her unfortunate attacker is also alive and getting the treatment she needs, I understand. Isn't that all true?"

"I reckon so," Madge agreed.

"Therefore," Tina Mary declared, "what you did is—how do they say it—a win/win. As a result, in my humble opinion, you deserve my thanks and a medal."

"Now that you mention it..." interjected Jack, who'd been eavesdropping on the conversation between his intrepid deputy and this incredibly wholesome and heartbreakingly attractive young nun. The sheriff stood up and banged his spoon against his coffee cup, signaling a request for the room's attention.

When everyone was silent, Jack continued, "As the mouse said when he was required to stand up in front of a crowd and give an account of himself: unaccustomed as I am to public squeaking..."

It took time to quell the groans welling up from his unappreciative crowd and, while the sheriff sought to restore order, he was gratified to see that Sister Tina Mary was carefully copying down the details of his lame joke.

I bet she'll have 'em rollin' in the aisles during Vespers, he thought. Pleased with himself, he caught the sister's eye and mimicked the fingers of one hand writing on the palm of his other hand in what he hoped was the universal pantomime for "I'll write it down for you."

Tina Mary seemed to understand Jack's message, because she smiled and nodded and silently mouthed the words "thank you."

"It's my great honor and pleasure," the sheriff continued, "in the presence of this-here assembled multitude..." He paused then and frantically signaled for Trinidad to open the conference room door. Jack wanted to admit the remainder of his Delta County squad—everyone not on duty, including two special guests: K-9 Cozy and her handler Officer Smiley. Once the door was open, a legion of well-wishers flooded silently into the room to form ranks behind Madge's chair. When all were in place, Jack made it official.

"Stand to attention, Deputy," he said as he eyed Madge with mock solemnity. Confused, but obedient, Madge got to her feet. "It's my pleasure to present to you, Deputy M.C. Oxford, the Delta County Sheriff Department's Medal of Merit for commendable service in defense of the public peace and safety and..."

Applause erupted as he pinned the gleaming medal to Madge's uniform, but Jack held up a hand for silence. Then he continued with a broad grin on his face.

"And last but not least, Deputy Oxford, I regret to inform you that you're out of uniform. So, allow me to present you with these lieutenant bars—awarded at my discretion as a field promotion for conduct above and beyond the call of duty. So, everybody, join me in welcomin' to our officer ranks, our most deservin' deputy, here-so-after to be known as Lieutenant Marjorie Carol Oxford."

An outbreak of rhythmic clapping morphed into a hearty chant as almost everyone shouted "Oi, Oi, Oi." Except for brave Cozy—she timed her barks to fill the intervals.

Chapter 52

Holes
(Friday, July 5)

"We're close," said Trinidad.

"I can move to the other side of the bed if you like," Anne suggested.

"Stay put," Trinidad instructed. "By 'close,' I mean we almost have the Koller case nailed down."

"You have a unique sense of timing," she gave him a contented kiss. "Are you certain you want to talk business at a time like this?"

"What better time," he observed, "when I know exactly where you are? In my arms and out of danger."

"Not entirely out of danger, I hope," she added.

"Hmm," he replied. "Humor me please."

"Always," she sighed and snuggled closer.

"When we listened to the audio of the Topper and Phillip Show—also known as the secret lives of the brotherhood of butlers—they filled in several holes," Trinidad recalled. "For one thing, we now know that the original Ruth Koller died years ago."

"Yup," agreed Anne.

"And we also know that, despite the multiple personalities rattling around inside her brain, our murder was committed by none other than her surviving daughter."

"Yup."

"And, if Phillip's conjectures are correct, granddaughter R-2..."

"Ruthie," Anne interrupted, "Isaac is calling her Ruthie."

"Have it your way," Trinidad decided. "Ruthie becomes the mysterious imaginary playmate who haunted White Quail Manor, interacted with the adopted Koller daughters, and made Phillip nervous..."

"And compelled Koller to abandon his manor house," Anne interrupted.

"Who's telling this story?" Trinidad inquired with mock indignation.

"Sorry, dear-heart," Anne whispered. "Please continue."

"Where was I?"

"Lying here in my arms," she purred.

"Stop it," he pretended to protest. "Oh yes..."

"And don't start marching around the room or initiate a concert," she interrupted again.

"What?"

"When you're pontificating about a case, you have a tendency to pace back and forth," she reminded him. "Either that or you start noodling on your harmonica. I'll only listen to this if you stay put and keep your harmonica out of it."

"As you wish," he agreed. "*Now*, may I continue?"

"I'm all ears, master."

"Well, I think I'm stumped for the time being," he admitted. "We're still missing some facts and those holes can only be filled by questioning Ruthie, who's crazy as a loon and sequestered in the nut house."

"To be more precise," Anne corrected, "that troubled young woman has, by court order, been confined to the Colorado Mental Health Institute for treatment."

"That's pretty-much what I said," Trinidad protested. "The point being that we can't ask the burning questions I'm dying to ask."

"Well, I'm not so sure about that," Anne suggested. "You know that her Uncle Isaac is a regular visitor and that he's interviewing Ruthie with an eye toward writing a more accurate account of the Koller saga, picking up where his evil father of a novelist left off."

"So?" Trinidad asked.

"So," Anne answered, "while we're still stuck in town as material witnesses, what if we send him a list of questions we'd like to have answered?"

"Got a pencil on you?" Trinidad inquired of his naked bed-mate.

"Are you kidding me?" she laughed as she rolled out of bed, put on her robe, and padded barefoot toward the dresser in search of a pad and pencil.

Epilogue

(September 23, Autumnal Equinox)

Working from a list of questions supplied by Trinidad and Anne, the budding novelist known as Isaac K. spent months quizzing his niece and preparing a series of answers. Sensing that the newlyweds would appreciate the closure which Ruthie's recollections represented, he mailed several pages to the couple on the occasion of their much-delayed honeymoon.

The package from America reached them in Ireland, arriving by messenger just after breakfast. The two detectives bundled up, emerged from their small honeymoon cottage, and carried the document box along the rocky trail which led to the shore. Finding shelter, they sat for a time, relishing the quiet, watching the water.

Trinidad and his bride nestled in the corner of an ancient stone wall, keeping warm. Before them stretched a wind-swept meadow—a broad expanse of emerald green which bordered the southern coast of Ireland. Cozy, the faithful German shepherd who had saved Anne's life, sat at their feet. The brave dog's K-9 career had been cut short in late summer by a criminal's stray bullet and the detectives instantly adopted her.

"Do you forgive the perp who plugged you?" Anne asked as she gave the dog a loving pat. Cozy looked up to nuzzle her mistress, then yawned and resumed her post. Anne yawned too and leaned closer to Trinidad.

It was shaping up to be a lazy day without drama.

Reaching Ireland and peace had been a challenge and the detectives were glad to have a respite. Their honeymoon abroad had been deferred. Omens portending the postponement had manifested themselves the instant Judge Purdy Smyth pronounced them man and wife. A summer cloudburst had sabotaged their outdoor reception and a somber process server had crashed their wedding bearing the bad-news documents.

Then, exactly one day later, a seemingly endless marathon of Koller depositions commenced, requiring the testimony of both detectives. An array of trials followed and, no sooner had those affairs ended, than the attending publicity landed the couple a basketful of lucrative cases. All this delayed their honeymoon for weeks and then a last-minute mountain of paperwork required to bring Cozy along for the ride ate up two more weeks. In the end, their June 2019 honeymoon trip morphed, by stages, into an autumn journey.

"Well anyway," Trinidad said as he gazed wistfully across the pearl and turquoise waves which formed the incoming tide of the Celtic Sea, "here we are at last."

"Yes," Anne sighed. "Here we all are: a laddie and his lassie and our little furry import."

Cozy stirred, looked up, and cocked her head as if to second Anne's sentiment. Apparently, the faithful dog was blissfully unaware of the indignity of having entered Ireland as airline cargo.

As they contemplated the peaceful setting, Trinidad balanced the document box on his lap. He kept one gloved hand on the topmost sheet, hoping the recurring breeze wouldn't snatch the loose pages and end up papering the Irish coast with Isaac's prose.

It had not escaped Trinidad's notice that he and Anne were on the cusp of closing the Koller case much as they had begun their inquiry months ago. The fledgling author's package had come by messenger, invoking memories of the several packets of evidence delivered to Lavender Hill Farm in the opening days of the Koller investigation.

The detectives had begun the Koller case by working their way through a massive pile of documents. Having examined all the evidence, and even after sitting through hours of courtroom testimony, the principal partners of the Sands Detective Agency still had questions. A month ago, they'd mailed a list to Isaac, hoping the old man's semi-literate son could extract answers from the old man's legally insane granddaughter. Having posed their questions, they turned their attention to planning their postponed honeymoon. Their letter to Isaac was forgotten until this morning's package arrived—an unexpected bundle which might contain the answers they'd been seeking.

Both detectives were curious, and yet the bulk of Isaac's work remained inside the FedEx box in which it had arrived. Cozy was lying on the discarded lid, which the opportunistic dog had crushed flat and fashioned into something which, on the damp and weathered ground, approximated a pet rug. Anne had extracted the topmost sheet, a handwritten note from Isaac, but it remained in her hand, unread.

Wanting Anne to take the lead, Trinidad waited patiently as she fingered the note. Here at last was what might prove to be the final chapter of the Koller saga and Trinidad wondered what effect the contents might have on his new bride. He hugged her tightly and sought to kiss her head. It was a sincere and loving gesture, though a bit off target. She was cloaked in cold-weather gear, so he only managed to touch his lips to the tassel which topped her wool cap.

Anne sat beside her husband holding Isaac's handwritten note—a single sheet of lined paper which she clutched in her gloved hand. Her oversized mittens complemented her floppy knit cap and huge sweater. Trinidad grinned to see her bulky outfit.

"I'm still cold," she complained.

"You look like a Cork County Michelin Man," he observed. "You want me to read Isaac's letter?"

"I'll do it," she said.

The letter was an apology, representing Isaac's humble efforts to make amends. Anne could almost see and hear the huge man speaking as she read his words.

"Sorry for scaring you all them months back. The gun wasn't loaded, but it was still a dumb and bad thing to do. I ain't that man no more. Anyhow, here is all that Ruthie remembers of that time when her brains was scrambled. So, they tell me that the thing to do on your 1st anniversary is to give you paper. Well, I know it ain't been a year yet, but here's your present early. Your friend (I hope), Isaac K. And P.S.: Ruthie says 'hey' and no hard feelings also."

Anne sniffed and used her gloved hand to absorb a single tear.

"The rest could wait, you know," Trinidad said.

"I know," she said, "but Isaac went to a lot of trouble to send the answers to us. And this introductory note of his really got to me. I'm all choked up, so I wonder, darling husband..."

"Yes, dear wife," Trinidad said.

"Can I depend on you to read to me?" she requested.

"Absolutely," he said. "Close your eyes and I'll tell you the rest."

The rest consisted of neatly typed pages. Isaac hadn't done the typing, of course, but the words were his own. Joel Signet had included an explanatory note which verified that every typewritten word had been faithfully transcribed from a combination of Isaac's handwritten notes and tape-recordings.

"Here's your answers," Joel explained. "Isaac's work ain't as polished as his father's prose, but the spark is there and the story he tells is dynamite. His writing captures Ruthie's turmoil and also channels the repressed passion of his own unhappy life onto the page. As a result, despite his unsophisticated style, he's faithfully reported his niece's adventures and documented her vivid recollections which run the gamut from fact to fiction. He not only reports the disturbed woman's lucid insights into her own madness, he also captures flights of fancy which channel her many adopted personalities. Anyway, here it is warts and all and—as far as I'm concerned—I wouldn't change a thing."

"The Koller Chronicles..." Trinidad began. "Catchy title..."

"We can do without the commentary, Mr. Editor," Anne chided.

"Got it," Trinidad agreed and he read the rest aloud as written without adding so much as a comma.

About the Author

Donald Paul Benjamin is an American mystery novelist. Born in Greeley, a mid-sized settlement on Colorado's eastern plains, he grew up writing stories about local characters and sketching animals on his family's small acreage. As a teen he worked on his high school newspaper. Upon graduation in 1963, he enlisted in the U.S. Army, serving three years as a military journalist, including a tour in Korea from 1965-66. Honorably discharged, he returned to Greeley to earn his teaching degree from the University of Northern Colorado (UNC). He taught first grade, then served as UNC's first campus ombudsman. In 1982, he earned a master's degree in college student services administration at Oregon State University. For more than three decades, he lived in Arizona and worked in higher education, most recently as e-advisor for Phoenix College. In 2014, he retired to the wild Western Slope of Colorado where he lives in the small town of Cedaredge. He works for the *Delta County Independent* newspaper as a contributing writer. In his spare time, he draws cartoons and fishes and hikes in the surrounding wilderness. Recently married, he and his wife, Donna Marie, have founded **Elevation Press**, a service which helps independent authors design and format books for self-publication.

Email: elevationpressbooks@gmail.com
Studio Phone: 970-856-9891
Mail: D.P. Benjamin, P.O. Box 603, Cedaredge, CO 81413
Website: https://benjaminauthor.com/
Visit the Author's Facebook Page under: D.P. Benjamin Author
Instagram: https://www.instagram.com/benjaminnovelist/

Titles in the Mountain Mystery Series

[Details at https://benjaminauthor.com/]

*The Road to Lavender (Book 1: July 2020)
A Lavender Wedding (Book 2: April 2021)
Ghosts of Grand Lake (Book 3: November 2021)
The War Nickel Murders (Book 4: March 2022)
Rare Earth (Book 5: May 2022)
Walking Horse Ranch (Book 6: July 2022)
A Lavender Farewell (Book 7: November 2022)

*Third-place winner in the 2019 Rocky Mountain Fiction Writers' Colorado Gold Contest and recipient of a 2020 award for cover design from the New Mexico Book Association.

CPSIA information can be obtained
at www.ICGtesting.com
Printed in the USA
FSHW020615070821
83853FS